"I hadn't reali██ ███████████████████ characters and putting them into knotty real-life situations. Nor what depths and emotions I'd find in *Falling For You*. If the sexual ten███ent in w██████ the plans for the Pearl Island B&B go forth, and suspense in the social repercussions of Chance and ███████████████ing."
—*Romance Reviews Today*

"I had a blast reading *Falling For You*, and enjoyed it so much that I'm really looking forward to her next book. As long as Julie Ortolon is writing books like this one, romantic comedy is in good hands."
—*All About Romance*

"A thoroughly delightful, fast-paced romance about what happens when opposites attract. Her characters are wonderfully appealing, even the supporting cast. And the setting is so vividly drawn, you feel part of the surroundings. A lovely story!"
—*Old Book Barn Gazette*

"A lively delightful contemporary romance of two opposites falling in love. The story line is fun . . . a charming vivacious tale."
—Bookcrossing.com

"Full of humor . . . Very entertaining and well worth your time!"
—*Huntress Book Reviews*

Dear Cupid

"*Dear Cupid* is so romantic it will make you melt! Julie Ortolon has perfected the art of the male/female relationship."
—Virginia Henley, author of *The Marriage Prize*

"Julie Ortolon does it again. What a fun, flirty, fantastic book!"
—Pamela Morsi, author of *Here Comes the Bride*

TURN THE PAGE FOR MORE ACCLAIM . . .

Drive Me Wild

Lead Me On

Julie Ortolon

St. Martin's Paperbacks

LEAD ME ON

Copyright © 2003 by Julie Ortolon.
Excerpt from *Don't Tempt Me* copyright © 2003 by Julie Ortolon.

ISBN: 0-312-98348-4

Printed in the United States of America

St. Martin's Paperbacks edition / January 2003

St. Martin's Paperbacks are published by St. Martin's Press, 175 Fifth Avenue, New York, NY 10010.

10 9 8 7 6 5 4 3 2 1

To Mom
For teaching me that family matters

Chapter 1

SCOTT FIGURED IF A GUY couldn't get lucky on Galveston Island during tourist season he had to be a loser. And luck was exactly what he needed right now—in more ways than one.

The thought made his grip tighten on the steering wheel as he pulled the black Jaguar to a halt before the Pearl Island Inn. The inn sat on a private island on the bay side of Galveston Island. He hadn't been to Galveston in years, and hadn't particularly wanted to come back now. But his situation had grown so desperate he was willing to try anything. "Take a break," his agent had told him. "Go somewhere and relax. Get laid if that's what it takes. But for God's sake do something to get your old charm back before your career goes down the toilet."

Get your old charm back. The words had brought the mansion on Pearl Island instantly to mind. Setting the brake, he looked up at the three-story Gothic structure with its gargoyles and gables, surprised at how much the place had changed since the last time he'd seen it. It seemed odd, seeing the old monstrosity with clean windows, fresh paint, and baskets of ferns hanging on the stone veranda.

Staring up at it, he wondered if he was nuts for coming here, nuts to believe in old legends about good-luck charms, and even more nuts to think a vacation fling would cure his recent bout of writer's block. If he had any sense left in his brain, he'd turn the car around and head straight back for his townhouse in New Orleans and force himself to write. Discipline was what he needed— not luck.

He reached for the gearshift—ready to call the whole plan off—but stopped when a movement on the veranda caught his eye. There in the shadows he swore he saw the figure of a woman. Her pale, gauzy dress gave her an ethereal quality that brought to mind every ghost story he'd ever heard about "the Pearl." Then the figure faded deeper into the shadows, making him wonder if he'd imagined her.

Stepping out of the air-conditioned car, he lowered his sunglasses and squinted against the glare of afternoon light. The salty breeze off the nearby cove ruffled his shirt and hair, relieving the humid heat along the Texas gulf coast.

The figure appeared again, this time stepping fully into the light. Definitely not a ghost, but a flesh-and-blood woman with the face of an angel and hair as black as French lace. The ghostly attire was actually a white cotton sundress that left her arms bare as she raised a pitcher to water one of the hanging baskets.

As she lowered her arms, she spotted him and smiled. "Hello" she called. "Are you Mr. Scott?"

Hello yourself, he thought as he gave one curt nod. Maybe his agent didn't have such a crazy idea after all. A little quality time relaxing on a beach with a beautiful woman might be just what he needed to clear the cobwebs from his brain.

Grabbing his laptop from the passenger seat, he headed up the oyster-shell path to the wide sweep of stone steps. "Yes, I'm Scott," he said as he mounted the steps to stand before her. Soft, shoulder-length waves framed her face, and he saw her eyes were a pale shade of blue, almost gray. "Although it's not Mister. It's just Scott."

"Oh, sorry." A blush tinted her cheeks. "My sister Rory took the reservation, so I wasn't sure. I'm Allison St. Claire." She held out her hand. "Welcome to the Pearl Island Inn."

Her Southern-lady accent gave his gut an interesting tug, even though he normally preferred women with voices like smoky blues on Bourbon Street, not mint juleps served on a veranda. Her handshake was friendly but impersonal. An innkeeper welcoming a guest.

"Come on inside, and I'll get you checked into your room." She took a moment to carry the pitcher to a shadowy alcove, then led the way to the ornate front door. Her walk was as ladylike as her handshake, nothing sultry about it. Even so, he tipped his sunglasses down again to better appreciate the feminine sway of hips beneath her loose-fitting dress.

"Do you want to bring your bags now?" she asked over her shoulder. "Or get them later?"

"Later."

As they stepped inside the wide, central hall, the cool air enveloped him. He noticed the large space had been converted into a lobby with Victorian sofas and chairs set before one of several fireplaces in the house. Rather than cobwebs and dust covering every surface, sunlight poured in through the doorways of the outer rooms, adding a soft, welcoming glow.

The stillness of the place seemed almost reverent with the three tall stained-glass windows that lit the stairway at the far end. The room to the left, the old library, had been turned into a gift shop.

"We have you booked into the Baron," Allison said as she led him into the parlor to their right. She took a seat at an ornate desk before a rose marble fireplace. "It's one of our larger rooms, and the only one with a desk, which Rory says you requested." She glanced at the computer screen. "You'll be staying through the end of the month?"

"Correct." *One month,* he thought, remembering his agent's advice and hoping that would do it. Although he never should have confessed to Hugh Ashton how long he'd been without a woman. Two years was an embarrassingly long time for a healthy man to stay celibate. Well, that was about to end. Hopefully.

The thought must have shown on his face since Allison St. Claire glanced up and froze. For a moment she stared back at him as awareness warmed the air between them. She was everything he liked in a woman: attractive face, slender body, a spark of intelligence in her eyes. The last was a must in his opinion, even for a temporary liaison. As he'd matured, he'd decided that sexual partners should be as stimulating out of bed as in—which probably had something to do with his long bout of abstinence.

Holding her gaze, he allowed an inviting smile to lift one corner of his mouth. Color flooded her cheeks and her eyes widened. She looked away, fumbling at the keyboard. "Yes, well, if you'll give me just a minute, I'll, um, have you checked in and can show you to your room."

Okay, so she was either shy or not interested, he thought. Or maybe he was so out of practice at smiling that he'd snarled at her instead. He knew his expressions could be intimidating at times, but the dark scowls were supposed to scare off blood-sucking leeches, not potential lovers.

Although, watching Allison St. Claire, he became almost relieved at her lack of interest. The woman had an aura of basic goodness that pegged her as the marrying kind. Which was *not* what he was looking for. Too bad. He would have enjoyed discovering the body beneath that dress.

"I, um . . ." A frown puckered her brow. "I see you reserved the room with a credit card, but some information's missing. Do you have the card on you?"

"Certainly." He knew exactly what information was missing—his last name. He'd intentionally rattled the person who took his reservation so he wouldn't have to give it. A last-minute impulse to pay for the whole trip with cash made him hesitate slightly before reaching for his wallet. He missed the privacy of those days when he'd first changed his name and, to the world, he'd been Scott Nobody.

Resigned, he laid the card on the desk ... and knew the moment she read the name.

"Scott Lawrence?" Her gaze shot up and awe filled her eyes. "*The* Scott Lawrence?"

He nodded curtly, disappointed at how quickly her chilly demeanor melted away.

"Oh my." A brilliant smile lit her face. The smile made her positively breathtaking, dammit. Why couldn't she have given him that smile before she knew his name? "I love your books!" she said. "All suspense novels really—the more hair-raising the better—but your books are some of my favorites! I know, you probably hear that all the time, but I can't tell you how often you've kept me up all night biting my nails." She leaned forward, her face glowing. "I especially like how you throw ordinary people into so much danger, and have them win over such impossible odds. You're a fabulous storyteller."

"Thank you." He frowned, surprised that someone so innocent-looking would actually have read his gritty suspense-thrillers.

"Oh goodness." Still smiling, she entered his name into the computer. "This is so exciting. Our first national celebrity. I can't wait to tell Adrian, he's my brother, and another big fan of yours. He's going to be so jealous that I met you first."

A weary sigh escaped Scott as he took back his credit card. He could already hear it coming, all the predictable questions people asked when they met a writer.

"So"—her gaze flickered to the case for his lap top—"are you going to write a book while you're staying here?"

"Not a book. Just a proposal." A seriously past-due proposal. And if he could manage to even start one, he'd be grateful to the writing gods.

She lowered her voice. "You know, I've always wondered, where do writers get their ideas?"

He nearly laughed, not just because that was the biggie—the number one most frequently asked question—but because at that moment he desperately wished he knew the answer. Instead he gave her his best deadpan look. "Personally, I order mine online from Plots.com."

She covered her mouth as laughter danced in her eyes. "Sorry. I guess that was a silly question."

"Not silly, just common." He gave her a lopsided smile.

She retrieved a sheet from the printer and laid it before him. "Here, if you'll sign this, we'll be done."

Setting the computer case down, he leaned over the desk to review the room charges. Alli had barely a moment to study him unobserved. Though his smile had faded, its effect lingered, for it had transformed the aloof expression of his wickedly handsome face into something that bordered on . . . mischief. Not boyish mischief, though. It was too carnal for that.

The look in his eyes as his gaze held hers had sent flutters of alarm rioting through her system. For a second, she'd thought he was flirting with her. Except men never flirted with her. They flirted with her sister, Aurora, all the time—not that Rory ever noticed—but Allison they treated with utmost respect or sisterly affection.

Then she'd seen his name, realized who he was, and knew she was being foolish. Someone as exciting as Scott Lawrence would hardly notice a background fixture like her. He was just being kind when he smiled. What a relief. And what a thrill to finally see what he looked like! His books never had an author photo in the back and the short bios revealed little about him.

As he signed the form with swift, bold strokes, her gaze skimmed over his short, dark hair and closely trimmed beard. He was younger than she expected for someone who'd achieved so much success, early thirties perhaps, and very fit for a man with a sedentary occupation. The short-sleeved black shirt and tan slacks accentuated his broad shoulders, narrow hips—

He straightened abruptly, and his whiskey-colored eyes caught her in mid-gawk. That sardonic brow of his lifted and she realized the beard did nothing to soften the razor-sharp edges of his face.

Her cheeks heated as she took the printout and set it aside. "Well then, I'll um . . . just show you to your room." She retrieved a key ring from a drawer and came around the desk to hand it to him. Oh my, he was taller than she'd first realized. Not as tall as Adrian, who was well over six feet, but he definitely towered over her less-than-impressive height. "My brother and I live on premise. Right downstairs. In the basement. Well, in an apartment in the basement. What I mean is, if you need anything, there's always someone here." Was she babbling? Surely not. She never babbled. Straightening her shoulders, she composed herself. "We lock up at night, so you'll need the gold key to get in the front door after dark. The silver key is to your room."

"Got it." He gave another lopsided grin and butterflies danced in her stomach. God, he was so gorgeous when he did that, like a movie star who would play nothing but villains and still have every woman in the audience swooning.

Trying to appear casual, she led the way back into the hall, describing the inn's policies. He nodded absently, seeming more interested in looking about than what she was saying.

"You've really fixed up the place," he said as they started up the stairs. "I never would have imagined it could be this . . . inviting."

Startled, she paused on the landing, where the stained-glass windows bathed them in colored light. "You've been here before?"

He shrugged. "My family vacationed in Galveston a lot while I was growing up."

"Really?" she asked, fascinated.

"It was a common enough dare for kids to sneak out here and see if they could stay all night without running scared from the ghost. My sister and I took it a step farther and broke into the house with sleeping bags and séance candles." As if realizing he'd just admitted to breaking and entering, he quickly added, "This was, of course, long before your family owned the place."

"*Ghost Island*," she breathed in awe. "Your first book."

"My first published book," he clarified.

"It was about three boys who broke into a haunted house on a dare, and wound up discovering a storeroom for international art thieves." She looked about, seeing the house through different eyes. "You based that house on this one?"

"Pretty much."

"Can we tell people that? I mean, would you mind?"

He shrugged. "Doesn't matter to me."

"Oh, this is wonderful. I think guests will be fascinated. So, did you make it the whole night?"

"Barely." He chuckled. The sound was even more appealing than his lopsided grins. "Although once the sun was up, I'm not sure if we were relieved or disappointed that Marguerite never put in an appearance."

She laughed nervously, suddenly aware of how closely they stood together—so close that she caught the faint scent of soap and his freshly laundered shirt.

"So, what about you?" he asked, tipping his head to study her. "Did you ever sneak out here as a kid to see if Marguerite would reveal herself?"

"No, actually none of us, Adrian, Rory, or I, ever did." To gain some distance, she started up the stairs again. "That probably sounds odd, since Marguerite is our ancestor and we had more reason than most to want to see her. I guess it was just too much of a sore spot for all of us."

"What do you mean?"

"The house wasn't ours by right of inheritance, as it should have been. We still wouldn't own it if it hadn't come up for sale on a bank foreclosure a year ago. Marguerite's husband, Henri LeRoche, left the island and all his wealth to his nephew rather than his daughter, Nicole."

"Except Nicole Bouchard wasn't Henri LeRoche's daughter. Otherwise, why would she have taken her mother's maiden name?"

Surprise stopped Alli at the top of the stairs. She knew people said such things behind their backs, but rarely to their faces. "I see you did spend a lot of time in Galveston to have heard that bit of old slander."

"We writers are a curious lot," he said, not sounding the least contrite. "Which is probably the answer to your question about where ideas come from."

"Well, you can let your curiosity rest on that subject. The rumors are nothing more than vicious lies against Marguerite, invented by the LeRoche family to justify keeping Nicole's inheritance."

"It can't all be lies. After all, Marguerite *was* trying to run off with her pirate lover the night she and her husband fought on these very stairs and she fell, breaking her neck." He gestured down the grand sweep of stairs.

Alli straightened, ignoring a sudden rush of vertigo. "First of all, Marguerite didn't fall. Henri pushed her down these stairs. And secondly, her lover, Captain Jack Kingsley, was a Confederate blockade runner, not a pirate or a Yankee spy, as Henri claimed."

"But he was her lover."

"That hardly means Nicole Bouchard was illegitimate. She was born years before Marguerite even met Captain Kingsley."

Scott started to argue the point further—amused to see the kitten had claws when her fur was rubbed the wrong way—but the scent of lemon polish and fresh flowers distracted him. Glancing around, he found the upper hall had been turned into a sitting room with comfortable chairs and a sideboard for serving coffee and hot tea. "Impressive."

"Thank you," she said in a crisp voice that made him hide a smile. What a shame Allison St. Claire was too sweet for him to even think about seducing, since she apparently had a spark of passion beneath the surface.

Turning, she headed across the sitting area, her back rigid.

"So, have you ever seen her?" he asked as they reached the door to his room.

She shook her head. "Marguerite never actually shows herself. She makes her presence felt in other ways."

"How so?"

Allison looked up in the process of unlocking the door. "I'm surprised you don't know, since you seem knowledgeable about everything else."

"Amuse me." He leaned against the doorjamb, which brought him closer to her eye level.

"Marguerite is considered to be a good-luck charm, because of a blessing from the voodoo midwife who birthed her."

"Well, I knew that. I was hoping you could offer some proof that the charm really works. Or at least tell me if it works for anyone staying in the house, or only the owners."

Confusion replaced the anger in her eyes. "Is that why you're here? To borrow some of Marguerite's good luck?"

"Maybe." He shrugged as if the matter were of little importance.

"I'm surprised a man with your talent would feel the need for magic." Her gaze flickered over his face.

He studied his fingernails to keep her from seeing any hint of desperation in his eyes. "In addition to being curious, writers are notoriously superstitious. If I thought it would get me a number one slot on the *New York Times* best-seller list, I'd write naked in the middle of Times Square."

"You've already done that."

"What? Write naked in Times Square?" He grinned at her.

"No!" A breathy laugh escaped her. "I mean you've made number one on the best-seller lists. Many times."

"Hey, it never hurts to hedge your bets." The vivid pink in her cheeks intrigued him, and he wondered what it would take to make her cheeks go all the way to red. "Who's to say the success of *Ghost Island* wasn't due in part to Marguerite? I did get the idea while staying here."

"I've always thought the power of a charm comes more from believing in it than anything supernatural."

"If it works, it works."

"True." With a jiggle of keys, she opened the door and headed for a bedside table where she clicked on a lamp.

Scott took in the paisley wallpaper, heavy four-poster bed, and other furniture that gave the room a masculine feel. Whoever had decorated the inn had a taste for quality antiques.

She flung open three sets of heavy draperies, revealing a wall of windows that faced the cove. Sunlight poured in as she rattled off the routine for laundry and room cleaning. She opened another set of draperies, revealing a door to the second-floor balcony. He knew a larger balcony, off the ballroom on the third floor, loomed

directly above. It was from that balcony Henri had fired
a cannon on Jack Kingsley's ship, killing his wife's lover.
The remains of the ship and Kingsley's ghost were said
to still be at the bottom of the cove ... with the two
ghosts forever looking for a way to reunite.

"You'll want to keep this door locked, since you
share the balcony with the Pearl."

"The ghost?"

"No." Allison laughed lightly. "The Pearl is what we
call Marguerite's old suite in the tower since she was
known as the Pearl of New Orleans during her days as an
opera singer. Just as we call this suite the Baron, since
'shipping baron' was the nicest term we could think of to
describe Henri."

"Makes sense." Scott nodded.

"I think that covers everything." She folded her hands
before her, looking perfectly composed except for the
color still glowing in her cheeks. "Do you have any questions?"

"Just one." He stepped back to see under the desk.
"Where's the modem hookup?"

"Oh, we don't have phones in the rooms. So many
people carry mobile phones, we decided it wasn't necessary. We do have a computer set up in the music room,
though, so guests can check e-mail."

He stared at her a moment. "No phones in the
rooms?"

"I'm afraid not." Worry flickered across her brow. "Is
that a problem?"

"Actually"—he smoothed his beard to hide a smile—
"that's the best news I've had in weeks."

"Oh." The comment obviously confused her. "Well
then, I'll leave you to settle in." He nodded as she made
her way to the door. "If you need anything at all, please
let us know."

"I'll do that."

The moment she left, he glanced about. "Hear that, Marguerite? If I need anything at all . . . Well, right now, I could use a damn good idea for my next novel."

Taking a seat at the desk, he booted up the computer, then stared at the blank screen. His mind remained equally blank. After several minutes he let his gaze drift back to the door. "Although, as long as I'm asking for 'anything,' how about you make your great-great-great-granddaughter a little bit less of a 'nice girl'?"

Chapter 2

ALLISON HURRIED DOWNSTAIRS TO SHARE her news with her brother and sister. When she entered the kitchen, her dog, Sadie, bounded up from her pallet in the corner with a happy bark. The sassy little sheltie trotted over to greet her, while Adrian and Aurora didn't miss a beat in their ongoing food fight.

"Come on, Adrian," Rory pleaded with one hand resting on her pregnant stomach. "I know you have some nuts in here somewhere."

"For the thousandth time, no," Adrian insisted. "And for the millionth time, the doctor told you to cut back on salty food to keep your ankles from swelling."

"It's not the salt I need. It's nuts. Any nuts."

"Still at it?" Alli whispered to Sadie as she squatted down to ruffle the sable and white coat. Sadie grinned back, her brown eyes twinkling.

"Waldorf salad," Rory muttered as she waddled past them on her way to the refrigerator. Because of her height, Rory's pregnancy had taken a while to become apparent, but now that she'd reached her final weeks her belly expanded daily.

Alli always marveled that she and her sister were so different in both temperament and looks. While she was reserved and petite and had the coloring of their French ancestors, Rory was as outgoing as one would expect of a woman nearly six feet tall with long tumbling curls of golden-red hair. As Rory rummaged through the fridge, their older brother shook his head in amused frustration.

"You already picked all the walnuts out of the salad last night," Adrian complained as he slid a batch of lemon poppy muffins into the oven. He wore a red T-shirt and wildly patterned chef's pants, but the long black ponytail and small gold earring made him look more pirate than cook.

"Pistachio almond ice cream," Rory said, moving from the refrigerator to the freezer.

"Apparently you ate the last pint some time during the night," Adrian said, "because it's all gone."

"Oh." Rory's shoulders slumped. "Chance didn't tell me it was the last one." Narrowing her eyes, she glanced about the massive kitchen with its red brick walls and aged rafters. The room held a homey scent that came from generations of cooking, a fragrance that had captured Allison's heart when they'd first toured the house. Now it held a year of memories as well, of their struggles to buy the neglected old mansion and restore it to its former grandeur. The place was so much more than a business to them. It was a symbol of family. A home where they could stay together, always, rather than scatter as most siblings did.

"Pecans." Rory nodded. "I can melt some chocolate, stir in some butter, sugar, a little cream . . ."

Adrian spread his arms to guard the cabinet that held his baking staples. "Don't even think it. I have three orders of brownies to fill for the other B and Bs."

"Beer nuts?" Rory tried, her blue eyes hopeful.

Adrian hesitated a fraction of a second. "Uh, fresh out. Really. I swear."

"Aha! You have beer nuts hidden somewhere." Rory waddled through a door that led to a back hall, where a food pantry was tucked beneath the main stairs. "Where are they?"

"Get out of my pantry this minute, Aurora St. Claire." Adrian hurried after her.

"Aurora Chancellor," Rory corrected.

"Whatever. Those nuts are for my poker game tomorrow night. Touch 'em and you're a dead woman."

"Just tell me where you hid them, Adrian, and no one will get hurt."

Allison buried her face against Sadie's fur to stifle a laugh as she listened to the two of them argue in the pantry.

"No, Rory, they're for the guys," Adrian insisted.

"Pleeeeease, I'm begging you. You're dealing with a desperate woman here."

"I said no."

"Okay, if not for me, how about for your niece? You wouldn't deprive an innocent, unborn child of peanuts would you?"

Allison heard a pause before her brother gave in. "Oh, all right, but I swear I'm getting a padlock for the pantry."

"Mmm, thank you. Mmm." Rory returned to the kitchen a moment later digging a hand into a canister with a homemade label. Adrian had written the word "poison" in black marker and even drawn a skull and crossbones, which should have been a dead giveaway.

Adrian reappeared, shaking his head in disgust. "We need to do something, Alli. Enroll her in Nut Eaters Anonymous or something. The situation is clearly out of control."

Allison gave Sadie a final pet before standing. "Somehow I think it will take care of itself once the baby's born."

"Man, I hope so," Adrian said.

"In the meantime . . ." Allison let a smile blossom over her face. "Guess who just checked in?"

Curiosity lit Adrian's eyes when he saw her expression. "Are we talking about someone besides the Mr. Scott we're expecting?"

"Nope." She shook her head. "But Scott isn't his last name."

"He showed up? Thank goodness." Rory sighed as

she lowered herself into a seat at the worktable. The windows at her back framed the sun-drenched trees and yard behind the mansion. "Although I'm still sorry for doing such a sloppy job taking the reservation. It's just that the day he called, I was about to go down for my afternoon nap."

"More like afternoon coma," Adrian mumbled.

Rory wrinkled her nose at him. "So I get a little tired halfway through the day. I swear, though, I didn't even realize I hadn't taken down his full name until I woke up. Which was when I realized I hadn't asked for his phone number either, so I couldn't even call him back." She settled deeper into the chair with the can of nuts on her stomach. "Sometimes I think being pregnant causes temporary brain damage. At least I hope it's temporary."

"Never mind that now." Allison gave her sister a sympathetic smile. "He showed up, so we didn't lose any money by holding the room. Now, try to guess who he is."

"Give us a hint," Adrian said as he carried the mixing bowl and baking utensils to the sink.

"Okay. One hint," Allison agreed as she automatically moved forward to help with the dishes. "He's an author."

Adrian tipped his head in thought as he grabbed a soapy sponge and started washing. "Well, it can't be F. Scott Fitzgerald, since he's dead."

"Unless Marguerite is inviting ghosts over," Rory pointed out. When Adrian gave her an older-brother-to-irritating-little-sister look she just shrugged. "It could happen."

"He's definitely not a ghost," Allison said, rinsing each item her brother handed her.

Adrian thought a bit more. "Orson Scott Card, the sci-fi writer?"

"No."

"M. Scott Peck?"

"No."

"Scott Lawrence?"

"Yes!"

"No kidding?" Adrian's eyes went wide.

"Would I kid about something like this?" Allison said. "And, get this, he says he's here to work, which I guess is why he's staying so long."

"So he's really staying a whole month?" Rory asked.

"Yep," Alli answered.

"Well, thank you, Marguerite, for small favors," Rory said, referring to the good luck Marguerite brought. The inn was taking off nicely, but they were still in the first year of business, when every penny mattered. Renting the Baron for a month would definitely help their cash flow.

Adrian let out a laugh. "Scott Lawrence writing a book while staying at our inn. Talk about publicity."

"It gets better." Alli smiled as she dried the mixing bowl. "He told me the house in *Ghost Island* is based on this house. He and his sister broke in here as kids and stayed the night. Which is what gave him the idea for the book."

"Oh man." Adrian looked to Rory. "That has to go in our brochure."

"You got it." Rory nodded since publicity was her department. They each handled a different area of running the business. Rory took care of promoting the inn and renting the rooms, her husband, Chance, served as book-keeper and business manager, Adrian cooked, and Alli ran the gift shop. When it came to making the guests welcome, though, they all pitched in as needed.

Just then, a dark blue BMW pulled up by the back entrance, and Rory's eyes widened like a kid about to be caught with her hand in the cookie jar. She glanced around for a place to hide the can of nuts. At the sound of the back door opening, she slammed the lid on the can and set it on the floor, then dusted any telltale evidence from her mouth. By the time her husband, Oliver Chancellor, entered the kitchen, she was sitting primly in the chair with a smile of pure innocence. "Hi, honey. How was your trip to the post office?"

"It was . . . a trip." Chance shook his head, his expression a bit dazed. With his tall, thin build, wire-rimmed glasses, and neat blond hair, he managed to look like a rich banker's son even when wearing shorts and a golf shirt. When Rory tilted her head back, he bent and kissed her lips, then pulled back with a frown. "Why do you taste salty?"

"Salty?" Rory batted her eyes. "I have no idea."

Allison saw her brother roll his eyes as she struggled not to laugh. Chance just growled playfully and kissed his wife again, longer this time.

In the midst of that perfect moment, filled with such happiness, fear whispered against the back of Alli's neck. She shook it away, determined to ignore it. Her sister and Chance were blissfully married and expecting their first child. Their business was going well and picking up daily. She had to quit looking around corners waiting for tragedy to jump out and destroy everything.

Chance straightened with a weary sigh and Rory's smile faded as she studied his face. "Something's wrong."

" 'Fraid so." He looked at all of them. "Apparently John LeRoche isn't too happy with our refusal to sell Pearl Island back to him. Because now"—Chance held up an envelope—"he's suing us."

"What?" Adrian and Rory demanded as Allison's stomach dropped.

"He's also suing the Liberty Union National Bank," Chance went on, referring to the bank his family had founded in the mid-1800s, then sold recently to an East Coast banking chain. "He's claiming there was some dirty dealing involved in the bank's decision to foreclose on his loan and seize possession of Pearl Island."

"But he's the one who put the property up as collateral, then fell six months behind on his payments," Rory protested.

"He's also claiming I personally used prior knowledge to help the three of you buy the property before he had the opportunity to rectify the situation."

"That's ridiculous!" Adrian dried his hands, then threw the dish towel on the counter. "You told us yourself that your father tried to give him first right of refusal, but he showed no interest back then. Why the sudden interest now?"

"Who knows?" Chance sighed.

"I think I do." Allison clasped her hands together to keep them from shaking. "Chance, didn't you say John LeRoche has had a string of financial setbacks since he lost the house?"

"I've heard rumors to that effect," Chance confirmed. "Apparently it started when he first took out the loan. He used the money for a business venture that failed, and everything he's touched since has gone sour. Still, it'll take a lot more than that to topple a fortune the size of LeRoche Enterprises."

"Even so . . ." Allison said. "I think he wants the Pearl back."

"That doesn't make sense." Adrian glanced from her to Chance. "If he believes in the Pearl, why didn't he take steps to keep the house a year ago when the bank started threatening to foreclose?"

"Maybe he didn't believe in the legend back then," Allison offered. "But once his luck with making money evaporated, he may have started blaming everything on losing the Pearl. So now he wants her back."

Chance rubbed his forehead. "If that's true, we could be in big trouble."

"Why?" Rory struggled up from her chair. "You're not guilty of anything. None of us are. Surely an investigation of bank records will show that."

"It will." Chance sighed. "But I still have to pay a lawyer to help prove I'm innocent."

"No, we pay a lawyer. This involves all of us." Rory glanced to her brother and sister. They both nodded.

"Now hold on," Chance said. "We need to be practical. The inn can't afford to fight this, but I can. It's basically a nuisance lawsuit, and John LeRoche knows it. Which means his goal isn't to win a settlement. It's to weaken us financially and run us out of business. If we go bankrupt, we'll have to sell the house, and he'll buy it back."

"Can he do that?" Rory paled.

"He can try," Chance said. "And let's face it, the man may be having some money problems, but he still has plenty of resources." Chance looked at each of them. "If he's determined to get the Pearl back, this could get nasty."

"So we should stand back and let you fight it with your own money just because you're a trust fund baby?" Adrian snorted. "I don't think so. When you married Rory, you became family. We fight this together."

Chance held up his hands. "Let's all be realistic about this. The three of you sank your entire net worth into this venture. You can't afford to fight a lengthy legal battle."

"Tough," Adrian said. "It's our inn, so it's our battle."

"It's my inn, too," Chance pointed out. "I bought a full one-fourth partnership before Aurora and I even married."

"Okay"—Adrian nodded—"then you can pay one-fourth the cost of fighting this bogus lawsuit."

Chance rolled his eyes. "Allison, Aurora, talk some sense into your brother, will you?"

Allison exchanged a glance with her sister, silently

telling her she sided with Adrian. Rory nodded and turned
to her husband. "Alli and I vote to fight this as a family."

"How do y'all *do* that?" Chance demanded, referring
to the way they communicated without words.

"We're sisters," Rory said. "If you weren't an only
child, you'd understand."

Chance shook his head. "I still say let me handle
this."

"Too late." Rory kissed him soundly on the mouth.
"The vote's been cast. You lose, three to one."

"But—"

"But nothing." Rory wrapped both her arms about
one of his. "Now if you really want to be useful, come
help me clean rooms."

When they'd gone, Alli looked to her brother, trying
to fight the panic. "This doesn't sound good."

"No, it doesn't. And Chance is right. It could get
nasty. Even if we let him use his own money, he's no
match for John LeRoche."

"What do we do?"

Adrian's cheeks puffed as he let out a heavy sigh.
"Hope Marguerite's magic is firmly on our side?"

Allison remembered what she'd said to Scott
Lawrence: A charm only works if you believe. Unfortunately, life had taught her that blind faith too often led to
shattering heartbreak.

Morning arrived much too early after a night of tossing
and turning and worrying over money, but that didn't
mean Allison could sleep in. By six o'clock, she and the
others were in the kitchen, preparing for "Show Time,"
as Adrian liked to call it.

As B and Bs grew in popularity, so grew the expectations of guests. With the former chef of Chez Lafitte
manning the stove, the Pearl Island Inn was more than up
for the challenge. Mouthwatering pastries, fluffy soufflés,

and poached eggs drenched in hollandaise were served alongside fresh fruit, homemade yogurt, and their own toasted granola.

At seven o'clock the first two guests had already come downstairs.

"Good morning," Allison greeted the couple cheerfully as she swept into the dining room with a wicker basket of pastries. Chance and Rory followed with silver trays to fill the serving stands on the sideboard. "I hope y'all slept well."

"Reasonably well," Colonel Grubbs, a retired army officer, answered as he took a seat beside his wife at the long table. "Considering Elsie forgot to pack my pillow."

"Oh, Arthur, stop complaining." His wife gave him an indulgent smile before turning to Allison. "I'm afraid my husband's never been much of a morning person."

Alli saw Rory and Chance exchange glances and roll their eyes. One thing they'd all learned about running a bed and breakfast was that innkeepers met a lot of people, from the delightful ones to the ones who took a bit more patience. With Colonel and Mrs. Grubbs, they had one of each.

"What do you two have planned for today?" Alli asked the couple as she took up a pitcher of fresh squeezed orange juice.

"We were thinking about the Texas Seaport Museum," Mrs. Grubbs answered.

"Oh, you'll like that," Rory said. "The *Elissa* is a beautiful old sailing ship that's been fully restored and the museum's display on smuggling is fascinating." As Rory, a former tour guide, launched into a list of other things to do down by the pier, the phone in the office rang.

"I'll get it," Alli said. With orange juice pitcher in hand, she headed for the office and reached the desk just before the answering machine would have picked up the call. "Pearl Island Inn. Allison speaking."

"Well, now there's a disgustingly chipper voice for

so early in the day," a deep voice grumbled.

"Sorry." Alli smiled. "I forgot it was before the chipper hour. How may I help you?"

"Run away with me to Tahiti?"

She laughed, wondering who the caller was. "I'm afraid that will have to wait until after I finish serving breakfast."

"Darn! Well, if you won't run away with me, how about patching me through to Scott Lawrence's room?"

"I'm afraid I can't do that, either."

"Don't tell me—the son of a bitch beat me to Tahiti."

"No." Her laughter grew. "We don't have phones in the rooms."

"No phones in the rooms? Man, no wonder he picked your inn. The jerk must be doing handsprings."

"Would you like me to give him a message?" Setting aside the pitcher, she reached for a pen and piece of paper.

"Sure. Why not? I'll give it a shot. Not that I expect it to do any good, but tell him Hugh called. As in Hugh Ashton. His agent in New York, in case he's forgotten the name. While I almost admire the way he's turned avoiding me into an art form, we do have some business to discuss. So, tell him I would appreciate him actually returning one of my calls sometime before Y3K. Got that?"

His agent! Calling from New York! "Y-yes, sir. Absolutely."

"Great. Now what did you say your name was?"

"Allison. Allison St. Claire."

"Allison, eh? Pretty name. Pretty voice. I don't suppose you have a face to match, do you?"

"Excuse me?" She couldn't believe she was talking to Scott Lawrence's literary agent.

"Are you good-looking?"

Why on earth would he ask that? Rattled, she grasped for a way to handle the situation, to seem sophisticated

rather than awestruck. An image of her aunt, the Incomparable Vivian, star of the stage on Broadway, rose in her
mind. How would Aunt Viv handle a flirtatious caller?
Alli tossed her head to help get into character and pitched
her voice low enough to sound husky. "Devastatingly gorgeous, darling."

"Oh, be still my heart. So, what do you think of
Scott?"

Confusion nearly made her break character. Why
would he flirt with her, then ask her what she thought
about another man? "I think he's a brilliant writer, of
course."

"No, what do you think about *him*?"

"Not bad on the eyes, I suppose. If you like the tall,
dark, and deadly type."

Hugh Ashton's laughter boomed forth, rich and full
like a man with a bawdy sense of humor who sorely
needed a chance to laugh more often. "Allison, I like you.
Please tell me you're not married?"

"Why? Are you proposing?"

"No, just being nosy."

"In that case, I'm single."

"Involved?"

"I . . ." Some of her initial wonder dimmed to caution. What an odd conversation. "I need to go."

"Wait! The message. Tell Scott his editor agreed to
another extension on the proposal, but she needs a title
suggestion and a short blurb about the premise and setting
so they can start on the cover concept. Tell him to fax me
something. Anything. Got it?"

She nodded as she wrote. "Yes, I have it."

"Good. Then bye for now, love. I'm sure we'll be
talking again soon."

After disconnecting, Alli stared at the phone. She'd
just talked to a real, live literary agent, and he wanted her
to play go-between for him and Scott Lawrence!

Celebrities normally didn't intimidate her—her family tree boasted too many stars of the stage for that—but Scott was fast proving to be an exception. Perhaps because he didn't just act out stories, he created them. She glanced toward the ceiling and wondered when he would come down for breakfast.

Breakfast! Snapping out of her haze, she picked up the orange juice, slipped the note into her apron pocket, and hurried back toward the dining room.

As if her thoughts had conjured him, Scott was coming down the stairs as she entered the hall. He wore a dark print, short-sleeved shirt tucked into black shorts. She stopped for a moment, wondering how he could possibly be more devastating to the senses than he'd been yesterday.

Breathe, she told herself. *And stop being such a ninny.* "Mr. Lawrence?"

He stopped on the last step, which made him seem that much taller as she approached. "Scott," he said, correcting her.

"Oh. Yes. Of course." She fished the note out of her apron. "I have a phone message for you. From Hugh Ashton."

"Well, that didn't take long." He took the sheet of paper she handed him without even glancing at the message.

"What didn't take long?"

"Nothing." He folded the paper several times and stuffed it into the pocket of his shorts.

"Aren't you going to read it? He said it was very important."

"I'm sure he did. Am I too early for breakfast?"

"No, not at all." She frowned, wondering if she should just tell him what it said. The agent had made the message sound so crucial . . . but it wasn't her place to get involved in guests' private business, she reminded herself. Forcing aside her avid curiosity, she gestured to the dining room. "If you'll follow me."

Chapter 3

IRRITATION TIGHTENED SCOTT'S JAW AS he followed Allison into the dining room. Calls from his agent hadn't always put him in a sour mood. In fact, he used to enjoy them. That, however, was before Hugh started calling every morning to say "So, did you get any writing done yesterday?" Did the man actually think daily prodding would help? And what was the point of leaving town to relax if Hugh was going to track him down and remind him of why he was stressed out in the first place?

He gave his shoulders a subtle roll to loosen them and turned his attention to something far more pleasant: the delightful view Allison presented as she walked in front of him. The shorts covered more thigh than he'd prefer, but they hugged her narrow waist and shapely behind very nicely.

"We serve breakfast buffet-style." She glanced back to explain. "Would you like me to pour you some orange juice while you grab a plate?"

"No, coffee will be fine," he said as he scanned the room. If his luck was turning, there would be some jaded but delectable creature among the other guests. Instead, he saw an elderly couple at the far end of the table where morning sunlight poured in through the windows. So much for his luck changing.

As for the room, they seemed to have made the fewest changes here, but then there hadn't been as much to change. The massive table and chairs had been there during his clandestine visit all those years before and he suspected they were original to the house. Their carvings of sea serpents and mermaids matched the molding that crowned the paneling.

The fresco on the ceiling depicted Neptune riding the waves in a giant shell drawn by sea horses as if charging to attack whoever entered the room. Scott didn't have to work his imagination much to see the formidable Henri LeRoche—with black hair and hawkish features—sitting in the thronelike chair at the head of the table. By all accounts, he'd liked to "hold court" over the rough seafaring men who had carried cargo for his shipping company.

"Rory, Chance," Allison said, distracting him. "You haven't met our new guest. This is Scott. Scott, my sister, Aurora, and her husband, Oliver Chancellor."

Scott turned toward the built-in sideboard, to find a young couple he hadn't noticed. His automatic greeting stuck in his throat along with surprise when he caught sight of Allison's sister. The two women looked nothing alike. Allison had a quiet beauty that whispered seductively to a man. The sister was a vision to incite wars. Helen of Troy. Tall with glowing skin and long golden-red curls. Unfortunately she was also pregnant. Very pregnant. And married to the skinny blond guy beside her.

"Good morning." The golden goddess wiggled her fingers in welcome. "Scott Lawrence, right?"

Scott nodded, but wished he'd had the forethought to ask them not to tell the other guests who he was.

"And this is Colonel Arthur Grubbs and his wife, Elsie, from Chicago," Allison continued, motioning to the older couple.

"Pleased to meet you." The woman smiled at him, with no flicker of recognition. Scott sighed in relief.

"Help yourself to as much breakfast as you want," Oliver Chancellor told him. "There's always plenty to go around."

"I'll do that." Scott nodded.

"Alli, if you have things covered here, we'll go help Adrian in the kitchen," the sister said.

"I'm fine."

As the two left the room, Scott crossed to the sideboard and found an amazing spread of food that sent his salivary glands into overdrive. Grabbing an antique china plate, he started down the line.

"Scott Lawrence . . ." Colonel Grubbs tested the name, and Scott's shoulders sagged in disappointment as he realized his relief had come too soon. "Any relation to the famous writer?"

Resigned, Scott glanced back at the man. "One and the same."

"Weeell," the colonel said, his bushy black brows rising toward his white crew cut. "This is an honor. I've read a book or two of yours, even though I normally prefer historical novels, Pearl Harbor, Civil War, you know, *real* books. In fact"—he pointed his fork at Scott—"I have an idea for a story based on my own experience in Korea that would be a surefire best-seller. If only I could find the time to sit down and write it."

Scott nodded gravely. "Yeah, I know what you mean. The lack of a free weekend keeps more blockbuster bestsellers from being written than you can imagine."

When Allison came closer to retrieve the sterling silver coffee urn from its warming stand, he leaned toward her and whispered in her ear, "I'll give you my idea and we can share the money."

She turned to him with a startled frown.

"Hey, I have a thought," Colonel Grubbs said. "I could give you my idea, you could write the book, and we could share the money."

Allison's eyes widened and Scott arched a brow, enjoying the moment of shared humor. Although, for one flicker of an instant, he actually considered the man's offer—proof that he was truly getting desperate. He knew from experience that ideas from non-writers were never doable. Especially when those ideas were based on personal experience.

Fortunately, he was saved from his moment of insanity when an attractive black couple wandered into the room.

"Good morning, Keshia, Franklin," Allison greeted them as she headed around the table with the coffeepot. "I see you're up early."

"Too early." The woman shook off the end of a yawn as the two of them joined Scott at the buffet. "Since we checked in so late last night, I was hoping to sleep until a reasonable hour. But, no, Franklin's eager to strap on our scuba tanks and check out the shipwreck."

"Come on, baby." Franklin slipped an arm around her waist. "You like scuba diving, too."

"Around coral reefs where there's something to see," she said. "Not in the murky water of Galveston Bay."

"Actually," Allison said, "our cove is protected enough that it's surprisingly clear. And who knows, you might get lucky and find some pirate gold."

Keshia frowned. "I thought the ship was a Confederate blockade runner, not a pirate ship."

"It was," Allison said. "But the captain, Jack Kingsley, was the grandson of one of Jean Lafitte's men. Some people think a portion of Lafitte's missing treasure was on the *Freedom* when she went down. Unfortunately, most of the ship is covered in silt from the nineteen hundred hurricane, so no one's been able to explore her completely."

"Pirate gold?" Keshia considered. "Okay, now that's worth getting up early."

Scott carried his plate to the chair where Allison had already poured him a cup of coffee.

"Well, treasure or not, I'm looking forward to seeing the ship." Franklin chose a chair across from Scott and extended his hand before taking a seat. "Franklin Prescott."

"Scott Lawrence." He shook the man's hand, deciding there was no sense trying for anonymity at this point.

"The author?" Keshia's brows shot up. When he nodded, she beamed at him and took a seat. "Well, isn't this my lucky day. I'm Keshia Prescott." She shook his hand. "News anchor for KSET in Houston. My producer was just talking about doing a series of author interviews as a special segment. I don't suppose you'd agree to an interview."

"Keshia, we're on vacation," Franklin complained.

"I know." She flashed her husband a dazzling smile that had probably won the hearts of thousands of viewers. "I wasn't talking about interviewing him right now, just setting it up." She turned back to Scott. "So, how about it?"

"I don't do TV interviews."

"Why not?"

For the same reason I don't have my photo on the back jacket of my books, he thought. He didn't want every Joe on the street recognizing him. Plus, in a live interview, he had less control. On the other hand, interviews did help sales. "I tell you what," he said. "I'll consider it on two conditions. One, we schedule it for the fall, when my next book comes out." Mentioning the release date sent a small streak of panic through him since he hadn't even started the book. "And two, I get to set some boundaries on what's off limits."

Keshia's eyes narrowed. "How strict are the boundaries?"

"We talk only about my books. No questions about my personal life." He could tell she didn't like that, since the personal angle was what all reporters wanted.

"All right," Keshia finally agreed. "Although there is one question I'd like to ask you now."

"Keshia . . ." her husband warned.

"It's just one question," she insisted, then turned back to Scott. "In *The Flier,* the one about the pilot whose daughter is kidnapped, I swear my heart stopped about ten times during the dogfight scene at the end of the book. How do you come up with stuff like that? Where do you get your ideas?"

Scott glanced at Allison and found her watching him, her eyes sparkling with laughter.

"Plots.com?" she suggested.

"Or the author's mail order catalogue." He smiled at her. "But you have to know the secret code word to subscribe."

"Okay." Keshia held up her hand. "I can take a hint."

To smooth over the moment, Allison introduced the Prescotts to the Grubbs. With the attention off him, Scott watched the others while he ate, mentally collecting fodder for future books. Even without the benefit to his writing, people fascinated him: their gestures, expressions, the cadence of their voices. It was one of the main reasons he liked living in the French Quarter. When his niece, Chloe, came to visit, they would sit on his balcony and play "What's their story?" for hours.

This morning, though, only Allison held his attention for long. She moved about the table with the posture and grace of a dancer, so he assumed she'd taken ballet. What other lessons had she taken? Piano, voice? He watched her hands as she refilled coffee cups and removed dirty dishes, her movements simple but agile. What would it feel like to have her trail those slender hands over his body?

He shifted in his chair as heat flowed through him.

"Can I get you anything?" she asked as she came around behind him.

"No, I'm done." He leaned sideways as she reached for his plate and her scent drifted to him—a subtle blend of fragrances he couldn't quite sort out. Lavender? Vanilla?

"Are you going to write today? Or see the sights?" She stepped back, leaving only a trace of her scent to tease him.

He thought about the laptop waiting upstairs—the screen as blank this morning as it had been yesterday afternoon—and about the message from his agent lurking in his pocket. He should go upstairs, lock himself in his room, and not come out until he had at least started a proposal. A page. A paragraph. A sentence! "I think I'll go to the beach over on Galveston."

"No need to fight the crowds at the public beaches," she said. "We have a very nice private beach here."

"Crowds don't bother me." As long as he didn't have to interact with anyone.

"Well, if you're going to the public beach, you'll want to get an early start. Even this time of year, parking spaces disappear in a hurry." Allison moved around the table to clear away more dirty dishes. "Do you want to use the phone in the office before you go?"

"Use the phone?" He stared at her.

"To return your call."

"I'll, um, get to it later." He dropped his napkin on the table as he rose and made a quick exit before she could say any more about the message from Hugh. As soon as he reached his room, he crumpled the note and tossed it in the trash unread.

What a total waste of a day, Scott thought as he returned to the inn that afternoon. He had sand in his Top-Siders, his skin felt gritty from the salt water, he was dehydrated, hot, and exhausted. All that to spend a day on the beach with married couples, shrieking kids, and self-absorbed coeds.

To think a day at the beach used to be one of his

favorite pastimes. Of course, that was back in the days
when he and his older sister had come to Galveston to
spend agonizing weeks trapped in the family beach house
with their bickering parents. The beach had offered escape. Plus, to a hormone-driven teenager, ogling coeds
had held vast appeal.

Okay, so ogling coeds still held appeal, but he didn't
feel the least inclined to actually strike up a conversation
with one and ask her out on a date. They all seemed too
young.

He climbed the front steps of the inn thinking fond
thoughts about a shower and a two-hour nap before he
faced going out for dinner and maybe hitting a few of
Galveston's night spots. Trolling for women was a lot
more work than he remembered from his younger days.
He much preferred the more adult liaisons he'd had since
where a couple of gourmet dinners with fine wine, long
talks about literature, travel, current events, a few movies,
maybe a concert, all led up to the Big Event: a night of
really hot, down-and-dirty sex—followed by more nights
of hot sex, until both partners got bored and moved on.
Unfortunately, those relationships took more time to develop than he had at the moment.

That and they didn't always end well. Sometimes
they ended with a lot of crying, shouting, and accusations
that left him feeling like a jerk. Who needed that? What
he needed was a quick, effortless, no-strings-attached vacation affair. Now if he could just find an attractive, reasonably mature, halfway intelligent woman who was
looking for the same thing he'd be set.

He stepped through the front door and sighed in relief
when the coolness of the inn enveloped him. Pulling off
his sunglasses, he waited for his vision to adjust.

"Oh, Scott," Allison called from the parlor-cum-
office. "I have some more phone messages for you."

Groaning, he started to tell her to toss them in the

trash and save him the bother. Besides, the last thing he needed was to face the ever-tempting Allison after the day he'd had. Then the sunspots cleared from his vision and he saw the person standing with her in the office. *Hel-lo!*

The tall, slender woman in a stylish pantsuit gazed back at him with equal interest. Short, brown hair framed a handsome face—not gorgeous, but attractive. He guessed her to be about his age, early thirties. But it was the expression in her eyes that got his attention. She looked directly at him in the manner of a woman who'd been around the block a few times and wouldn't mind another trip.

He stepped into the office on the pretext of gathering his messages. "Thank you," he said to Allison, holding out his hand without really looking at her. Looking at Allison St. Claire was not a good idea since it put too many lust-filled ideas in his head.

Allison frowned at his rudeness, and the fact that he didn't bother reading the messages—again.

"Checking in?" he asked the new guest.

The woman made an affirmative humming noise as her gaze moved boldly down Scott's body. Alli blushed on his behalf. But rather than take offense, he let his gaze take a trip of its own, down to the woman's left hand to check for a ring. Well, at least he cared enough to see if she was married. When he didn't see a ring, he smiled.

"Are you here for business or pleasure?" he asked.

"Pleasure." The woman all but purred. "You?"

"Definitely pleasure. I'm Scott, by the way."

"Dr. Linda Lovejoy." She held out her hand.

And I'm Alli, she wanted to say. *Remember me? The person who is standing right here watching all of this?*

Scott set the messages down as he shook the woman's hand. "Doctor? As in M.D.?"

"Ph.D. Forensics specialist."

"Oh really?" Scott arched a brow. "Police?"

"FBI."

"Are you kidding?" His face lit up, like a boy who'd just been given a pony for Christmas. "You know"—he propped one hip on the desk—"crime scene analysis is one of my favorite subjects."

"I'll bet." The woman laughed.

"No, I'm serious."

Alli watched in amazement as Dr. Lovejoy, who had been all business a moment ago, tipped her head and smiled at Scott through her lashes. "Let me guess," Linda said. "You're either a cop, private investigator, or a writer."

"I've been known to dabble at writing."

Dabble? Alli choked.

He must have caught the sound, because he glanced at her, then shifted his body to block her out completely. As if she didn't already feel like a third wheel.

"So," he said to Linda, "is this your first trip to Galveston?"

"Yes. You?"

"Not hardly. I've spent so many summers here, I'm practically a local. How long you staying?"

"Three days." Linda toyed with her necklace. "Two nights."

"I'd be happy to show you around in exchange for the chance to pick your brain."

Oh right, Alli snorted, *like that's all he's interested in. Her brain.*

A smile softened Linda Lovejoy's face. "I might be interested."

"Good." Scott straightened, which at least got his backside off the desk. "Why don't I let you get checked in while I wash off a few pounds of sand? I'll meet you downstairs and we'll talk about where to have dinner."

"All right." Linda watched him go, her gaze openly straying to Scott's buns as he walked away. Okay, so he had some pretty incredible buns, Alli decided.

"God Almighty," Linda breathed when he was gone. "Is he for real?"

"I'm not sure," Alli said, hardly believing what she'd just witnessed. The man walks in, says "Hi, I'm Scott," and two minutes later he has a date!

"I wonder if he'd mind skipping dinner so I can eat him instead."

Alli's jaw dropped so far her chin nearly hit the desk—and the messages he'd left there.

Chapter 4

SCOTT WAS JUST GETTING OUT of the shower when he heard a knock at the door. Dr. Lovejoy must be more eager than he thought. "Just a minute!" he called as he pulled on a pair of trousers. Still drying his hair, he opened the door.

Instead of the tall, leggy Ph.D. he found sweet Allison St. Claire. Her eyes widened at the sight of his bare chest before her gaze darted away. A pink blush stained her cheeks and he felt an answering flush of heat spread low in his belly. *Damn,* she shouldn't be able to do that to him now that he had somewhere else to focus his attention.

"You, um . . ." She cleared her throat. "You forgot your phone messages."

She held out the same three slips of paper she'd tried to give him earlier. He stared at her slender fingers and the heat coiled into a knot. *Down, boy,* he told his body, *good girls are off limits.* He plucked the messages from her hand, careful not to touch her. "From Hugh, I presume."

"Actually," she said in that sweet Southern-lady accent, "one is from your editor asking if you've sent the fax she needs. Another is from your publicist wanting to know if you'll agree to an interview with *Publishers Weekly*. The last one is from Hugh Ashton. He wants to know—"

"Look, I don't mean to be rude, but—" He cut himself off as he remembered that rudeness had always been a good defense in the past. "On second thought, do me a favor."

"All right." She looked up at him with innocent blue eyes that widened when he started ripping up the messages.

"Tell my editor and my publicist I checked out and you don't know where I went. As for Hugh, tell him to *back off*." He leaned toward her and her scent filled his nostrils, making him want to shake her and tell her to back off, too. "Remind Hugh I'm down here trying to follow his advice, which is to take some time to do some serious relaxation. I can't very well do that if he's calling me five times a day. Can you tell him that for me?"

"Yes, certainly."

He pulled back to a safer distance. "Speaking of 'serious relaxation,' what room is Dr. Lovejoy staying in?"

If possible, Allison's eyes went even wider as his meaning apparently sank in. "The Crow's Nest. There." She pointed to a door at the top of the stairs, catty-corner from his suite. "Although . . ." She trailed off, frowning.

"Although what?"

She surprised him by glaring back. "Although I hardly think an intelligent woman like Dr. Lovejoy would be flattered to learn you consider her as nothing more than a means to aid your 'relaxation.' "

Scott laughed. "You think only stupid women enjoy recreational sex?"

Her cheeks went all the way to red: fire-engine, I-can't-believe-you-said-that red. "I—I wouldn't know."

"Let me tell you something, sweetheart. Some women aren't any different from men when it comes to sex. Unless I'm way off the mark, Dr. Lovejoy is down here looking for the same thing I am. If that notion bothers your delicate sensibilities, I suggest you not watch."

"Yes, well . . ." She gathered herself up to her full height, which didn't even come to his chin. "If you'll excuse me."

She turned with dignity, and walked toward the stairs.

Guilt hit him full in the face. God, he really could be a bastard sometimes. Well, if nothing else he didn't have to worry about her tempting him anymore with her dainty manners and sexy sweetness. She'd probably give him a wide berth for the rest of his stay.

Anger and embarrassment followed Alli all the way down to the apartment in the basement. She would simply forget the last few minutes ever happened or that Scott Lawrence even existed. The rude, arrogant, obnoxious . . . *toad*!

"Hey, Alli," Adrian called from the sofa where he lay sprawled out in shorts and a muscle shirt, drenched in sweat. Fortunately, he'd spread a towel to protect the furniture so she wouldn't have to fuss. "You'll be happy to know Chance and I finished the jogging trail today. It now runs completely around the island. Of course, after working on it all day, Chance wanted to try it out. God, I swear, he might be a skinny geek, but he can run even me into the ground. He's a total klutz at t'ai chi, though, so I guess we're even."

"Does everything with men have to be a competition?" she demanded hotly as she moved around the combination counter/bar that divided the kitchen from the dining and living area.

"Long day for you too, eh?" Adrian said, apparently noticing she was not in the best of moods.

"Yep." She slammed a metal mixing bowl onto the counter.

"You want some help with dinner?"

"No, it's my turn," she answered as she took out a package of ground beef. She dropped that onto the counter beside the bowl and started gathering the other ingredients for a meat loaf.

"Wanna tell me about it?" He came off the sofa and took a seat on a barstool across from her.

"What makes you think there's something to tell?"

She grabbed a meat cleaver and chopped an onion in two with one brutal stroke.

"I don't know, but I sure am glad I'm not that onion."

She looked up with the knife still in her hand. "I just want to know one thing. Am I ugly? Do I have a huge wart on my nose that everyone but me can see? Do I have body odor? What?"

"That's more than one question, but the answers are no, no, no, and what the hell are you talking about?"

"Men!" She attacked the onion, chopping with a vengeance.

"Uh, since I happen to fall in that category, do you think you could put the meat cleaver down before we continue this discussion?"

"There's nothing to discuss." She set the knife aside and scraped the onion into the bowl.

"Good. I'm too tired for a discussion that starts off with a woman saying 'Men!'"

"Blind cretins. Or maybe I'm invisible." She added bread crumbs and an egg, and started working them into the meat with her hand. "They never even look at me, much less ask me out, or so much as make a pass at me."

"Are we talking about a general 'they' or a specific 'they'?"

"We're talking about a Scott Lawrence 'they.'" She shook some spices into the meat mixture. "He wants to have sex."

"*Excuse me!*"

"Scott Lawrence came to Galveston hoping to play a little beach blanket bingo."

"*He told you that?*" Adrian came halfway off the barstool.

"Sure did."

Adrian plopped back down, stunned. "Do you want me to beat him up?"

"Yes, actually I do." She continued squeezing the ingredients through her fingers. "I want you to break both his kneecaps for insulting me."

"I can't believe he propositioned you."

"He didn't."

"Okay, now you lost me." Adrian held his hands up.

She glared at her brother. "Scott Lawrence told me he needed to do some 'serious relaxing,' which apparently includes recreational sex. The thought of having it with me, however, never crossed his mind."

Adrian gave his head a quick shake, as if to clear it. "Let's back up here. How do you know it didn't cross his mind?"

"Because . . . he didn't even try to make a pass at me." She pulled out a Pyrex baking dish and transferred the meat mixture into it.

"That doesn't mean he doesn't want to," Adrian said. "More likely, he just figured out you're not the beach-blanket-bingo type. You're more the 'Let's buy a house with a picket fence and have a couple of kids' type."

She narrowed her eyes at him. "You're saying a man can tell that after a few brief encounters?"

"Nooo, I'm saying a man can tell that after a few seconds. Like that hot number who checked in a few minutes ago—now there's a candidate for beach blanket bingo."

"Well, apparently Scott agrees with you, because they have a date tonight."

"Man." Adrian gave a low whistle of admiration. "Touchdown on the first play."

"Cretins," she growled and stalked to the sink to wash her hands. Yet all the questions whirling in her head wouldn't go away. "Adrian . . ."

"Yes?"

She shouldn't ask. It was too embarrassing. But this was her brother, and if she couldn't ask him, who could she ask? Drying her hands, she turned to face him. "Is there really such a thing as recreational sex? I mean, I know you men claim you can do it without any emotion involved, but . . . do you think it's possible for a woman?"

"Sure." He shrugged. "For some women, anyway."

"What do you mean, 'some women'?"

"People want different things out of life. Some women are focused on their careers, or they haven't found Mr. Right, or they've just come out of a bad relationship and don't want to get seriously involved for a while, or any number of things. But not wanting emotional involvement doesn't mean they want to do without men altogether. As much as women like to bitch about us, admit it, there are times when y'all like a man's company. Especially when it comes to what a man can do for you in the bedroom. Well"—he backpedaled—"not you personally."

"No, of course not me." She suppressed a twinge of hurt. Her experience with sex was so limited and so far in the past, she was likely a born-again virgin. "Adrian . . . do you think there's something wrong with me? Something that repels men?"

"No, there's nothing wrong with you. I assumed you didn't date because . . ." *Because you were so badly hurt the one time you did.* The words hung between them, unspoken, but there. "Because you didn't want to."

"I'm not sure what I want." She dropped her gaze to the towel and continued wiping her hands. "I know I'm not interested in getting married."

"Why not?"

"I'm just not." She looked up and saw the doubt in his eyes. "I'm serious. I have no interest whatsoever in marriage. But lately I've been wondering . . . don't you think it's unhealthy to be completely asexual?"

"I don't know." He shrugged. "Nuns do it all the time. Or rather, nuns don't do it."

"I'm not a nun."

"No, you're not." He sighed. "But if you're thinking of having an affair with a man based solely on sex, don't. You're not cut out for it."

"How do you know?"

"Alli, I've known you your whole life. You aren't capable of sharing something that intimate with a man and not getting emotionally involved. Which is why men don't hit on you. When the right one comes along, though, you'll both fall like rocks, and live happily ever after, just like Rory and Chance."

"I told you, that's not what I want."

"Of course it is. All women want that, eventually."

"God. Men!" She tossed the dishcloth onto the counter. "You think you know everything."

"That's because we do." He grinned at her. "Now, are you going to actually cook that meat loaf, or leave it sitting on the counter all evening?"

Fuming, she slid it into the oven, and went to the refrigerator to decide on what vegetables to cook. If her brother was right, that men had been avoiding her all these years because they thought she was after marriage, they were all dead wrong.

The sound of a car door slamming woke Alli during the night. She was used to guests coming and going at all hours, and had learned to roll over and go right back to sleep. Then she remembered: Scott and Linda. They'd left early in the evening, both of them dressed for a night on the town.

Against her will, Alli lay there listening. With the house so close to sea level, the basement was mostly above ground, allowing for windows. Her window was situated beneath the veranda, so she had no trouble hearing the footsteps on the oyster-shell walkway, followed by feminine laughter.

"What a crazy night," Linda Lovejoy said. "Wasn't it crazy?"

"It was that," Scott's deep voice answered. "But right now, I think we need to move this little party upstairs."

"Oh no, not yet. Let's dance. Come on, don't you want to dance with me in the moonlight?"

"Actually, what I really want to do is get you into bed."

"I just bet you do." Throaty laughter floated on the night air, followed by silence.

Allison lay perfectly still, trying not to picture what was going on right outside. Unfortunately she could imagine it all too clearly: the two of them locked in a passionate embrace. What would it feel like to be kissed by Scott Lawrence? To run her hands freely over his hard body. To have his hands move up her back so he could bury his fingers in her hair, or down to cup her bottom and hold her tightly to him . . .

Dr. Lovejoy murmured something low and hungry sounding, and Allison felt her insides stir.

"Another time, perhaps," Scott said. "Let's get you upstairs and into bed?"

"I don't wanna go to bed. I wanna go skinny-dipping."

"Up we go." Shoes scraped on the stone steps to the veranda. "Whoa, let's wait until we get upstairs before you undress, okay?"

"Okay."

She heard the opening and closing of the front door, the light tapping of Linda's shoes, the heavier thud of Scott's boots, then the sounds faded. Would they go to his room, or hers?

Images flashed through Allison's mind of naked bodies moving together on tangled sheets. She rolled to the side, pressing her thighs together to ease the aching in her loins. But the fantasies still came—Scott's hands on her own bare skin, his mouth moving over her breasts. Her hands touching every inch of him she could reach. She'd tried so hard to squelch such thoughts, to not think about sex, but there were times the act was so vivid in her mind she felt as if it were actually happening.

Did men honestly think she never had such thoughts? Never felt her insides turn hot and liquid as she imagined the feel of a man thrusting deep inside her? She would have to be abnormal to never think about it. Did they really believe her so pure of mind she'd be affronted if they mentioned such things in her presence? Or, heaven forbid, asked her to participate?

She was not pure of mind at all. She thought about sex a lot, yearned for it to the point of physically aching. But she'd never sought to relieve that yearning, because she'd feared the greater pain of a broken heart. She knew too well how it felt to lose someone she loved, or to trust and have that trust destroyed. She would rather do without love completely than ever risk that kind of devastation again.

But what if Scott and Adrian were right? What if a woman could detach herself emotionally to satisfy her physical longings for the sheer pleasure of it? What if she could ease the constant ache to feel a man's touch, without risking her heart?

She lay in the dark, considering the idea, and imagining herself upstairs in Scott Lawrence's bed.

Chapter 5

GAWD, SCOTT THOUGHT, *THIRTY-TWO YEARS old and already an old man.* Lying on the beach towel, flat on his back, he didn't even care that the sun was burning through his eyelids in a red haze. If he lay there long enough, maybe the heat would burn away his hangover and the memory of last night.

The hangover was mild, barely even noticeable now that he'd guzzled some coffee from the upstairs sideboard and taken a dip in the cove. Unfortunately he'd missed breakfast, but probably couldn't have faced Allison anyway after his rudeness yesterday. As for the memories . . . He scrunched his face in an effort to block them. Sometimes he thought life should be like writing, so you could go back and edit a scene that didn't work the way you'd hoped. Or, better yet, delete the scene completely.

One of the first things he'd rewrite was everything he'd said to Allison when she'd come to his room. He'd spent half the evening distracted by thoughts of whether or not to apologize. He owed her one, no doubt, but in order to give it to her, he'd have to talk to her. Just the thought of being in the same room with her made his pulse pound, so not a good idea.

"Hey, there," someone called.

He snapped his head up, fearing it was Allison. Instead he saw Linda Lovejoy in a swimsuit cover-up coming down the azalea-lined path that led from the inn to the private cove. He stifled a groan. As much as he didn't want to see Allison, he wanted to see this woman even less, but for entirely different reasons.

Physically, Dr. Lovejoy was attractive enough, but as

long as he was rewriting yesterday, the second thing he'd
edit out were the tattooed dragons that covered the
woman's upper back and shoulders. He'd seen enough of
them last night when she'd removed the jacket to her
spaghetti-strap dress.

"So, how's the water?" she asked when she reached
him.

"Wet." He frowned as she spread a towel next to his.
"I'm surprised to see you up before noon."

"Vacations are too short to waste time sleeping in."

He squinted against the sunlight while she tossed
aside the cover-up, revealing a tiny, leopard-skin string
bikini. "No ill effects from last night?" he asked as she
started applying suntan oil to her arms, stomach, and legs.

"I never get hangovers."

He dropped his head back with a groan. It should be
illegal for someone to drink as much as she had and not
suffer the next day. He hadn't had anywhere near as
much, and he'd awoken with a splitting head to add to
his nagging guilt over his rudeness to Allison. At least
the headache had subsided. Perhaps the guilt would too.
In time.

"Wasn't that a great club last night?" Linda said.
"There's just something about disco music."

He nearly snorted as he remembered the retro bar
they'd gone to, complete with mirrored ball over the
dance floor, flashing colored lights, and dry ice. "Personally, I had enough of the Bee Gees the first time around."

"You aren't old enough to have been clubbing back
then."

No, but you probably are. When he'd first seen her
yesterday, he'd thought she was about his age, maybe a
couple years older. But the more he'd studied the hardness
around her eyes and mouth, the more years he'd added to
his guess.

"Do my back?" she asked.

With a sigh, he sat up and took the bottle of oil from her. She stretched out on her stomach and he stared in disbelief. The dragons and wicked-looking fairies didn't just cover her upper back. They covered her *entire* back. "Aren't you worried the sun will fade all that ink?"

"Tattoos don't fade." She laughed at him over her shoulder. "Aren't they great? The artist really did a fabulous job."

If you say so. He poured oil in his palm and started rubbing it in. It wasn't that he objected to all tattoos. In fact, he'd seen some small, tasteful ones that were very sexy. But a whole back covered with fairies who appeared to be . . . He peered closer. "What the hell?"

She smiled at him again, her eyes hooded with sexual knowledge. "What do you think?"

He stared at the ink fairies who seemed to be practicing some very kinky S and M bondage on the dragons. "Are they doing what I think they're doing?"

"Ever try it?"

"Bondage? No." He may have thought about it from a curiosity standpoint, but he'd never seriously considered trying it—even in the wildest days of his misspent youth.

She shrugged and laid her head down on her forearms.

He finished oiling up her back, and returned to his own beach towel with his back to the sun. The next time his agent suggested he take a vacation, he'd shoot the man. Nothing that had happened so far was remotely relaxing. Not returning to a place that stirred up old memories. Not his instant attraction to a woman who was entirely too innocent for him. And definitely not his night on the town with Dr. Strangelove.

"You know," she murmured, as if already sleepy from the effects of the sun. "It was very sweet of you to play the gentleman last night, but it really wasn't necessary."

Oh yes it was. He wasn't about to break a two-year stretch of celibacy with a woman who was slobbering drunk. "Don't mention it."

He tried to listen to the lapping of the water and enjoy the breeze against his skin. Maybe if he didn't say anything, the woman beside him would fall asleep.

"So," she said. "Have you ever wanted to try it?"

"Try what?"

"Letting a woman tie you up?"

"No." Something like that required way too much trust from both partners for his comfort zone.

"Okay, no tying you to the bedposts, but how about . . . spanking?"

He opened one eye. "Giving or receiving?" Not that either appealed to him.

She smiled slowly. "Receiving."

"Okay, I'm out of here." He stood, gathering his towel and shirt.

"Hey," she called as he picked up his Top-Siders and headed for the inn. "I didn't mean to scare you off."

"You didn't." *You turned me off.* This whole trip had been a mistake. He might as well pack up his computer and head back to the French Quarter. At least he expected the women there to be weird.

First, though, he'd apologize to Allison. If he was leaving, there wasn't any reason not to see her since she'd soon be too far away to tempt him. He'd just have to get through a few minutes without grabbing her and kissing her so hard and deep they both went weak in the knees.

He stepped into the cool relief of the central hall, and stood for a moment, waiting for his eyes to adjust. The inn was quiet, since the other guests were apparently out sightseeing. Should he seek Allison out now, or wait until he'd showered? Although, since the morning was fairly cool, and he hadn't been down at the beach long, he was presentable. He might as well get it over with.

A noise to his left drew him into the gift shop, where sunlight drifted through the lace curtains. A colorful array of knickknacks and books filled the built-in shelves while porcelain teapots sat on a small linen-covered table. The smell of scented candles and those bags of leaves and twigs women seemed to like filled the air. Inhaling, he recognized the scent as Allison. It wasn't perfume she wore, but the fragrance of her shop that surrounded her.

Turning, he saw a table displaying dolls with delicately painted faces and frilly dresses. He picked up one with curly black hair and bright blue eyes. How like Allison to sell dolls and tea sets.

"In the market for a doll?"

Ah, that voice. A tingle of arousal raced down his spine as he turned to face her. She stood in the corner with an armload of books and filtered light shining off her hair. She gave him a mildly challenging look.

He glanced back at the doll in his hands. "I have a niece who'll expect a gift when I return to New Orleans." Although Chloe would snort in disgust if he gave her something so "girly."

He set the doll down as Allison turned her back to him to shelve the books, her movements jerky with anger.

"Rory took a few phone messages for you this morning," she said. "But don't worry, I've already tossed them in the trash for you."

"Thank you." He moved toward her, cautiously, since she reminded him of a kitten ready to hiss and spit at the household dog. If he got too close, he'd probably get his nose scratched. "Look, I, um, need to let you know I'm checking out early."

"How early?" Startled, Alli whirled to face him. With the lawsuit pending, they couldn't afford to lose the month's rent he would bring. All thought of money faded, though, when she saw him at such close range. The fantasies of last night returned in a warm rush.

"Today, actually."

"But . . . *why*?" The unbuttoned black shirt left his stomach and chest exposed: a remarkable chest, with swirls of black hair that tapered downward, dividing his hard stomach. She squelched thoughts of touching him and forced her gaze back to his face. "Is it something we've done?"

"No, of course not. I'm just . . ." He made a restless gesture with his arms that caused his shirt to gape even more. "I'm not finding this trip as relaxing as I'd hoped."

She glanced at the window, toward the beach where Dr. Lovejoy had headed mere moments ago. Anger returned with the memories of how he'd shunned her for another woman, how she'd lain awake listening as they'd kissed in the moonlight outside her window. Then his words sank in, and she wondered if she'd been mistaken. Maybe the two of them hadn't slept together last night. Confusion and relief struggled to break through the hurt. "Are you saying you're leaving because one of our guests wouldn't . . ."

"Wouldn't what?" He raised a brow.

"Nothing." She clamped her lips together. She would not add mortification to the other emotions battling inside her.

He studied her face, then laughed. Actually laughed, the toad! "If you're thinking I'm leaving because Linda wouldn't put out for me, you're wrong."

"Oh." So they had been together! "I see."

"See what?"

"That you— That—" She tried to hold her anger back, but after his rudeness yesterday, she saw no reason to mince words. "That you got what you came for, so there's no point in staying. Well, we have a twenty-four-hour cancellation policy, so we'll have to charge you for tonight whether you stay or not."

He narrowed his eyes. "For what it's worth, I didn't 'get what I came for.' "

"But you just said she didn't turn you down."

"She didn't. Unfortunately, I seem to have developed an annoying quirk in the last few years where I have to at least like a woman before I go to bed with her."

"I see." The yo-yo emotions, spinning from jealousy to relief, left her dizzy.

"Look, before I pack, I um . . ." He seemed suddenly unsure of where to put his hands and wound up resting them on his hips while he stared at his feet. Oh God. The shirt gaped wide, showing his trim waist above the black swim trunks. "I want to apologize for yesterday. I had no right to talk to you the way I did. It's obvious you're a woman who isn't used to being spoken to so bluntly. If I offended you in any way, I'm sorry."

"Apology accepted." She clutched the books to her chest, wrapping her arms tightly around them.

He tipped his head. "But you're still angry."

"Yes." She swallowed hard. Hating him for being so attractive. Hating herself for wanting him so badly. "Because you have no idea how greatly you offended me."

His gaze dropped back to the floor. "I don't know what to say, other than I'm sorry."

"But you're apologizing for the wrong reason!" she snapped. His head came up and she wanted to slug him. "You stood there yesterday and told me you came to Galveston looking for a woman to . . . to—"

"I know what I said, and I apologize for being so blunt—"

"—to have an affair, yet *not once* did you even attempt to come on to me."

"*What?*" He drew back, blinking with a comical look of shock.

She should stop now, simply shut up and go back to shelving books, but the hurt wouldn't let her. "I want to know why. Why didn't you even attempt to find out if I was interested?"

"Because I . . . I didn't want to get my face slapped, for one thing."

"What makes you think I would have slapped you?"

"You're not the kind of woman a man propositions for casual sex. If I'd asked you out, you would have assumed I was interested in something more."

"Like marriage, I presume." She nearly growled in frustration. "You men can be so stupid sometimes! You judge a woman by what you see on the outside without bothering to ask what she wants or expects. I'll tell you something, Scott Lawrence. You're only right about one thing. If you'd asked me out before yesterday, then yes, I would have thought you were interested in something more than casual sex—and I would have told you no." She watched his eyes widen as she stepped toward him, her body shaking with fury. "I would have said no, because marriage, or any relationship that could even remotely lead to it, is the last thing in the world I want. If you'd taken the time to spell it out, to tell me exactly what you were after, you might have gotten a different answer."

He stared at her, dumbfounded. "What are you saying?"

"That you offended me by treating me as if I were a—a stick of furniture. What is so wrong with me, I'd like to know?"

"Nothing is wrong with you." He raised his hands, looking lost at sea. "I just don't want to lead some innocent woman on and have her end up getting hurt."

"God, what an ego! Do you honestly think you're so irresistible that a woman can't go out with you without falling madly in love? Trust me, after yesterday, I'm in no danger of falling under your spell. I still find you attractive physically—more fool I—but quite frankly, the rest of you *needs some work!*"

"I know." He nodded. "I'm a regular bastard. A woman would have to be crazy to get tangled up with me."

"Either that, or in it only for the sex."

He held her gaze for a long moment before responding quietly. "Too bad you're not the type."

"You don't know anything about me or what I want."

"No. But I know what I want." He raised his hands and framed her face. His mouth descended to cover hers and heat shot through her like a liquid bolt of lightning.

Shock came first, followed by a wild rush of need as all the longing she'd suppressed for years surged upward. She dropped the books and flung her arms about his neck, returning the kiss with more eagerness than skill.

He gathered her hard against him as he slanted his head and deepened the kiss. Her body molded more tightly to his as she welcomed his tongue with a moan. His hand swooped down to clasp her bottom. The evidence of his response pressed hard against her stomach, making her light-headed with relief. She wasn't repulsive after all. He did want her. She moved against him, trying to ease the needy tightness inside her.

He groaned and walked her back until she came up against the bookcase. The shelves pressed into her spine, but she didn't care. She moved her hands to his chest, marveling at the feel of hot skin and crisp hair. His breathing turned labored as he kissed her neck and stroked her sides with his fingers. When his hand moved up to cup her breast, she gasped at the pure thrill of it.

Oh yes! she wanted to shout. *Touch me, touch me.* She took his jaw in her hands and brought his mouth back to hers, trembling at the feel of his beard against her palms, his lips and tongue. He lifted her until she sat halfway on a shelf and she wrapped her legs about his hips. The hard bulge in his swim trunks made contact with the center of her aching need.

A strangled cry caught in the back of her throat when he pressed harder into her. *Oh yes, right there, just a tiny bit more—*

"Alli, have you seen—Oh!"

They both froze at the sound of Rory's voice. Alli opened her eyes, and found his open as well with their mouths still fused together. She broke away, and tried to scramble down from the shelf but her body rubbed hard against his and he gripped her thighs to hold her still.

"Don't . . . move," he said between clenched teeth and squeezed his eyes shut as if in pain.

Panicked, she looked past his shoulder and found her sister standing in the doorway, staring in shock. The expression turned to concern when Scott didn't let her go.

"Everything okay?" Rory finally asked.

Alli nodded even as her cheeks flamed and her pulse pounded.

"Oh. Well then . . ." Rory cast one more worried look at Scott and started to back out. "Sorry. I'll just . . . be going."

As soon as Rory left, Alli dropped her forehead to Scott's chest.

"Holy shit." He took a deep breath and let it out in a loud rush. "You all right?"

She gave a squeak she hoped he took as a yes.

"Gawd Almighty." He exhaled again. "I guess you are 'that kind of girl' after all."

"I guess so." Even drowning in embarrassment, she laughed. The laughter eased the tension between them, and she felt his erection subside a bit. She sighed in both disappointment and relief.

"Well," he said, loosening his death grip on her thighs.

She leaned back enough to cast him a sheepish look through her lashes. "Well, indeed."

He chuckled. "You have the most prim voice I have ever heard."

She straightened as much as possible, considering she was sitting inside a bookcase straddling a man's hips. "Do you have a problem with that?"

"Nope." The grin spread to his eyes. "In fact, it turns me on."

He moved back and helped her down, then held her hands like a gentleman while the strength returned to her wobbly legs. "So, you think you can tear up the bed sheets with me without falling in love, huh?"

She raised her chin, hoping for a look somewhere between cocky and seductive. "If other women can have flings, why can't I?"

"No reason I can think of." He glanced around. "Not here, though. Just my luck, your brother will walk in on us next time, and I'll wind up with a broken jaw. How about I drive into town and get us a room at the Hotel Galvez? Dinner reservations for eight o'clock okay with you?"

She opened her mouth to speak but nothing came out. He was asking her to check into a hotel. Her stomach did a joyful back flip at the thought even though she knew she should refuse. But then doing what she should was getting her nowhere in life. "Eight will be fine."

"Great. I'll be back at seven-thirty to pick you up. Pack an overnight bag and wear something nice for dinner." He gave her a quick, closed-mouth kiss. "Nightgown optional."

She stared as he turned and strode toward the door. What had she just done? "Scott, wait."

He glanced back with one brow raised.

"Does this mean you're still checking out?"

He pondered the question for a moment. "No. I think

I'll stay the full month after all." He wiggled his brows. "Maybe Marguerite's charm is finally starting to work."

"Maybe so," Alli whispered when she was alone, since it looked like both of them were about to get lucky.

Chapter 6

"WHAT IN THE WORLD IS going on?" Rory demanded.

Setting her jaw, Alli glanced up from the black cocktail dress she'd laid out on the bed to find her sister standing in the doorway looking like an outraged Viking warrioress. She'd already had one fight with her big brother; she didn't need another one with her baby sister.

Rory came forward, her hands accenting her words. "I find you kissing one of our guests in the gift shop this morning, and once I recovered from my shock, I thought, 'Good for you! About time you got involved with a man.' And woo-wee, what a man! I mean, Scott Lawrence. Wow! He's rich, he's famous, you love his books, and he's gorgeous, if you like the brooding type. So the whole time Chance and I are running errands in town, I'm so happy for you, I'm about to bust into song.

"Then we get back, and Adrian's in an uproar, banging pots about the kitchen. I ask him what's wrong, and he tells me—Well, never mind what he told me. He clearly misunderstood something you said, right?"

"He didn't misunderstand."

"But . . . he said you asked for tomorrow morning off, because you're going out with Scott and don't plan to be back in time for breakfast, which again, good for you. It's fast but sometimes it happens that way. Except Adrian has some notion that Scott's just using you for sex, and you're going to let him. He's wrong though, isn't he?" Anxiety lined Rory's face. "I mean, he's just being overprotective like he always is, right?"

"Scott isn't using me."

"See, I knew it." Rory sat on the bed.

"I'm using him."

"What?" Rory shot back up.

"Well, actually it's a mutual use, I guess."

"What are you talking about?"

"Nothing." She sighed. "Look, Scott and I are attracted to each other, but neither one of us is interested in a relationship."

"So you're going to check into a hotel and have sex?" Rory's voice rose an octave.

"Something like that."

"Are you insane?" Rory stared at her. "You can't just check into a hotel with a man to have sex."

"Why not?" Dressed in her pink floral bathrobe, Alli took a seat at her vanity and glanced over her scant supply of makeup. "Other women do."

"You're not 'other women.' You're—"

"Too prudish and nunlike?" She applied blusher to her cheeks in angry strokes. "Well, I'm sick of living that way, of having men treat me like an old maid. I've finally found a man who finds me enticing. If I want to have an adult relationship with him, that's my business."

"Allison, listen to me." Rory came up behind her, pleading with her reflection in the mirror. "Don't do this. You're going to get hurt."

"No I won't, and that's the point. I'm going into this with my eyes open. Not romanticizing it, like I did . . . before."

"With Peter, you mean?" Rory said, speaking the forbidden name. "Is that what this is all about? Alli, that was years ago."

Allison went cold inside. "Exactly, and it's time I got over it."

"What, by sleeping with a man you don't care anything about?"

"Yes." She closed the makeup case with a snap. "Peter hurt me, because he lied to get me to sleep with him.

Scott's honest enough to be up front about what he wants, and we both agreed this is just physical."

"You actually discussed it?" Rory nearly squeaked.

"Yes, we did," she responded with calm resolve.

"Alli, you have to listen to me."

Allison met her sister's gaze in the mirror. "You mean the way you listened to me when I told you not to get involved with Chance because he'd break your heart?"

"That was totally different," Rory insisted. "I was in love with Chance. And in the end, we proved you wrong. He didn't break my heart."

Not yet, anyway, Allison thought, suppressing the fear that tried to clutch at her heart. How did any of them know Chance wouldn't die of a heart attack or develop cancer? Or die in a car crash like their parents had. "Maybe this time *you're* wrong," Alli said. "Even if you're not, it's none of your business. And it's none of Adrian's business." Rising, she went back to the bed and started packing the casual clothes she'd picked out for tomorrow. "I'm doing this, Rory, and I would appreciate you and Adrian butting out."

The shock that registered on Rory's face stirred her instincts to soothe and coddle, but she ruthlessly resisted.

Adrian appeared in the doorway with a dark scowl. "Your 'date' is here."

Her breath snagged in her throat. Could she really do this, or was she as crazy as Rory said? "Tell him I'll be right up." Her hands shook as she picked up the cocktail dress she'd laid on the bed. When Adrian was gone, she turned back to her sister. "I realize you don't understand this, but I'm sick of feeling damaged inside. I know I'll never heal completely from what happened with Peter, I'll never be able to fall in love like most people, nor do I want to. But at least I can have this. Please try not to hate me for it."

"Oh, Alli, I could never hate you." Rory hugged her

awkwardly over the mound of her stomach. "I just don't want you to get hurt."

Alli closed her eyes as fear whispered through her mind the way it did more often with each passing day. Rory was so happy with her marriage and the baby on the way it scared her. What if something happened to destroy that happiness? Or worse, far worse, what if Fate stole Rory from them? What would they do without Aurora, the Sunshine Girl, who brought light and laughter into the lives of everyone she touched?

Damn life for being so cruel. And damn love for allowing it to hurt.

Squeezing the fear away, Alli pulled back and offered a reassuring smile. "I won't get hurt, because I could never fall in love with someone as arrogant as Scott Lawrence. Admire his talent, yes. Love him romantically? No."

Ten minutes later, though, she wasn't so sure. She entered the central hall and saw him leaning his forearm against the mantel of the hearth as he scowled at the cold grate. At the sound of her approach, he looked up and the scowl vanished. A smile slowly took its place as he straightened, and the sight of him standing there, so virile, took her breath away. He'd dressed in a charcoal-gray Italian suit with a dark shirt and tie. The look was saved from being stuffy by a pair of eelskin cowboy boots. His whiskey-colored eyes took in her simple black dress and high-heeled sandals, and he lifted a brow in approval.

"You look . . . incredible," he said, coming toward her.

"Thank you." Dropping her gaze to the floor, she tucked a curl behind her ear. She tried to think of something pithy to say, but the butterflies in her stomach made thinking impossible.

"I'll take that." He reached for the overnight bag. "You ready?"

She squared her shoulders and met his gaze directly. "Yes."

"So . . ." Alli cleared her throat but couldn't bring herself to look at anything but the menu before her. "How do we . . . I mean . . . I need to know . . . how does this work?"

Scott leaned toward her as if planning a conspiracy. "You tell the waiter what you want, and he brings it to you."

She looked up, into his smiling eyes, and a strained laugh escaped her. "No. Not ordering dinner. Having an affair. I've, um . . . never had one."

"Allison." He dropped his voice to a whisper. "I sort of guessed that already."

Was he laughing at her, or trying to get her to laugh with him? She turned back to the menu, struggling to make sense of the whole evening. Scott had played the part of the perfect gentleman since the moment he'd picked her up, opening doors, carrying her bag.

Her stomach fluttered as she remembered the few brief minutes in the posh room upstairs. She wasn't sure what she'd expected—maybe for him to grab her the minute they were alone—but nothing could have prepared her for what she'd found. He'd bought flowers. Two dozen fragrant white freesias. They were there on the coffee table in the sitting area of their room. The sight of them had shocked her far more than the box of condoms she'd seen sitting on the nightstand, or the fact that either he or the maid had already turned down the bed.

When he'd seen her staring at the flowers, he'd pulled one stalk from the vase and handed it to her before he presented his arm to escort her downstairs.

She looked at the flower now, lying on the linen tablecloth next to her plate. He'd said he wanted sex and nothing else, but then he'd bought a vase of flowers. And asked the maitre d' for a table in a quiet corner. She'd assumed he'd picked the hotel restaurant for convenience, but now she wasn't so sure. She dared a quick peek over the menu at the candles on the tables. Real silver and crystal stemware gleamed in the low lighting. Romance drifted on the air to the soft cadence of chamber music and the friendly murmur of other diners.

Why would he give her flowers and take her to a romantic restaurant if this evening was only about sex?

Her heart began to pound as she returned her gaze to the menu. "I need to know how this works. Are there rules? You said no emotions would get involved, but . . ." She looked up at him, searching for a way to put all her fears into words. "You've been treating this like a date. Like a real date."

"It is a real date." The look he gave her made her feel stupid. "Just because we're not going to fool ourselves into thinking love is involved doesn't mean we won't enjoy each other's company." He took her hand and squeezed her cold fingers before he kissed her knuckles. The heat of his lips rippled through her. "I definitely plan to enjoy you. On several levels."

"Oh." She gazed at his mouth as images danced through her mind, of him kissing her neck, her shoulders, her breasts. With a jolt, she pulled her hand free and went back to staring at the menu.

He sighed, as if disappointed or impatient with her naïveté. "You know, there's no rule that says lovers can't also be friends."

"But . . . how does it work?" she asked a bit desperately. "How do we enjoy each other's company, get to know each other, become friends, but stop the emotions from going any further?"

"One way is to keep the association brief."

"How brief?"

He folded his menu and set it aside. "A weekend here and there. Which is one of the reasons long-distance affairs work well if you don't want anything serious. You get together for a night or two when you're both in the same town, then go back to your separate lives. What you each do between weekends is none of the other person's business. Sort of the 'don't ask, don't tell' policy."

"I thought that applied to gays in the military."

"It applies to a lot of things in life. Especially casual affairs. You only reveal so much of yourself and never press your lover to bare their soul. Keep things on the surface, and no one gets close enough to hurt you."

"And you keep it brief."

"Exactly."

She thought about that. "Perhaps we should specify a time limit up front. If you're staying for the full month, will we continue to . . ." The words stuck in her throat.

"Sleep together that whole time?" He raised a brow, and she nodded. "That could get a bit awkward with your brother around. Correct me if I'm wrong, but when I picked you up earlier, I got the distinct impression he wanted to chop me off at the knees."

Allison cringed inwardly at her memory of her fight with Adrian. "He and Rory are worried I'll get hurt. I told them not to, that I'm in absolutely no danger of falling in love with you, but you know how protective siblings can be."

He made a noncommittal sound.

"You're right, though," she said. "I'd feel awkward being with you at the inn. Maybe we should say this is only for tonight. Tomorrow, when we go back to Pearl Island, we'll return to being innkeeper and guest, nothing more."

"One night?" He stared at her as if she'd lost her mind. "That's not much of an affair."

"I just think it would be best. Seeing each other as lovers for a solid month could be emotionally dangerous. Don't you think?"

He didn't appear too happy, but sighed in resignation. "Very well. One night it is."

The waiter arrived to take their order.

"Appetizer?" Scott asked her.

"Yes. An appetizer would be lovely." She set her menu down and folded her hands in her lap. Beside her, Scott smoothed his beard, but she still saw the smile he was trying to hide at her prim manner. Did it really turn him on? Or had he been making fun of her?

"We'll have the spinach and artichoke dip," he said, then glanced over the wine list before turning back to her. "Will you be ordering steak or seafood for dinner?"

"I haven't decided."

He picked a Chardonnay, claiming it went with anything. "Besides," he told Allison when the waiter was gone, "red wine makes me sleepy. If we're only going to have one night, I don't want to waste it."

Nerves skittered deep in her belly, even as arousal sent out a flush of heat.

The waiter returned with the wine and Scott went through the ritual of tasting, then nodded his approval. He watched Allison closely as she took her first sip and wondered if she could even taste it, she was so nervous. Leaning back in his chair, he studied her over the rim of his wine glass. She sat perched in her chair, back ramrod-straight, legs crossed tightly at the ankles with her feet tucked under the chair. He figured if he made one wrong move, she'd bolt.

Except, she'd said she wanted this. And so did he. He couldn't remember the last time he'd been so turned on just sitting next to a woman watching her play with the stem of her wine glass. Her delicate hands looked perfectly suited for serving tea in those fancy porcelain cups she sold in her gift shop. But all he could think of was getting those hands on his body.

If she bolted at the last minute, he'd probably keel over from frustration.

By the time their appetizer arrived, he decided he could do one of three things: call the whole thing off and take her home; talk about something neutral to help her relax; or . . . he could seduce her with words until she was equally eager to go upstairs. He was good with words. He knew their power to stir thought, emotion, physical response.

His eyelids lowered as he watched her nibble at a tortilla chip with a scant amount of spinach dip. Taking a chip, he trailed it through the dip. "Here," he said, leaning toward her. "Some things are better when you indulge all the way."

She jumped slightly, then started to take the chip from him.

"Naw-ah." He pulled it back. "Trust me. Now open wide."

Her gaze met his as she opened her mouth. *Oh, sweetheart, you do take direction well.* His groin tightened as he placed the chip on her tongue and watched her lips close about it.

"You know," he said, holding her gaze. "There are reasons men like to take women out to dinner."

She blushed and swallowed. "I know. I'm sorry. I'm normally better at making conversation. I'm just . . . nervous."

A smile tugged at his lips. "No. I wasn't talking about conversation. I was talking about . . . anticipation."

Her eyes widened.

"You see"—he leaned in close—"while we sit here looking very proper and dignified, the well-dressed couple out on a civilized date, I'm visualizing all the things I plan to do to you the second I get you upstairs."

She dropped her gaze, and stared at the table so hard, he expected the linens to burst into flames. Okay, maybe a verbal seduction wasn't such a good idea. Instead of exciting her, he might frighten her off. But if she were going to change her mind, he'd rather she do it before he had her in bed.

He rested one elbow on the table as he swirled the wine in his glass. The position brought his mouth close enough to her ear for him to talk softly. "I've always had a very vivid imagination. Do you want to know what I'm imagining right now?"

She sat perfectly still, but her breathing turned fast and shallow.

"I'm imagining how much I'm going to enjoy peeling that little black dress off your very nice body to discover what you have on underneath." He took a sip, savoring the oaky flavor. "My guess is something white and virginal, with lots of lace and a tiny pink bow between your breasts."

She nearly stopped breathing altogether and her gaze remained fixed on the table. Well, he supposed that was answer enough. She definitely was not up to this. He set his wine down as disappointment settled over him. At this rate, he might as well drive her home as soon as their meal was over.

She whispered something very low that sounded like the word "lavender."

"Excuse me?" he asked, not even sure she'd spoken.

"My underwear. It isn't white." Her lashes lifted revealing dilated eyes. "It's lavender. With black lace."

A punch of desire hit him low and hard. "Describe it."

She took a shaky breath. "The bra is . . . mostly lace, but with some satin. I've always enjoyed . . ."

"Yes?" he prompted.

She reached for her wine glass and took a deep sip. "I've always enjoyed the way satin feels. Like . . . decadence."

He shifted to accommodate his arousal as he imagined the cool, smooth fabric beneath his fingertips. "Are your panties satin?"

She nodded. "They're cut high on the leg, and have lace insets on the sides."

Oh man. He took a slow breath to keep from pulling her to the floor then and there. The response worried him since he'd never been this desperate to touch one particular woman. Ever. "Do you always wear sexy underwear?"

"No." Her throat moved as she swallowed. "I usually wear white cotton. A while back, though, I saw this set in a store window, and I bought it on impulse. But I've never worn it."

Until now. The unspoken words hung between them. Frightening in their implication. She was the innocent he'd suspected in so many ways, but with a streak of hidden passion she'd never let out. He felt suddenly torn between the desire to seal her in a glass case to protect her from all the world's vices, and a potent urge to help her explore every naughty thought she'd ever entertained in the privacy of her mind.

"Are you ready to order?" the waiter asked, making them both start.

Scott glanced at Allison.

She stared at him, her gray eyes dark, her lips slightly parted. "To be honest," she said at last, "I'm not very hungry."

"Neither am I." He pulled his attention away from her long enough to ask for the check, and for the wine to be recorked so they could take it to their room.

Chapter 7

WHAT HAVE I GOTTEN MYSELF into? Scott wondered as they rode up in the old elevator. Every bachelor survival instinct he had was screaming for him to run like hell. The woman who stood quietly beside him watching the numbers change was far more complex than he'd bargained for, and his fascination for her had grown all out of proportion to what he was used to handling.

The elevator came to a jarring halt and the doors slid open to reveal the ornate hall with Art Deco chandeliers. Allison glanced up at him, her smile timid. Shifting the bottle of wine to his other arm, he took her hand and gave it a reassuring squeeze. *Everything will be fine,* he told himself as they started down the hall. *You've spelled out the rules. She's agreed. Nothing to worry about.*

Except he'd never been this nervous about making love to a woman. Or this aroused so early in the game. Just holding her hand made his pulse jump. Once he'd matured past the selfishness of adolescence, he'd learned to take pride in pleasing his partners. But what if he was so rusty he'd forgotten how?

He brushed that possibility aside as ridiculous. No one "forgot" how to pleasure a woman.

As for the fact that she intrigued him more than any other woman he'd ever met, it didn't have to mean anything. They were two mature, consenting adults about to share a little mutual gratification. Period.

When they reached the suite, he dropped her hand to unlock the door with the card key. "I hate these things," he muttered when he couldn't get it to work.

"Here, let me." She took the card from him and got

the green light to flash on the first try. He turned the handle and opened the door for her.

Allison's knees shook as she walked to the center of the sitting area, clutching her purse. Soft light from the courtyard came through the sheer curtains, giving the room a peach-colored glow. Behind her, she heard the jangle of loose change and keys hitting a hard surface. She turned and found Scott standing by a marble-top table near the door, emptying his pockets. It was such a simple male ritual that suddenly seemed very intimate—the sort of thing a wife would watch her husband do at the end of each day.

He set the bottle of wine on the same table, then looked at her. He appeared more shadow than reality, with his dark beard and hair, the darkness of his clothing. But his eyes captured the light in a way that made them gleam. Wolf's eyes, she thought with a shiver.

"Would you like some wine?" he asked.

"No," she said, barely above a whisper. She wanted him to kiss her and end the wondering and the waiting.

He came toward her and her body began to tremble. When he reached her, he pried the purse from her hands and dropped it to the coffee table. The height and breadth of him dwarfed her as she tipped her head back to meet his gaze.

He raised his hands and cupped her face. "Do you have any idea what you do to me?"

She closed her eyes as his mouth descended, the contact so soft it was hardly a kiss at all. He held her there, his warm palms cradling her face as his lips brushed and retreated, then brushed again.

A tingling heat spread downward from his hands, relaxing her chest, then her stomach, as hunger unfurled. He deepened the kiss while his hands held her still for the onslaught of need he poured into her. She rose on her toes and pressed her body to his, gripping his shoulders as a demand for more.

He kissed her cheeks, then spoke against her temple. "I take it you're excited too?"

She nodded, her throat too tight for her to speak.

"Say it," he coaxed. Raining kisses over her face. "I love the sound of your voice. Tell me you want this."

Squeezing her eyes shut, she summoned the courage to voice her desire, but a quiet "yes" was all she could manage.

"Louder." He brushed his lips over hers.

"Yes," she whispered. "I want you."

He rewarded her with a hard, searing kiss as his hands traveled down her back to cup her bottom. He pulled her against him, letting her feel the strength of his erection. With a whimper, she rubbed against him as excitement rolled through her.

"Oh yes," he breathed in approval. "Talk to me. Tell me what you like, what pleases you. If all we have is this one night, I want to make the most of it, for both of us."

"I . . . can't." Embarrassment made her pull away. "I'm too nervous."

He chuckled and kissed her forehead. "If it makes you feel better, I'm nervous, too."

"You are?"

He gave her a lopsided grin that seemed oddly self-deprecating. "I'm afraid I'm a little out of practice here, so I'd be a whole lot more comfortable if you'd agree to tell me when I do something you like, or don't like."

The embarrassment softened to tenderness. She didn't believe he really was nervous, but it was sweet of him to try to put her at ease. "I'm afraid I'm a *lot* out of practice. And"—she dropped her gaze to his chest—"I'm worried I'll disappoint you."

He lifted her chin with a knuckle. "Not a chance, sweetheart. Just tell me if I do something that feels good.

If there's anything you want to do, tell me that, too."

She lowered her lashes to hide her eyes. "There is one thing."

"Yes?" He kissed the corners of her mouth.

"It's just . . ."

"What?"

"Every time I look at you, I try to imagine you"—her cheeks flamed, but she forced the words out—"naked. I wonder what it would be like to . . . touch you. Simply run my hands all over you. That probably sounds ridiculously tame, but I fantasize about touching you. A lot."

She waited for him to laugh, or puff up with arrogance. Instead, he removed his jacket, then raised his hands and undid his tie. Next he unbuttoned his shirt. Her mouth watered as the shirt parted, revealing first his chest, with its gorgeous muscles and mat of black hair, then his taut stomach. She swallowed hard as he pulled the shirttails from his trousers, removed the garment completely, and tossed it aside.

She stood there, mesmerized, until he took hold of her wrists and placed her hands on his chest. The texture of his hair thrilled her. She spread her fingers to touch as much of him as possible and heard him draw a breath through his teeth. The breath made his chest expand, and she moved her hands in a slow circle to learn the shape and feel of him. Drawing her hands downward over his stomach, she leaned forward and pressed her lips to the center of his chest, where the hair formed a little swirl. His muscles twitched against her lips as his masculine scent filled her.

He ran his hands through her hair, pulling it out of the way, and she could feel him watching her. Giving herself over to impulse, she turned her head and caressed one of his nipples with her tongue.

With a groan, he pulled her head back and covered her lips in a full, openmouthed kiss, explosive with pas-

sion and need. She stroked him with her hands, petting
his stomach and chest. He arched her head back farther,
exposing her throat to his hungry mouth. His lips found
a pulse point and the pressure of his mouth made her heart
pound harder.

"Tell me," he rasped, "does this fantasy of yours in-
volve me touching you as well?"

"Yes."

"Say it."

"I want . . . I want you to touch me. I want to feel
your hands on my body."

He reached for the zipper at the back of her dress and
drew it down slowly. "First I want to see this underwear
of yours."

He stepped back enough to let the dress fall to her
feet. With her body tanned from living on the coast, she
wore no hose, nothing but the satin and lace bra that
barely covered her aching breasts, the French-cut panties,
and high-heeled sandals.

His gaze moved over her, thoroughly, and when he
lifted his eyes, she saw a desire that made her feel exot-
ically beautiful. The look emboldened her enough to hold
out her hand. He took it and led her to the bed. "Kneel
on the mattress," he told her.

She slipped off her shoes and did as he asked, facing
him as he stripped off the rest of his clothes. Watching
him, she realized this was no clumsy adolescent, eager to
get to the deed as quickly as possible, but a man in his
prime, with the restraint to linger and savor. The idea sent
a shiver of excitement racing through her.

When he was nude, he knelt on the mattress as well,
so they faced each other. This time, she placed her hands
on his chest by herself as he cupped her lace-clad breasts.
Like mirror images, they touched and tasted, each seeking
out sensitive spots that made the other suck in a breath or
moan for more.

He removed her bra, and bent his head to suckle her breasts. Closing her eyes, she let her head fall back, gloried in the heady rush of pleasure as he slipped a hand inside her panties and found her aching center. A purr sounded deep in her throat.

"You like that?" he whispered as he caressed her.

"Y-yes. I— Oh yes."

His touch grew bolder, making her bones feel weak. As the pleasure built, she felt faint and would have collapsed backward onto the pillows, but he caught her and held her to him. Then he was the one talking to her, whispering, telling her how beautiful she was, how much she excited him as his touch drove her higher. She closed her eyes, listening to his thrilling words as the tension grew tighter and tighter in her belly.

Then the tension snapped. Gasping in shock, she clung to him as she splintered into a thousand pieces.

Slowly, the world settled. She opened her eyes, startled and dazed, to find him smiling at her. When he saw her expression a chuckle rumbled in his chest. "First one?"

Her blush must have told him he'd guessed right.

He kissed her sweetly, smiling against her lips. "Well, it won't be your last."

The kiss deepened as he lavished her body with attention, stripping off her panties. By the time he stretched out on the bed, powerfully built and beautifully male, she'd lost all her inhibitions. Almost.

The shyness returned when he reached for a condom, removed it from the foil wrapper, and held it out to her. She stared at it, both surprised and curious since she'd never seen one in person. She'd definitely never touched one. Her gaze shot to his.

He smiled, that lazy lopsided grin that had attracted her from the beginning. "You said you wanted to touch me."

She took the condom from him, praying she didn't give her inexperience away, but her first attempt proved a dismal failure.

"Like this," he said, and covered her hands with his own.

She closed her eyes to savor the feel of him, so hard and hot within the circle of her fingers and palm, while his hand guided hers.

"Jeez." His breath hissed through his teeth. In one swift move, he pulled her down beside him and was looming over her, staring at her with his intense amber eyes. "I already loved watching your hands. Now I won't be able to look at them without getting hard."

Nibbling her jaw, he shifted until he lay with his hips cradled between her thighs. "Talk to me, sweet Alli. Tell me what you want."

"You," she said, as her heart began to pound. Everything inside her felt wild and reckless. She arched beneath him, telling him with her body as well as with words that tumbled from her lips how desperately she wanted him inside her. He answered with a hard nudge that made her gasp. He pressed again and she bit her lip because he didn't seem to fit.

"Gawd, you're tight." His expression looked pained as he started to pull back.

"No!" She wrapped her legs around him, holding him close. "I want you. Now, please, now. I want you." She kissed his neck, feeling his beard against her cheek and his rapid pulse against her lips.

With a groan, he pressed forward again, forcing his way inside her one small thrust at a time. Her head arched back on a gasp of both pleasure and pain.

"Please tell me you're not a virgin," he said between clenched teeth.

"No."

"Thank God." He moved a hand to her thigh, adjusting one of her legs higher on his hip. "Hang on." He drove himself to the hilt with one brutal thrust. She gasped in shock and wonder at the feel of having their bodies joined. He kissed her mouth, her face, her neck, waiting for her to adjust to him.

When she did, he moved over her, inside her.

She held him tight as the world fell away and words tumbled from her lips. *Yes, please yes, now, right there. Oh. Yes. Right. There.* She arched again, as sensations crashed through her, more shattering and glorious than before. She felt him stiffen against her, heard his strangled cry of pleasure, and then she melted with a sigh into the mattress. She didn't even care when he collapsed on top of her, as boneless as a hot, heavy blanket.

For the first time in years, she didn't feel damaged inside. She felt . . . womanly, powerful, and free. Hugging him to her, she smiled.

Chapter 8

ALLI STIRRED AT THE SOUND of running water and wondered why Adrian was using her shower instead of his. Moaning, she rolled over in hopes of a few more minutes of sleep. Then morning sunlight landed on her face and she bolted upright thinking she'd overslept. She tossed the covers aside, felt a blast of cool air against her naked breasts, and jerked the covers back.

Her surroundings registered: pale green and white wallpaper, elegant gold draperies, soft light seeping through sheer curtains. Memory returned, heating her cheeks. She glanced sideways to find Scott had already left the bed, which explained the shower noises coming from the bathroom.

Dropping back to the mattress, she clutched the sheet to her chest while she tried to decide if she was relieved or disappointed that he wasn't there. Relieved. Being alone gave her a minute to adjust to the reality of waking up naked in a hotel room with a man in the shower.

How did a woman behave the morning after? Did she act as if nothing unusual had happened? Or did she compliment the man on being a fabulous lover? Which Scott certainly was. Even with her limited experience, she knew he was good. Very, very good.

She closed her eyes to savor the memories. She'd assumed their first time would be it, but twice more during the night he'd pulled her to him and brought her nearly to the point of screaming and begging. Okay, so she had begged all three times, but she'd only screamed once. He'd seemed to enjoy every sound she made, so it hadn't embarrassed her at the time. But that was in the dark during the throes of passion. Remembering all the intimate details in the light of day was a bit . . . disturbing.

And titillating.

A little smile tugged at her lips as heat flickered to life in her belly. Daylight or not, she wouldn't mind having him bring her to flash point a few more times before they checked out of the room.

Which proved how wrong people were about her. She could have recreational sex without falling in love and getting hurt. Once she left this room, that would be it, no expectations from either one of them that the affair would continue.

She waited for relief to follow. But the only thing she felt was a vague discomfort. And a little hollow inside. Okay, so maybe sex without emotions took a little getting used to. But if she had to pick between her previous experience with Peter and last night with Scott, sex with Scott would win hands down for a lot of reasons. His honesty being high up on the list. Along with his skillful hands and the way his kisses made her head spin.

Smiling, she sat up . . . and saw that he'd draped one of the white hotel robes across the foot of the bed. And he'd laid a flower on it.

The sweetness of the gesture made her smile fade. *Why does he do things like that?* she wondered as she stared at the flower. It didn't make sense. The world-weary cynic who could be generous in bed, that she understood, because he benefited from his own generosity. But the thoughtful romantic? No, that didn't fit. Nor did she want it to. She liked it better when he was arrogant and rude.

Nudging the flower away with the tip of her finger, she donned the robe and went to the window to look outside. The hotel offered a perfect view of Seawall Boulevard and the beach beyond. A few joggers and bicyclists

moved along the wide sidewalk at the top of the seawall—
a massive concrete retaining wall that had been built after
the nineteen hundred hurricane. When the wall had been
completed, dirt had been pumped in, raising the level of
the island's east end several feet. Confidence in the for-
tifications was so high that the Hotel Galvez had been
built to replace the Grand Hotel, and when another hurricane swept over the island a few years later, the cream
of Galveston society had gathered in the ballroom to
dance in defiance of the storm.

Allison had always liked that image, of women in
lavish gowns, men in black formal dress, dancing beneath
crystal chandeliers while a dangerous storm raged around
them. It made her feel safe to know that even after the
heartbreaking devastation of the Great Storm, life could
go on within the safety of strong walls. How appropriate
that she had come to that same hotel to resume her own
life, to dance in defiance of the previous pain she had
suffered.

Behind her, the shower turned off, and a few minutes
later, Scott stepped out of the bathroom wearing another
of the hotel's robes.

"You're up," he said.

"Yes." She turned with a smile, determined to act
sophisticated. Then her gaze dropped to the deep V of
exposed chest and her cheeks heated.

"I hope I didn't wake you," he said.

"No, I'm used to getting up much earlier than this."
Although she wasn't used to losing so much sleep during
the night to make love. She glanced back out the window
as her stomach fluttered.

"Hungry?" he asked as he went to the nightstand and
retrieved his wristwatch.

"I suppose."

"Me too." He gave her a lopsided grin. "We never
did get around to eating last night."

Her cheeks grew hotter. "No, we didn't."

"Why don't I order room service while you shower?"

Nodding, she headed for the sanctuary of the bathroom.

Scott let out a sigh of relief when the door closed behind her. He always dreaded mornings after sex. If a woman was going to morph into a clinging vine, or turn bitchy with regret, that was when it happened. Allison had seemed . . . shy. A little edgy and embarrassed, maybe, but that was all. No morning-after theatrics. Thank God.

Crossing to the phone, he ordered two plates of sausage, bacon, eggs, biscuits, and toast, and a pot of coffee. Then he added some yogurt and fruit, since women seemed to like that stuff, and remembered orange juice at the last minute. The B and B served fresh-squeezed orange juice every morning, so Allison probably liked it.

By the time she emerged from the bathroom, he was arranging the food on the coffee table.

"Ah, perfect timing. I was just—" He glanced up and forgot what he was about to say. She stood in the doorway, looking angelic in the white robe. Her wet hair had been combed back from her face, emphasizing her delicate bones.

"Is breakfast here already?"

"Hmm? Oh yes." He glanced down at the dishes. "I wasn't sure what you'd want."

"Whatever you ordered will be fine." She moved forward and perched on the edge of the sofa, looking for all the world like a lady about to partake of afternoon tea. He watched in fascination as she selected a slice of toast. Rather than leave it dry, like so many stick-figure women who claimed they were fat just so people would tell them they weren't, she slathered it with butter and jam. "I only see one glass of juice, did you want it?"

"No, I ordered it for you."

"Oh. Thank you."

He watched her as he took up one of the plates, trying to connect the prim woman beside him with the abandoned temptress who'd caught fire in his arms several times during the night. She had so many facets, he wondered how long it would take a man to discover them all.

Settling back into the corner of the sofa, he tried to imagine her as a character in one of his books. He toyed with the idea a bit, waiting for a scenario to present itself. Would she be the hero's weakness or his strength? Would she be the fragile beauty who drove him to protect her at all costs? The key to solving a mystery? Or an equal partner on a dangerous mission? He could easily see her as all those things, but what sort of man would he pair her with?

Blank. Dammit. His mind went blank.

He tried again to form some glimmer of a plot, but Allison began to fidget under his focused regard. After a while, she cleared her throat, but didn't look at him. "Can I ask you a question?"

"Sure," he said, distracted by his thoughts.

"Do you always buy flowers for your lovers?"

"Not always," he answered carefully rather than admit almost never. He remembered walking past the gift shop in the lobby after checking in and seeing the vase of fragrant white flowers. Everything about them reminded him of Allison, so he'd bought them on impulse hoping she'd like them. From the way she was frowning at the vase, though, he wondered if he'd made a mistake. "Why do you ask?"

"It just seems odd. Like you're trying to court me."

He set his plate aside, unaccountably stung that she didn't like his gift. "Don't read anything into it, Allison. All it means is I was in the mood to buy a woman flowers. So don't start thinking I'm a nice guy. I'm not. I'm a selfish son of a bitch. And I'm not trying to court you."

"Thank goodness." She visibly relaxed, and gave him

a shy, sideways smile. "You had me worried."

He realized she meant it. She really didn't want anything more from him than sex. The thought should have put him at ease. Instead, he felt oddly perturbed. Taking up his coffee, he studied her over the rim. "Okay, you asked me a question, now it's my turn."

Her smile vanished. "Oh?"

"Last night when you said you were a lot out of practice, what exactly did you mean?"

She looked away. "Just that I haven't . . . been with anyone for a while."

"Define 'a while.' "

"A while. A long time."

"I'm looking for a figure here. One year? Two?"

Her chin came up in a regal gesture. "I thought we weren't supposed to ask personal questions."

"So I'm breaking one of the rules. Sue me. But first answer the question."

She gave him a mutinous stare. "How long has it been for you?"

She clearly didn't expect him to answer. Which would let her off the hook. Damn. He took a sip of coffee. "Two years. And before that it was off and on, with increasingly long periods of off."

"Why increasingly long periods?"

He narrowed his eyes, debating whether or not to answer, but the more questions he answered, the more she'd have to. And maybe those answers would help him unravel the mystery of her. "The last woman I dated was a pharmaceutical sales rep from Baton Rouge. Divorced, two kids, constantly on the road. Her career and family came first. Just as my career has always come first for me. However, we both enjoyed movies, live music, and Cajun food, so she'd call me up whenever she was in New Orleans. What we had was friendly and convenient. Nothing more."

"So, what happened? Why'd it end?"

"The last time I saw Kelly, all we did was go to dinner where she told me she'd met someone. Even though she'd sworn to me a million times she never wanted to remarry, she had high hopes the relationship would become serious. Personally, I've never understood how people can change their minds about something like that, but I wished her well and haven't heard from her since."

A frown line formed between Allison's brows. "Did it hurt? For her to end things?"

"Not at all," he lied. The truth was, Kelly's decision had cut his ego right to the bone. Not that he blamed her. He couldn't give women the emotional sharing they seemed to want, and he knew it. "I miss her company whenever there's a movie I want to see, but other than that, I really do hope she's happy."

Allison nodded as she digested that.

"Okay, your turn," he said. "How long's it been and who was he?"

She folded her hands in her lap and stared at them for several seconds. "Ten years. And the details are none of your business."

"Ten years?" His mind raced. "How old are you?"

"I told you, it's none of—"

"How old?" he demanded.

That chin of hers went up again. "Twenty-six."

"You haven't had sex since you were *sixteen*?" He nearly sloshed coffee all over his lap.

"It's none of your business." She started tidying dishes. "And I don't want to talk about it."

Scott remembered details from last night, her nervousness and uncertainty. "He was the only one, too, wasn't he?"

She continued straightening the coffee table.

"I take it you were in love."

She glared at him.

"Okay." He held up his hand. "I won't press for all the gory details, I just want to know if you were in love with the kid. I assume he was a kid."

"He was a spoiled little rich boy carving notches in his bedpost. And yes, I thought I was in love. Except the boy I loved was an illusion."

"How long did you date him before you figured that out?"

"Four months," she answered through gritted teeth, her gray eyes flashing.

"Have you dated anyone since?"

"No."

"At all?"

"No!"

"God, no wonder you were desperate to have sex." He regretted the words the instant they left his mouth. She rose and crossed to the window, staring outside with her arms wrapped about her stomach.

With a sigh, he rose as well and came up cautiously behind her. "I'm sorry."

"Why? It's the truth. I'm desperate and pathetic. You're the first man in ten years who has even wanted to take me to bed."

"I doubt that."

"It's true." She wiped her cheeks with the sleeve of the robe.

"No it's not. It's impossible." He laid his hands on her shoulders and felt her stiffen. "You just intimidate men, is all."

She snorted. "Oh yes, I'm *so* intimidating."

"If you only knew." He massaged her shoulders, to help her relax as he remembered first meeting her. The primness of her manner had warned him to keep his distance. Now he knew part of that stiffness came from old hurt, magnified through years of perceived rejection. How ironic that the shield she used to protect herself only compounded her pain. He bent his head to nuzzle her hair. "You're so beautiful, the shy ones probably assume you'd turn them down flat, and you're way too sweet for the selfish bastards of the world. Except me, apparently." He kissed her temple. "Which proves I have even fewer scruples than I thought."

"You're not that bad."

"Well, thanks for the vote of confidence, but I have to disagree." He turned her and gathered her against him. "I had no business bringing you here. You should be dating some nice guy who'll take you on picnics and long walks on the beach, then get down on one knee and beg you to marry him so he can spend the rest of his life giving you babies and making you happy."

"No!" To his surprise, she buried her face against his chest. "I told you, I don't care about that. I'm just tired of feeling unwanted."

"Hey, hey." Tipping up her chin, he brushed the tears from her cheek with his thumb. "You are anything but that."

"Prove it." She looked at him with translucent eyes. "Make me feel wanted."

An alarm sounded inside his head, warning him he was entering dangerous waters. He should turn back and swim like hell for shore. But he couldn't resist the plea in her eyes. He lowered his head and kissed her lips, wishing he could kiss away whatever demons tormented her. Her arms slipped up around his neck as she molded her body to him.

Hunger stirred eagerly to life. Last night they'd enjoyed each other with abandon, each glutting their senses in a carnal feast. This time, though, would be for her.

He swept her into his arms and carried her to the bed, where he laid her down among the rumpled sheets. Tossing his robe aside, he settled beside her. Her own robe parted as he trailed kisses down her neck, over her body. He focused all his attention on pleasing her, on seeking out every sensitive spot that made her gasp and sigh. Her pulse drummed against his lips as she writhed beneath him.

"Scott," she whispered and reached for him. "I want you. Now."

"No." He brushed her hands away and continued his path down her stomach. He pressed his lips to the heated skin just below her belly button and felt her muscles quiver. Raising his head, he smiled at her. "I'm going to show you just how desirable you are by doing all the things I've wanted to do since the moment I first saw you."

He moved his hand down over her belly and between her thighs. Her eyelids went heavy as he teased her heated flesh with slow, bold caresses. "Yes," she whispered, and relaxed her legs, giving him free rein to pleasure her however he wished. And pleasure her he did, oh so beautifully, before giving in to the demands of his body and seeking his own release.

Chapter 9

HER BODY WEAK AND SATED, Allison lay facing Scott. His eyes were closed, giving her the freedom to study his face. Life was so full of surprises. Three days ago, she'd almost resigned herself to living vicariously through others. She had the inn, the gift shop, family and friends. She'd told herself that was enough to balance the lonely nights in her empty bed. Yet now, here she was—lying in bed with a gorgeous, compelling man who delighted in making her wild with pleasure. The thought brought a smile to her lips.

"What's that grin about?" he asked in a lazy rumble, and she realized his eyes weren't completely closed.

"That life is never what we expect."

"Oh?" He arched a brow.

He looked so irresistible when he did that, even though she suspected he was trying to look dark and cynical. She propped her head on her hand and trailed her fingertip through the swirls of black hair on his chest. "When I was young, I used to dream about exactly what you described—dating, marriage, children."

He tucked an arm behind his head and studied her. "So what happened?"

She shrugged, hedging.

"Come on," he coaxed.

"Loving someone makes you vulnerable. And the more you love, the more it can hurt when you lose them. I have no choice with Adrian and Rory, and my aunt Viv. I already love them, but I don't want to let anyone else into that circle."

"What about your parents? I've never heard you mention any."

She kept her gaze fixed on her fingertip as she made precise circles. "They died when I was five. Mom and Dad were both actors, performing on stage in Connecticut. We were in an accident, returning to our hotel one night after one of their performances."

"You were with them?"

She drew more circles, each one smaller. "Adrian and I were asleep on the back seat. Mom had made a bed for Rory on the floorboard. It was a head-on collision."

"Oh God, I'm so sorry. That must have been horrible." He tried to gather her close, but she remained rigidly where she was, refusing to get emotional.

"People think kids are resilient, that they can bounce back from something like that and go on with life. But some things you never get over." She took a breath and blew it out slowly to help keep the pain down deep where she'd buried it years ago. "So . . . what about you? Why don't you want a wife and kids?"

He shrugged one shoulder. "Because even I'm not that big of an SOB."

She gave him a questioning look.

"Genetically I'm a bad risk. The men in my family, for as far back as anyone can remember, have practically been legends for two things: their greed, and their emotional cruelty toward women. Indifference and infidelity were my father's specialties."

She cocked her head to study him. "You don't really think something like that is passed down through the genes, do you?"

"Ask my mother. She'll be happy to tell you how I'm just like my father, that I don't care about anyone but myself, I'm selfish and thoughtless and a terrible son."

"What an awful thing for a mother to say!"

"Yeah, truth is a real bitch, ain't it?" His mouth

twisted with sarcasm. "But even if I weren't a chip off
the ol' block, I wouldn't want marriage. The whole idea
of happily-ever-after is a myth. People pretend they have
a great marriage because they don't want others to know
the truth. They don't realize *everyone* is pretending. If
we'd all be honest and admit no two people can live together long term and stay happy about it we'd all be better
off. I grew up watching what hate does to people, and I
don't want any part of it."

"Your parents' marriage was that bad?" she asked,
shocked that he thought all marriages were like that.

"Why do you think I became a writer?"

"I don't understand."

"It's the perfect way to escape. When I'm writing,
I'm not even part of the real world. I mentally enter a
world of my own making. It's like being the god of my
own universe." He wiggled his brows, suddenly playful.
"Characters live and die by my whim. And if one of them
dares to irritate me, I can end their miserable existence in
some ghastly manner." He gave a diabolical laugh.

Her brows shot up. "Have you talked to a therapist
about this god complex and violent streak of yours?"

"And risk ruining my career?" He feigned horror.
"What would my readers say?"

"You're right. Forget I said anything. As one of your
readers, I much prefer you slightly insane." She kissed his
shoulder. "Speaking of your books, are you going to tell
me about the one you're writing now?"

For a heartbeat, his face went blank. Then he narrowed his eyes. "So, this was all a dastardly plot to relax
me with sex, catch me off guard, and wheedle information
out of me." His voice took on a German accent. "Confess
ze truth and I may let you live. Someone put you up to
zis, eh?"

Her eyes widened. "I'm innocent, I swear."

In one swift move, he had her on her back, her hands

pinned to the mattress above her head. "Who are you spying for, *Fräulein*?"

"No one."

"Ve have vays to make you talk." He transferred both her wrists to one hand and tickled her ribs until she convulsed with laughter. "Vas it another author who vants to steal my brilliant ideas?"

"No, no." She writhed beneath him, laughing so hard, her sides ached.

"My editor, *Frau Kommandant*?"

"You'll never torture it out of me." She thrashed her head from side to side, tears of mirth wetting her lashes.

"Aaah, I know. It vas my agent. Ze two of you devised zis scheme together."

"All right, I confess. It was Hugh Ashton. He asked me to run away with him to Tahiti and I couldn't resist."

"Aha! I knew it." He rolled on top of her, his body pressing her into the mattress. "And now, you must be punished for consorting with ze enemy." His mouth took hers in a deep, drugging kiss.

She was dizzy by the time he lifted his head. "No more," she sighed, stretching up toward his mouth. "I can't take it. Have mercy."

"I have no mercy for traitors." He kissed her again.

She melted beneath him, enjoying the way he made her body sing with excitement. When he moved to her neck, she pressed her lips to his ear. "So, what *is* your book about?"

Groaning, he rolled off her and sprawled on his back staring at the ceiling.

She propped her head on her hand and wrapped a bit of chest hair around one finger. "Ve have vays to make you talk." She gave a warning tug and his hand covered hers.

"No." His eyes lost their teasing light as he looked up at her. "I'm officially taking the day off. No talk of writing. For today, I don't even want to think about writing."

"All right." She tried to hide her disappointment that the playful mood had ended. "What do you want to think about?"

"That depends." He came up on both elbows. "What are we going to do today?"

"I assumed we'd go back to the inn once we checked out."

"Do you have to go straight back?"

"I should." Her shoulders slumped. "There's always rooms to clean, towels to wash, and the gift shop to dust and straighten. Although I've hardly taken any time off since we opened."

"In other words, you could get away with playing hooky if you wanted to."

"Hooky?" The word piqued her interest.

"You know, like you did back in high school."

"I never played hooky."

"You're kidding." He stared at her. "Man, and I thought my childhood was deprived."

"So, how's it done?" she asked eagerly.

"First, name something you'd really like to do that you haven't done in a while?"

"Anything?"

"Well, anything we can do together."

She blushed, and glanced down at his body.

"Besides that, you wanton thing."

She thought a minute. "I don't suppose you ride horseback."

"Are you kidding?" He snorted. "When my family came here in the summer, riding horses on the beach ranked right up there with surfing and ogling babes in bikinis."

"Really?" She sat up with the sheet tucked loosely

about her. "I wonder if the stable out on Stewart Road still rents horses by the hour."

"We could find out," he said. "Do you have the right clothes to wear?"

"Well, not on me."

"Obviously." He grinned at the portion of breasts visible above the sheet.

"But I still have some jeans and riding boots at my aunt's house. That's where we were living until we moved into the inn. We haven't bothered to move everything out since Aunt Viv isn't using the place."

"Aunt Viv?" Scott's eyes narrowed. "As in the Incomparable Vivian Young, star of Broadway, right?"

"You've heard of her?"

"I'm a hopeless addict of movies, plays, and other people's books." He touched his forehead. "If memory serves, you've had several famous performers in your family, all the way back to Marguerite."

"True." She nodded. "In fact, Adrian, Rory, and I are the first generation who haven't had any interest in the stage."

"Now there's bound to be a story behind that statement."

"I guess, but I doubt it would hold your interest."

He gave her a wry look. "I'm always interested in hearing a story. I have to warn you though, anything you say may be used in my next book."

She smiled. "All right then. Take me horseback riding, and I'll be happy to bore you to tears."

"You got it, sweetheart." He tossed back the covers and leapt from the bed, gloriously nude. "You get dressed while I call the stables."

Half an hour later, when Scott emerged from his turn in the bathroom, Allison was dressed and hanging up the phone from calling the inn.

"Everything all clear?" Scott asked.

"Yep." She gave him a stiff smile. "Adrian isn't happy, but he's taken off more days than I have, so there wasn't much he could say."

Nodding, Scott headed for the closet and pulled on jeans and a black T-shirt.

"Do you always wear so much black?" Allison asked as she dug through her luggage for a pair of sandals to go with her yellow tank top and tropical-print skirt.

"Pretty much." He sat on the bed and pulled on the black cowboy boots he'd worn the night before. "But before you go thinking it's some political statement or social commentary, let me assure you it's just laziness on my part."

"How so?"

"Every day I have to make a million decisions, not just about plot twists but character names, physical descriptions, mannerisms, and what the hell *they're* wearing. The last thing I want to think about is my own clothes. Plus, when I travel for research, it's easier to pack if everything is either black or something that goes with black."

"You forgot one thing."

"What's that?"

She grinned at him. "It's very sexy."

"You think so, eh?" He pulled her down onto his lap and kissed her full on the mouth, sending her senses reeling. The minute she wrapped her arms about his neck, though, he pulled back. "Stop that, woman. Or you'll wind up taking a very different kind of ride."

"I could be persuaded."

He gave her lips a quick smacking kiss. "Enough. We'll never get out of here if you keep attacking me."

A few minutes later, they'd checked out of the hotel and tossed their bags in the back of the Jag. Scott headed for the house where Allison had grown up. It was just a few blocks due north from the hotel, but the scenery changed subtly as they crossed the line from the newer development along the gulf side of the island into the historical district on the bay side. The old nineteenth-century buildings that made up downtown and the residential areas immediately surrounding it were all that had survived the Great Storm.

Pulling to a halt before the Bouchard Cottage, Scott admired the quaint one-story white house with its picket fence and green shutters. The flower beds had grown wild with neglect, but the place had charm to spare.

He didn't need to read the historical marker mounted on a pole in the front yard to know the cottage had been built by Henri LeRoche for his wife's daughter, Nicole, when he banished her from Pearl Island. He knew enough about Galveston history to know Marguerite's descendants had lived there ever since. But while the descendants of Marguerite were well known to everyone in Galveston, they were definitely not part of respectable society. Actors were still considered nothing more than "privileged servants" in certain circles.

"This'll only take a minute," Allison said as she jumped out of the car. "Why don't you come inside and have a seat while I change?"

"You got it." Scott climbed eagerly from the car since he'd always wanted to see the inside of the cottage.

As they made their way to the front porch, she frowned at the overgrown flower beds. "I really need to get over here more often and take care of things."

"Can't your aunt hire a lawn service?"

She looked at him. "Why should she do that when she has the three of us living nearby?"

"Because you have an inn to run, for one thing." He held the screen door open while she fished the key out of her purse.

"True, but Aunt Viv made a lot of sacrifices to raise us after our parents died. A little mowing and weeding is the least we can do in return. Besides, I've always loved this place." Opening the door, she led the way inside. The dark entry held the musty heat of spring on the gulf coast. "Here, let me open a window."

Scott followed her into a small parlor filled with a hodgepodge of antique furniture. Sunlight flooded the room as she threw back the heavy curtains. Glancing around, he saw a multitude of framed photographs, playbills, and theater props. Generations of family history covered the walls and every flat surface, including the piano that stood near the archway to the dining room.

This one small house, with its untended gardens and cluttered parlor, held more welcoming warmth than any of the mansions he'd lived in growing up. How very different her childhood was from his.

"I'd offer you something to drink, but the kitchen's completely bare." She wrestled a window open to let in some fresh air and the sounds of sparrows squabbling in the shrubs.

"I'm fine," he assured her.

"Well, if you'll wait here, I'll go change."

He hid a smile as she headed through the dining room toward the back of the house. After everything they'd done in the hotel room, it seemed odd to wait for her in the parlor like a high school sweetheart come to pick her up for a date.

To pass the time, he studied the pictures. Mixed with the live-action shots to promote stage productions were studio head shots of her various ancestors. On the mantel, though, he found some candid shots of Allison with her brother and sister at various ages.

What a skinny little thing she'd been, he thought as he picked up a photo of her sitting on the front steps with her sister. He knew Aurora was the younger of the two, but even at this early age she'd been taller and more filled out than Alli. Aurora was flashing the camera a playful smile with her back arched and her bright hair tumbling about her budding figure. Alli, on the other hand, sat beside her, solemn but poised with her hands folded neatly in her lap. She reminded him of a gazelle with her slender limbs and long neck. Her smile was timid, and her eyes held a sort of acceptance that made her seem sad and serene at the same time.

She couldn't have been more than fourteen or fifteen, and already she'd been a complex blend of layers. Who was Allison St. Claire? And what made her such an intriguing study in contrasts?

"Okay, I'm ready."

He turned as she walked into the room wearing faded blue jeans tucked into black English riding boots and a white T-shirt. The outfit did a fine job of showing off her slight curves, and the riding boots were enough to inspire a few fantasies.

"How 'bout you, cowboy?" She gave him a cocky grin. "You ready to ride?"

Oh, honey, am I ever.

Alli laughed as the wind whipped through her hair. Her knees gripped the saddle as the gray mare flew over the packed wet sand. Glancing over her shoulder, she saw Scott chasing after her on his powerful bay gelding. She leaned over the mare's neck and urged her mount faster. Her heart beat in time to the pounding of hooves as they splashed through the surf. The waves came and went beneath her in a blur as they raced along the water's edge. A flock of sea gulls took flight, screeching in protest while sandpipers scurried out of the way.

The sounds and scents brought back so many memories. As a girl she'd ridden as often as she could, loving the freedom, solitude, and total connection with nature.

Thunder sounded nearby, and at first she thought it came from the clouds crowding the sky over the gulf.

Then she glanced back to see Scott closing the gap, his smile wicked and triumphant. She thought of urging her mount to a faster pace, but drew back instead, letting him charge past.

Laughing, she reined her mount in a wide circle, so the mare could catch her breath. When Scott realized she'd ended her mad dash down the beach, he reined in as well. Turning his mount, he trotted back to her, a lone dark figure against the beige sand, frothy waves, and pale blue sky. "You should have warned me you wanted to race."

"That wasn't a race," she said. "It was . . . freedom." She patted the mare's neck and continued on down the beach at a jaunty walk, making him turn again to follow her. "Oh, I have missed this," she said, lifting her face to the salty breeze that held a promise of rain. "Since we bought Pearl Island, I haven't had time for things like riding."

"You should make time," he said, nudging his horse alongside hers.

"I wish I could. But running a bed and breakfast isn't like a normal job. It's twenty-four hours a day, seven days a week."

He laughed. "I can definitely identify with that. But trust me when I say if you don't get away from it now and then, you'll burn out, big time. Even on something you love."

She cast him a sideways glance. "Is this the voice of experience?"

"Hey, I do things besides write."

"Like what?"

He frowned as if unable to think of anything. "So, when are you going to tell me why none of you went into the theater?"

"Are we changing the subject?" She tried to mimic his single-brow arch, but knew she wasn't even close.

"That was the deal." Teasing her, he raised one brow, and she wondered how he did that. "We go horseback riding, you tell me a story."

"It's not much of a story." She tried again to get her brows to move independently, then decided to give up until she had a mirror to monitor her success. "I already told you both my parents were in the theater. They loved it. The whole lifestyle, traveling, performing, everything. Even when Adrian hit school age, we rarely stayed in one place. By the time he was in the second grade, he'd gone to three different schools in New Jersey, Massachusetts, and here in Galveston. When summer came, Mom would pack us up and off we'd go again, living like Gypsies."

"I take it the three of you weren't thrilled with the arrangement."

"Part of the time we were." She combed her fingers through her horse's coarse mane. "There's an excitement to life backstage, and a joy to being with your parents while they're working. Dad was a wonderful actor. I may have been young, but I distinctly remember sitting in Mom's lap watching him, and feeling a swell of pride along with that warm fuzzy feeling."

"Warm fuzzy feeling?"

"You know, that feeling you get when everything in the world is just as it should be?" Like now, she thought, taking in the kiss of the sun on her cheeks, the scent of the gulf . . . and the fascinating, sexy man at her side.

" 'Fraid I don't know that one."

"Just as well." She shrugged. "It usually comes right before tragedy strikes and destroys everything. Just one of life's cruel quirks, I guess. Anyway, I had lots of moments like that when I was little, but there were other times when I wasn't happy. Like when us kids had to sleep on the floor because the hotel didn't have enough rollaway beds to go around. Or when we ate stale sandwiches that some stagehand brought in. I loved my parents, but . . ." She looked out over the gulf.

"What?"

"Nothing."

"Come on," he wheedled. "The story doesn't count if you leave something out."

"Sometimes . . . I think it was selfish of them to raise us that way." She watched the gulls as they dipped and rode on the wind. "After they died, and we came to live with Gran'ma, Adrian promised Rory and me we'd never have to sleep on the floor or eat baloney sandwiches again."

"I thought you said your aunt raised you."

"That was after Gran'ma died. I still miss her." She smiled fondly. "She told the most wonderful stories about Marguerite and Nicole, and the rest of the family. Not that there's that many of us. With everyone's devotion to the theater rather than starting a family, it's amazing the Bouchard line hasn't died out."

"When did your grandmother die?"

"When I was eleven. Rather than pack us up and move us to New York, Aunt Viv put Broadway on hold to work in Houston for a while. We were on our own a lot during those years, but Adrian turned out to be a pretty good mom."

Scott grinned at her. "I'm not sure I would say that to his face."

"Oh no, Adrian is very proud that he can cook and clean and do the laundry. Although the fact that he excelled in every sport and was so good-looking he had girls hanging all over him in high school kept the other boys from teasing him too much."

"So *that's* where I went wrong in school," Scott said. "I never took home ec."

She laughed. "Somehow I doubt you had much trouble finding a date for the prom."

His expression sobered. "I wasn't much into things like the prom."

"What were you into?" She cocked her head as the wind picked up.

"Nothing much."

She started to say that wasn't fair, but noticed how far they'd ridden and pulled to a halt. "We need to turn back."

He glanced at his watch. "No, we've got time left, and there's a really great inlet up ahead where we can dismount and let the horses cool off a bit."

"No. I never go any farther than this."

"Why not?" He turned his horse to face her.

"That house there." She pointed to a modern structure with soaring glass walls and a flat roof that sat atop a man-made mound rather than on stilts like the other houses along the beach. The retaining wall that surrounded it on the front and sides made it look like an ultra-modern castle. "That's the LeRoche family beach house."

"So?"

"So, I'm not comfortable riding by it." She rubbed her bare arms, noticing that the temperature had dropped. "What if one of them is out by the swimming pool in back and they wave? I'd have to wave back like I was some friendly stranger, since I doubt they'd recognize me. Why would they? It's not like people as rich as the LeRoches bother to keep up with their distant, middle-class cousins."

"Do I detect a touch of animosity?" He raised that blasted, sexy brow again.

"Try outrage," she answered. "And if we didn't have cause to hate them before, we sure do now."

He rocked back in the saddle. "What do you mean?"

"John LeRoche, the current patriarch on that branch of the family tree, is suing us."

"What?" Scott demanded. "On what grounds?"

"He claims we made some underhanded deal with Chance's bank to get them to foreclose on Pearl Island."

"What do you mean, 'Chance's bank'?"

"Oliver Chancellor's family founded the First Bank of Galveston, which is now the Liberty Union National Bank. Even though his father had already sold the bank, Chance was still working there when the foreclosure took place. John LeRoche is claiming Chance talked the bank into foreclosing because he knew we wanted to buy Pearl Island. And that Chance used prior knowledge to help us get the property."

"Did he?"

"No! Of course not." Allison batted hair out of her eyes as the wind swirled. "Chance is one of the most honest, upright people I can imagine. Besides, he and Rory weren't even involved until after the foreclosure. That's how they got to know each other, by us trying to get a loan from his bank to buy the place."

"Then you have nothing to worry about."

"Legally, maybe not. It's a bogus lawsuit, and John LeRoche has no chance of winning. But if he drags this out, it could get costly, and Chance thinks that's his real goal. John LeRoche wants to drive us out of business so we'll have to sell the house." The thought of losing Pearl Island after all the work they'd put into it tore at her heart. And it wasn't just the work, it was the connection she'd always felt to the house, even before they owned it. "What makes me mad is he doesn't care about Pearl Island. None of the LeRoches do. They only want to own it because of the good luck Marguerite has brought them in the past. The Pearl was like a Midas touch for them, which is how they got to be so obscenely wealthy in the first place. Now that they've lost possession of the charm, John LeRoche is having all kinds of financial problems. He's desperate enough to do anything to get the house back."

She shook her head as fear filled her heart. "I don't know what we'll do if we lose it. Not just the house, but the business. It means more to us than I can tell you, to have something that's *ours*. Something that can't be taken away from us. At least I thought it couldn't be taken away." She looked back at the beach house. "God, I hate the whole LeRoche family sometimes! They did *nothing* to deserve Pearl Island. They left the house abandoned for years. And now that we've put in all the work, invested every dime to our names, they want to steal it back."

"So what are you going to do?" he asked quietly.

"Fight," she answered without hesitation. "No matter what it takes. Pearl Island is rightfully ours, and we're not giving it up."

Scott looked out over the gulf, his expression thoughtful. "Actually, you're right, we should be getting back. That storm is rolling in faster than I thought."

Chapter 10

SCOTT WAS STRANGELY QUIET ON the drive back to the inn. Deciding to leave him in peace, Allison turned her attention to the drama of the storm.

The clouds that had been bumping around on the horizon a mere hour before now covered the island like black mountains blocking out the sun. The first fat raindrops quickly grew into a downpour, pounding on the roof of the car. Scott turned on the windshield wipers and headlights as traffic slowed.

Then they turned onto the private bridge to Pearl Island, and Allison's stomach tightened at the thought of facing Rory and Adrian with all of them knowing she'd slept with Scott last night.

"Pull around back," she told him as they approached the house. A variety of vehicles crowded the parking lot near the front, letting her know most of the current guests were inside. But then, few people would be at the beach or antiquing in town in weather like this. "If you don't mind using the back entrance, we won't get as wet."

He turned into the small, oyster-shell lot behind the house and parked between Chance's BMW and the old Jeep she and Rory shared. Adrian's motorcycle had been pulled up onto the back porch. The pounding of the rain seemed louder when Scott killed the engine.

"Well," she said, "I guess this is it. Back to reality."

"Yeah. Guess so." Lightning flashed, followed by a blast of thunder that shook the ground.

They looked at each other, and she wished he would kiss her one last time. Instead, he looked toward the house where lights shone from every window. "I need to use the phone in the office for a private call, if that's all right."

"Certainly." She frowned at his stiff manner after the openness they'd shared for the past twenty-four hours. But that was part of the deal, she supposed. One night only. She turned back toward the house. "Shall we make a dash for it and leave our bags for later?"

"Definitely." He peered out at the rain. "You ready?"

She nodded and they moved together, jumping from the dry safety of the car into the deluge. They raced for the back porch, splashing through puddles before they ducked beneath the protection of the overhang. Sheets of rain fell about them in a gray curtain, closing them in that small space as they shook water from their hair. Allison plucked at her wet T-shirt, thankful it wasn't wet enough to have gone completely transparent. With Scott crowding in behind her, she maneuvered around the motorcycle and reached for the door.

"Wait," he said.

She turned toward him as best she could. Though his body blocked the wind, the intensity of his gaze made her shiver.

He cupped her face in his hands, holding her there as he lowered his mouth to cover her cool lips with a hot kiss. She swayed into him, absorbing every sensation as he wrapped his arms about her. Her fingers slid into his wet hair as the taste and scent of rain filled her. A part of her wished the exhilarating freedom of the past two days could go on forever. It had been a time out of time, where she could be as bold as she dared.

Wanting to cling to that an instant longer, she pressed into him. He groaned as he kissed the raindrops from her cheeks, her neck, then returned to her mouth, taking her back to that place of greedy giving. Her body trembled as he lifted his head. She looked up into his eyes, and saw the same blaze of desire that burned inside her.

He banked it slowly, pulling back inside himself before he stepped away physically. "Okay." He nodded, his voice raspy but firm. "Now I'm ready."

The words were an ending. She nodded, knowing it was best but feeling an odd sadness as she led the way inside. The air-conditioned back hall raised goose bumps on her arms. A murmur of voices came from the kitchen, letting her know the whole family was gathered there. She let out a sigh as she and Scott took off their muddy boots.

"I guess I'll need to get fitted for a new pair," he said, frowning at his black cowboy boots. They were eel-skin—meant for dress wear, not horseback riding—and they looked frightfully expensive. They were also scuffed beyond repair.

"Sorry," she offered.

"Don't be." One corner of his mouth lifted. "The ride was worth it."

Sadie let out a bark and came charging toward the sound of their voices. "Hey there, sweetie." Allison bent forward and ruffled the dog's long fur. "Did you miss me?"

"Who's this?" Scott asked, smiling at the dog.

"Sadie." Allison looked up at him. "We keep her in the kitchen or downstairs most of the time, since not all guests care for dogs."

He gave the sheltie a scratch beneath the chin, winning her over instantly. "She's a pretty thing."

Sadie cocked her head and barked.

"And she knows it." Allison laughed, then straightened. Bolstering her courage, she stepped into the open doorway to the kitchen.

Silence descended. Adrian, Rory, and Chance sat around the worktable, their expressions grave.

Allison's stomach tensed. "Is something wrong?"

Adrian glanced meaningfully at Scott before answering. "Family matter. We've been waiting for you to join us."

"Oh." Her gaze flew from one frowning face to the next, wondering what had happened. Or were they simply planning to berate her again about last night, this time en masse? "I'll be right with you."

Rather than walk through the kitchen and butler's pantry, she motioned for Scott to follow her to the small servant's door that led straight from the back hall into the central hall. "The phone's this way. No, Sadie, you stay."

Sadie barked in protest and Allison quickly closed the door on the sound. Turning, she was glad to find the central hall free of guests, since she looked a bit worse for wear in her stocking feet and wet T-shirt. A couple sat in the music room, across the hall from the dining room, watching the TV they'd tucked into an armoire, but they were too absorbed in their show to pay any attention to her and Scott.

"So how much grief are they going to give you?" he asked as they headed for the office.

"I don't know. It could be something else."

He nodded and let the subject drop.

"The phone's here on the desk," she said as she turned on a floor lamp. "We have a block on the line to prevent anyone but us from making long distance calls, so you'll need a calling card."

"No problem." He reached for his wallet. "I just need a few minutes of privacy."

"Take your time. I'll be in the kitchen if you need anything." She stopped long enough to pull the sliding pocket doors together, closing the room off.

Scott let out a breath when she was gone, but his temper began to simmer again as he dialed the number for his sister's house in New Orleans. Everything Allison had told him on the beach kept playing through his mind. He had expected some ill will between Nicole's descendants and the LeRoche family, but the extent of her animosity stunned him, as did the reason behind it.

His sister answered on the first ring, sounding frantic. "Chloe?"

"No, it's Scott." He frowned at Diane's tone.

"Scott? Oh, thank God! I've been trying to get in touch with you all day. Why don't you ever listen to your damn answering machine?"

"Diane"—he sighed—"do you think we could skip the latest episode in your soap opera life just this once so I can ask you a favor? I don't have my address book on me and I need the number for John's lawyer. Can you look it up for me?"

"Not now. Scott, I need your help. Something serious has happened with Chloe."

He went on mild alert, since "serious" was a relative term with his sister. "What this time? Did she dye her hair green? Pierce her navel?"

"She's missing."

"What?" The mild alert jumped up to code red. "What do you mean missing?"

"She's run away!" his sister wailed. "I found a note . . . on the kitchen table when I got home. Oh Scott, how could she do this? Where could she be? Doesn't she realize how worried this would make me?"

"Okay, slow down, back up." He pinched the bridge of his nose. "What time did you find the note?"

"When I got home."

"What time!"

"I don't know. About ten this morning."

Jesus! His sister had left her twelve-year-old daughter alone all night while she was out, clubbing most likely. Even for Diane, that hit new lows of irresponsibility.

"Scott, please tell me she's with you."

"Why would she be with me?"

"Because her note said she was going to live with

you, that you were the only person who cared whether she lived or died. How could she say that? Doesn't she know how much I love her? How can she hurt me like this?"

Scott refrained from commenting as his sister fell to pieces. All the lectures in the world would do no good unless Diane miraculously decided to grow up. "Don't panic," he said when she wound down. "I'll find her."

"Thank you," she sniffed, not bothering to ask how. "You always know what to do."

He gritted his teeth in frustration. "Just do me one favor while I'm finding Chloe."

"What?"

"Look up the number for John's attorney."

"Do I have to do that now?" she whined.

"Well, not this minute, but sometime in the next twenty-four hours, yes, I would appreciate it."

"Why? So you can tell them to cut off my allowance?"

"Diane . . ." He struggled to control his temper. "This isn't about you, okay? I just need to talk to John's attorney."

"Why?"

"Because John LeRoche, our asshole of a father, is wreaking havoc on the lives of some very decent people, and I want to stop him."

"What do you care? You disowned all of us years ago."

I care because he's hurting Allison. "Just get me the number, will ya?"

"Oh, all right! But promise you'll find Chloe."

"I'll find her." His mind raced as he hung up. If his niece had gone to his townhouse, she'd found it empty. She had a key, but Chloe alone in the French Quarter was not something he wanted to think about.

The kid was smart, though, and resourceful. Plus he'd

given her a surefire way to contact him in case of emergencies. She had his agent's phone number, and Hugh had instructions to help the kid if she ever needed to find him.

Dialing his agent's office, he glanced at his watch and saw it was just after four o'clock. Five New York time. *Please be there.*

"Hugh Ashton."

Thank God. "Hugh, it's Scott."

"Scott? Now why does that name sound familiar? I remember! I used to know someone named Scott many moons ago, but I think he fell off the ends of the earth."

"Will you can it and listen? My niece, Chloe, is missing. Has she called there?"

"Actually, yes, she has."

"When! What did she say?"

"She called this morning while I was in a meeting. Refused to leave a number for me to call her back. She finally got through to me about an hour ago."

"What'd she say? Did she sound all right?"

"She sounded fine. And surprisingly mature. I thought you said she was just a kid."

"She is a kid. She's only twelve."

"Well, she sounded older."

"What did she say?"

"Only that she needed to talk to you. So I gave her the name and number of the inn where you're staying. That's okay, isn't it?"

"Yes, that's perfect." Relief washed through him. "I need to go so I can find out if she's called here. Do me a favor, though. If she calls you back, find out where she is. Then call me immediately."

"Will do. But remember this the next time I ask *you* to call *me* back."

"Yeah, yeah," Scott promised absently. After hanging up, he headed back to the kitchen.

Allison was seated with the others around the table.

Conversation stopped instantly and all attention turned on him.

"Does anyone know if my niece has called here in the last hour or so?" he asked. "Her name's Chloe."

Allison looked at the others.

"The only phone call you've had was from your editor," Rory said. Though her voice was civil, her expression held no warmth. "I left the message on the dresser in your room."

"You're sure it was my editor, not a young girl? Chloe sounds very mature for her age."

"Yes, I'm sure," Rory answered. "Unless your niece would be calling to ask why you haven't faxed in a title suggestion for your next book."

"All right. Thank you." Fear churned in his gut as he turned away.

"Scott, wait." Allison rose. "Has something happened?"

He shook his head, having no wish to air his problems before her scowling family. "It's nothing. I need to make a few more phone calls, though, if that's okay?"

"Of course."

Allison watched him go, sensing there was something he wasn't telling her. At the moment, though, she had her own problems to deal with. John LeRoche had been interviewed on the midday news in Houston about his company's recent financial problems. LeRoche Shipping, the foundation company of LeRoche Enterprises, was closing their warehouse in Houston, putting hundreds of people out of work. During the live interview, the subject of the foreclosure on Pearl Island and subsequent lawsuit against the Liberty Union National Bank had come up.

According to Chance, who'd watched the whole segment, John had been as calm and smiling as a politician caught in a scandal. But when he was asked about the lawsuit, anger had taken over. He said he'd had a strong working relationship with the Galveston bank for years, which was why he was surprised when the bank president's own son used his influence to help three complete idiots with no business experience to buy the property to open a B and B. He'd gone on to say he wanted the house back because it had "sentimental significance." Then he'd added: "Frankly I pity anyone gullible enough to stay at the Pearl Island Inn, because that house is too run-down to ever make a decent bed and breakfast. The fools who bought it only wanted it because of an old grudge against the LeRoche family."

Allison looked at Chance, still trying to take in everything he had just told her. "I can't believe he said all that."

"I can't either," Chance told her. "It was really stupid on his part, because he opened himself up for a big fat slander suit. Not that it will be easy to win, but that's what we've been discussing."

"Have you asked Malcolm for his advice?" Alli asked, referring to the attorney Chance had hired on their behalf. "What did he say?"

"I called him the minute the interview ended," Chance told her. "He said it looks pretty good in our favor. We can't sue him for calling us fools. That's opinion. But his comments about the house show 'malicious intent' to harm the reputation of our business. Malice is a hard thing to prove, though, and filing the suit could just bring more attention to his inflammatory remarks. We've already had the local paper calling up wanting our reaction."

"What did you tell them?" Alli asked.

"I told them exactly what Malcolm told me to say, 'no comment.' And that's what all of us need to say to anyone who asks about this. Especially if we file a slander suit. We don't want John LeRoche to be able to file a countersuit because of something one of us says in a moment of anger."

Allison turned to Adrian. "What do you think we should do?"

"I think we should sue his ass for everything we can get. And if it attracts media attention, fine. Bring 'em on."

"Rory, I assume you're with Chance on this?" Allison said.

"Absolutely." Rory nodded. "Although I may have to duct-tape my mouth shut to keep from telling people what I think of John LeRoche."

"Well, okay then." She took a deep breath, battling her aversion to any kind of confrontation. "I vote we should do it."

"Fine." Chance nodded. "I'll call Malcolm tomorrow. In the meantime, we have other business to discuss." He opened a folder.

Rory groaned at the sight of the computer printouts, each one filled with neat rows of numbers. "Do we have to talk about money? I'm already depressed."

"Sorry." Chance gave his wife a sympathetic smile. "Although it's not all bad news."

"Well, that's a relief." Adrian sat forward to look over the figures.

"Of course, it's not all good news, either." Chance handed each of them a report. Allison cringed at the amount of red ink. "Our occupancy rate is only averaging fifty percent."

"Well, that's up from our first quarter," Rory offered. "And this is only our first year. We expected to lose money at first."

"I know," Chance conceded. "But I've been running some numbers, and our operating costs are too high. We either need to cut costs or raise our rates."

"Or increase our guest capacity," Rory said.

Adrian arched a brow. "You mean divide up the ball-room on the third floor?"

"Oh, Rory, no," Alli said, her heart sinking at the

thought. The third floor was like a beautiful music box with whimsical frescoes and ornate plasterwork. "We all agreed to leave the ballroom intact, so we could rent it for private parties and day conferences."

"Only we're having trouble booking conferences, because we don't have enough rooms. So I was thinking"— Rory's eyes sparkled as she looked at each of them— "what if we go ahead and build the bungalows we've discussed now instead of waiting?"

"Not practical." Chance shook his head. "We already have too much invested in this venture. We can't possibly borrow any more money until we start showing a profit."

Rory disagreed, and the debate was on. Allison chewed her lip as she listened to both sides, fretting over what they should do. Chance's argument for caution was sound, but Rory had a point. Too much caution could spell failure. They were either committed to succeeding or they weren't. Of course, Rory looked at everything as an all-or-nothing proposition, and the thought of failure rarely entered her mind.

The debate headed quickly for a stalemate. To appease both sides, Allison agreed to look for ways to cut costs and increase income with the gift shop.

"Well, I'm not cutting back on anything that jeopardizes the quality of the food," Adrian insisted, setting off a new debate between him and Chance.

Allison closed her eyes as a dull throb started behind her forehead. Why couldn't there be an answer that pleased everyone and guaranteed success? "If y'all will excuse me," she said, "I think I'll go clean up, then do some inventory work in the gift shop."

Adrian frowned in concern as she rose, but didn't object to her leaving.

By the time Allison finished showering and changing into a clean T-shirt and denim jumper, Adrian had come downstairs. She could hear him in the room they'd meant to be Rory's bedroom. When Rory had married, she and Chance had built a small house on the island, secluded from the inn by a stand of trees. Adrian had turned the spare room into a workout room with free weights along one wall and mirrors covering another.

Crossing to the doorway, she watched her brother go through the graceful movements of t'ai chi. "I take it Rory and Chance have headed home?"

"They have," Adrian answered without breaking stride.

"Would you like me to fix some dinner before I go upstairs?"

"I'll get something later." He moved into a pose meant to increase balance and improve concentration— shutting her out completely.

She stood a moment, hurt by his cool behavior. Her brother had always been there for her, offering unquestioning support and understanding. Even though his workouts required focus, he never shut her out like this.

"Adrian, you're not mad at me, are you? I mean, I know you're worried I'll get hurt, but you're acting like you're . . . angry." She laughed, waiting for him to say that was nonsense.

Instead, he moved into another stance, not meeting her gaze.

"I don't understand why you're being this way." She shook her head. "You didn't disapprove when Rory was spending every night over at Chance's apartment. You worried, yes, but you weren't mad."

He finally looked at her, his eyes cool. "Rory was in love with the man she was sleeping with."

That stopped her for a moment, until anger took over. "Oh, and I suppose you've been in love with every woman you've taken to bed."

"That's different."

"Why, because you're a man?"

He shot her a scowl, then picked up a towel to dry his face. "Okay, so maybe I haven't been in love with them, but I have the decency to be sure they won't expect more than I'm willing to give."

"How is that different from the way Scott is treating me?"

"It's just different."

"Because I'm your sister?"

"Yes, dammit!" He tossed the towel aside, his muscles flexing in anger. "And I don't want you getting used by some man who sees you as nothing more than a new 'Flavor of the Week.'"

"Adrian . . ." She pressed her fingers to her temple. "I'm not a kid anymore. I don't need you to protect me. I know the score and I won't get hurt."

"The hell you won't. I know you, Alli. You're lying to yourself if you think you can handle this sort of a relationship. In fact, I'll bet money you're half in love with the guy already."

She dropped her hands. "I told you, I don't want that. I don't want marriage or children, or any of that."

"This from a woman who collects dolls."

"What does that have to do with anything?"

"Honestly?" As he studied her, she saw his anger shift to caution. "I think you're trying to replace the baby you lost."

The unexpected words hit her low and hard. They never talked about the miscarriage and Rory didn't even know. It had happened so long ago, but suddenly the pain returned, clamping about her chest until she could barely breathe. "If you'll excuse me"—she turned away—"I have work to do."

"Alli . . ." he called. She turned in time to see his shoulders sag. "I'm sorry. I—"

"Don't." She squeezed her eyes shut. When her composure returned, she looked at him calmly. "I think it's best if we let this whole subject drop. Come on, Sadie, let's go upstairs."

Chapter 11

IN THE BACK HALL, ALLI pressed a hand to her stomach and waited for her body to stop shaking. Sadie whined and looked at her with worried brown eyes.

"I'm okay." She squatted down to soothe the dog. "Big brothers think they know everything, but they don't."

Sadie tilted her head, listening. The gesture was so dear, Alli's throat threatened to close. Big brothers might not know everything, but hers had known a puppy would make the perfect get-well gift ten years ago when Aunt Viv had brought her home from the hospital. Nearly eleven years now, she realized as she noticed a trace of gray around Sadie's muzzle.

"You're still young, though, aren't you, girl?" Sadie's eyes twinkled with life as Alli scratched beneath her chin. "Tell ya what, if you promise to be good, you can sit in the gift shop while I work. Would you like that?"

Sadie barked and twirled in a circle.

"No! No barking. You have to be good." Standing, she opened the door a crack to be sure no guests were about. When she found the first floor empty, she headed for the sanctuary of the gift shop where she could lose herself doing inventory and poring over catalogues.

Halfway there, she noticed the doors to the office were still closed and light was shining beneath them. Curious, she veered that way and slid one panel open. The floor lamp by the desk had been left on, casting a faint glow over the room. Lightning flashed, drawing her attention to the curved alcove formed by the tower. She saw Scott seated on the settee, his forearms braced on his knees. He lifted his head and the haggard expression on his face startled her.

"Scott?" She stepped into the room, grabbing Sadie by the scruff before the dog could charge forward to greet her new friend. "What is it? What's going on?"

"It's nothing. I'm just waiting for a call. Is it okay if I wait in here?"

Before Allison could answer, Sadie wiggled free and dashed straight for Scott, planting her front paws in his lap, her tail wagging.

"Sadie, get down!" Allison hurried forward. Sadie sat at Scott's feet, completely confident of her welcome. Allison put her hands on her hips. "You are so spoiled rotten." To Scott, she added, "Now you know why we don't let her around guests."

"I don't mind." Scott smiled sadly as he petted Sadie. He still had on the clothes he'd worn riding, and the faint but pleasing scent of horse and leather tickled her nose.

"Are you sure nothing's wrong?" Alli asked.

"I'm fine."

She thought about leaving, but could tell something was definitely wrong. Cautiously, she sat beside him, folding her hands in her lap. "I thought you said it wasn't fair to withhold information."

"That's only when you're telling a story. Real life is exactly the opposite."

Rather than point out that her "story" had been real, she tried a different tack. "So, tell me a story."

He started to shake his head, then glanced at the phone. "My niece, Chloe, ran away from home. She's been missing since sometime before ten this morning."

"Oh, Scott . . ." She laid a hand on his thigh, longing to absorb some of his worry. "I'm so sorry. What can I do?"

Gratitude filled his eyes as he stared at her. "You just did it."

"What?"

He covered her hand with one of his. "You did nothing. You didn't ask for anything, blame me, or demand that I fix the problem. You did . . . nothing."

She sat quietly as his thumb brushed her knuckles. In that moment, gazing into his eyes, she felt closer to him than she had last night even when their bodies had been joined.

He looked away. "The worst part is, all I can do is wait by the phone. The police have put out a BOLO, 'be on the lookout,' but runaways aren't something they actively investigate. So I have to wait and hope either Chloe calls and tells me where she is, or my sister calls to tell me the kid's been found."

"Do you know where she may have headed?"

"Yeah. She left a suitably dramatic note saying she wanted to live with me, so it's a safe bet she headed for my townhouse." He rubbed his forehead. "I live in the French Quarter, for God's sake. I don't even want to think about my twelve-year-old niece wandering around that area by herself."

"What do you think she did when she found out you weren't there?"

"She was smart enough to call my agent, who told her where I'm staying and gave her the phone number. Since she hasn't called, I assume she's taken it into her head to come find me. Oh, man." He leaned forward, and buried his face in both hands.

Worry came off him in waves, reminding her of her brother when he went into protective male mode.

"If she's hitchhiking I swear I'll kill her. Surely she's not that stupid, though. She's a smart kid. She'll try to take a bus, right?" He looked at Allison, his eyes beseeching. "The driver will notice she's a minor traveling alone and turn her in, right?"

Her heart ached, knowing all the things that could

happen, or might already have happened. "I'm sure she'll be fine."

He nodded and stared at the phone as if willing it to ring.

Allison petted Sadie absent-mindedly as she wondered what to do. "Can I get you something to eat?"

"I'm not hungry."

"How about something to drink? We have white wine in the refrigerator."

He laughed. "Now that I'll take."

Nodding, she headed back for the kitchen to get a bottle of Pinot Grigio. When she and Sadie returned, he raised a brow at the second glass. She shrugged. "I figured I might as well keep you company while you wait."

"Thanks." His whole face relaxed with a smile. "You know, Alli, I don't care what anybody says, you're okay."

She laughed as she poured them each a glass. "Such lavish praise."

"Try and not let it go to your head."

She sat beside him and Sadie settled in at their feet. "Tell me about Chloe."

"Oh, she's a handful." He laughed. "Smart, stubborn, a tomboy trapped in a body destined to be a heartbreaker. I've been totally nuts about her since the day she was born, and she knows it."

"You spend a lot of time with her?"

"Not as much as I'd like, but more time than her father does."

"Oh?" Allison frowned at the bitter edge to his voice.

He settled back into the corner of the settee, facing her with an ankle resting on the opposite knee. "My sister has a real knack for picking men. Chloe's father is a prime example, suave, charming, and a total user. That was Diane's first husband and the marriage lasted all of one year. She's been married twice since then and is currently accepting applications for asshole number four. Chloe has a way of getting lost in the shuffle."

"So you step in as surrogate dad."

"Something like that. I like having her around, even if she is a major distraction." He took a sip of wine. "The irony is, Diane loves to complain about how our parents were so wrapped up in their own lives, they totally neglected us as kids. Yet she's doing exactly the same thing. It drives me insane."

"Have you talked to her about it?"

"Oh yeah." He snorted. "Unfortunately, Diane's whole life is an optional illusion."

"An 'optional' illusion?" Alli settled back into her own corner of the settee.

"You know, you get to pick and choose your own reality. She's quite creative at altering the facts to fit her fantasy."

"Maybe she should have been the writer in the family."

"Gawd." He shielded his eyes. "I can just imagine the kind of books she'd write—high drama with lots of angst. There would be the misunderstood glamour queen who marries one lying, cheating playboy after another, the child who takes her for granted, and the friends who only care about her money and connections. No one really loves her, or gives her the attention she deserves."

"Sounds dysfunctional enough to be a blockbuster movie."

"That's it!" He snapped his fingers. "She writes a book, Hollywood picks up the movie rights, and Diane becomes even more impossible to deal with than she is now."

"No." Allison shook her head. "She marries the leading man. Finds him in bed with a starlet. Murders him, and goes to jail."

Scott raised both eyebrows. "Maybe *you* should be a writer."

"Wait, I'm not finished." She waved her hand as she took a sip of wine. "In prison, her roommate is a cat burglar who teaches her the tricks of the trade. They stage a daring breakout, then go about the country stealing from all the men who ever did them wrong."

"With Diane that would have to be all over the world. Asshole number three was an Italian tennis pro."

"Italy, hum? Even better. They can graduate from stealing jewels to stealing internationally famous art objects."

He grinned, getting into the spirit of the story. "And since they both hate men so much, they become lesbian lovers."

"Oh, that's good." Alli laughed. "What happens next?"

Scott wiggled his brows. "Diane finds her new lover in bed with another woman. No wait." He held up his hand. "In bed with her Italian ex."

"Ooo, you are cruel."

"It's an author's job to torture his characters."

"Okay, so which one does she kill this time?"

"Neither one." Scott leaned forward, lowering his voice. "The lesbian lover and the Italian ex don't know they've been found out."

"Ah, so she plots revenge?"

He nodded. "She steals a famous bronze—"

"And pins the crime on them."

"Exactly." He toasted her.

She clicked her glass to his. "Then what?"

"She sells the bronze for a bundle and retires to a tropical island, of course."

"Where she finds the only man who can make her happy," Allison added. "A gorgeous cabana boy who doesn't speak a word of English but worships her like a goddess."

"Now *that* would make my sister happy." He toasted her again. Then his face went strangely blank and he stared into space. "I don't believe it."

"Don't believe what?" Concern made her straighten.

"I actually came up with a story. Okay, so it was completely ludicrous and you thought of half of it, but it was something." He burst out laughing.

"I don't get it." She looked at him, wondering if he'd gone a little mad. "Surely you come up with stories all the time."

"Not lately. Oh man, you can't imagine what it's like to have writer's block. At first, I just couldn't think of a decent idea—at least not one I thought my editor would approve—but for the past several months, I haven't even been able to come up with a bad idea. Every time I try to force my mind in that direction, my brain shuts down. Like hitting a wall. *Wham!* Nothing. Total blank." He slipped a hand behind her neck and gave her mouth a hard, smacking kiss. "Thank you!"

"For what?"

His slow grin made her heart flip. "For helping me relax. Maybe Hugh was right and that's all I needed."

"Oh." The word came out on a little breath of wonder. He was so close, she could feel the warmth of him. "Does that make me your muse?"

"I guess it does." His gaze wandered over her face before dropping to her mouth. "Which means we need to renegotiate your term of one night only."

She almost forgot to breathe as he lowered his mouth to hers. Desire flowed through her, hot and sweet, as he took her glass away, freeing her hands. She twined her arms about his neck, sliding down with him onto the cushion.

"Oh yeah . . ." He kissed her cheek, her neck, sending

shivers down her spine. "We definitely need to rethink the one-night-only clause."

Her mind surfaced from the haze of pleasure long enough to realize what he was saying. And how badly she wanted it. Wanted many nights of making love with this man, of waking in his arms in the morning, of kissing him and touching him the way she was right now.

Her brother's words echoed in the back of her mind: *I'll bet money you're half in love with the guy already.*

Panic streaked through the haze of pleasure.

"Wait." Pressing a hand to his chest, she pulled back to stare at him as fear replaced desire. "We can't do this."

"Oh, yes we can." His body moved over hers, so virile and male.

"No, really." Her mind raced for a convincing reason to stick with their agreement. "How do you know being with me cured your writer's block?"

"What else could it be?" He nibbled at her lips, making her heart race.

"It could be Chloe's running away."

"What?" He pulled back, his confusion comical.

"Think about it." She wiggled backward to get some space between their bodies, hoping her heart would stop pounding. "You told me you started writing to escape the stress of real life. Well, having your niece run away is pretty stressful, right?"

"Oh man." He sat up. "I hope you're not right."

"What does it matter, as long as you're able to write?"

"Because if I had to pick between making love to you to get my muse back, or calling my sister so she can dump a boatload of stress in my lap, which do you think I'd choose?"

She gave him an apologetic look. "Well, I guess it could be one other thing. Maybe it's Marguerite's magic."

A chill traced down Scott's spine as if someone

standing directly behind him had touched the back of his neck with a cold finger. He jerked around, but saw nothing between the settee and window. Outside, full night had fallen, with only flickers of lightning to break the blackness.

"What is it?" Allison asked, looking toward the windows, then back at him.

"Nothing. I just . . ." He shivered to shake off the feeling. "That was weird."

She studied him with knowing eyes. "I've never told anyone this, but sometimes I think I feel Marguerite's presence in this room. I can almost picture her standing here at the window, staring out at the cove as if waiting for Jack to come to her."

He wanted to scoff at such a claim but remembered why he'd come back to Pearl Island. It wasn't just to follow Hugh's advice. He'd come to be near Marguerite. His writer's block had gone from worrisome to total panic the day he'd learned his father had lost the house. When Diane had told him, he'd realized the block had started about the time John had put the house up as collateral. Coincidence? Probably. But the mere possibility that it wasn't coincidence, that his success as a writer hadn't been due to talent and hard work, but due to some old voodoo magic and a ghost trapped inside an old house, had rocked his confidence to the core.

"If you're right, I have another problem."

"What's that?" she asked.

"What if I have to come stay here every time I have trouble with my writing?"

"Would that be so bad?" She smiled.

If it meant keeping his hands off Allison every minute of every day, it would be like living in hell. While riding on the beach, the idea of lengthening their relationship to something like what he'd had with Kelly had danced around in the back of his mind. Galveston and New Orleans were fairly close, how hard would it be for them to get together a few times a year?

Then she'd mentioned the old feud between their families, which he'd assumed had died out generations ago, and he realized she hated the very blood that ran through his veins. If she found out he'd changed his name to Lawrence when he'd left home at eighteen, that he'd been born Scott LeRoche, she'd probably kick him out of the inn, and out of her life.

And if he touched her again knowing that, he'd deserve all the anger she cared to toss his way.

He heaved a sigh. "You realize this conjecture is all premature."

"How so?"

"I haven't exactly come up with a decent idea for my next book. All I had was one moment of mediocre creativity."

"It'll come back to you, though." Total confidence shone in her eyes. "I'm sure of it."

"God, I hope so. Because you have no idea how close I am to watching my career vanish. I'm contracted for a book that's due out in October, and I haven't even started it."

"You're kidding." The confidence turned to surprise. "Can you write that fast?"

"When I have an idea, I can finish a book in eight weeks, if I have to. I prefer three to four months, but when I'm under the gun, I can do it in less. The problem is, I don't have an idea that has a chance of getting past my editor. She shot down every proposal I sent her back when I was able to still write proposals."

"What happens if you don't come up with an idea?"

"I have to give back the portion of the advance they paid me when I signed the contract. Which would sever my relationship with my current publisher and put a big black mark next to my name. I'd have to find a new publisher willing to take a chance that it wouldn't happen again, and to do that, I'd need an idea. Which puts me right back to square one."

"It'll work out, though. Look at how many wonderful books you've written. In fact, I bet all those ideas your editor rejected would have been fine. She just didn't trust you."

"You're right. She didn't. And she drives me nuts. She used to be my old editor's assistant, so when Lisa retired, they made Penny my editor. When she was an assistant, we worked together fine. But now that she's reached full editor status, she questions everything." He rubbed his forehead. "It's like trying to write by committee."

"Maybe she's just nervous. You should tell her to trust you."

"I've *tried* telling her that. And my agent's tried telling her that." He looked at the woman sitting beside him with absolute faith in her eyes. "Maybe I should have *you* call her."

"Well, maybe I just will," she said in that prim voice of hers that always made him want to kiss her.

How in the world would he manage to stay at the inn for a whole month without getting his hands on her body one more time?

Chapter 12

SCOTT WOKE WITH A JOLT to find the dark shadow of a man bending over him. He pressed back, ready to come up fighting.

"Whoa!" The figure straightened with hands held up. "I'm just waking my sister."

As his head cleared of sleep, he recognized Allison's brother in the faint glow of dawn coming through the windows. He looked about, disoriented. The last thing he remembered was sitting on the settee listening to the sleepy murmur of Allison's voice as she tried to distract him from worrying. They must have fallen asleep. She stirred on the narrow cushion, her back moving against his front. His body responded to the accidental caress, and he tightened his arm about her to hold her still.

"You know, our guests usually sleep in their rooms," Adrian told him.

"I was waiting for a call." Scott glanced toward the phone. It remained as silent as it had all night.

"Adrian?" Allison mumbled, and Sadie's tail thumped against the floor.

"Yeah, it's me." The brother's voice softened with affection. "Time for work, kiddo."

"Too early," she groused and snuggled closer to Scott.

Adrian's eyes narrowed at Scott before he looked back at his sister. "Actually, you've overslept. It's six o'clock."

"Six o'clock!" She tried to sit and elbowed Scott in the gut. "Why'd you let me sleep so late?" Pushing her hair off her forehead, she glanced around. Her eyes widened with surprise when she realized she was in the parlor. "Oh." She turned and stared at Scott, and he wondered if she could feel the erection pressing against her bottom. Although how could she not?

"Hi." He managed a lopsided smile.

"Hi." She blushed.

Glaring at Scott, Adrian gathered the empty wine bottle and glasses from the coffee table. "I'd tell you two to take your time, but the other guests will start coming down for breakfast soon. Sadie, you come with me."

Sadie scrambled up to follow Adrian out the door.

"I guess we fell asleep," she said as they both sat and straightened their clothes.

"Guess so."

"Chloe never called?"

"Not yet."

She glanced around, looking a bit disoriented. "Do you want any coffee?"

"I'd kill for a cup of coffee," he said, longing for a shower as well.

"Adrian's probably already put some out upstairs."

"I'll be sure and check it for arsenic before I drink any." Standing, he stretched his back, then cringed when his muscles announced their opinion of the sleeping arrangements. "Oh man, if you're thinking about renting the sofa to guests, I wouldn't."

"It's not something we normally do." A smile tugged at the corners of her mouth.

He held out a hand and helped her stand. "Thanks for sitting up with me last night."

She nodded. "If you want to take a shower and get some rest, I'll listen for the phone."

"Shower, yes, but I don't think I could go back to sleep. I will wait in my room, though, so the other guests don't wonder who the crazy guy is sitting in the parlor staring at the phone."

Understanding softened her face. "I promise to get you the moment your sister or Chloe calls."

"Thanks." He cupped her cheek, wanting to kiss her so badly, he could almost taste her mouth. He pressed his lips to her forehead instead.

Lack of sleep pulled at Alli throughout the morning, making her mind and body sluggish. By noon, she was stifling yawns as she waited on guests in the gift shop. From outside came the sound of car doors slamming. She glanced out the window to find a young woman with shoulder-length dark hair standing beside a taxi. The smashing red pantsuit showed off a figure that would make men drool and women green with envy. Big sunglasses hid the upper part of the face while bright red lipstick accentuated the pouty lips. The woman studied the house while the driver unloaded a full set of Gucci luggage.

Alli frowned in confusion as the woman headed toward the veranda wobbling slightly as she navigated the oyster-shell path in high-heeled red leather sandals. The only guests they were expecting were a couple from Iowa who had said they'd be in late, so who could this be?

"Will you excuse me for a moment?" she said to the guests in the gift shop and stepped into the hall just as the woman entered. "Welcome to Pearl Island. May I help you?"

"Oh, hello." The woman pushed the sunglasses to the top of her head, revealing large brown eyes and a heavy application of makeup. In contrast to the rest of her appearance, the nails were ragged and free of polish. "I'm looking for Scott Lawrence. Is he in?"

"Yes, he is." Alli's frown vanished as she wondered if this was his sister with news about Chloe. But why would she come in person rather than call? "May I tell him who's here?"

"Please do." The woman turned to the driver as he lumbered in with his heavy burden of luggage. She waved a hand. "Right there will be fine."

The man stacked the suitcases as the woman opened her tiny purse, carefully counting out the enormous fare the driver named.

Alli watched the exchange with growing impatience, a thousand questions flying through her head. Finally the driver left and the woman turned back. Before she could speak, though, the sound of someone running down the stairs made them both turn.

Scott stopped on the bottom step, staring in disbelief. "Chloe?"

Chloe? Alli turned back in time to see the woman raise a hand and wiggle her fingers.

"Hey, Uncle Scott. Surprise."

"Oh, thank God!" He rushed forward, past Alli, to sweep his niece into his arms. His embrace lifted her off the floor as he buried his face in her hair.

"Not so tight!" the woman/girl squeaked. "I can't breathe."

He released her abruptly and held her at arm's length. "What the hell do you think you're doing!" he bellowed. "Do you have any idea how worried I've been?"

"So you knew I was coming, huh?" The cultured voice had vanished.

"Your mother is hysterical—"

"Gimme a break. Mom's always hysterical—"

"We've called the police. And—" He looked down at her clothes. "What are you wearing?"

"I borrowed some of Mom's clothes. Do you know how hard it would have been to buy a plane ticket if they'd known I was a kid?"

"You *flew* here?"

"What'd' ya think, I'd take a bus? Pu-leez." The girl rolled her eyes. "I borrowed Mom's driver's license and a few credit cards, and booked a flight to Houston."

"Why didn't you call when you got there so I could come get you?"

"It was the middle of the night and I didn't want to wake you. So I got a hotel, grabbed some sleep, then called a cab."

"You think I actually slept last night!" he demanded, then recovered enough to remember where he was. A quick glance confirmed they had an audience; not just Allison, but two guests stood in the doorway to the gift shop watching with wide eyes. "Come on." He grabbed Chloe by the wrist and headed for the stairs, his heart pounding with every step.

"Uncle Scott, slow down. I'm gonna break both my ankles in these stupid shoes."

"Good! Then you'll have a matched set, your ankles and your neck since that's the first thing I'm going to break. Right after I spank you."

"What?" She stumbled up the stairs, losing a shoe on the landing.

When he reached his room, he dragged her inside and slammed the door with enough force to shake the walls.

"Uncle Scott, I—"

"Shut up!" He held up a hand, struggling to rein in his temper. "Don't say one word."

Her face blanched beneath the heavy layer of makeup, but she closed her mouth.

Stalking to the bathroom, he wet a washcloth, then returned and tossed it at her. "Wash that gunk off your face. You look like a prostitute."

She lifted her chin. "I'm not wearing any more makeup than Mom wears."

"Is that what you want? To be like your mom?"

"Of course not."

"Then stop acting like her."

"I'm not!" Chloe's eyes filled with hurt. "I only

dressed this way so I could travel without people knowing I was a kid."

"I'm not just talking about the clothes." He ran his hands through his hair and realized they were trembling. "I'm talking about this stunt you pulled. Running away, leaving a note specifically worded to hurt Diane, not calling me even though Hugh gave you the number, then showing up here looking all proud of yourself like I should be happy to see you. Right down the line, everything you've done is exactly like one of the dramatic things your mother does to make herself the center of attention. Well, Chloe, you got my attention, because I have never been angrier or more disappointed in you *in my life!*"

"I'm sorry." She blinked as tears welled along her lashes. "It's just that everything's been so awful lately. I'm tired of being in the way, of knowing Mom doesn't want me around. That she doesn't . . . love me."

"Stop it!" He held up a finger when the tears started to spill down her cheeks. "Don't think you can get off the hook by crying. And don't you ever, *ever* say your mother doesn't love you, because you know that's not true."

"It is true!" Chloe wailed. "She's so wrapped up in herself, she barely knows I'm alive."

"Good God, you really are turning into my sister, blaming all your problems on your mother, on being neglected, on everyone and everything but yourself."

"Don't say that!" Chloe wiped her cheeks with the washcloth. "You don't know what it's been like. I can't go back there. Please, Uncle Scott. Don't make me go home. I'd rather *die!*"

"Jesus." He turned away. "I can't deal with this right now. We'll finish this later." He headed for the door, needing to get away until he could think straight.

"Uncle Scott! Please! Don't make me go home. *Please!*"

He slammed the door on her anguished pleas and stormed down the stairs. Allison was on the landing, holding Chloe's shoe to her chest, her eyes huge with shock. He went right past her and out the front door of the inn.

Allison watched him go, not sure what to do. Chloe's broken sobs finally drew her up the stairs, but the closer she got to the door, the more her stomach tightened with uncertainty. She stood for a while listening, every maternal instinct urging her to comfort the child on the other side of the door. But she didn't know this girl, and felt certain Chloe would yell at her to go away even if she offered a shoulder to cry on. But what if the girl didn't? What if she welcomed her comfort? The mere possibility made her palms sweat. Quickly setting the shoe by the door, she turned and fled downstairs.

Adrian, Rory, and Chance had all come into the hall and were standing around looking like witnesses to a car wreck. "What the hell was that about?" Adrian asked when he spotted her.

"Scott's niece," she answered.

"So I gathered. What'd he do, beat her?"

"No! Of course not." She saw the doubt on everyone's faces and her spine stiffened. Why was her family so quick to think the worst of Scott when they didn't even know him? "If you'll excuse me . . ." She crossed to the front door, needing to find Scott to be sure he was all right.

Chapter 13

SCOTT HEARD SOMEONE CALL HIS name, but didn't bother responding. He sat on a driftwood log staring at the portion of beach he could see through the tangled trees. The blue waters of the cove stretched out to meet the bright morning sky. No trace of the storm remained except for the scent of dampness that clung to the shadows. Allison appeared at the opening to the clearing, backlit with sunshine. He wasn't surprised she'd found him, since he'd surely left a trail of footprints in the sand, but he was surprised she'd looked.

"Hi," she said in a tentative voice.

"If you came to chew me out for making a scene in front of your other guests, you can save your breath. I've already taken care of it."

She came forward, into the shadows, and sat beside him. "I came to see if you're all right."

"I don't know." He rubbed his face. "Christ. I've never done that before. Yelled at her like that. Ever. I don't know what got into me."

"My guess would be fear."

"Fear?" He gave her a startled look. "I wasn't afraid while I was yelling at her. I was furious. I can't remember the last time I've ever been so angry at someone. Even so, she didn't deserve that. A good talking-to, yes, but not having the one person she thought she could depend on yell at her until she cried."

"Maybe she did deserve it after what she put you through."

He stood and moved to the edge of the shadows,

where the leaf-strewn ground gave way to sandy beach. The breeze rustled through the trees, promising a perfect spring day. Down on the pier, two scuba divers were suiting up, checking their tanks. With the sunlight sparking off the blue water, the white beach contrasting with green lawn, the scene looked like a commercial for a tropical vacation. *Pearl Island, a place to escape all your troubles.*

"You remember what I said about life being filled with false expectations?" he asked.

"Yes."

"Well, Chloe is a perfect example. She thinks every kid in the world except her got *Leave It to Beaver,* and she's mad because she thinks she got a raw deal. How can I make her understand we all got a raw deal? She needs to stop searching for something that doesn't exist."

"Maybe it does exist for some people."

"Yeah, right. There's as much chance of people finding a happy home life as there is of those scuba divers finding Lafitte's lost treasure."

"You don't think anyone in the world is happy?"

"I didn't say that." He turned to her, leaning his back against the trunk of an oak tree. "The people who have learned to stop striving for the impossible at least find contentment. The rest—people who keep thinking that love is this grand prize that will solve all their problems— are destined to suffer one big disillusionment after another."

"You talk as if love doesn't exist."

"Oh, it exists, in all its varied forms. Like with Diane and Chloe; they love the hell out of each other, but it solves nothing for either one of them. It just gives them more freedom to hurt each other."

"That's very sad." She looked at him with a confused frown as if destructive relationships were a foreign concept to her. "I guess it depends on the people involved, as to whether love makes them weaker or stronger. But you are right about love making you vulnerable to pain."

"Yeah," he said, glancing back toward the cove just as the scuba divers stepped off the pier and splashed into the water.

His mind shifted away from the problem of Chloe to wondering what sort of story he could write about scuba divers. Rather than stopping at the familiar blank screen, his mind continue to drift, anything to keep from thinking about the problem at hand. Vague images began to gather: a hunt for sunken treasure, underwater action scenes . . .

He straightened off the tree trunk when he realized a story was forming in his brain. *"Shit!"*

"What? What's wrong?" Allison hurried toward him.

"I just realized you're right. My writer's block isn't from too much stress in my life. It's from not having enough."

"You have an idea for a story?"

"No. But it's there. Right there." He tapped the back of his head. "I don't know what it is yet, but I can feel it."

"Well, at least something good came out of this, then."

He raised a brow at her. "I just discover I can't write unless my life is filled with stress, and you think that's a good thing?"

"It's better than never being able to write again, isn't it?"

"I'm not so sure. If I have to go through something like the last twenty-four hours in order to come up with a story idea, maybe I should just give back the advance and retire."

"Retire from writing? You can't! I love your stories. You can't do that to your readers."

"Alli, there are other writers in the world."

"I know, but if you don't keep writing, I'll never be

able to walk into a bookstore and have the thrill of finding a new Scott Lawrence novel on the shelf. You have to write."

"You sound like my agent." He shook his head, even as pleasure blossomed in his chest. "And while I love the praise, I have more important issues to deal with at the moment, like apologizing to my niece for losing my temper and calling my sister to let her know Chloe is safe."

"You're right. I'm sorry."

"Don't apologize. A little ego boost is always good for a writer's soul." He cocked his head, studying her as he realized she was good for his soul all the way around. "You know, I appreciate you sticking by me through this. Most people are far more interested in what I can do for them, not the other way around."

Her brows drew together. "Maybe you should hang out with more giving people."

"Maybe I should." He smiled into her pretty gray eyes and thought how much he'd love to kiss her right then, in the cool shadows with the sound of the surf behind him.

"Would you like for me to walk back with you?" she asked.

An image rose in his mind of walking along the beach, hand in hand with Allison. Such an innocent image, but entirely too tempting. He promptly thrust both his hands in the pockets of his shorts. "No, I'm fine."

"Come on," she coaxed and slipped an arm through his.

Rather than fight it, he let her tug him out of the clearing into the glare of sunlight and they headed down the beach together.

Scott stopped by the office long enough to call his sister and let her know Chloe was safe, but he wanted to talk to his niece before deciding on the best way to get her home. Going upstairs, he cautiously opened the door to his room.

"Uncle Scott?" Chloe sat up on the bed with her hair tangled, the silk pantsuit wrinkled, and mascara smeared down her cheeks.

"Hey, kid." Not knowing what to say, he simply closed the door and sat on the bed with his arms open. She threw herself against his chest and burst into tears.

"I'm so sorry," she cried. "Please don't hate me."

"I don't hate you." His chest constricted as he smoothed a hand over her hair. "I could never hate you."

"But you yelled at me."

"I know and I'm sorry. I was just . . ." He started to say angry, but remembered what Alli had said. "Frightened, okay? I stayed up most of the night worried sick, imagining all kinds of things. Then suddenly there you stood, all safe and sound, and I wanted to strangle you for scaring me."

"At least you care enough to get mad."

"Your mother's pretty upset, too."

"I'm surprised she even noticed I was gone."

"Chloe, look at me." He eased her away and took both her hands in his. "I know Diane isn't the greatest mother in the world, but she's doing the best she can. That's all any parent can do. She has her own baggage to deal with, and yes she can be self-absorbed, but she does love you very much. This stunt of yours has really hurt her."

"You're not going to make me go back, are you?"

"I have to."

"Why?" she asked in earnest. "Why can't I live with you? I wouldn't be any trouble. I swear."

"Well, for starters, I'm not at home. I'm in Galveston."

"But not for long, right?"

"Through the end of the month."

"Oh." Her shoulders slumped. "Do you have to stay so long?"

He thought about cutting his trip short. But his writer's block was finally lifting, he could feel it. What if being here, on Pearl Island, was tied to that? It would probably sound ludicrous to anyone but another writer, but you never messed with your mojo. If wearing a certain shirt and sitting in a certain chair facing east while Ravel's *Bolero* played in the background worked, you stuck with it. No matter how stupid it sounded to others.

"Yeah," he sighed, "I'm afraid I do need to stay."

"Then let me stay with you."

"Chloe, I can't do that. If it were summer, and school were out, maybe."

"What does that have to do with anything? Mom takes me out of school all the time when she wants to go skiing in Aspen or fly out to L.A. to go shopping with friends."

He pulled back in surprise. "I thought you stayed with Mom when Diane went out of town?"

"Only if she's going someplace boring that I don't want to go."

"But how does that work?"

"You know, like, private school? E-mail?" Chloe gave him her adults-are-so-stupid look. "As long as I keep up with my assignments, I don't have to actually be in the classroom. So, please, Uncle Scott, let me stay."

"I don't know . . ."

"*Please.* You don't know how bad it's been. Mom's seeing this new jerk and he's all she cares about. Ralph this, Ralph that. Well, excuse me, but Ralph is married. How can she do that? She always goes on and on about how much she hates John for cheating on y'all's mom, and how much she hates my dad and the others for cheating on her, and then she turns right around and dates married men. It doesn't make sense."

"I know." How could he begin to explain the psychology behind his sister's obsessive need to be the center of a man's attention? How Diane had felt neglected as a child because her father had lavished his lovers with attention that should have gone to his family. And how in some twisted way, this was her way of making up for that neglect. "It doesn't make sense to me, either."

"If you want my opinion," Chloe said in a deadly serious, adult voice, "Mom needs psychotherapy."

"Either that or a frontal lobotomy." He smiled slowly, making her laugh.

"Agreed." Her expression turned worried. "So can I stay with you awhile? Just until this thing with Ralph blows over? You know it won't last long. Her affairs never do."

Scott let out a long breath thinking the word "affair" shouldn't even be in a twelve-year-old's vocabulary. "Okay, I'll talk to your mom. I'm not promising anything—"

"Oh, thank you, Uncle Scott! Thank you!" She threw her arms about his neck. "You are the best uncle in the whole world!"

"Just don't strangle me for it, okay?"

"Okay." She pulled back to smile at him. "I love you."

Oh man. His insides turned to mush. How did she always do that to him? Shaking his head, he pulled her back against him and rubbed his knuckles on her head. "I love you, too, brat. But this isn't a done deal yet, okay?"

"You'll work it out. Once you decide to do something, you always do it."

If only he had her confidence, Scott thought as he left the room. He found Allison in the music room, setting out cookies on the rococo grand piano. On the frescoed ceiling, cupids took aim at frolicking women and mermen from behind pink and gold clouds. Two guests sat at a

Victorian card table working on a puzzle while a TV
played quietly in the background. He noted the computer
on the small desk in the corner, and realized that solved
one of his problems; Chloe would have e-mail access and
a place to do homework.

He pulled Allison aside and asked if there was a room
available. She said the First Mate was open for the next
two weeks. After that, they'd be booked solid for a while.

Nodding, he went to the office and braced himself for
another conversation with his sister, who was still in full
Drama Queen mode. Only the memory of how close
they'd been growing up kept him from losing his patience.
Halfway through the hour-long call, Chloe ventured into
the room. She'd changed clothes and looked more like
herself in ratty shorts, a New Orleans Saints T-shirt, and
her hair pulled through the back of a ball cap. She paced
before the windows, chewing her nails and listening to his
half of the conversation. Finally, he hung up with a sigh,
completely drained.

"Well?" Chloe asked.

He gave her a smile. "You get to stay for two
weeks—"

"Yes!" She bounced over to him and threw her arms
about his neck. "I knew you could do it."

"But we need to set some ground rules." He glanced
around to be sure they were alone, then lowered his voice.
"First, you have to keep something to yourself. The St.
Claires don't know Lawrence isn't the name I was born
with, and I want it to stay that way."

"What's the big deal about that?"

"I'll explain more later, but basically our family used
to own Pearl Island until John lost it in a bank foreclosure
last year. Now he's trying to get it back, so the current
owners don't like anyone connected to him very much.
So, not a word, okay?"

"Sure." She shrugged, all trace of anxiety gone. "Hey,

do you think we can go scuba diving while we're here?"

"Chloe . . ." He stared at her, dumbfounded. "If you think you just earned yourself a two-week, fun-filled vacation, think again. You're staying with me to give you and your mom a short break from each other. But I am not going to reward you for what you did. In fact, in addition to keeping up with your homework, I want you to write a ten-page paper on why it was wrong to run away."

"Ten pages?" Her jaw dropped. "You gotta be joking!"

"Do I look like I'm laughing?"

"Mom never makes me do extra assignments."

"I'm not your mother. You want to stay with me, you follow my rules."

She scrunched up her face. "Okay, but if I do the paper, can we go scuba diving?"

"I'll think about it. But diving around Galveston isn't going to be like Cozumel. The water's murky and there's no coral reef nearby."

"But other people are diving out in the cove. See?" She turned back to the window. "I've been watching them."

"They're just going down to see the old shipwreck."

"There's a shipwreck? Wow, how cool is that!"

He started to tell her the bare bones of the legend, about Marguerite and her lover, the rumors of pirate treasure, when suddenly it hit him, like a lightning bolt straight through his forehead, filling his mind with images.

"That's it!" he shouted. "That's *it!*"

Chloe frowned at him. "That what?"

"The idea for my next book!" He scooped her up and twirled her around. "That's it! That's it! *That's it!*"

"Scott, what's wrong?" Allison rushed in. "Has something happened?"

He released Chloe and grabbed Allison to waltz her

about the room. "I have an idea. I have an idea."

"For a book?" Her face lit up.

"Yep." He stopped dancing to explain. "Basic premise, a group of young underwater archeologists are invited to a secluded island to search for sunken treasure. There'll be a mansion owned by the villain, who's pretending to be their gracious host. Only the archeologists learn he's using the island as a base for his band of modern-day pirates. Drugs, arms, you name it. Once his cover's blown, the drug lord holds some of the archeologists hostage and forces the others to keep searching for the treasure, planning to murder all of them once it's found."

She frowned at him. "Didn't you do something similar in your first book, *Ghost Island*?"

"No, that was kids and art thieves. This will be different. Adults, male and female. More room for some interesting relationship twists. Lots of stuff to work with. But finally, I have an idea!" He cupped her face and gave her a hard kiss on the mouth that was too quick to give her time to react, but too long and full to be mistaken as a platonic peck. "Oh yes, lots of room for interesting relationship twists. I need to write this down while it's all still there. Will you help Chloe get settled in her room?"

"Yes, of course."

"Chloe, I'll expect that paper first thing in the morning, so have Allison show you the work station in the music room." He gave Allison another quick kiss. "Thanks."

"But . . ." She watched him stride out the door. The room fell silent as if all the energy had gone out with him. She turned and saw Chloe's disgruntled smirk.

"Great." The girl planted her fists on her hips. "If I'd wanted to be ignored, I could have stayed home."

Allison bit her lip, wondering what to say. She had no experience with adolescents since she'd spent the last ten years avoiding children. "Would you like for me to help you carry your bags to your room?"

"Might as well." Chloe gave a long-suffering sigh. "Lord knows when Uncle Scott will return to earth. Once he starts a book, it's like his brain is living on another planet."

Allison frowned at that. If Scott was holed up in his room writing, who would take care of Chloe for the next two weeks?

Chapter 14

WHEN SCOTT ENTERED THE DINING room the next morning, Allison was the only one there. "Where is every-
body?" he asked.

She turned from the sideboard, where she was setting
up the buffet. "You're up early."

"Am I?" He glanced at his watch and realized she
was right. "Oh. Well, got any coffee ready?"

"I'm brewing some now. I can bring you a cup when
it's done."

"That'd be great." He grabbed a chair and opened the
legal pad he'd brought down with him. The story churning
in his brain had kept him up half the night and woken
him at dawn. Clicking the pen, he started scribbling out
the next scene in the cryptic shorthand he'd developed
over the years. Later, he'd transfer it to the computer,
fleshing it out as he went.

Lost in the flow of action and dialogue, he barely
registered the sounds of Chance and Aurora helping Allison set out breakfast. Guests filed in and out, but he
ignored the buzz of conversation and the clatter of dishes.
A writer didn't survive in the French Quarter without
learning to focus even if a Dixieland jazz band were
marching down the street.

Oddly, it was the quiet that finally distracted him. He
looked up to see he and Allison were once again the only
people in the room, only now the remains of breakfast lay
strewn across the table, like the carnage of a well-fought
war.

"Welcome back." She smiled at him, clearing away

the dirty dishes. "Can I get you a pastry or something to go with that coffee?"

His gaze shot to the sideboard, and he saw that most of the food had been taken away. "Man, I missed breakfast."

"I'll get you a Danish," she said, clearly amused as she headed for the basket of pastries.

"Thanks." He stretched to work a kink out of his back. "Although I also came down to check on Chloe." He frowned, wondering if she'd come and gone while he'd been off scuba diving in South America. "Did I miss her?"

"No, she hasn't been down yet."

He glanced toward the stairs, wondering if the girl was sulking in her room, or just sleeping late. She'd certainly sulked last night when he'd taken a break to check on her. He'd found her in the music room watching a movie. Since she'd been the only guest in the room, he'd turned the set off and told her no TV until she finished the assignment he'd given her. Then he'd suffered through her protests as they headed into town to grab dinner.

Deciding to just wait her out, he started to turn his attention back to his writing when she came clopping down the stairs in baggy jeans and T-shirt, her ball cap pulled down nearly over her eyes.

"Well, speak of the devil." He flipped the legal pad closed. "You're finally up."

"Up and starving," she said enthusiastically.

"Did you finish your paper?"

"All ten pages." She handed it to him with a flourish. "Am I too late for breakfast?"

Allison set the Danish next to Scott. "We put away the hot dishes, but there's plenty of cereal, fruit, and yogurt. Help yourself to as much as you want."

While Chloe headed for the sideboard and piled a plate with pastries, Scott read her paper. She'd written a paragraph of essay, then launched into a list of one hundred bad things that could have happened, spacing each item out to be sure the list filled ten sheets of paper. Okay, so maybe that was cheating a bit, but he nodded in approval that she'd included worrying her mother, worrying him, getting hurt, kidnapped, or even killed. As he continued down the list, though, he couldn't help but chuckle. By the time he reached the bottom, he was laughing outright. "You might have been run over by a one-eyed octogenarian in a souped-up wheelchair?"

"Yeah, I kind of liked that one, too." She gave him a cheeky grin as she took a seat across from him, licking sugar from her fingers.

"Okay, I'll knock your grade down to a B for laziness, but I'll add a plus for knowing how to spell octogenarian."

"You're going to grade me?" Her eyes bugged out. "Sheesh, this is worse than school."

"Remember that the next time you want to run away." He leaned across the table to hand her back the paper, then snatched the ball cap from her head.

"Hey!" She grabbed for it, but he put it on the chair beside him.

"No hats at the table."

"That only applies to boys."

"You dress like a boy, you follow the same rules. And don't slouch."

"Jeez," she grumbled, but sat up straight.

He saw Allison struggle not to smile as she continued clearing the table. Settling back in his chair, he sipped coffee as he pondered how to handle the next two weeks. Remembering how he and Diane had been at that age, he knew the only way to keep an adolescent out of trouble was to keep them busy. Too bad his parents hadn't cared enough to figure that out. "So, Chloe, how'd you like to help me with my book?"

Her eyes narrowed in speculation. "What kind of help?"

"Research assistant."

She snorted. "Sounds like more homework."

"What if I said the job includes scuba diving?"

"You mean it?" Her face brightened.

"What I need researched is how to hunt for sunken treasure. I figured we'd start by checking out the shipwreck here."

"Man, you got it!"

Allison cocked her head with interest. "Does this mean you're setting another book here on Pearl Island?"

"Yes and no," he answered. "Galveston isn't remote enough for what I need, so I'm moving Pearl Island to somewhere off the coast of South America. But I'd like to use your ghosts for background color, if you don't mind."

"You'll have to ask Marguerite and Jack, not me." Alli smiled.

"Since I didn't hear any ghostly moans or chains rattling last night, I assume Marguerite's fine with the idea. As for Jack, I guess I'll get his opinion when we check out the ship."

"Wait a sec." Chloe held up her hand. "What's this about ghosts?"

"The house and cove are haunted by two ghosts," Scott explained. "Since they were in love, the general belief is they're trying to find a way to reunite before they can pass on to the hereafter."

"Really?" Chloe's eyes went round. "That is like way cool. So when do we go diving?"

"As soon as you finish breakfast we'll check into renting equipment."

"We rent gear here." Allison glanced at Chloe. "If you're certified."

"I got my open water certificate on my last birthday,"

Chloe answered proudly. "Since I'm *finally* twelve."

"All right." Allison eyed the girl as if measuring her body. "If you need to borrow a wetsuit, I think mine will fit you." She turned to Scott. "Would you like me to ask Adrian if you can borrow his?"

"No," he said, imagining her brother's reaction to the idea. Adrian would probably want to weight it with lead and toss Scott in the middle of the gulf with no air tanks. "I'll dive in my swim trunks."

"Are you sure?" Alli said. "You'll be much warmer in a wet suit."

"I'm positive. Now, on to more important matters." He turned to Chloe. "After the dive, we need to head for the library and start looking for a plausible treasure for my adventurers to be going after."

"Why not use Lafitte's missing treasure?" Allison suggested.

"The one that supposedly went down with Jack's ship?" He shook his head. "No, I want something more distinctive than a chest of Spanish doubloons."

"Well," Alli said, "the story of Lafitte's treasure in connection with Jack and Marguerite is actually twofold. There is the traditional treasure people speculate Jack inherited from his grandfather, who was one of Lafitte's men. But there was also Marguerite's necklace, an enormous teardrop-shaped pearl that once belonged to Jean Lafitte. It was given to her by the voodoo midwife who birthed her, as part of the blessing that gave Marguerite her magic."

"Whoa, wait a minute, sit down." Scott came to attention and pointed to a chair. "Let's start from the beginning. First, how do you know all this?"

"Marguerite wrote about it in her diaries." Setting the dishes aside, Allison took a seat beside Chloe.

"Marguerite kept a diary?" Scott flipped open his legal pad to a clean page.

"Several of them. We have the originals, which are written in French, and the English translations my great-grandmother did."

"Okay, so tell me about this necklace."

"Marguerite's mother was a—" Allison stopped and looked at Chloe.

"Professional woman," Scott supplied for her, since the woman had been a French prostitute.

"Exactly." Allison nodded in thanks. "She planned to give her baby to an orphanage. The old voodoo woman who acted as midwife didn't want that to happen, because she feared the child would be neglected or abused. So she named the baby Marguerite, which means 'pearl,' then blessed her saying, 'Whoever keeps this pearl shall have good fortune.' Then she draped a pearl necklace about the baby and told the mother the necklace had to stay with the child in order for the blessing to work."

"So that's how she came to be considered a good-luck charm." Scott shook his head, jotting down notes. "I've never actually heard the whole story."

Allison nodded. "The mother was greedy enough to keep the child, just to see if the blessing worked. Sure enough, a wealthy patron of the . . . establishment fell madly in love with her and set her up in a house with a generous allowance. His own fortune grew dramatically, so the mother told him the story of Marguerite's birth, which proved a powerful incentive for him to keep both of them under his protection. There are other stories of how Marguerite brought wealth to everyone around her, but for her the blessing was more of a curse."

"Why is that?" Chloe asked, wide-eyed with interest.

"Because as word of Marguerite's magic spread, more and more people befriended her solely in hopes that they would grow rich by being near her. Henri LeRoche was the worst of the lot, though, and courted her relent-lessly. Her instincts told her not to trust him, but he wore her down with endless vows of undying love until she finally gave in and married him. She truly wanted to believe he loved her, but on their wedding night, all his pretense dropped away. When she realized he'd been lying, she threatened to have the marriage annulled. He beat her and told her she belonged to him now and he'd never let her go. Apart from the physical pain, she was destroyed emotionally, and vowed never to trust or love again."

"Until she met Jack Kingsley," Scott said.

"Yes, but he had a tough time convincing her his love was real after all the others who had lied to her and used her."

Chloe turned startled eyes to Scott, silently asking if that were true.

"Let's get back to the necklace," he prompted, wanting to avoid talk of Henri LeRoche in front of Chloe. Having John LeRoche for a grandfather was bad enough. She didn't need to know she had a distant uncle who was a wife beater.

"When Marguerite was still living in New Orleans, an old Creole woman stopped her on the street and asked her where she got the necklace she was wearing. That's when she found out the midwife had died the night she was born, because the woman's friends couldn't find the necklace even though she'd worn it constantly since the day it was given to her. Then the woman on the street told Marguerite the story of how the midwife came to own such a fabulous pearl. First, though, how familiar are you with Jean Lafitte's life?"

"I live in New Orleans, and I'm insatiably curious." Scott grinned at her. "How well do you think I know it?"

"Okay, then, in her younger years, the voodoo woman used to make medicinal potions for Marie Villars to give to her, um, gentleman friend."

"Marie Villars?" Scott tapped his forehead to jog his

memory. "Pierre Lafitte's quadroon mistress. Mother to his numerous children."

"Very good." She smiled at him. "During the year Pierre spent in prison on charges of piracy, Jean was frantic to win his brother's freedom. Pierre's health was very poor since he suffered a stroke early in life, and his friends feared he'd die under such ill-treatment."

"That was right before the Battle of New Orleans, right?" Scott asked. "Jean promised the U.S. support toward fighting the British in exchange for his brother's release but the local government ignored him. Pierre ended up escaping prison, although no one knows how."

Allison nodded. "Well, I don't know all the details of his escape, but the voodoo woman had a vision that great danger was coming to New Orleans, and the Lafitte brothers would rise up to protect the city. So she went to the prison and somehow helped Pierre escape and return to Jean's stronghold on the island of Barataria, outside New Orleans. Jean was so grateful to have his brother safe, he presented her with the pearl necklace. He said the pearl was one of the first prizes he'd ever taken and he thought it held great magic, so he gave it to her, saying he hoped it brought her as much luck as it had brought him."

"Cool!" Chloe said. "So what about the vision? Did that come true?"

Scott looked at her. "What do you mean, did the vision come true? Jean Lafitte? Andrew Jackson? The Battle of New Orleans? Does any of this ring a bell with you?"

"Uhhh, Andrew Jackson." Chloe scrunched her nose. "The statue of the guy on a horse in Jackson Square?"

Scott rolled his eyes. "Your second paper will be a report on the Battle of New Orleans. And yes, Jean Lafitte helped to repel the British. When Andrew Jackson arrived on the scene and saw how poorly the city was prepared to defend itself, he had no problem taking Jean up on his

offer of men and arms. Without him and his band of pirates the city would have fallen."

"So he's like a hero?" Chloe asked.

"In that one instance, yes, people consider him a hero.
No doubt, he's one of New Orleans's most colorful characters in history, dashing and charismatic and all that. Personally, though, I think he should have been taken out
and shot rather than merely run out of town."

"Because he was a pirate?" Chloe asked.

"No, because I've read some of his letters, and anyone who writes prose that purple should be put before a
firing squad."

Allison pressed a hand to her mouth to keep from
laughing.

"You think I'm joking?" He lifted a brow. "Bad prose
is no laughing matter, I'll have you know."

"Of course not." She bit her lip, drawing his attention
to her mouth.

Don't go there, he told his wayward thoughts. *Off
limits, remember?* "Let's get back to the necklace."

"All right." She nodded. "In her diary, Marguerite
talks about one of her rendezvous with Jack where he
asked her about the necklace. After telling him the story,
she asked if it were true that he had Lafitte's treasure. He
laughed and said, yes, his grandfather had given it to him
before he died, and that he kept it in his cabin to remind
himself what he came from, because he didn't want to be
like that. He wanted to be a better man, which was why
he'd given up smuggling and only carried legitimate
goods for Henri."

"Wait a second," Scott interrupted. "He kept Lafitte's
treasure in his cabin? How did he keep his men from
stealing it?"

"I don't know. I'm only telling you what Marguerite
wrote in her diary."

"Okay, go on."

"It was also during that clandestine meeting that Jack told Marguerite about his decision to start running blockades for the Confederacy. Afraid for his life, she took off the necklace and gave it to him, saying she hoped it brought him luck and kept him safe. He said he'd put it with the rest of Lafitte's treasure to help him remember all the reasons he wanted to be a better man."

"Apparently the charm wasn't strong enough to protect him from a jealous husband," Scott muttered, still making notes.

"No, it wasn't."

"Doesn't matter. This is great." He tapped his pen against the legal pad. "Perfect, in fact. Not only is the item valuable from a monetary and historical standpoint, it has magical powers. My drug lord is going to be insane with greed to have it. I don't suppose you'd let me read Marguerite's diaries, though, since I'm using her as the background story?"

Allison hesitated. "I don't know. We've never let anyone outside the family read them."

"I swear I'll be careful with them." He held up a hand. "Scout's honor."

"You were a Boy Scout?" She asked in surprise.

"Uuh, no. But I do have lots of experience handling old documents."

"I'll think about it."

"Fair enough." He nodded and turned to his niece. "In the meantime what do you say we check out this shipwreck?"

By the time Allison headed down to the pier with Scott and Chloe the day had warmed considerably. "We have everything you'll need stored out here," she said as they stepped from the beach onto the wooden pier. Waves lapped at the old pilings beneath them as they made their way to the end. A pelican sat atop one of the storage bins that doubled as a bench, and she had to shoo it away to lift the lid.

"The water's pretty murky for the first twenty feet," she said. "Then it gradually starts to clear. Below forty feet, you could have excellent visibility depending on how much the storm the other day stirred things up."

"How deep is the cove?" Scott asked as he looked over the various tanks.

"Close to sixty feet, the deepest in Galveston Bay," Allison answered. "The ship is directly ahead of us, pretty much smack-dab in the middle of the cove. This chain here"—she pointed to a chain attached to the end of the dock that disappeared into the water at an angle—"will lead you to the ship. It has depth markers for your stops coming back up. As for the ship, it's resting partially on its side, and most of it is buried under silt, but you'll be able to see some of the forecastle and quarterdeck."

"How'd it get buried?" Chloe asked, tugging on the shortie wetsuit she'd borrowed from Allison. The suit fit her snugly, and showed off a figure that was far more developed than that of the average twelve-year-old.

Scott gave his niece a disbelieving look. "Ever hear of the Great Storm?"

"No. Should I have?" Chloe asked.

Scott rolled his eyes. "Okay, your third report will be on the hurricane that nearly wiped Galveston off the map."

The girl's face fell. "Damn, Uncle Scott, how many papers are you gonna make me write?"

"What, three isn't enough?" He raised a brow. "I'll be happy to add another on why young girls shouldn't curse."

"No, three is fine." She held up her hands. "More than enough. Really."

"Okay, if you insist." Scott picked out an air tank,

weight belt, and fins for Chloe, then helped her get them on.

"This stuff always makes me feel like a turtle with a whole house strapped to my back." Carrying the fins, she plopped down on a second storage chest so hard she nearly toppled backward.

"Careful." Scott chuckled as he peeled off his shirt, tossed it aside, and presented his beautifully nude back to Allison.

The sight struck her dumb—just when she'd been congratulating herself on how well they'd slipped back into their proper roles of innkeeper and guest. Now he stood before her, with sunlight shining off his tan muscles, and she wanted to run her tongue right up the middle of his spine.

He glanced over his shoulder. "You going to help me with the tank?"

"Oh. Sorry." Laughing and blushing, she lifted the air tank so he could slip his arms into the buoyancy vest.

"What sort of shape is it in?" he asked, turning to face her. His biceps rippled as he fastened the buckles to hold the vest and tank in place.

"Great shape," she breathed, then cringed. The ship. He was asking about the ship. "I mean—it's in great shape considering it suffered two direct hits from a cannon." Her gaze strayed back to his chest as he fastened the last buckle. "I wish you'd let me ask Adrian if you could borrow his wetsuit. You're going to freeze in nothing but swim trunks."

"The water's not that cold."

"Tell me that after you've been down at sixty feet for half an hour."

He glanced up, straight into her eyes, with a lopsided grin. "I'm tougher than I look."

"Okay, well." She blew out a breath and tried to focus. "One thing we ask all the divers is that you try not to stir up the bottom."

"You don't want me to stir things up?" The double meaning sparkled in his eyes and she realized how close they were standing.

"No, I . . ." She stepped back and caught the heel of her sandal on a wooden plank.

Scott grabbed her arm, steadying her. Time hung suspended as he looked into her eyes.

Her gaze moved to his lips and he longed to lean forward and kiss her.

"Uncle Scott, are we going in or not?"

He dropped his hand. "I'm coming."

Turning away, Scott slipped on his mask and clamped the mouthpiece for the breathing regulator between his teeth. He held them in place as he giant-stepped off the end of the pier. The water engulfed him in a whoosh of bubbles. When he surfaced, he patted the top of his head to signal that he was okay and for Chloe to follow. She jumped off the pier like a cannonball, sending a giant splash onto the dock. Allison shrieked and barely jumped back in time. Scott held up his hands in a gesture to apologize.

As soon as Chloe surfaced, they went through their safety checks. Satisfied, he glanced at Allison and gave the thumbs-down signal to tell her they were going under. She nodded and waved as he deflated his vest and sank slowly into the murky brown haze. The salty taste of it slipped into his mouth around the regulator as bubbles gurgled past his face mask.

They swam slowly at a downward angle, following the chain. As Allison had predicted, the water cleared as they descended. It also grew colder. At forty feet, the haze all but disappeared. Enough light filtered down for him to see reasonably well. Even so, he turned on the dive light and hand-signaled Chloe to ask how she was doing. She wiggled her head to pop her ears, puffed a bit of air into her mask to compensate for the water pressure, then signaled back that she was okay. Nodding, he continued toward the center of the cove.

They came upon the ship all at once. One moment there was nothing in the beam of his light but an occasional fish and specks of suspended silt. Then suddenly, there was the bow of a nineteenth-century sailing vessel rising out of a cloud of silt stirred up by careless divers.

He glanced sideways and caught Chloe's look of excitement before they swam in for a closer look. A carved mermaid greeted them from beneath the jibboom, her face still proud in spite of the cracks of age. Swimming past her, Scott reached out a hand to feel the rough texture of barnacles that covered the ornately carved railing of the forecastle.

They swam up and over the rail as a school of small fish darted through the beam of light in flashes of silver, then turned and dipped out of sight. He swept the light along the broken relic as they floated slowly toward the stern. A single mast had endured, rising at an angle, like a giant cross. Chloe flipped her fins and headed over to explore the crow's nest as he continued straight ahead.

Reaching the quarterdeck, he saw it lay at an awkward angle, not quite lined up to the bow. Had one of the cannon blasts ripped the vessel in two? Or had it been the explosion of gunpowder in the cargo hold?

His mind conjured images of what that night must have been like based on tales handed down from the surviving crew. Marguerite had sent a message to Jack through a servant, telling him that Henri had found out about them, and that she feared for both her and her daughter's lives. When the servant told Jack that Marguerite had been badly beaten and locked in her room in the tower, he'd set sail straight for Pearl Island.

Had he thought Henri would let him land? That a

man that ruthless would hesitate at murdering a whole crew of men in a jealous rage?

What had Jack Kingsley thought in the instant when he saw the flash of the cannon on the upper balcony, felt the impact shudder through his ship? Scott turned at the wheel and a chill brushed his skin as he passed through a cold spot. He cast his light back over the wreckage, picturing the frantic crew, the black sky filled with violent bolts of lightning.

Kingsley had been helpless to return fire against a house filled with innocent people, Marguerite among them. His first mate had hollered at him to turn away, to try and escape, but he'd held his course, appearing intent on running the ship right onto the beach. Had it been an act of angry defiance from a man used to facing danger, or desperation to reach the woman he loved?

When a second blast ignited the cargo of gunpowder, Kingsley had shouted orders to abandon ship. But rather than join the crew racing for lifeboats, he'd headed toward his cabin. The first mate tried to stop him, but Jack had shouted that he wouldn't leave without the treasure, a mistake that cost him his life, since the back of the hold exploded as he was racing down the cabinway. The concussion from the blast had killed him instantly.

The first mate dragged his body onto a lifeboat, but many claimed his spirit remained behind. Whether it was trying to reach the riches hidden in his cabin or still trying to rescue Marguerite depended on who told the story.

The fact that he'd been running toward the treasure in his cabin certainly lent credence to the first theory. But what if sentiment rather than greed had sent him into that passageway? What if he'd been going back for the necklace?

Was that it, Jack? Scott silently asked. *Did you love her to the point you couldn't bear to lose even that small part of her?*

The cold seeped into his muscles as he tried to imagine what Jack Kingsley had felt, tried to put himself in the man's place. An eerie ringing started in his ears, drowning out the swoosh of air through the regulator. The water pressure squeezed tighter about his chest as a frightening rush of grief and loss filled him.

And he knew, in that moment, exactly what Kingsley felt, as if the man's spirit had slipped into his body: a loss so devastating it defied description.

A hand touched his shoulder, and he jerked around as bubbles erupted from his mouth. Chloe's eyes widened behind her mask, and if he hadn't been sixty feet underwater, he'd have burst out laughing. Clearly he'd been thinking about ghosts way too much in the last few days.

Chapter 15

ALLISON REMAINED ON THE PIER for several minutes before she turned and headed up the azalea-lined path to the house. The bulbs she'd planted in the flower beds to either side of the steps were starting to come up, providing a pretty splash of color at the top of the vivid green lawn. If she finished cleaning rooms early enough, maybe she'd have time to do a little gardening.

Reaching the steps, she saw Rory sitting in one of the veranda's wicker chairs with a glass of iced tea and a magazine. She hesitated with her foot on the first step, her hand on the stone rail. On any other occasion, she would have called out a greeting on her way to the front door, or even joined her sister to enjoy the spring day for a few minutes before going in to clean rooms.

But things had been strained between her and her siblings since the night she'd spent with Scott. No one had said a word since her last flare-up with Adrian, but the subject hung in the air. With a sigh, she accepted that the burden of defusing the awkwardness lay on her shoulders.

She mounted the wide sweep of steps and headed for her sister. As she drew nearer, she saw Rory had a pen and was circling items in the magazine. Rory didn't read well, but she enjoyed flipping through magazines to look at the pictures.

"Hi," Alli offered tentatively. "Mind if I join you?"

Rory glanced up, and paused for the barest fraction of a second. "Of course not."

She took a seat in the wicker chair beside her sister, not sure how to proceed. "What are you doing?"

"Planning a wedding, if you can believe it." Rory laughed as she held up the magazine so Alli could see the cover of *Modern Bride*.

"Oh? Who's getting married?"

"Chance and me."

"But you're already married."

"That's what I keep telling him." Rory reached into the bag beside her for a handful of salted pecans. "He says after the baby comes, he wants us to have a real ceremony. Apparently he doesn't think the quickie service before the judge when he found out I was pregnant is sufficient. Oh!" Rory jumped, then patted her tummy. "Yes, we're talking about you."

Alli felt the familiar ripple of fear as she watched her sister talk to the baby nestled inside her, but she pushed it back down. "When did all this come about? The wedding, I mean."

"Oh, he's been badgering me about it for some time. Last night, I asked Adrian what he thought, and he said we should go for it."

"I see." Her sister had discussed it with their brother, but not with her.

Rory eyed her, apparently hearing the tinge of hurt in her voice. "What do you think?"

"You know I'm for whatever makes you happy. Do you want to get remarried?"

"I don't know." Her sister let out a sigh of frustration. "A part of me thinks it's silly. But then I think it might be fun to have a real service. As long as it's a very *small* service."

Alli nodded, knowing Rory had a phobia about being the center of attention in large groups, not that Rory let her fears hold her back. She plowed ahead with a courage Alli had always admired. "Well, if you decide to do it, what do you have in mind?"

"A garden wedding." Rory flipped to a dog-eared

page and turned the magazine so Alli could see the two-page photo spread of a fairy-tale arbor covered in climbing roses and surrounded by pots of flowers. "We could build one of these over there beneath that stand of oaks. Maybe have the service on our first anniversary, which will give me time to get my figure back. Only . . ." Worry lined Rory's face. "Will you help me with what to wear? You know I'm clueless about such things."

"I'd love to help however I can."

"Thank you." Rory's shoulders sagged with relief. "Adrian said he'd give me away. So, as long as we're getting all traditional, will you be my maid of honor?"

"Of course." Allison's heart squeezed.

"Great." Rory smiled. "Now, as for guests, I'd like to keep it to Chance's parents, Aunt Viv, if she can come, and Bobby and Paige—if you don't think it's weird for me to invite Chance's former girlfriend to our wedding."

"She invited all of us to her wedding," Alli pointed out.

"Yeah, but that was a huge society affair with half of Galveston invited. Wasn't it hilarious, though, seeing all the country club set sitting all proper and stiff on the bride's side, then all of Bobby's drinking buddies and dockhands sitting on the groom's side?"

"It was." Allison nodded. "But what an awkward moment when the ushers asked us where we wanted to sit, since we're friends with both of them."

"At least we had Mr. Manners, Chance, there to smooth things over." Rory settled back with a sigh and popped another nut into her mouth. "Funny how all that worked out, don't you think? When I first met Paige, I hated her guts."

"When you first met Paige, she and Chance were practically engaged, so of course you hated her."

"True. But I never—not in a million years—would

have imagined her falling for a total bad boy like Captain Bob."

"I don't know." Alli smiled slowly. "Bad boys have their charm."

"Apparently." Rory cocked her head, studying her. "Speaking of bad boys, can I ask you something?"

"What?" Alli went still, feeling the shift in mood.

"This thing between you and Scott. One minute you claim it's purely physical, then I see the two of you together, and there seems to be something more, something that goes beyond simple lust. So what's really going on?"

"We're friends. Sort of."

"Friends who sleep together."

"Not ongoing, it was just that one night."

"One night? Yeah, right." Rory let out a snort of laughter.

"I'm serious." Alli frowned at her sister. "We agreed that while he's staying here, we'd be nothing more than innkeeper and guest."

"And he's staying here how long?" Rory's eyebrows lifted.

"Three more weeks."

"Uh-huh." Rory nodded. "That's what I thought."

Alli straightened. "I'm not going to sleep with a guest right here at the inn. It wouldn't be proper."

"And Chance didn't mean to sleep with me at all. You can't get much more proper than Oliver Chancellor, and we all can see how long those good intentions lasted." She patted her tummy.

"What's going on between Scott and me isn't anything like that."

Rory's teasing turned to confusion. "Do you want it to be?"

"No! Heavens, no." Fear skittered through her heart at the mere thought of it. "I'm not interested in falling in love."

"Okay . . ." The confusion deepened. "Do you want to sleep with him again?"

She opened her mouth to say no, but nothing came out. Did she want to sleep with him? Silly question—she mentally rolled her eyes—of course she wanted to sleep with him again. "It wouldn't be wise."

"There's a lot of things in life that aren't wise. That doesn't keep us from doing them." Rory hesitated. "Like me getting all shocked and telling you what you should and shouldn't do. I'm really sorry about that, and I hope you can forgive me."

"Rory . . ." Alli stared at her. "I thought you were the one mad at me."

"I wasn't mad. I was stunned! I always pictured you settling down with some sweet, quiet guy. And while Scott might not be the most talkative guy in the world, there is nothing 'sweet' about that man."

"Actually, Scott is very sweet at times."

"Maybe," Rory conceded. "I still don't trust him, mostly because he's messing with my sister, but if you want to pursue whatever is going on between you two—even though you seem to think it's only sex—I say go for it."

"You're joking." Alli rocked back in her chair.

"I'm dead serious. Something wonderful and unexpected might come of it. Even if it doesn't, you were right when you said it's your life and Adrian and I should butt out. So that's what I'm going to do." She popped another nut into her mouth. "Unless he breaks your heart. Then I plan to chop him up into tiny little pieces and use him for shark chum."

"Well, you needn't worry. I have no intention of letting him get close enough to break my heart."

"If you insist." Rory grinned.

• • •

As the days passed, her conversation with Rory kept playing in the back of Alli's head. She refused to believe anything as dangerous as love would grow between her and Scott. They were too different. But what of the other: the thrilling lust that tingled through her whenever she so much as looked at the man? Or even thought about him, which she seemed to do constantly.

Would it really be unwise to sleep with Scott again? Assuming he even wanted to. The night she'd sat up with him to wait for news about Chloe, he'd expressed serious interest in "renegotiating" the terms of their one-night affair. Since then, though, his attitude seemed to have changed. Polite but distant described it best.

Had she done something to turn him off? The fact that one night with her had apparently been enough after all hardly flattered her ego. Perhaps he was just respecting the boundary she'd set, but he could at least try a little bit to seduce her again.

Rearranging merchandise in the gift shop to make room for a new display of dolls, she thought about that night on the settee, remembered the way he'd kissed her. What would have happened if she hadn't stopped him? Would he have made love to her right there in the office? With her brother downstairs and the inn full of guests? The wicked images that played in her mind sent a shiver of excitement racing through her.

She closed her eyes and let the fantasy play out in her mind.

"Hey, Allison."

With a squeak, she whirled around to find Chloe standing in the doorway. "Oh, Chloe. You startled me." She held a hand to her cheek, and prayed her thoughts didn't show on her face. "Did you need something?"

"No. I'm just bored. Uncle Scott is holed up in his room pounding away on the computer. I swear, if I died, it would take him a week to notice."

"Chloe, that's not true!" Allison gasped at such a statement.

The girl smirked at her. "You have no sense of humor, do you?"

"Oh." She frowned, having no idea what to say to that. But then she never knew what to say to Chloe. The girl put too many things into uncomfortable perspective. Alli had spent the last eleven years picturing the child she'd lost as a nameless infant. She didn't even know if that child had been a girl or boy, since the doctor had referred to it only as "the fetus," as if sensing she couldn't bear to know.

Truth was, if her baby had lived she'd be dealing with a person barely younger than Chloe. The reality made her ache for what she'd lost—yet it also made her think of how much time she had spent grieving. Years had passed with her life on hold.

"I wanted to go to town, but I guess I'll have to wait till he takes a break." Chloe sauntered about the room, eyeing the tea sets as if viewing objects from another world. In profile, her face struck Alli as classically beautiful, even though she did her best to hide it beneath the ever-present ball cap, just as she hid her well-developed body with baggy T-shirts.

"So, um, how's your schoolwork coming?" Alli asked to make conversation. "Do you need to use the computer to e-mail anything today?"

"Later." The girl picked up a gardenia-scented candle to sniff. Scrunching up her nose, she set it down and tried another.

"You know . . ." Alli said hesitantly. "If you're really bored, I could give you something to do."

"Like what?"

"You could help me here in the gift shop." She pointed to the box on the counter. "I was just about to unpack a shipment of dolls."

"Dolls?" An amusing blend of horror and intrigue contorted Chloe's face.

"It would give you something to do."

The girl pondered the idea, then shrugged. "Okay, sure. Why not? What do you need me to do?"

"Why don't you unpack the dolls and I'll check them off the invoice and make up price tags?" When Chloe nodded, Allison set the box on the multi-tiered display table she'd cleared, then pulled the barstool from behind the cash register. Hopping up onto the stool, she settled a clipboard on her lap to use as a desktop.

Chloe pulled the first doll out of the box and removed the protective plastic. Her eyes went wide as the doll stared back with movable glass eyes set in a hand-painted porcelain face. The doll's rose-pink mouth formed a little pout and a hint of color had been brushed onto the cheeks. The green bonnet that sat atop the silky black curls matched the velvet spencer and bell-shaped skirt.

"Kids actually play with these things?" Chloe made a face. "How do they keep from messing them up?"

"Oh, they're not to play with. They're for collecting."

"You mean like baseball cards?" Chloe asked.

"Something like that." Alli smiled. "The name will be on the tag sewn into the back collar of the dress."

Chloe turned the doll over and read the name. For a tomboy, she handled the dolls with surprising care, taking the time to fluff the dresses before setting them on the table. One doll in particular caught her attention. She held it awhile, studying the satin and lace ball gown that captured the romance of the Old South. "So, are these the kind of dresses Marguerite would have worn?"

"Um-hum." Allison nodded. "Pretty, aren't they?"

"I guess." Chloe smirked, but her fingers lingered on

the lacy trim. Allison suspected that when the girl hit sixteen, she'd be tossing out her baggy clothes in favor of form-fitting dresses, testing out lipstick and dabbing perfume behind her ears. The boys in New Orleans wouldn't stand a chance. "Can I ask you a question?"

"I suppose." Allison checked the name off the packing list.

"What was Captain Kingsley like?"

"Oh, let's see." Allison stared into space. "Marguerite describes him as tall, broad-shouldered. He had long, black hair that he wore in a queue—"

"A what?"

"A ponytail, tied with black ribbon." Allison motioned toward her own nape.

"Like Adrian?" The girl's eyes lit with interest.

Allison nodded. "He wore full-sleeved white shirts with lace spilling from the collar and cuffs and a dashing red coat. His tight black breeches were tucked inside tall black jackboots that came up to mid-thigh."

"Wow," Chloe breathed, as if her hormones had made another leap toward adulthood. Then she narrowed her eyes. "You're making that up."

"No, he was the quintessential captain of the high seas, only a lot cleaner and better smelling than most of the men who worked for LeRoche Shipping." Alli wrinkled her nose at the girl, hoping for a laugh.

Chloe stared thoughtfully at the doll, her brow creased in a frown. "Was Henri really as mean as you say?"

"I'm afraid so." Allison sighed. "He deceived Marguerite in every way. He overwhelmed her with romantic gestures the whole time he courted her, hiding his true nature until after they were married. Then he treated her as nothing more than a beautiful object for him to adorn in fine clothes and jewels and parade before the band of smugglers who worked for him."

"Why didn't she leave him?"

"Unfortunately, back then women had little or no recourse for escaping abusive marriages. She was a prisoner in this house. When Jack Kingsley came into her life, offering her acceptance, love, and understanding, she was afraid to trust him, to believe his love was real. She'd been lied to so often, she doubted him, and that was her downfall."

"What do you mean?" Chloe reached in the box for another doll.

"If she'd trusted Jack Kingsley and run away with him when he first asked her to, or if he'd fought harder to convince her, they both could have lived to grow old together."

"Why didn't he fight harder, if he loved her?"

"I don't know. That's always puzzled me."

"Maybe he was scared she didn't really love him," Chloe pointed out.

"I never thought of that." Allison straightened. "But that's so silly. She loved him desperately, which was why she was so scared. If his love had turned out to be false, it would have hurt her far worse than any of the other times people betrayed her."

Chloe grew silent for a while. "Do you really believe in ghosts?"

"I don't know." Allison glanced about. "Sometimes I feel things inside this house, sorrow, regret, longing, and I wonder if it's Marguerite's emotions I'm feeling, or my own."

Footsteps sounded in the hall, and she turned just as Scott appeared in the doorway. The sight of him quite simply stole the air from her lungs, as it did every time. He wore a short-sleeved dark print shirt hanging open over a black T-shirt and jeans. Her mouth watered at the thought of running her hands up under the T-shirt to feel his warm skin against her palms while she buried her nose in the crook of his neck and breathed in his scent.

"Hey, Chloe." He waved. "I was wondering where you were."

"Just here playing with dolls." The girl held one up.

Scott's eyes widened. "You feeling okay?"

"Yes." The girl smirked at him.

"Oo-kay." He turned to Alli. For one heart-stopping instant, their gazes held. She knew he saw the desire in her eyes and an answering hunger flickered in his own. Then the impersonal mask dropped over his features, breaking the connection. "I need to use the phone, if that's all right."

"Help yourself." She watched him turn and cross the hall, all her earlier questions tumbling through her mind.

"Are you sleeping with my uncle?" The question took a second to register.

"Chloe!" The clipboard nearly slid off Allison's lap. She grabbed for it, fumbled, then finally had it clasped to her chest. "You don't ask things like that."

Chloe looked at her with too much knowledge for such young eyes. "So, you are?"

"No!" she answered too quickly, and flushed with guilt. Then realized it wasn't a lie. Outside of her daydreams and nighttime fantasies, they hadn't been together since that one night. "Even if I were, you simply don't ask people such things."

"I just wondered, is all." Chloe shrugged. "I see the way you look at him, and I figured you were after him. Lots of women are, you know. He's rich, he's famous, and he's good-looking. Not as good-looking as Adrian, but definitely not bad."

"Well, I'm not after him, I assure you. I like your uncle, yes, and we've become friends, but that's all." She set the clipboard back on her lap. "Now, where were we?"

"He looks at you that way, too."

"What?" A little thrill tingled to life deep in her belly

before she could squelch it. "Never mind. Let's get back to work."

"Okay." Chloe shrugged hugely. "I just thought you'd want to know, 'cause it really is kinda funny."

"What's funny?" The question popped out on its own.

Chloe grinned. "It's like he'll be fine one minute, just everyday Uncle Scott, then you walk into the room and his brain shuts off because all he can do is try to watch you without you catching him. Worst case of google-eyes I've ever seen."

So he did still want her. Allison looked away, caught in the unexpected pleasure of it.

"Hello." Chloe waved a hand before her face. "You wanna set up this display or not?"

"Hum?" She blinked.

"We're done unpacking the dolls. You wanna arrange them on the table?"

"Oh, uh . . . no, I'll do it later."

"Google-eyes." Chloe shook her head, looking thoroughly disgusted. "I think I'll go see what Adrian is cooking. Maybe I can help him in the kitchen."

"Yes, all right." Alli nodded and followed Chloe to the doorway. "Thank you for your help."

When Chloe disappeared, she stared across the hall. Did Scott really watch her with "google-eyes"? The term in connection to someone so masculine should have made her laugh. Instead, she stood, breathlessly wondering.

From the office, she heard his voice. Just the sound of that deep rumble tugged at her. She cocked her head, not meaning to eavesdrop, but unable to resist listening.

"No, Hugh," she heard him say. "I am not negotiable on this. I know my contract says I have to turn in a proposal, but you and I both know what will happen if I do. Penny Nichols will start picking it apart, questioning everything, and this book will never get written. Besides, we don't have time for the proposal stage."

Silence fell as he listened to his agent and she found herself moving toward the doorway.

"I know that. But have you stopped to consider that this whole process is largely to blame for why I've been so blocked lately? I just want to write the book, turn it in, *then* let her pick it apart. I don't mind revisions, within reason, but I am sick to death of her questioning everything ahead of time."

She could see him pacing before the settee with the cordless phone pressed to his ear. Even dressed casually, he had a way of moving that spoke of confidence, cunning, and an aloof sort of power, as if he were apart from ordinary men.

Unattainable.

The word popped into her head, and she realized that had been his appeal all along. He was unattainable, not because his fame and fortune put him out of reach—she had too many famous relatives to think that—but because he was self-contained and had no desire to be otherwise.

How wonderfully safe that made him.

Smiling, she leaned on the doorjamb and took full advantage of the opportunity to watch him unobserved.

"Yes, I have an outline for my own use, but I'm not showing that to anyone. Are you nuts? It's just a bunch of handwritten gibberish. I gave her a title, the setting, and basic premise for the art department to start the cover. That's all she's getting."

He turned to face the windows, presenting her with a view of broad shoulders. Too bad his loose shirt hid the way his back tapered down to the tight set of buns inside his jeans. She knew they were there, though, could remember quite clearly the feel of those buns in her hands as he'd driven inside her.

"Hugh, that's blackmail! I thought you worked for me, not them." He paced some more, then stopped before the coffee table as something caught his eye. "Okay, fine."

He bent forward to scoop up a hardcover book, teasing her with one quick glimpse of his denim-covered back-side. "If Penny is that stuck on doing everything according to the letter of the contract, tell her the outline is on its way . . . Yes, I'm serious. In fact, I'll send it right now."

Lowering the phone, he hit the off button and turned. He froze when he saw her, and she blushed at being caught gawking.

"I um, I was just . . ." She made a vague gesture with her hand. "I couldn't help but overhear. I take it there's a problem?"

"Don't ask." He sighed. "Look, can I bum a piece of paper?"

"Certainly." Frowning in confusion, she went to the desk and took a seat so she could retrieve a sheet out of the printer.

He carried the book over to the desk, placed it down on the piece of paper, then took a pen and traced around it. Setting the book aside, he bent forward to write something. She was struck by the memory of the day he'd arrived, and felt as breathless now as she had then.

"Here." He straightened abruptly and handed the paper to her. "Will you fax this for me? To the name and number I've written on the back. I'll pay for the call, naturally."

She glanced at the paper before she placed it in the fax tray. Within the rectangle, he'd written the words "A Novel by Scott Lawrence" in bold block letters. When the document was on its way, she looked up at him. "Care to tell me what this is all about?"

"My publisher's threatening to cancel my contract."

Shock came first. "Why would they do that? It doesn't make sense. You're a huge bestseller."

"They're publishers." He shrugged. "They don't have to make sense."

"But can they get away with it?"

"If they can prove I broke even one minor clause, they can do anything they want." He started pacing again. "The stupid thing is, until I heard from Hugh yesterday, I was on a roll. Since then, every scene I've written stinks. Why is it so hard for them to leave me alone and let me do what they're paying me to do?" He hung his head in defeat. "Maybe I should quit writing. Nothing is worth this much grief."

"You don't mean that." She came around the desk, half afraid he did mean it this time.

"It's just that writing a book is mentally grueling enough. Why do they have to make it even harder?"

Recognizing a creative spirit that needed pampering, she stepped closer, placed both hands on his shoulders, and began to massage. "What can I do to make it less hard?"

He gave a dry laugh. "Not that, I assure you."

She concentrated on kneading the stiff muscles to either side of his neck. "You really are tense. Why don't you sit down and let me give you a back rub?"

"Allison . . ." He took hold of her wrists. "This is not a good idea. Believe me."

She looked up, confused, until she saw the look in his eyes. Hunger. Heat. "Oh."

"Yeah, 'oh,' " he repeated and rubbed his thumbs against her wrists, making her pulse jump. "I'm not a saint. So if you want me to stick to our agreement, you need to keep a little distance, okay?"

"I see." Recklessness battled back good sense. "About our agreement . . . I've been thinking . . . maybe we should do what you suggested and 'renegotiate.' "

He stared at her, his expression guarded.

Licking her lips, she forged on. "It's just that, well, you really aren't going to be here all that long, so I was thinking, how dangerous would it be if we . . ."

Her courage faltered and she fell silent, gazing up at him, waiting for a response.

Scott told himself to pull away. She had no idea he was the son of the man who was trying to destroy her inn, and he had no right to take advantage of her ignorance. True, he had been keeping steady tabs on the lawsuits, trying to reason with his father through the lawyers, but that didn't change the facts. In Allison's eyes, the LeRoches were all the same, and when she found out he was one of them, she'd see his silence as deceit.

But gazing down into her hopeful gray eyes, it was hard to think about their family history or future consequences. He could only think of now. A now that had Allison standing a hairsbreadth away, wanting to be kissed. When he continued to hesitate, a flicker of hurt entered her eyes, and he couldn't bear it.

Telling himself it was only a kiss, just one last kiss, he lowered his mouth to hers. Sweet. God in heaven, she was so unbelievably sweet. With a moan, he gathered her in his arms and let himself sink. She returned the kiss with all the unschooled passion that drove him mad. Closing his eyes, he drowned in the pleasure of holding her again. In the back of his mind, his conscience shouted a warning but need outweighed good intentions.

He cupped the back of her head and kissed her endlessly, thinking he could live forever on the taste of her mouth alone. His hunger spurred her own and she moved against him, like a kitten rubbing him with her body, demanding to be petted. He leaned back against the desk, pulling her with him until she stood between his thighs, her soft belly cradling his arousal. The warning screamed louder, but he refused to listen as the rip current pulled him under.

Her head fell back with a moan of pleasure when he kissed her neck. "Yes," she whispered. "We definitely need to rethink the rules. One night isn't enough."

No, it wasn't. A million nights wouldn't be enough with her. He wanted to fill his life with loving her.

The thought stopped him cold.

Opening his eyes, he stared at her and realized the alarm clanging in his brain had very little to do with the possibility of her hating him. It had to do with the things she stirred inside him, an intensity of longing that went beyond lust. An unfamiliar emotion ballooned inside him until suddenly he couldn't breathe.

He jerked back and nearly toppled onto the desktop.

"Scott?" She braced her hands against his chest to keep from falling on top of him. "Are you all right?"

"Yes." *No!* He pushed her back to arm's length as his heart pounded. "I'm fine. It's just . . . we can't do this." When she frowned, his mind raced. "We can't because . . . the door's open."

An impish grin pulled at her lips. "We could always close it."

"And have your brother walk in on us?"

"You're right. We'll have to be discreet." A wicked gleam sparkled in her eyes. "What if I come to your room tonight, when everyone else is in bed?"

"No! You can't."

"Why not?" She frowned.

"Because I . . ." *I what?* Nothing came to mind, and he watched the confusion turn slowly to hurt.

"Oh, I see." She pulled away, looking mortally embarrassed. "My mistake. The other night you said . . . never mind . . . I just thought you were still interested—"

"Of course I'm interested." How could she doubt that after the way he'd nearly devoured her whole? "It's just that I'm . . . busy." *Okay, that worked.* "I'm really, really busy right now."

She stared at him as the embarrassment in her eyes turned to disbelief, then anger. "You're too busy for sex? Since when is any man too busy for that?"

So maybe the busy excuse didn't work. "Allison, I—"

The phone rang and he sagged in relief.

She reached around him and jerked up the receiver. "Pearl Island Inn." After listening to the person on the other end, she held the phone out to him with a fumigating look. "It's for you."

He took the phone gratefully. "Scott, here."

"What is this!" Penny Nichols squawked, and he'd never been so happy to hear his editor's nasally voice.

"What is what?"

"This fax you just sent."

"You said you wanted a book outline, so that's what I sent you. The outline of a book."

He watched as Allison stalked toward the door, then stopped to give him one last glare over her shoulder. Her anger was good, he told himself. Much better than having her warm, tempting, and willing in his arms. But the look she gave him cut straight through to his heart.

"Cute, Lawrence," his editor said. "What's your point?"

His gaze held Allison's as he answered. "The point is, I need you to trust me."

Allison's mouth thinned before she turned and left him standing there.

"All right," Penny growled. "You win. I'll authorize payment of your outline-approval check. Are you happy?"

"Ecstatic," he said, even though nothing could be further from the truth.

He glanced in the direction Allison had gone and remembered that strange, unfamiliar sensation that had moved through him, and the panic threatened to return. If that sensation was what he feared, he had a much bigger problem than he realized. He'd always considered falling in love akin to losing one's sanity. But for him to fall for Allison St. Claire would be emotional suicide. Thank goodness he'd spotted the danger in time. Now he just needed to stay as far away from her as possible.

Chapter 16

TOO BUSY TO HAVE SEX? Ha! Like she was going to believe that. She wanted to wring Scott's neck. Here she'd agonized for days about sleeping with him again, wondering if he wanted to, worrying about the complication. A torment of indecision. Then, when she finally makes up her mind, he says he's too busy?

She couldn't believe it.

She didn't believe it.

Not after that kiss!

Only, why would he lie about such a thing? She pondered it for the rest of that day as the hurt of rejection wrestled with anger. By the following morning, though, anger had won out. How dare he lie to her? He had a right to tell her no, but he could have the decency to give her a reason rather than a ridiculous excuse. As petty as it was, she wanted him to pay for that. Not in a huge way—she wasn't that childish—but she did want him to pay just a tiny bit for the days of soul-searching he'd put her through, only to be rejected with a lie.

Finally, she hit upon a subtle yet perfect way to extract revenge. Unfortunately, her plan would only work if he really did still want her. If he didn't, she was about to make a colossal fool of herself.

Trying not to think about the potential humiliation, she carried a bucket of cleaning supplies and fresh linens to his room and gave the door a brisk knock. "It's Allison. You decent?"

"Yes, come in," he called.

Squaring her shoulders, she opened the door. He sat at the little desk by the windows that overlooked the cove.

Afternoon sunlight filled the room. As if oblivious to it, he stared at the laptop screen—as he always did when she came to clean his room.

"Making progress?" she asked, her voice cheerful.

"Some." He answered without looking up.

So, he was going to pretend nothing had happened yesterday. Her eyes narrowed with determination. "Well, don't mind me, I'll be out of your way in a jiff."

"Take your time."

Humming a tune, she carried her bucket of cleaning supplies into the bathroom first, not that the room needed much cleaning. Scott was one of the neatest guests they'd ever had. Once the sink area and shower were sparkling, she headed back into the main room to change the sheets.

She watched him in the mirror on the armoire as she bent forward to strip the sheets. She'd worn a gauzy sundress without a slip. While it wasn't indecent, she hoped the hint of her silhouette would attract his attention. At first, he didn't look. Then his gaze strayed to her backside and the heat that smoldered in his eyes bolstered her courage. "Google eyes," as Chloe would say.

Oh yes, Scott Lawrence wanted her, all right. To torture him just a bit, she bent over as frequently as possible as she finished making the bed. The minute she straightened and turned, though, his attention snapped back to his computer screen and his fingers started clicking away at the keyboard.

Swaying her hips, she headed for the sitting area with a feather duster. His fingers stilled on the keyboard when she moved by him, leaving a faint trail of the perfume she'd dabbed on before coming upstairs.

Scott's nostrils flared in an effort to catch the scent. Winsome and mysterious, like some rare night-blooming flower.

"Do you want me to dust off the desk?"

"No!" he answered abruptly. Pushing her away yesterday had nearly killed him. No way did he want her that close again.

"Very well." She moved about the sitting area, shaking out curtains and fluffing the little decorative pillows on the settee. Sunlight poured over her, making her look as ethereal as she had the first time he'd seen her. Then he realized the light shone straight through her dress, outlining her legs. *Oh God.* A bolt of desire shot to his groin.

He dipped his head forward and shielded his eyes with one hand.

"Scott?" she said, and the sound of his name spoken with that proper, lady-of-the-manor voice sent another jolt through his senses. "I know you're terribly busy, and I hate to bother you, but I've been wondering about something."

"Yes?" *Just don't look at her*, he told himself. *Don't look and you'll be fine.*

"It's about my voice. You said it turned you on, something about it making you ... 'hot.' I believe that was your word ... so I was wondering, do you think it has that effect on other men?"

Slowly, he raised his head and looked at her over his hand. She stood there, her expression so innocent, she all but blinked her eyes at him. "Why do you ask?"

"I just thought it would be a good thing to know. If my voice does turn men on, maybe I could learn to use it more effectively. You know, practice some of the words and phrases that would get a man excited. Like phone sex, where a woman can get a man so aroused just with words that he ..." Color stained her cheeks.

"Is satisfied?"

"Tactfully put." She sighed a bit in relief, but the determined glint in her eyes had him on full alert. "That seems like a useful skill, as useful as knowing how to touch a man in ways that make his blood rush and his body ... quiver."

Her voice dropped in pitch on the last word, making him want to do exactly what she said. Quiver. He cleared his throat. "Yes, words are powerful, but then, I suspect you know that."

"Actually, I never thought about it before, but they really are, aren't they?" The newfound power sparkled in her eyes, an irresistible combination with her flushed cheeks and the sunlight glowing in her hair—and through her skirt. "When you hear something described, you can almost feel it physically. For instance, if I said something like, 'I want to taste your skin against my tongue and feel the heat of your body covering mine,' would that get a man aroused?"

He groin went so hard he grimaced. "Yeah, I'd say that would pretty much do it."

She moved closer, graceful and seductive. He leaned back, bracing his hands against the desk. "But surely that's only the beginning. I wonder how one learns to talk provocatively enough to send a lover . . . over the edge."

"Somehow I don't think you need lessons."

"So you think I could excite a man, get him hot and hard, with words alone?"

"I think it's possible, yes."

"Hmm." She purred, stroking her throat with her fingertips, making him long to kiss her there and feel her pulse pound against his lips as he breathed in her mind-numbing scent. "That gives me something to think about." A smile as mysterious as Mona Lisa's curved her lips. "Thanks for taking the time to answer. I'll, um, let you get back to work. Since I know how very 'busy' you are."

She gathered the dirty sheets and the bucket of cleaning supplies and left.

He dropped his face into his hands. *Help.*

A memory flashed in his mind from the day he'd arrived, when he'd asked Marguerite to make Allison a

little less of a nice girl. Lifting his head, he looked about
the room. "Is it too late to change my mind?"

Allison's campaign to get back at Scott worked so well
that by Saturday, she was practically singing, and would
have been except she'd discovered she was wielding a
double-edged sword. True, he looked more flustered each
time she questioned him about the finer points of "verbal
sex," but each encounter left her itchy all day and restless
at night.

It was worth it, though. Especially since now he'd
started to sweat the minute she entered his room, before
she even said a word.

A feline smile curved her lips as she topped bowls
of crisp lettuce with chilled shrimp. Scott was on the
verge of begging her to sleep with him and she was going
to have the supreme pleasure of telling him she was "too
busy."

"What next?" Chloe asked. The girl had become a
regular little helper around the inn, offering to do odd jobs
to keep from being bored. And—Alli suspected—to get
Adrian's attention. Ah, the agony of a first crush. At
twelve, it was still innocent enough to be sweet.

"Let's see." She pulled her mind away from Scott to
concentrate on making shrimp Caesar salad for the crowd
that had just descended upon them. Each Saturday they
served lunch on the veranda as part of Captain Bob's Big
Bay Boat Tours. "Parmesan cheese. You should find a
block of it in the fridge."

Chloe crossed to the refrigerator just as Paige entered
the kitchen—petite and blonde and graceful as always.
She might help her husband run the tour boat, but she still
looked like she should be lounging at the country club.
She even made the tour-guide uniform of white shirt and
navy-blue shorts look like the latest designer fashion,
complete with diamonds at the ears and a tennis bracelet

that could blind a person in strong sunlight.

"Good morning," Paige said brightly.

"Good morning to you," Allison answered with a smile.

"Well, you're in a good mood," Paige noted. "And here I thought to rescue you by offering to help."

"On a Saturday, I'll always take help," Allison laughed.

Chloe pulled her head out of the refrigerator to hold up a block of hard white cheese. "Is this what I'm looking for?"

"That's it." Allison nodded toward a drawer. "The grater's in there."

Paige raised a brow as she joined Allison at the center island that functioned as a workstation. "I didn't know you'd hired help."

"Well, sort of." Allison transferred salad bowls to a large serving tray. "Chloe's actually a guest, but she enjoys helping out. Chloe, meet Paige."

"Pleased to meet you," Paige said as she fell easily into the rhythm of assembling salads. "I noticed Aurora working in the gift shop. That's a switch." Normally Allison worked the shop on Saturdays, dressed in her Southern belle costume, while Adrian and Chance waited tables in their pirate costumes. Rory had been working the kitchen the last few months, since she couldn't fit her stomach into her own costume.

"Her ankles are so swollen lately, she has trouble standing for long periods," Allison explained. "We all thought the gift shop would be less taxing for her right now."

"I guess she's getting pretty close to her due date? How's she feeling?"

"Fine, she says." Allison's happy mood dimmed as she fought the growing urge to turn and run every time the subject of the baby came up. When she thought of

Rory in labor, of all the possible complications to both the mother and child, fear slid beneath her skin like ice.

"Hey there, Paige." Chance came striding in wearing a big-sleeved white shirt, wide leather belt, and tight pants tucked into black boots. He set a tray on the counter and started filling the sink with dirty soup bowls. "That's quite a crowd you brought today."

"And tourist season isn't even in full swing." Paige shook her head in amazement. "Bobby wants to talk to y'all about adding a dinner run this summer."

Chance blew out a breath. "Let's wait until after the baby comes, then maybe we can all think straight enough to talk. Alli, do you have a tray ready?"

She finish grating cheese over the salads. "Take it away."

He shouldered the full tray as if he'd been waiting tables for years, rather than working behind a desk at a bank.

Adrian came in next, looking every inch the dashing pirate with his ponytail, small gold earring, and jackboots. Chloe stopped work and sighed out loud. Allison hid a smile at the girl's obvious crush.

"We're going to need more iced tea," he said.

"I'll get it!" Chloe offered and rushed to the commercial-sized coffee maker they used for brewing tea as Adrian balanced a second tray on one hand over his head and headed out.

And so it went for the next half hour: soup, salad, homemade bread, and huge slices of sigh-inducing chocolate cake went out while dirty dishes came in. As the tourists finished their meals, they wandered into the gift shop or down to the cove for a walk along the beach.

The steady pace kept Allison's mind off Scott . . . until he strolled into the kitchen just as she was finishing the dishes.

"Hey, Uncle Scott." Chloe brightened at the sight of him. "How's it going?"

Allison's heart jumped as she glanced toward him. He stood in the doorway, wearing a black polo shirt, black shorts, and the sort of befuddled expression she imagined a bear would have emerging from hibernation.

"Okay." He nodded. "I take it from all the noise it's Saturday again."

"It does tend to come once a week," Allison said. She almost laughed when she saw him stiffen.

His head turned slowly toward her, the muddled look giving way to wariness. "I thought you'd be in the gift shop."

"Rory and I are trading places until the baby comes."

"Oh." He glanced back toward the door, as if he wanted to bolt. *Poor frightened bear*, she thought, even as she let her gaze flow over him. *Big sexy black bear*.

"I hope we didn't 'disturb' you in any way," she said as her gaze took a leisurely journey back up to his face.

"No." He cleared his throat. "Not at all."

She watched color rise up his neck, and marveled that she could affect him so easily. She didn't even have to be overtly suggestive. The simplest words, with just a hint of sexual connotation, were enough to raise his blood pressure.

"I, uh, just thought I'd grab one of the Cokes I left in the fridge, then do some research on the Internet about salvage ships."

"Actually, I'll do you one better," Alli said. "This is our friend Paige, who has an absolute passion for all things nautical. If you have a question about boats, she's the one to ask."

"Really?" Scott eyed the former debutante with only a hint of skepticism showing.

"You must be Scott Lawrence." Paige smiled back. "Chance and Rory told me you were staying here. You know, I've always wondered where writers come up with their ideas."

He gave Allison a deadpan look. "We get them from sadistic muses, who find inventive ways of making us pay."

Allison bit her lip to stop a grin.

Scott turned back to Paige. "I don't suppose you'd have time to answer a few questions?"

Paige looked at her slim gold Rolex. "Bobby's probably about ready to shove off."

"Maybe later, then?" Scott said.

"Actually . . ." Paige hesitated, then smiled. "I don't see any reason he can't take the boat back by himself. I've already done my tour-guide bit, and he can certainly dock by himself."

"That would be great." Scott glanced at the table by the window, then back toward Alli. "Maybe we should go sit in the music room, where we'll be out of the way."

Amusement tickled Allison's cheeks as she watched them leave. Oh, he wanted her, all right—but he was fighting it. Why she had no idea, she just knew he was.

She dried her hands on a dish towel. "Hey, Chloe, I'm done with these dishes. You want to keep me company while I clean rooms?"

"As long as you don't ask me to pitch in and scrub toilets."

"Deal." Alli pulled on the bill of the girl's ball cap, then headed for the closet in the back hall to get the bucket of cleaning supplies.

As she moved through the rooms making beds for guests who were staying, changing sheets if they were checking out, Chloe kept up a running monologue about the baseball game she'd watched the night before with Adrian over at Chance and Rory's house. This was news to Allison, since she'd spent the evening downstairs re-reading one of her favorite Scott Lawrence books. He really was an amazing storyteller, drawing the reader into an adventure where spine-tingling danger built with every page. Where *did* he come up with all those twists and turns, and characters that seemed so real?

When they reached Scott's room, they found the usual organized clutter: neatly stacked piles of papers on the desk, reference books on the coffee table in front of the settee. Wherever his ideas came from, he wrestled them onto the page in a very methodical manner.

Reaching the bathroom, she had to shake her head. The toiletries sat on the counter in the same regimented order she found them every day.

"Is your uncle always this neat?" Allison called to Chloe, who had flopped down on her uncle's bed.

"Pretty much," Chloe called back. "If the writing is going really, *really* well, he'll slide a tiny bit on the neat-freak routine, but otherwise, clutter bugs the heck out of him. He says it's distracting."

Shaking her head, Allison opened the shower door to clean in there, but stopped at what she saw. Several pairs of boxer shorts hung on the retractable clothesline. They were the lightweight silk variety preferred by people who did a lot of world traveling because they packed small and could be washed in a sink and dried overnight. They came in two colors, solid white and solid black. Naturally Scott's were black. She couldn't help but laugh. "Look at this. He even wears black boxers."

"Black is his favorite color for clothes." Chloe appeared in the doorway. "So he doesn't have to make decisions when he's getting dressed."

"Yes, I know." She realized how personal that sounded. "I mean—I noticed. I just didn't realize he carried it through to his underwear."

"Sad, isn't it?" Chloe clucked her tongue. "Poor Uncle Scott. Heaven forbid he should get up in the morning and have to decide what color boxers to put on. He'd probably have a coronary."

An idea flickered to life in Alli's mind. A wicked, devious . . . *tempting* idea. "Oh no, I couldn't."

"Couldn't what?" Chloe asked.

"Nothing. I just had a silly thought. But no, it's too childish. I couldn't possibly . . ."

"Couldn't possibly what?"

She looked at Chloe, trying to suppress a smile. "Play a practical joke on Scott."

"What? Tell me."

"Okay. I'm not saying we should do it, but here's my idea . . ."

Chapter 17

SCOTT WALKED PAIGE DOWN THE path to the dock when they spotted the tour boat returning. "Thanks again for all your help."

"It was my pleasure," she assured him as they reached the pier. Shading her eyes, she waved at her husband as he steered the large pontoon toward them. "Not many people are willing to listen to me talk about boats for hours on end. I just wish I could have helped you more with underwater salvage techniques."

"Well, there's always the library."

"Hey, I have an idea. Bobby has a friend, Jackie Taylor, in Corpus Christi whose father was a treasure hunter. The father spent years going after Lafitte's treasure and even named her Jackie, after Jack Kingsley."

"Oh really?" Scott raised a brow in interest.

"Jackie has sworn off treasure hunting and runs a charter boat now, a fabulous old Baltimore schooner, but I bet she could answer your questions."

"Hey, sweetheart!" the boat driver called as he cut the engine. The pontoon bumped gently against the pier, sending waves to slosh against the pilings.

"Hey, yourself." Paige's whole face lit up as the driver tossed her a mooring line. For a moment the two of them beamed at each other, while Scott did a bit of staring himself. After spending the afternoon with Paige, he'd expected her husband to be cultured and refined. The man smiling at her from the platform of the pontoon looked like he could wrestle alligators with one arm, while swilling beer with the other. Thick black hair curled around the edges of his battered captain's cap and the sleeves of his white shirt stretched taut around massive biceps, while the front hung open to reveal a hairy chest.

"Bobby, this is Scott Lawrence," Paige said, holding the boat in place with the ease of someone familiar with the task.

"Pleased to meet ya." The man leaned over the rail and offered a massive paw. Suppressing the writer's instinct to protect his hands at all costs, Scott surrendered to the crushing handshake, then flexed his fingers in a subtle check for broken bones. Everything still worked.

"Honey, do you have a phone number for Jackie Taylor?" Paige asked.

"I have it somewhere, why?" After Paige explained, he ducked into the cabin at the back of the boat and came out with a wrinkled and stained brochure. "Here you go." He handed it to Scott. "I'm not sure how willing she'll be to talk to you about her father's treasure hunts, though. It's kind of a sore subject with her."

"Well, it never hurts to ask." Scott glanced at the brochure—which pictured a majestic old ship with billowing white sails on the front—before he slipped the pamphlet into his pocket.

"You ready to shove off?" Bobby asked his wife. When she said yes, he took a seat behind the wheel and the engine came to life with a puff of blue exhaust.

"Let me know if you have any more questions," Paige said as she stepped nimbly onboard.

"I will." He waved as the pontoon boat pulled away from the pier and headed across the sparkling water to the mouth of the cove. Only then did he realize how far the sun had dipped in the sky. He and Paige had literally talked the afternoon away. She'd fascinated him, though, with her knowledge of boats, from old sailing ships to the stealth boats used by modern-day pirates and drug smugglers. Amazing information.

With his mind still sorting through what he could use,

he started back for the inn. As he reached the end of the pier, he saw the jeep that belonged to the St. Claires heading up the drive with Allison at the wheel. She'd breezed downstairs earlier with Chloe and said the two of them were heading into town on an errand. The mischief in her eyes had made him wonder what sort of errand, but he hadn't asked. After the last few days, he didn't dare ask her anything for fear of what might come out of her mouth. Whoever would have guessed someone who looked as shy as Allison could have such a wicked way with words?

God, she was killing him. And she knew it. Just that morning at breakfast, she'd leaned over his shoulder to heat up his coffee by topping off the cup. With her lips close to his ear, she'd dropped her voice to a seductive purr and asked if there was anything else she could heat up for him. He'd let a groan slip, which had made her laugh.

Not up to facing her right then, he turned and started walking along the beach toward the trail that circled the island. Maybe a walk would give him the time he needed to decide how to handle Allison.

He'd never been so drawn to a woman before, or so intrigued, which made it imperative that he keep the situation under firm control. Unfortunately, he needed a better plan than simply avoiding her. Even when she wasn't physically in the room driving him nuts, she lingered in his mind in a most unsettling way. Just thinking about her made butterflies dance about his stomach—something he'd never experienced before.

Reaching the start of the trail, he stepped gratefully out of the sun into the cool shade of sprawling live oaks. Palm trees rustled overhead while a tangle of yaupon and scrub oak protected him from the steady gulf breeze. The crushed granite trail crunched beneath his Top-Siders as he turned the problem over in his mind.

The way he saw it, he had three options. One, he could tell her who he was, which would promptly put an end to her efforts to seduce him. Of course she'd likely kick him off the island as well.

He shook his head, rejecting that idea, since nothing about it appealed to him. Not only would he lose his connection to Marguerite, Allison would be hurt, and he couldn't bear that.

Two, he could keep resisting her. He snorted at that idea since it stretched the bounds of believability a bit too far—even for someone with a vivid imagination.

Three, he could give in to temptation and keep his mouth shut.

He stopped abruptly and stared straight ahead, down the winding path through light and shadow. What would happen if he spent time with Allison the way he wanted, both in and out of bed, without telling her he was John LeRoche's son? His body cheered enthusiastically at the idea, but how long could he keep her in the dark?

He could pull it off easily for the rest of his stay at Pearl Island, he realized as he resumed walking again. Yes, it could work. It would be wrong to take advantage of her ignorance, but it could work. And if she never found out, she'd never be hurt.

What about afterward, though? He'd never pull off the deception long term, assuming he wanted to keep seeing her. *Did* he want to keep seeing her?

He stopped as his heart pounded in an uncomfortable blend of desire and dread. Yes, he did. She was funny, sexy, sweet, and surprisingly passionate. She made him laugh, drove him mad with lust, and brightened his mood just by being near. Of course he'd want to keep seeing her . . . if things were different.

But things weren't different.

If he continued seeing her long term, she'd find out the truth. The longer it took, the angrier she'd be. Unless

. . . unless she came to care for him enough to forgive his one lie-by-omission.

Could he make her care for him? Should he even try?

He rejected the idea instantly—along with the whole plan of sleeping with her again. If he gave in to temptation and spent time with her, he'd want to keep seeing her that much more. He did not want to open himself up to that. Every person he'd ever counted on or cared for had let him down sooner or later. Far better to keep her at arm's length. If he did anything else, they'd both wind up hurt, and frankly, he could do without the pain and guilt.

Allison and Chloe hurried upstairs. They'd seen Scott down at the dock with the boat leaving. He could walk through the front door any minute.

"Do you think we have time?" Chloe asked in a stage whisper.

"We'll have to be quick." Reaching Scott's room, Allison motioned Chloe toward the window. "Go see if he's still by the pier."

"Okay." Chloe darted to the windows. "I don't see him!"

"Go check the stairs. See if he came in after us. If he's on his way up, stall him." Allison ducked into the bathroom and took down the black boxer shorts. Then she reached into the bag from Savers Mart and started hanging up the boxers she and Chloe had bought, creating a jolly chorus line of chili peppers, happy faces, polka dots, and one pair with bright red lipstick kisses. "Perfect."

"He wasn't downstairs." Chloe appeared in the bathroom doorway, slightly out of breath. "Maybe he went for a walk."

"No matter. I'm done." She gathered up the black boxers and stuffed them into the bag. "Let's get out of here."

"Wait, I want to see." Chloe opened the shower door. "I love it!"

"Come on, hurry," Alli coaxed as she closed the shower door.

"This is so funny." Chloe giggled. "What do we do now?"

"Head for the gift shop. And wait."

Together, they clattered down the stairs and were both laughing when they entered the gift shop. Rory, who'd been working in the office, crossed the hall and frowned in confusion. "What's up with you two?"

"Nothing," Allison answered sweetly as she stuffed the bag on the shelf beneath the cash register. Her sister gave her a questioning look as Chloe raced for the window.

"He's coming!" The girl turned to her. "What should we do?"

"Just act natural." Alli started straightening a display of souvenir pens.

"Okay"—Rory put her hands on her hips—"something is obviously going on."

The front door opened and Alli struggled back a laugh.

"Hello, Uncle Scott," Chloe called as he appeared in the hall. "Did you have a nice walk?"

"I suppose," he said. "How was your trip into town?"

"Boring." Chloe faked a yawn. "Very, very boring."

Allison turned away to hide her grin. When she heard Scott head for the stairs, she winked at Chloe.

"How long do you think it'll take him to notice?" Chloe asked.

"I don't know, but when he does, we both act clueless and blame it on ghosts or gremlins, okay?"

"Notice what?" Rory demanded.

"We replaced Uncle Scott's black boxers with the

wildest ones we could find. He is so going to freak."
Chloe rolled her eyes.

Rory frowned. "I don't get it."

Chloe explained but Rory still didn't understand the
joke.

"I guess you just have to know him to understand,"
Chloe finally said.

"I suppose so." Rory rubbed the small of her back,
making her stomach protrude. "Although if you two
pranksters don't mind, I think I'll head home."

"You okay?" Allison asked in concern. Rory looked
so tired, and her stomach had gotten huge.

"I'm fine. I just want to see if Chance is back from
talking to the attorney." On the advice of their lawyer,
they'd offered to drop the libel suit if John LeRoche
would drop his suit against Chance and the bank. They
had yet to receive an answer and the waiting was beginning to wear on all their nerves.

"Yes, go," Allison told her. "And put up your feet.
You need to rest."

"Don't worry, I will." Rory smiled as she waddled
out. After she'd left, Alli and Chloe waited in the gift
shop for nearly an hour before Scott finally came back
downstairs.

"Hey, Chloe," he said. "You ready for some supper?"

In unison, Allison and Chloe stared at him, looked at
each other, then back at him. He didn't show a flicker of
reaction to what they'd done. "Uh, sure," Chloe said.

"Well, come on," he said. "We can decide what we
want on our way in to town. That is, if you're finished
helping Allison."

Chloe looked at her again, but all Allison could do
was shrug. "Fine with me."

As Allison watched them go, her shoulders slumped
in disappointment. Maybe he hadn't opened the shower

door yet. Although surely he would notice when they got back, tomorrow morning at the latest.

The evening came and went without a word. Chloe ventured into the kitchen just before bedtime. "How could he not notice?"

"I don't know." Allison poured them each a glass of milk and fixed a plate of brownies. "Maybe we should have left the shower door open."

"You mean, we have to wait until morning when he takes his shower?" Chloe asked.

"Looks like it."

"I hate waiting." Chloe took a big bite of brownie.

"Me, too. But remember, act clueless when he does notice."

"You got it."

The following morning, Allison waited eagerly for Scott and Chloe to come down for breakfast. Chloe came down first, beating most of the other guests. She fidgeted in her chair and giggled each time she looked at Allison. By the time Scott came down, breakfast was in full swing with guests sharing their plans for the day over the clatter of dishes.

Allison glanced up from pouring coffee, saw him enter the room, and froze as she waited for his reaction. He simply went to the sideboard, fixed his plate, and sat down. She couldn't believe it. Nothing!

She stared at Chloe who gaped back at her. He had to have noticed by now. His damp hair proved he'd taken a shower, yet he didn't say one single word about it. He just questioned Chloe about her schoolwork.

Okay, she decided, if he was going to pretend nothing had happened, so would she.

"I can't believe he didn't say anything," Chloe complained later when she joined Alli in the gift shop.

"Me, either."

"He must be up to something. I bet he's known since yesterday, and he's plotting his revenge."

"You think so?" Allison thought that over as she dusted off a display of miniature sailing ships. "But what could he do?"

"Heck if I know, but we better be careful until we figure it out. Remember, we're dealing with a man who drags his characters through snake-filled jungles and shark-infested waters. Heaven only knows what torments he's capable of in real life."

"Oh, come on, Chloe, that's just fiction." Allison laughed nervously. "What's he going to do, hide snakes in our beds?"

"I'm just saying we're dealing with a man who makes a living scaring the living daylights out of people."

"You're right." Allison bit her lip.

The thought of what Scott might be planning soon had her jumping at every noise. Scott gave nothing away, though. He came down to the kitchen at noon to make lunch for Chloe and himself from the groceries he kept in the refrigerator, then went into town to do research at the library.

That evening, Allison sat in the music room, helping Chloe with her homework. Quiet had settled over the house with most of the guests in town. Rory and Chance had gone home for the day, and Adrian was playing poker at a friend's house. Scott appeared in the doorway, startling both of them.

"What are you two up to?" he asked, as casual as ever.

"Nothing," Chloe said, looking a bit like a deer caught in the headlights.

He turned to Allison. "I have a huge favor to ask. I'm really on a roll with the writing and don't want to stop. So, do you think you could take Chloe out to dinner? On me, of course."

"I . . ." She hesitated at the unusual request. "I suppose."

"Great." He reached in his back pocket for his wallet, and pulled out a credit card. "I really appreciate this."

She took the card, still frowning.

"Yep, he's up to something," Chloe said when he was gone.

Night had fallen by the time they returned, both of them pleasantly stuffed with seafood. They stopped at the base of the stairs, taking in the quiet creaks and pops of a house settling in for the night. Allison hadn't seen any lights on upstairs besides Scott's so any guests who had returned from town had apparently gone to bed already.

"Well, I guess this is it," Chloe said, looking up the stairs.

"You want me to go up with you?"

Chloe seemed to consider it, then squared her shoulders. "No. I can take it. Besides, like you keep saying, how bad can it be?"

"Okay, but check your shower before you go to bed."

"Yeah, good thinking. You, too."

"Right." Allison waited at the base of the stairs until she heard the door to Chloe's room close. When no scream followed, she took a deep breath and headed down to the apartment in the basement. Adrian hadn't returned from his poker game, and probably wouldn't for hours.

She turned on all the lights in the main room, then eased open the door to her bedroom on its creaky hinges. How could such a new door make that eerie noise? Nothing seemed out of place, though, so she ventured inside, moving carefully to the threshold of the bathroom. She needed to wash her face before going to bed, but her gaze landed on the shower curtain and she remembered the scene from one of Scott's books where the villain had hidden inside the shower with a knife in hand, watching the woman as she stripped off her clothes.

Logically she knew he would never go so far as to act out that scene, yet nerves skittered up her spine as she sidestepped into the room, never taking her eyes off that curtain. She bent sideways to reach the plunger by the toilet. Chanting the words "there is nothing behind that curtain, there is nothing behind that curtain," she swiped it open.

And screamed.

Then instantly laughed because there was nothing behind the curtain. She was alone in the apartment, and being utterly foolish. Too unsettled to wash her face, she went back into her room and sat on the bed. Maybe she and Chloe were wrong. Or maybe his revenge was as simple as making them wonder what he was planning. That sounded diabolical enough to be true. What better way for him to get back at them than to let their imaginations do it for him?

Then again . . . Her gaze wandered to her dresser. On a hunch, she crossed the room, stood with her head craned back just in case something jumped out, and eased the top drawer open.

Nothing jumped out.

She chanced a peek inside and her eyes went wide. Rather than neat stacks of cotton undies, she found a pile of slinky black lingerie! Sheer bras, lacy panties, garter belts, and stockings. All of it black.

Laughter bubbled up as she scooped up a handful. His revenge was perfect. Brilliant. Holding up a pair of crotchless panties and a bra that seemed to be missing the requisite cups, she laughed even harder. She'd swapped his black underwear with wildly tacky colors; and he'd swapped her sensible cottons with black underwear so sexy it fell over the border into raunchy.

Gathering up the whole pile, she headed upstairs and rapped on Scott's door.

"Who is it?" he called cheerfully.

"Who do you think?"

"The underwear thief?"

"*Me* a thief?" She tried the knob and found the door unlocked. "What about—" The minute she stepped into the room, she froze. Scott sat on the bed with his legs crossed at the ankles, dressed in nothing but the pair of boxers with the lipstick kisses. Mounds of her prim cotton underwear surrounded him. "Oh, my God!" She slammed the door, afraid one of the other guests would pick that moment to walk into the hall.

Whirling back to face him, she watched him dangle one of her many pairs of white panties printed with butterflies and flowers.

"Very sweet." He gave her one of those laconic smiles that made her heart bump. "This is much closer to what I expected you to wear than that sexy number you had on at the Hotel Galvez. Although"—he considered the panties—"I'm not sure which is sexier."

"Give me that." She lunged forward, spilling black lingerie onto the bed.

"Not a chance." He held the panties away from her, making her climb onto the mattress. "I'm keeping all of it as my spoils of war."

"I'll spoil your war." She lunged again and fell across his chest. "I want my panties back."

"And I want my black boxers."

She pressed her forearms against his chest to prop herself up. "You need variety."

"And you don't?" He scooped up a fistful of cotton undies. "Come on, Alli, I've never seen so many flowers and butterflies outside a garden."

"I like flowers."

"So do I." His amber gaze shifted, making her aware of the warm skin beneath her palms, the crisp mat of black hair, the honed muscles. "But I also like you in black."

Taking up a scrap of satin, he brushed it against her cheek. Heat flowed through her. "I like you a lot in black." Cupping the back of her head, he applied the slightest pressure, not jerking her to him, but leaving the decision up to her. The moment hung, shimmering with anticipation and all the reasons they shouldn't do this.

Slowly, she lowered her lips for a tantalizing brush, the barest taste.

Scott closed his eyes in surrender. Consequences be damned. He wanted her. Whatever happened afterwards, he'd deal with it when the time came. For now he just wanted her. He tightened his hand in her shoulder-length curls and gave himself over to the moment, the utter joy of holding her, touching her, breathing her in.

"Tell me you want this," he managed between nibbles. "I want to hear you say it."

"So you can reject me again? Tell me you're too busy?"

He pulled back, stared at her. "You know I want you."

"Maybe I'm the one who needs to hear you say it." Color rose up in her cheeks.

"You want to hear me say how much I want you? How I can't think about anything but you? I lie awake at night fantasizing about touching you." He ran his hand down her throat to cup her breast through her T-shirt. His thumb rubbed small circles over her nipple and her eyes went heavy. "You want words, I'll give you words." He turned to press her onto the mattress where she lay surrounded by innocent white cotton and provocative black lace. The contrast more than suited her.

"The very thought of you is enough to make me hard." He nibbled at her lips. "When you walk into a room, I can't think about anything but how much I want to get inside you." He moved his mouth to her ear and whispered. "I want you beneath me, so lost in your own passion, in the things I'm doing to your body, you can't stop calling my name and begging me to take you."

"Yes," she sighed as her body trembled. "I dream of the same thing, where you touch me and take me, hard and fast, and I'm helpless to stop you because I want you so much."

Hunger coiled inside him at the words, along with a desire to give her any fantasy she wanted. Before they parted, she'd likely hate him, but at least he could give her this: physical pleasure to remember for a lifetime. He searched through the garments scattered across the bed, until he found what he wanted. "Put this on."

She stared at the bra that was all straps, underwires, and very little else, her eyes going wide with shock at the idea of wearing it.

He kissed her neck, teasing her pulse with his tongue. "Trust me." He inched up her T-shirt, running his palm over the warm flesh of her stomach. With light kisses and teasing touches, he coaxed off her shirt and reached for the back clasp of her sensible cotton bra. It gave with a satisfying snap.

"Put it on," he said again, handing her the black bra.

She hesitated, then sat up, with her legs tucked demurely beneath her in the middle of the bed. Her breathing turned shallow as she realized she wanted to don the scandalous garment. Taking it from him, she bent forward to fasten it and felt the wires snug up under her breasts. The quarter cups ended below the nipples, lifting her breasts and putting them on display.

The sensation was wickedly thrilling as she straightened and looked down at him.

Lounging back on one elbow, he stared a moment before he dragged his gaze up to her face. "Now lie down," he said. She stretched out beside him, not quite sure what to expect. He took her hands and raised them to the headboard. "Hold on here. Don't let go." His smile was slow, sexy, and just a bit dangerous. "Trust me."

Her heart pumping, she did as he said and gripped the headboard as he stripped off her shorts and panties, then did away with his boxers. He came back to her, all dark, aroused, and potently male. His gaze dropped to her breasts, laid before him like a feast. Then, slowly, he bent and suckled each nipple until she whimpered with need. His hands moved downward, opening her thighs, teasing between them.

As his fingers slipped inside her, he spoke in husky tones about what he was doing, how her response excited him. He enthralled her body, enslaved her senses as she arched and writhed beneath him. By the time he positioned himself between her thighs, every fiber in her body sang like a tightly drawn bow string expertly plucked by a master.

Then he drove inside her with a force that made her gasp. With his lips against her ears, he told her how good she felt, as he moved steadily, driving her higher. She closed her eyes, returning his thrusts and gloried in the pleasure of the giving and taking.

Trust me, he'd said, and she did, absolutely. In that moment, she trusted him to take her anywhere. It was fate she didn't trust.

Chapter 18

THERE WAS NO GOING BACK, Scott realized as he lay staring at the ceiling with Allison's head resting on his shoulder. Someone was going to wind up hurt; it was only a matter of when.

Stroking his hands through her hair, he enjoyed the fit of her warm body against his. "For the record, I want to state that I did try to be noble."

"I didn't want you to be noble."

"Then I guess you got your wish." He tipped his head to see her face. "Remember that, okay? No matter what happens, remember that you wanted this and I never meant to hurt you."

"I won't get hurt." The trust in her smile wrenched his heart. "I know you're not interested in anything serious or long term, and neither am I. But like you said, we can still enjoy ourselves and enjoy each other, can't we?"

"I'm not sure it's that simple."

"Stop worrying. I'll be fine." She kissed him lightly and snuggled closer. "Besides, I couldn't leave you alone. I'm your muse."

"I thought we agreed stress was my muse."

"No, I'm your muse. I just use stress to inspire you."

"And you do it so well." A chuckle rumbled in his chest.

"So, how is the book going?"

"Very well, actually." His hand trailed lazily over her soft skin. "Although Marguerite and Jack keep trying to take over the story."

Her eyes widened and she lowered her voice. "Do

you think they really are ghosts? That they're trying to tell their story through you?"

He started to say no, that his minor characters frequently tried to steal attention away from the main characters, but he hesitated—remembered that moment underwater, when he'd felt . . . something. "I don't know. Ever since I went down to the ship, I've been thinking about things from Jack's point of view. I mean, I always try to put myself in each character's skin to understand them better, but I really do wonder about Jack. If he loved Marguerite as much as everyone claims, why did he leave her here so long? Why wasn't he more forceful in talking her into leaving Henri? And if her marriage was as bad as you claim, why didn't she go?"

"For her, it was lack of trust and too much fear of being hurt again. As for Jack, I agree, he should have fought harder. Although, in his defense, he didn't know how bad her marriage was. Like a lot of battered women, she couldn't bring herself to tell anyone."

"You'd think he'd notice the bruises if they were getting naked together."

"They didn't really 'get naked' that often." She propped her head on her hand. "Their affair started slowly, and wasn't physical at all for a long time. She was Catholic enough to want to keep her vows. Plus she was deathly afraid of Henri. And Jack, I think, from the way she describes him, put her on a pedestal. He worshipped her. They didn't actually make love until they'd been in love for a long time. That was the night she gave him the necklace."

"No wonder he went back for it."

"Yes, I suppose you're right. He would have cherished it as part of her, part of their love. So, if he thought it was a matter of running to his cabin and grabbing it before abandoning ship, he'd have gone."

"I'd still like to read the diaries. Understand what happened in Marguerite's own words."

"I don't know. We've never let anyone outside the family read the diaries."

"What if I swear to guard them with my life?"

"No, really . . ."

"I'll read them while I'm here. They won't leave the inn, so you wouldn't really be letting them out of your control."

"Scott, they're too personal. They're her diaries. I really couldn't."

He studied her. "I'm not going to let up on this."

"You have two weeks to try and persuade me." Her lips turned up in a slow grin.

"Is that a challenge?"

"Maybe." She trailed a fingertip down his chest.

"Because, as of yesterday and your Great Underwear Caper, all bets are off." He rolled her onto her back, covering her body with his. "No more Mr. Noble on my part."

"The part didn't suit you anyway." She ran her hands down his back to cup his bottom.

He closed his eyes as his body hardened. "Just be warned"—he bent down to nuzzle her neck—"I plan to take full advantage of the next two weeks." Cupping her breast, he rubbed the nipple with his thumb as he spoke. "You come into this room in the middle of the day bending over to make the bed in your see-through dresses, don't expect to leave untouched." He retrieved a foil-wrapped packet from the nightstand drawer. "I don't care if there are people in the hall, or if your brother comes knocking at the door. I will have you."

"Promise." She opened her legs to cradle him between her thighs.

"You can bet on it." He slipped inside her, enjoying the purr of contentment that rumbled in her throat.

•   •   •

"Okay, I can't stand the suspense anymore," Chloe said to her uncle as the three of them stepped out of the old-fashioned candy store licking ice-cream cones. Scott had decided to take the day off and go shopping with Alli and Chloe in the historic district. "I know you know about the boxer shorts, so when are you going to retaliate?"

Allison's gaze shot to Scott as her cheeks heated. Nearly a week had passed since they had made love on the underwear-strewn bed, but the memory was still fresh in her mind. Along with several other tantalizing memories of encounters that had followed.

"Who says I'm going to retaliate?" Scott countered calmly.

"Oh, come on," Chloe whined. "It's not like you to do nothing."

He affected a sinister look. "Perhaps that's my revenge. To leave you wondering for the rest of your life, glancing over your shoulder, waiting for me to strike."

"Now that is like you." Chloe's eyes widened as she turned to Alli. "I told you he was clever. Only, he'll have to catch me first." The girl took off like a power walker down The Strand.

Smiling at each other, Scott and Alli followed at a slower pace past the gift shops and art galleries. Brightly painted buildings stood beside stately red-brick and colorful blossoms filled planters and flower boxes. A few of the merchants had even set a sampling of their wares out on the sidewalk to take advantage of the springtime weather. The day would be perfect, Allison decided, if not for the cloud of the lawsuit hovering in the back of her mind.

John LeRoche had rejected their offer to drop the slander suit if he'd drop his suit. Their attorney's confidence about their chances of winning seemed to dwindle daily, but they'd voted to stick to their guns. The thought of a court battle made Alli's stomach churn. But then Scott casually took her hand in his, and her anxiety vanished.

Just walking down the street with him, hand in hand, filled her with contentment. Over the past week, not a day went by that he didn't find a way to get her alone. Sometimes in his room as he had warned, but he'd also coaxed her down the walking trail late one night where he took her against a tree. The following night, they'd left the house separately and rendezvoused at the far end of the beach, where they'd made love on a blanket with the stars overhead and moonlight shining on the cove.

A smile tugged at her lips as she licked her cone, savoring the icy vanilla and chunks of chocolate.

"What's that smile about?" he asked.

"I was just thinking I might need to . . . um . . . clean your room when we get back to the inn."

He raised a brow, then chuckled. "You know, Alli . . . I sure hope you aren't expecting Santa Claus to bring you any presents this year." When she looked at him askance, he leaned closer and lowered his voice. "Because you are a very naughty girl."

She licked her cone, smiling up at him. "I do believe I'll take that as a compliment."

"As it was intended." They stood for a moment, staring into each other's eyes as tourists moved around them on the sidewalk. A horse-drawn carriage clopped down the street, harnesses jangling, as the driver regaled his passengers with the history of Galveston. "Yeah"—Scott ran his thumb over her knuckles—"I think my room could use a little extra dusting when we get back."

"Hey, guys, come look!" Chloe called, waving toward the windows of the Strand Emporium. "Check this out."

With twin sighs, they continued down the sidewalk.

"What'd you find, kid?" Scott asked.

Chloe thumped the glass with her finger. "Look at that old baseball mitt."

Allison smiled at the girl. "One of the vendors specializes in sports memorabilia." When Scott looked at her, she explained. "I used to work here."

"Can we go in?" Chloe asked.

"Finish your ice cream first." He took another lick of his own cone, as his niece gobbled hers down.

"All done." Chloe held a hand in front of her full mouth.

"Hang on." Allison dug through her purse for a hand wipe. "The dealers get very annoyed when people come in with sticky hands and start touching everything."

Chloe wiped her hands, then held them up for inspection. "Can I go in now?"

"Yes," Scott said, "but don't touch anything until we get in there, okay?"

"Yeah, yeah." The girl disappeared through the door, making the bell over it jingle.

"She is such a tomboy." He shook his head, smiling.

"She'll outgrow it. Trust me."

"Oh?" He looked at her. "Do you speak from experience?"

"No, I was never a tomboy, but I see the way she looks at pretty things. She just doesn't know what to think about all the changes going on inside her. Growing up is scary business."

"Yeah, it is," he said quietly.

"What were you like growing up?"

"You done with that cone?"

She cocked her head, wondering why he always changed the subject if she asked him anything the least bit personal. At first she'd thought it was part of the rules, to not get too close, but a disquieting current had started flowing just beneath her contentment.

Peter had been equally evasive, never wanting to open his whole life to her. Except . . . that's what she *wanted* with Scott, wasn't it? So why did it bother her?

Rather than push, she polished off the cone, then dug out two more hand wipes. She didn't need to know Scott's entire past history to enjoy his company for the next week. And that's all they had left. Just a little over one week.

With a sigh at how quickly time could speed by, she headed through the door Scott opened for her. The scents of old books and aged wood greeted them.

They spent nearly an hour rummaging through stalls of antique clothing and jewelry, furniture, books, and collectibles. Allison was at the counter in the center of the shop, visiting with some of the people she used to work with, when Paige came through the front door.

"Thank goodness I found you!" Paige said, hurrying toward her.

"What?" Allison felt the blood drain from her face. "What's happened?"

"Adrian called to say Rory's in labor. Chance just took her to the birthing center an hour ago, but apparently it's progressing really fast."

"Is something wrong?" she asked. "Is Rory okay?"

"I assume she's fine. Adrian didn't say," Paige explained as Scott joined them, carrying a stack of rare books. "He just told me you were down here on The Strand and for me to find you. He'll meet you at the center. He's already called your friends the McMillans to have Betsy watch the inn. Do you want me to give you a ride?"

"I'll take her." Scott deposited his books on the counter and reached for his wallet. "Just give me a moment to check out. Chloe, come on. We're going."

Chapter 19

SCOTT WATCHED ALLISON FROM THE corner of his eye as he drove. She sat with her hands clasped tightly in her lap, leaning forward, as if willing the car to go faster. "Alli, relax. We'll get there in plenty of time, I promise. These things take somewhere between forever and infinity."

She nodded, but didn't say anything.

"I remember when Chloe was born. My sister was in labor for at least a week."

"She was not," Chloe protested, but Allison paled.

"That was a joke." He reached over and covered her clenched fists, startled by the chill of her skin. "Hey, she'll be okay."

Allison kept her eyes trained straight ahead as she gave instructions on how to get there. When they reached the birthing center, Scott parked between Adrian's motorcycle and Chance's blue BMW. The one-story building looked like a cross between a house and a doctor's office.

"You don't have to come in," Allison assured him.

Scott stared at her, trying not to laugh. "Alli, you're a nervous wreck. Let me get you safely to your brother, then Chloe and I will get out of your hair. Promise." He went around the car to open Allison's door, since she made no effort to get out on her own. "Ready?"

She took the hand he offered, and he helped her from the car.

"I thought men were supposed to be the jittery ones at times like these," he teased, but even that didn't get a reaction from her. Frowning, he squeezed her hand. "Let's go find your brother."

The front room had been set up as a reception area, with a desk and chairs. Since no one was around to greet them, Scott stepped through a door on his left and found what looked like an apartment living room complete with a kitchenette. Adrian sat on a sofa, reading a magazine.

"Looks like we found the place," Scott said, pulling Allison in behind him.

"Hey, sis." Adrian put the magazine aside. "You made it." He gave Scott a surprisingly cordial nod. "Thanks for bringing her."

"Not a problem." Scott nodded back.

"How's Rory?" Allison asked.

"Doing great. You want to see her?"

Allison paled further as she glanced toward a door that stood ajar. "Is it all right?"

"Sure, come on."

She hesitated, gripping Scott's hand. He tucked a stray curl behind her ear. "Why don't Chloe and I wait here while you say hi to your sister?"

She nodded, then released his hand to follow her brother.

"Will it really take hours?" Chloe asked.

" 'Fraid so."

"Do you think we can stay for a bit, just in case it happens faster? It'd be cool to see the baby."

"Let's play it by ear. We don't want to interfere with family."

"What was it like when I was born?"

"Well"—Scott took a seat on the sofa and Chloe sat beside him—"I was your mom's labor coach, so I was there the whole time. Got to see you scream at the world the very first time. And boy, were you loud." He tugged on his ears.

Chloe frowned in thought, and he waited for her to ask why her father wasn't Diane's labor coach. He'd never discussed the details with her, but maybe she'd al-

ready learned her father had been in Aruba with his play-
mate du jour at the time. Diane wasn't exactly discreet
when complaining about her ex-husbands.

But then a cocky grin replaced Chloe's frown. "I bet
I was a great-looking baby."

"The cutest ever in the entire history of babies."

"Yeah, that's what Mom says."

"Too bad you went straight downhill from there."

"Watch it." She punched him, and he obliged her
with a grunt.

Allison hesitated at the door, afraid she'd find operating
room lights glaring off stainless-steel surfaces. Instead,
lamps set on end tables lent a homey glow to the room.
Two women in scrubs were there, one in a rocking chair
near the bed, the other hovering in the background near
some medical equipment. Allison's eyes darted away from
the monitors and landed on Rory. Her sister lay on her
side in the bed with Chance sitting on the mattress, rubbing her back. "How's that?" he asked her quietly.

"Better." She lifted her head to smile at him and saw
Allison. "Hi. I'm glad Paige found you."

"How do you feel?"

"Like I have a cannonball pressing down on the small
of my back." Rory shifted into a half-sitting position while
Chance stuffed pillows behind her back.

"Can they give you anything for the pain?" Alli
moved to the side of the bed, reminding herself that this
day had nothing in common with her experience years
ago. Rory was birthing a healthy, living baby who would
be welcomed by everyone.

"It's not that bad yet." Rory blew out a breath. "Although someone remind me again why I decided to do
this the natural way."

"You're doing great, sugar," the midwife assured her.

"Just remember what you learned about riding with the pain, rather than fighting it."

"Right." Rory gave a dry laugh, then took Allison's hand and laid it on the protruding mound of her stomach. "Here, want to feel? That's her head."

Allison stiffened in shock. She'd managed to avoid this very thing for months, couldn't bear the thought of feeling the baby squirm with life one day, then go horribly still the next. As Rory pressed her hand down, though, a hard shape nudged her palm. Her breath caught in her throat.

Rory smiled. "She's been wiggling around like crazy for the past hour. Here, feel her little bottom."

Mesmerized, Allison let her sister move her hand to the other side. Rory's gaze lifted, and she smiled. "Can you feel it?"

"No, I can't." As if in answer, the baby kicked hard, making her jump.

"Oh boy." Rory blew out a breath. "Here we go."

"I got you." Chance slipped his arm around her shoulders, supporting her weight as she curled forward between her raised knees. Allison stumbled backward, colliding with Adrian. Memories swelled up from the dark place where she'd buried them: pain, fear, blood. So much blood.

She tried to shake free of the past as the midwife checked her watch. Chance focused all his attention on Rory, encouraging her and soothing her as she panted her way through the contraction. Alli's own stomach cramped in empathy. Oh God, it hurts, she thought. It hurts so much.

When it was over, Rory collapsed back against the mound of pillows, her hair sticking to her damp face. "Wow, they're coming closer together."

"They're supposed to," Chance told her as he wiped her face with a washcloth.

Tears clogged Alli's throat as she thought of all the things that could still go wrong. For the hundredth time, she wished Rory had opted for a hospital.

"You okay?" Adrian squeezed her shoulders.

She nodded, swallowing hard.

"Hey." He turned her slightly, studied her face. "If this is going to be too tough for you, you can wait at home."

"No, I want to be here." She looked back at her little sister. "I need to be."

"You sure?"

She nodded. "I just need a minute."

"Of course." He gave her shoulders another squeeze. "Let me know if I can help."

She fled the room before she could upset Rory by bursting into tears.

Scott came to his feet when he saw her. "You okay?"

She pasted on a smile. "I'm not the one in labor."

"You look a bit pale." He glanced toward the tiny kitchenette. "Can I get you something to drink?" Without waiting for an answer, he moved to the apartment-sized refrigerator and opened it. "Let's see, we have canned orange juice and . . . canned orange juice."

"I'm fine."

He pulled out the can, found a Styrofoam cup in the cabinet, and poured her some. "Here. Drink up. It's good for you."

"It's canned." She wrinkled her nose but took a sip.

He cocked his head. "You know, if you want some of the fresh squeezed from the inn, I could take Chloe back, gather up some drinks and eats and bring it all back here. What do you say?"

"That would be nice." Her voice nearly cracked, so she took another sip of juice. "Betsy McMillan, the inn-keeper from the Laughing Mermaid, is there. She can help you put together some leftover pastries from breakfast. I

imagine Chance's parents are on the way, and Bobby and
Paige will probably come later, so we'll need quite a bit."

"Just leave it to me. I'll take care of everything." He
turned to Chloe. "You ready?"

"Do we have to go?" Chloe protested.

"Yep. Com'on, you can help me raid the kitchen."

Allison fought the urge to call Scott back as he and
his niece headed out the door. He wasn't part of the family, but she wanted him with her. Needed him by her side.

"Well, at the rate things are going, we'll be holding
our niece before we know it," Adrian said, joining her.

She tried to smile, but could tell the effort didn't fool
her brother.

"Come here." He opened his arms. She slipped into
the familiar comfort of his hug. "I know this is hard on
you," he said.

"I just hate seeing Rory in pain."

"Hey, it'll be okay. Rory's always been healthy as a
horse. The doctor said she was a perfect candidate for
natural birth, and if anything goes wrong, there's a hospital right down the street."

"I know. I'll be okay." She pulled herself together
enough to straighten. "Did you call Aunt Viv?"

"She said her understudy broke her leg, literally,
while skiing in Vermont, so there's no way she can
come."

Alli nodded.

"Where'd Scott go?" Adrian asked.

"He went to take Chloe back to the inn, but offered
to gather up some food and drinks and come back. I figured we'd have a small crowd before long."

"Now why didn't I think of that?"

"Because you're nervous, too." She smiled at him.

He just laughed. "Caught me."

As they settled on the sofa, a low keening moan came

from the other room. Alli chewed her lip, part of her wanting to rush to her sister's side and hold her hand through the next hours. Another part of her wanting to run from the barrage of memories.

"You know, Alli . . ." Adrian said, pulling her attention away from the half-opened doorway. "I've been meaning to talk to you about Scott."

She turned to him, startled, then let out a groan of her own. "Not now, Adrian. I'm really not up to one of your big-brother lectures."

"Actually, it was going to be an apology, but if you're not interested . . ." He sat back.

"Apology?"

"Yeah." He turned almost sheepish. Well, as sheepish as her six-foot-plus hunk of a brother could get. "I think there's an outside possibility, a slight one, mind you, that I may have been wrong about the guy."

"What do you mean?"

"I thought he was using you—taking advantage of your inexperience."

"I've already told you—"

He raised his hand, silencing her. "I know what you told me. That it was a mutual use."

"A mutual agreement."

"Whatever you want to call it, I'm not blind. I can see there's something pretty powerful going on between you two, and I just want to say, about time. You deserve a man who's crazy about you."

She sat there stunned. "There's nothing 'powerful' going on between us."

"Alli, how stupid do you think I am? Do you honestly think I don't know you two have been going at it like rabbits for the past week?"

Her cheeks heated with embarrassment. "But that's just sex."

"That's not 'just sex.' Trust me. When it's just sex,

you do it once or twice and move on. When two people become clothing challenged for days on end, there's a whole lot more going on than a mutual desire to get horizontal."

Her embarrassment grew as she remembered some of the times they hadn't even bothered with the horizontal part, or getting completely undressed. She concentrated on smoothing her dress over her knees. "Okay, I'll admit, we enjoy each other's company. It doesn't have to mean anything."

Adrian opened his mouth as if to argue, but apparently changed his mind. "I just wanted to say, whatever is going on between you two, knock yourselves out. You'll get no more grief from me. Not that you need my approval, but well, there you go."

"Thank you," she said, wondering why his approval bothered her more than his disapproval.

Chapter 20

SCOTT RETURNED TO FIND THAT Bobby and Paige had
arrived along with an older couple who were introduced
to him as Chance's parents, Ellen and Norman Chancellor.
The names gave his heart a bit of a lurch. He'd heard his
mother, who'd grown up in Galveston, speak of Ellen
Chancellor as a mild acquaintance. John had done business at Norman Chancellor's bank for years, although the
relationship had clearly been severed over the Pearl Island
foreclosure.

As he returned their greeting, he reminded himself
the Chancellors had no reason to connect Scott Lawrence
to John and Deirdre LeRoche, or DeeDee, as his mother's
friends called her. Her maiden name had been Howard,
so DeeDee wasn't so bad, but he'd always thought that
paired with LeRoche it sounded like a stripper name. Not
that he would ever tell his mother that, but how could she
not think it herself?

Adrian took the bag of pastries from him, and somehow the two of them wound up working side by side in
the kitchenette, filling cups with ice and pouring tea and
juice for everyone.

Scott glanced over his shoulder at Allison, who sat
in a chair away from the others, looking small and lost.
"Is Alli all right?"

Adrian hesitated slightly. "She's just worried about
Rory."

"Is there some complication I don't know about?"

"With Rory, no. Although . . . if you could stick by
Alli, keep her distracted, I'd appreciate it."

The words startled Scott. Over the last week, Allison's brother had thawed a bit toward him, but to actually encourage him to spend time with his sister set a new precedent. "Sure. I'll do what I can."

"Thanks." With a friendly nod, Adrian took drinks over to Chance's parents. They were a handsome couple, with the polished manners of old money.

Norman Chancellor scowled at the cup. "I don't suppose you have anything stronger to put in this."

"Sorry." Adrian laughed. "I'm afraid iced tea and fruit juice are all we have."

Scott carried a cup to Allison and squatted down by her chair. "Any news on how she's doing?"

Allison blinked as if pulling herself out of her own thoughts. "Ellen went in a bit ago and said it was going really fast." Her gaze wandered toward the door. "I should probably go in, too. Sit with her."

He tipped his head, noting the lines of stress etched about her mouth. "You can do that later. How about you and I go for a walk to help pass the time?"

"No. I want to stay here. I need to be near my sister."

"All right." Glancing around, Scott saw a straight-backed chair against the wall and dragged it over to sit by Allison. "So, is this your first birthing to sit through?"

She hesitated, then nodded.

"It's my second. Although, so far, it seems a whole lot more boring sitting out here than being in where all the action is going on. You want me to tell you about it? Minus the gory details?"

"You've been through this before?" Ellen Chancellor asked.

"With my niece," Scott said, and regaled the room with how his sister had called him in the middle of the night to say it was time and for him to come get her. He'd shown up in a rush, tires squealing, heart pumping, only to find her in the bathroom putting on makeup. She'd stopped to have a contraction, then proceeded to do her hair.

Before long, he had the room laughing at the story of Chloe's birth.

"Your sister sounds like my best friend Marcy Baxter, Paige's mother," Ellen said, giving Scott another mild start. He knew that name, too. Marcy and his mother had been girlhood friends. They'd drifted apart when Marcy married a brash land developer after college and DeeDee married the heir to the LeRoche business empire and moved to New Orleans.

Ellen smiled at Paige. "Marcy was just as bad when you were born, refusing to go to the hospital until your father opened the suitcase she'd repacked three times already, and stuffed in yet another nightgown she'd bought the day before."

As Ellen talked, Scott watched how her husband sat quietly beside her, nodding and smiling, a look of genuine affection in his eyes. Bobby stood behind Paige's chair, his hand on her shoulder, completely absorbed in the tale about his wife's birth. The scene struck Scott as oddly intimate, as if he were getting a glimpse into these people's private lives, seeing them as they truly were. They were nothing like what he'd always imagined couples and families to be.

He tried to picture the same scene with his family, and couldn't. For one thing, his sister had asked him not to call either of their parents until after it was over. Upon hearing the news, their mother had rushed to the hospital on a cloud of French perfume, complaining about the luncheon she was missing and criticizing Scott for not calling her sooner. She'd made some comment about babies looking like tiny old people, all toothless and bald, then swept out again claiming she was late for her manicure. At least she'd shown up. Their father had sent an extravagant but useless gift—most likely purchased by his personal assistant—and a note expressing his deep regret for not being able to come in person. John had always been good at sending notes to express his deep regret. In fact, Scott often thought that was where he'd inherited his talent for writing fiction.

No, Scott couldn't imagine this same scene with his family as the players. These people actually liked one another. It wasn't an act for the outside world. It was real, and warm, and without warning it exposed a huge gaping hole inside him he hadn't even known was there.

This was what was missing from his life. *This* was the void he'd tried to fill with his writing.

When he was lost in one of his stories, he didn't have to examine his real life too closely. Yet sitting in this room, witnessing family and friends interacting with warmth and caring, he realized how empty his own life had always been and still was.

A strangled cry of effort and pain came from the other room, followed by one of the midwives telling Rory to push.

Ellen's eyes widened and she glanced at her watch. "If they're already telling her to push, it won't be long now."

Scott glanced at Allison, and found her deathly pale. He reached over and took her hand as Rory cried out again. Adrian stood abruptly to pace. "How do women go through this?"

No one answered or spoke as the sounds from the other room grew louder over the next several minutes: Chance's encouraging voice, the commands of the midwives, and Rory's straining cries as she struggled to push the child from her body.

Allison rocked back and forth as Adrian continued to pace. The room hummed with the combined focus of everyone there as they waited with breaths held.

Suddenly, a cheer rose from the other room, followed

by the thin, reedy cry of a baby. Tension rushed out of Scott, making him light-headed. He glanced around at the smiles and tears. Ellen hugged her husband, crying and laughing. Turning to Allison, he expected to see the same relief.

Instead, she stood abruptly, clutched a hand to her mouth to stifle a sob, and rushed from the room.

"Alli!" Adrian shouted and ran after her. Shocked silence followed.

"Is she all right?" Ellen asked, wiping her cheeks.

"I don't know." Paige looked to Scott as if he should know the answer.

"I'll, um, go see." Scott stepped into the front room, but saw no sign of them, so he headed outside. Night had fallen, but the parking lot lights cast a soft, yellow glow over the area. He found them sitting on the curb at the end of the sidewalk, Allison with her face buried against her brother's neck, Adrian holding her tightly and rocking.

As he approached, he heard Adrian speaking against Allison's hair. "I'm so sorry. I should have known this would be too hard for you."

"I thought I could handle it."

Gravel crunched beneath Scott's boots and Adrian looked up, then nodded for Scott to join them.

When he sat, Allison lifted her head, then ducked it back down to hide her tears.

"You okay?" Scott asked when neither of them spoke.

"Yes. No." With a watery chuckle she swiped at her cheeks.

Not knowing what to say, Scott decided to let her brother handle it.

Adrian helped her dry her face. "Do you want me to take you home?"

"I can't ask you to do that." Alli sniffed. "I know you want to be with Rory and see the baby."

"Can you handle going back inside?" Adrian asked.

She shook her head and glanced at Scott, misery and embarrassment swimming in her eyes.

"I'll take you home," he offered.

She nodded, and took his hand so he could help her stand.

Scott didn't ask any questions on the way to the inn, and Allison was grateful. She felt too raw inside to speak. She just wanted to get home, climb into bed and escape into the oblivion of sleep.

When they reached the inn, he parked near the back door, so she wouldn't have to walk through the main hall and chance running into guests.

"Allison? Is that you?" Betsy McMillan called from the kitchen.

Scott squeezed her hand. "If you want to go straight downstairs, I'll talk to her."

The offer was tempting, but she shook her head. "No, she's too good a friend for me to do that." She stepped into the kitchen where Betsy and Chloe sat at the table playing cards and waiting for news.

"Hey, kid." Scott greeted his niece. "I thought you'd be in bed by now."

"No way." Chloe looked eagerly at Allison. "Well?"

Betsy's eyes also twinkled. "Is the baby here?"

"Yes." Allison swallowed down the lump that rose in her throat. "She arrived just a few minutes ago."

"Oh, I'm sure she's beautiful." Betsy clasped her hands together. "So, give me the details. How much does she weigh? How long is she? And how's Rory doing?"

Unprepared, she looked to Scott for help.

"Rory's fine," Scott answered for her. "Unfortunately,

Allison isn't feeling well, so we had to leave before the weighing and measuring part."

"I'm sorry, dear." Betsy stood and came forward. "Can I get you anything?"

"No." Alli rubbed her temple, refusing to break down again. "I just need to lie down."

"Well, you go on downstairs." Betsy made a shooing motion with her hands. "I'll lock up tight before I leave."

"Thank you, Betsy. We really appreciate your watching the inn for us."

"It's no problem at all. At least this way, I got to be the first one in our group to hear the news. Now go on, off to bed."

"You, too," Scott told Chloe.

"Can't I wait until Adrian comes home?" Chloe begged. "He'll probably know more."

"Tomorrow is soon enough to get the details. Now come on upstairs." Scott cast Allison one last look, asking if she would be all right alone.

She nodded and watched him leave. After thanking Betsy again, she headed down the narrow stairs that led to the apartment. Sadie came to greet her, then whined when Allison barely acknowledged her.

The trembling started again as she crossed to her room. By the time she reached the narrow bed, she collapsed onto the coverlet, too exhausted to undress. Sadie jumped up beside her, whimpering in empathy. Allison buried her fingers in the dog's long fur, absently kneading as memories rolled through her like nausea.

When she heard the scrape of boots approach her open door, she lifted her head, expecting to see Adrian. Instead, Scott stood silhouetted in the faint light from the living room. With a groan, she dropped her head back to the pillow, willing him to go away. Instead, he came forward, closing the door behind him, leaving only the moonlight spilling through the window over her bed.

"You don't have to talk if you don't want to," he said. She felt his hands slip about her ankles as he removed her sandals. Then he chased Sadie off the bed and pulled Alli to a sitting position.

Her head ached from holding back tears, so she docilely obeyed as he undressed her down to the gauzy black bra and panties she'd worn that day with thoughts of seducing him. With no desire to be sexy and provocative, she covered her chest with one arm and looked away. The sound of drawers opening and closing penetrated her numbness. Then he stood before her, holding out a white cotton nightgown.

"Thank you," she whispered, her throat tight with grief. Rising, she clutched the garment to her, willing him to leave. He turned his back and busied himself with turning down her bed, silently telling her he wouldn't go away until she was tucked into bed. Giving in, she changed into the nightgown. He held the covers and she climbed beneath them, pulling them to her chin. "I'm okay now. Really."

"No one said you weren't." He calmly proceeded to take off his boots. She squeezed her eyes shut as emotions quivered beneath the surface of control. If only he'd go away, she could force the memories and pain back down, lock them away. He tapped her lightly on the hip. "Scoot over."

She thought about arguing, but didn't have the energy. So she moved closer to the wall, which gave him barely enough room on the single bed to stretch out beside her. His blue jeans felt rough against her thighs as he gathered her in his arms.

"Although, if you want to talk . . ." He left the invitation hanging.

"No," she whispered, then pressed her lips together to make them stop shaking. "I just want to forget."

"All right." He stroked her hair and back for several

long seconds. The soothing motion relaxed her muscles, weakened her defenses. She could feel the memories welling up again and this time was helpless to stop them.

She closed her eyes as they engulfed her. "I had a miscarriage. When I was sixteen."

"Oh hell." His arms tightened around her. "I was hoping that wasn't it."

"I wanted the baby." The force of that wanting tore through her body. "I wanted it so much even though Peter pressured me to have an abortion."

"Peter?"

"The boy I told you about."

"You seem to have left out a few details. Care to tell me the whole story?" When she shook her head, he fit her body more tightly along his. "Come on. I've got you. Tell me what happened."

The first rush of pain subsided enough for her to take small breaths. "He—he's the only one who ever noticed me."

"Somehow I doubt that."

"Oh, I had friends who were boys." She rubbed the heel of her hand against her cheek. "Well, Adrian's friends, really, but they weren't 'boyfriends.' Then one day, Peter was hanging around my locker. My heart just about stopped, because I had such a huge crush on him. All the girls did. He was beautiful and popular, on the football team. All the girls talked about him endlessly, and then suddenly there he was, standing by my locker."

She settled her head on Scott's shoulder and let herself drift back to that day. How clear it seemed, even though she hadn't thought of it in years. Hadn't let herself think about it. "I tried to be calm, not gawk and drool and make an idiot of myself. But then he looked at me, looked right at me, and smiled. I don't even remember what he said, just that he was talking to me, and then he took my books and walked me to my next class, and everyone was looking at us. I'd never been the center of attention before. It was frightening. And the most wonderful thing that had ever happened to me.

"The next few weeks were a fairy tale. Peter poured attention on me. I met all the popular kids. I mean, I knew most of them, because Adrian was . . . well, Adrian—Mr. Jock—and the girls were even more crazy over him than Peter—a fact that always seemed to make Peter mad." She frowned, because she hadn't realized that then, but it seemed quite clear now. Peter had always become irritable when her brother's name came up. "No matter. The important thing is, I wasn't just Adrian's shy sister anymore. I was wearing Peter Basset's letter jacket.

"I was so in awe. And so stupid." She balled her hand into a fist against his chest as tears filled her throat. "He told me . . . he loved me. And I believed him! God, I was so stupid. He was Peter Basset, part of the Galveston elite, the country club set. He talked about us being together forever. And I believed him!"

Scott's arms tightened and he murmured against her hair. "Come on, let it all out."

"The first time I let him . . . the first time we . . . were together . . . it was awful. I felt so empty afterward. I'd expected it to be wonderful, for it to fill some void inside me, but it just hurt and felt all wrong. I told myself that it would get better, and when it didn't, I told myself it was my fault. There was something lacking in me, that I expected too much. Peter was perfect, and I was this mousy little nobody."

"You are not mousy," he said fiercely. "And you are not a nobody."

"But I felt like nobody." She sniffed against a new rise of tears. "Even when I was with him. So, I concentrated on pleasing him and I dreamed about the future. I spent hours writing my married name in my school notebooks. Allison Basset. Mrs. Peter Basset. Mr. and Mrs. Basset.

"When I realized I was pregnant, I was frightened, but I was also excited. Because I thought we wouldn't have to wait until we were older to marry. We'd marry right away, I'd cook and clean for him while he went to college, then we'd get a house, raise a family, and everything would be wonderful."

She lay very still for a while, focusing on the feel of Scott's hand stroking her hair. "We had a date that night. I floated through the whole evening, smiling at his friends, thinking they would be my friends, too. They'd attend our wedding, as Peter and I would attend theirs. We'd all raise our children together.

"Then Peter took me home, stopping at one of his favorite 'parking' places on the way." She clung to Scott, wishing she could stop the memories now, but they kept coming. "We made out in the back seat of his Camaro. I felt as empty as ever when it was over, but told myself it was okay. Lots of girls don't enjoy doing it. I loved Peter. That's all that mattered.

"Afterward, I told him about the baby. Oh God." She buried her face in Scott's chest. "He was horrified. I tried to reassure him, to tell him we'd work it out, and that's when . . . That's when he . . . he started to laugh."

She swiped the hair away from her face, clenching her teeth. "He said he couldn't believe I took anything he'd said seriously. I was a Bouchard. That's how the old families in Galveston always think of us, no matter our last name. We're theater people, descended from a French prostitute. Surely I never really believed he'd want to marry me. He said . . . he said the only reason he asked me out in the first place was because the other football players said I wouldn't 'put out' for anyone."

She squeezed her eyes shut. "I was nothing but a challenge to him, a way to prove to the rest of the team

how macho he was. He told me I had to get an abortion.
Ordered me to. But I refused.

"The next few weeks were so awful, I can't even
remember them correctly. I told Adrian I was pregnant,
and he talked me into telling Aunt Viv. But we never told
Rory. She still doesn't know." She looked at him, suddenly frantic. "So you can't tell her. You can't tell anyone."

"Of course I won't."

She dropped her head back to his shoulder. "Aunt
Viv was furious. Not at me. At Peter. She wanted to con-
front his parents and file a paternity suit. I swear, if he'd
been older, she'd have filed statutory rape charges, but I
talked her out of it. I just wanted my baby. It wasn't
Peter's anymore. It was mine." She clutched her fist to
her breast. "I wanted it so badly.

"I remember the first time I felt it move. For nearly
a month, I dreamed and worried over the life growing
inside me. Oh God, I wanted my baby!"

Tears scalded her cheek and dampened Scott's shirt,
but he still held on to her. "One night, I woke up with
terrible cramps and I was bleeding. Aunt Viv rushed me
to the hospital. There was nothing they could do. I wanted
my baby. I wanted it so much."

Her shoulders jerked with sobs and her throat closed.
As Scott rocked her and cooed against her hair, she let go
of all the pain, let it flow out of her as he held her tightly
to him and let her cry.

Chapter 21

SCOTT STARED INTO THE DARKNESS, listening to Allison's quiet breathing. She'd cried herself to sleep hours ago. And sometime during the night, he realized he'd done the unthinkable. He'd fallen in love with her.

With his arms loosely about her, he turned his head so his lips rested against her forehead. Last night, as she let down all her defenses, revealed her sorrow and the depth of her pain, his own guard had crumbled completely. All the emotions that had been building inside him rushed out of his heart and filled him.

He loved her. The knowledge so awed him, his eyes stung. Never in his life had he felt an emotion so strong his body ached with it.

But with the love came fear. Even if they managed to get past his connection to John LeRoche, sooner or later one of them would let the other down. Every relationship he'd had worked that way. His arms tightened a fraction and he squeezed his eyes shut. *I don't want to hurt you.* Yet, how could he tell her he loved her without hurting her? She didn't want this, and now he knew why. She'd been hurt enough.

Sensing he was awake, Sadie whined beside the bed. He reached a hand down to quiet her with an ear-scratch and noticed the illuminated numbers on the bedside clock read four forty-eight. The house would be waking soon. As much as he wanted to stay with Allison, he knew he'd serve her best by making his way quietly to his room upstairs, before her brother woke and realized where he'd spent the night.

Shifting, he eased himself out from under her. When

she moaned in protest, he pressed a kiss to her forehead.
"Sleep."

She relaxed into the pillow with a sigh, her hand resting in the spot where he had lain. The faint light through
the window fell softly over her face and hair and a physical longing rose inside him to stay with her. Fighting it,
he picked up his boots and padded to the bathroom. Sadie
nosed her way past the partially closed door as he
splashed water on his face. He turned and found the little
dog rubbing her eyes with a front paw, and had to smile.

"I agree," he whispered and squatted down to pet her.
"It's way too early to be up."

The sheltie eyed him with her sleepy brown eyes.

"Tell you what. You stay here and watch over Alli.
I'll make a clean getaway to keep her out of trouble."

Sadie let loose with a huge yawn.

"I'll take that as a yes."

Rather than put on his boots, he headed upstairs in
stocking feet, hoping to get to his room without waking
Adrian. Considering the early hour, he figured that
shouldn't be a problem. Unfortunately, the minute he
reached the back hall, he realized the kitchen was filled
with light, the clatter of pans, and the smell of baking
bread.

Well hell. Allison's brother was already up and cooking breakfast. While Adrian might have softened toward
him some, Scott doubted Big Brother would be thrilled to
find a man sneaking out of his sister's bedroom in the
wee hours of the morning.

He stood still, debating his chances of sneaking past
the kitchen doorway and straight into the main hall. On
his first step a floorboard creaked, making him cringe.

"Alli?" Adrian appeared in the doorway, his con-
cerned expression going flat when he saw Scott standing
there with boots in hand. "Oh."

"Uh, good morning." Scott braced himself for anything. A fist in the face wouldn't surprise him.

"How's she doing?" Adrian asked with a total lack of hostility.

Okay, so that surprised him. "Sleeping now. She's pretty wrung out."

Concern lined Adrian's face as he glanced toward the stairs. "I wish I could let her sleep in, but with Chance still at the birthing center, she's all I've got."

"Is there anything I can do to help?"

Adrian snorted. "Make coffee, set up the buffet, serve guests."

"Okay."

"I was joking."

"I wasn't." Scott bent forward to pull on his boots. "If I can help out, I'm game."

"Well, that ought to give the other guests a thrill, to be served breakfast by a world-famous author."

"You know"—Scott straightened—"I've never understood why people think the minute you get published you forget how to perform the basic functions of life. I assure you, I manage to cook and clean and do my own laundry, just like every other bachelor. Probably a hell of a lot better than most."

"All right." Adrian nodded cautiously. "You're on. Coffee beans are over there. We fill the carafe for upstairs first. Dishes and silverware for setting up the buffet are in the butler's pantry."

Scott headed for the counter with the grinder and commercial coffee maker. Over the last few weeks, he'd learned his way around the kitchen fairly well, but always felt ill at ease about invading someone else's space. Especially with Adrian manning the stove with the skill of an accomplished chef.

Once he had coffee dripping into the first carafe, he turned back to Adrian, debating how far he should push this new friendly attitude. "Mind if I ask you a question?"

"Depends on what it is."

"This guy, Dick, does he still live in Galveston?"

"Dick?" Adrian frowned over his shoulder, whisking eggs in a metal bowl.

"The one who hurt Alli when she was sixteen."

"Oh. You mean Peter."

"Dick, Peter. Same thing."

Adrian chuckled. "I like that. But no. Last I heard, he's living in California working for some fancy law firm."

"Too bad."

"What were you going to do, go beat him up for something that happened more than ten years ago?"

"The thought crossed my mind." Scott calmly lifted a brow even as anger churned in his gut.

Adrian studied him a moment, then nodded in approval. "Well, if it makes you feel better, I took care of it back then."

"I trust you did a good job."

"Good enough to get arrested for assault. Fortunately Aunt Viv had enough dirt on Dickhead's father to get them to drop all charges. Not that any of that helped Alli. She was broken up about it for a long time. Still is, apparently. More than I realized."

"Yeah, still is." He thought about the way she'd cried last night, and felt the burn of helpless rage. The coffee maker gurgled, bringing him back to the duties at hand. He screwed on the lid to the carafe, and headed for the door.

"Hang on. Take this, too." Adrian filled a second carafe from a small faucet that dispensed steaming hot water. As he handed it to Scott, he gave him a hard, assessing look. "About you and Alli . . ."

Scott stiffened, but remained where he was, willing to take any anger Adrian cared to get off his chest.

"Whatever's going on between you, I just want you to know one thing. Allison feels things more deeply than most people. She doesn't give her heart lightly, because when she loves someone, she does it completely. And when she's hurt, she takes a long time to heal." Adrian's gaze bored into his. "I'd hate to see her hurt again."

"Message received." Taking the carafe, he headed upstairs. The last thing in the world he wanted to do was hurt Allison, but was there really any way around it at this point?

On his way back down, he stopped to set up the sideboard, a task that took a while since he had to search through all the drawers and cabinets in the butler's pantry to find everything he needed.

That done, he swung back into the kitchen. "Okay, now what?"

Allison turned with a start from the refrigerator. "Scott, what are you doing in here?"

He saw surprise, but thankfully no embarrassment. His heart clutched, though, seeing her pale face and the slight swelling around her eyes. Everything in him wanted to go to her, take her in his arms and kiss away the sorrow. But not with Adrian standing there. "You should be in bed."

"Why?" She frowned at him. "I'm not sick."

"No, but you're exhausted."

"Exhausted or not, breakfast has to be served." She sighed and pulled some bacon out of the fridge.

"I'll take care of it." He took the packet from her and carried it to Adrian at the stove.

"Scott . . ." she protested. "You're a guest."

"Chloe's a guest, and she helps."

"Yes, but you're . . ."

"A helpless celebrity?" he asked. Deciding to simply override her objection, he turned to her brother. "What do you need done next?"

Adrian didn't hesitate. He pointed to a wicker basket filled with muffins. "Take that out to the sideboard."

"Got it." Scott picked up the basket and headed back out.

The guests were already filling the table when Chance came through the back door, surprising them. "Sorry I'm late," he said, looking a bit rumpled and dazed.

"Late?" Adrian stared at him as he flipped blueberry pancakes. "We didn't even expect you."

"Oh." Chance gazed around the room as if he'd never seen a kitchen before. "Well, I'm here."

"He's useless," Adrian whispered to Scott just as Allison returned from the dining room with an empty tray.

"Chance?" she said, coming up short. Emotions moved over her face, shadows of anxiety from the night before. "Is Rory okay?"

"She's great," he said with a look of wonder. "So's Lauren. I got to watch Aurora feed her this morning. God, she's beautiful. And so tiny." He held out his arm. "Her head doesn't even fill the palm of my hand. I had no idea she'd be so tiny. I just . . . had no idea."

Allison carried the tray to Adrian by the stove, her back to Chance as he continued talking about the baby in minute detail. Scott glanced at Allison, taking in the tense shoulders, the carefully guarded expression, then noticed Adrian watching her as well.

"Will you be able to bring them home today?" Adrian asked, as he filled the tray with pancakes.

"I think so," Chance answered. "The midwife said it was one of the shortest labors and easiest deliveries she's seen in years."

Allison lifted the filled tray and headed for the dining room.

"Here, let me help with that." Scott followed her into the butler's pantry and slipped a hand about her arm to stop her. He waited for the door to swing closed and give them privacy. "You okay?"

"I'm fine," she said, as if trying to convince herself.

"I just have to get used to it, since I can hardly expect them to not talk about the baby when I'm around. They're excited, and so am I. It's hard for me, yes, but I am glad for Chance and Rory."

He rubbed her arm, wishing he could do something to make things easier for her. "They're a nice couple."

"Yes, they are." She nodded. "And they're deliriously happy together."

"I've noticed." He smiled.

She cocked her head. "I thought you didn't believe in happy marriages."

"I've decided to revise that statement and say that happiness is granted to those rare people who are decent and deserving when they treat each other with respect. You seem to have a high percentage of decent people in your life."

"I have been blessed with that, at least." She smiled.

"You've been blessed in a lot of ways." He studied her, wondering what life would be like surrounded by a warm loving family. "So, how will you handle it when Chance brings Rory and the baby home?"

"I just will," she stated firmly. "I'll start by apologizing to Rory for running off like that last night. She must be wondering why I didn't want to see the baby."

"Will you tell her what happened to you?"

She dropped her gaze. "I don't know."

"Allison." He tucked a stray curl into place. "I realize it's hard for you to talk about it, but if you tell them about the miscarriage, they'll be more sensitive around you."

"I'll think about it. Right now, though, I need to get through breakfast, and then lunch." She blew out a breath. "It is Saturday, you know."

"Ah yes. As someone once told me, it does come once a week." He shook his head, wondering where the week had gone. "If you want, Chloe and I can help."

"Thanks. I appreciate it. And if Chloe wants to help,

I'll gladly accept. You, however, have a book to write, and I've taken up enough of your time."

He started to protest.

"No, really, I'll be fine. Now, if you'll excuse me"— she lifted the tray—"I need to get this on the warming stand."

He watched her paste on a smile and head into the dining room. His heart grew heavy in his chest at her last words. After everything they'd been through, she still thought of him as a guest she happened to be sleeping with. Temporarily.

"Sadie, wait for me," Allison called as the little dog raced ahead of her on the trail to Rory and Chance's house. The dog turned and charged back, a blur of sable and white fur moving through patches of shadow and light. Allison laughed at such exuberance and envied the pure joy of the moment.

Sadie fell in step, prancing beside her, as they continued down the shaded path. Up ahead, she could see the wood frame house tucked beneath the trees and the tightness returned to her chest. Scott was right. She needed to tell her sister everything.

Telling Scott had been painful, but it had also been cathartic to let all the ugly emotions she'd held down so long rush out of her. It had left her drained, but strangely lighter, as if a physical weight had been lifted from her. Falling apart that way in front of him should have embarrassed her, but they'd grown too close over the past week for that. She felt comfortable with him in a way she'd never been with anyone before.

The realization had a whole new worry gnawing at the edge of her mind but she pushed it away as she stepped onto the porch that wrapped around two sides of the house. While the low-pitched green metal roof made the house nearly invisible from the inn, the porch that faced the cove offered a panoramic view. Rocking chairs, a porch swing, and baskets of colorful flowers created a peaceful spot to enjoy the gulf breeze. A wind chime danced merrily as songbirds squabbled at the birdfeeder.

Gathering her courage, Allison rapped on the screen door. Chance appeared a moment later, his smile and dazed look still firmly in place.

"Hi, Alli, come in. Aurora's been waiting for you to come by." He held the door so she and Sadie could step into the light and airy living room. The two-bedroom house offered only a small kitchen and breakfast nook, since Rory and Chance ate most of their meals in the kitchen at the inn.

"Sadie, no barking, okay? You be good," she admonished the dog as they headed down the short hall to the master suite. Sensing her nervousness, Sadie stuck close to her side. When they reached the room, they found Rory standing by the bassinet in front of the windows. The light through the sheer curtains bathed her in a soft glow, giving her the look of a guardian angel with her long golden-red hair and the full-length peach satin robe.

"Is she awake?" Chance asked, sounding hopeful as he joined Rory. They stood arm in arm, staring down into the white-wicker bassinet.

"No, she's still sound asleep. I guess the ride home wore her out." Rory smiled at Allison, but concern shone in her eyes. "Are you feeling better? Adrian said you weren't well last night."

"I'm fine."

"You're not contagious, are you?" Rory asked.

"No." Allison laughed lightly at that. "I'm not contagious."

"Well then, come see your beautiful niece."

Allison forced herself to move forward, to stand by the bassinet and look inside. Baby Lauren lay on her back, as perfect as a china doll with smooth white skin and rosy cheeks. Her pink lips moved in a sucking motion that was so endearing, tears filled Allison's eyes.

"Alli?" Rory laid a hand on her arm. "What's wrong?"

She wiped her wet lashes, wishing she could run back to the inn and hide in her room. "I—I need to talk to you."

An awkward moment passed as Rory and Chance exchanged a look.

"I'll go check on the casserole Adrian stuck in the oven when he came over." Chance kissed Rory's forehead.

"Sadie, you go on with him," Alli said, deciding the sensitive dog didn't need to witness another emotional scene. "Chance will give you a treat."

The little sheltie barked once, then trotted after Chance.

"Let's sit down," Rory said when they were alone. Moving gingerly, she climbed into bed where a stack of pillows had been propped up against the headboard. "I've been worried about you ever since Adrian said Scott had to take you home last night. And then when Adrian came to the birthing center today and you didn't, I was afraid something was really wrong."

"I'm sorry, Rory. I didn't mean to upset you." She sat on the bed, facing her sister, but couldn't quite look at her. "There's something I need to tell you. Something I should have told you a long time ago." She smoothed the fabric of her sundress. "Do you remember when I was sixteen and had to go to the hospital?"

"Yes. Aunt Viv said it was some sort of female problem, but never really explained. Then there was so much else going on when Adrian got into trouble, I was afraid to ask." Rory took hold of her hand. "So what did happen?"

Allison kept her gaze fixed on their joined hands,

holding on tight. "I had a miscarriage." Her sister said nothing, and she looked up to see the shock on Rory's face.

"You had a miscarriage?" Rory's shoulders sagged as if she'd taken a blow. "And you never told me?"

"Rory, you were only fourteen."

"But that was nearly eleven years ago." The words held an edge of accusation. "I can't believe you never told me."

"It was too painful for me to talk about."

"What about Adrian?" Rory glanced about, as if trying to get her bearings. "Does he know?"

She nodded as tears clogged her throat. "That was why he attacked Peter in the locker room. When I found out I was pregnant, I told Adrian first. I was so scared. Peter wanted me to have an abortion, but I wanted to keep the baby. Adrian talked me into telling Aunt Viv, but we wanted to wait awhile to tell you. You were so young. Then I lost the baby, so there wasn't any need. Adrian was upset but tried to let it go. Then he overheard Peter bragging to some of the boys on the football team. He never told me what Peter said, but I can imagine. Something in Adrian just snapped. It scares me to think what would have happened if the coaches hadn't come to break up the fight."

"Well, at least now it makes more sense. I was so shocked when it happened, because it's not like Adrian at all. He's just not the violent type."

"Normally, no, he's not. But when he's pushed, we both know he has a temper."

"True." Rory shook her head, as if trying to take it all in. "I can't believe none of you ever told me."

"I'm sorry," Allison whispered.

"Well, you should be. To think all these years, y'all have kept this from me, as if I weren't really part of the family. How could you not tell me? If not back then, then when I got pregnant. Jeez—" She rubbed her forehead. "That's why you've been so distant about the baby all this time. Here I've been talking about it in front of you, going on about how excited I was, and all the while . . . Oh, Alli." Rory hugged her with all the fervor and lack of grace she'd had as a child. "I'm so sorry."

"Don't be." Allison sniffed, hugging her back. "I'm the one who's sorry for not sharing your excitement more. I am happy for you and Chance. It's just difficult. I think about all the things that could happen to you or the baby, and I just feel this . . . this horrible fear."

"Fear?"

"Yes." Just mentioning the frightening possibilities had them rushing up inside her, threatening to choke her. "I love you so much." She tightened her arms about her sister. "I don't know what I'd do if anything happened to you or Adrian. I worry all the time that y'all will leave me, like Mom and Dad did. I couldn't handle it, Rory. I couldn't handle losing you. Now suddenly, there's Lauren, and I don't want to love her and have to worry about her, too. I just wish I could go through life not caring about anyone, so that no one I love will ever leave me again."

"Oh, Alli . . ." Rory pulled back, her face stricken. "I didn't know you felt that way. How can you not want love? Do you wish you'd never loved Mom and Dad?"

"No. I just . . ."—her throat constricted—"sometimes, I think, if I'd loved them less, it wouldn't have hurt so much to lose them. And if I'd wanted my baby less, that wouldn't have hurt so much, either. It hurts to love, that's what I'm saying."

"Alli . . ." Rory sat back, staring at her.

"I'm sorry." She sniffed back tears. "I didn't mean to dump that on you. I've never even said all that aloud before."

"But you've thought it. How awful to feel that way."

"Forget I said anything." She wiped angrily at her

cheeks. "I'm sorry. Here's your happy day, and I come along and upset you with things that happened a long time ago. I needed to tell you, though."

"I'm glad you did. You need to talk about this." Rory took her hand. "This is why you said you never want to marry, isn't it? You think if you don't let yourself love anyone, you'll never be hurt again."

She nodded as more tears clogged her throat.

"It's not that easy, though." Rory smiled with a wisdom far beyond her years. "You can't live that isolated and be happy. I know you, Alli. You have too much love inside you to be that stingy with it. I don't remember Mom very well, but I remember you, always taking care of me, reading me stories, teaching me to roller-skate . . . or trying to. You filled my life with love. Now you're saying love causes you nothing but pain?"

"I didn't say that. I said I worry constantly about losing you." She tightened her hands around Rory's. "And that causes me pain."

"I wish I could promise not to die before you do, but that would be ridiculous. None of us knows what the future holds. All we have is here and now. Right here, right now, you have me and Adrian. You have Chance, too, who loves you like a sister. And now you have Lauren. Would you turn your back on all that, push us away, because the future doesn't come with any guarantees?"

"You make it sound silly."

"Not silly, but very sad. Alli, can't you just enjoy now?"

"I don't know."

"Can you try?"

She struggled past the terror of opening her heart, and even that was a big step. She instantly wanted to pull back and hide. Then she thought of how many times Rory, with her fear of crowds and making mistakes, moved full steam ahead. Could she do any less? She swallowed the lump in her throat. "Okay, I'll try."

A mewing sound came from the cradle.

"She's awake." Rory's whole face lit with joy. She got up and lifted the little blanket-wrapped bundle from the bassinet, cooing softly. When she turned, she smiled at Alli. "Do you want to hold her?"

Alli thought about it, then nodded. "Yes, I do."

Rory juggled the squirming baby until she could place her in Alli's arms. "Lauren, this is your Aunt Allison, who's going to be the best aunt in all the world."

"Hello, Lauren," Allison whispered.

Lauren went still at the sound of her voice, blinking up at her with huge blue eyes. And Alli tumbled head first into a whole wide ocean of love.

Chapter 22

SCOTT SAT AT THE DESK, staring at his computer screen. He didn't know why he bothered trying to write when he couldn't think of anything but Allison. He glanced out the window and saw the sun was starting to set. Was she still with her sister?

His mind drifted back to that morning and what Adrian had said, that Allison felt things more deeply than most people, and when she gave her heart she gave it completely. The thought actually gave him hope. If he could make her care for him before she learned the truth, maybe they'd have a chance at building something that would last.

The trick would be winning her heart in the first place. Why would someone so wonderful want to take a chance on him when he knew nothing about healthy relationships?

God, he sounded pathetic, and more insecure than he'd have ever imagined. Which made him doubt his ability to win her even more. His moodiness was only a minor strike against him compared to this new and frightening self-doubt. Women might say they liked "sensitive, vulnerable men," but from personal observation, he'd found quite the opposite to be true. Women flocked to men who treated them with indifference, while men who worried too much about pleasing women were considered wimps.

The problem was, he did want to please Allison. He wanted her to care for him. And for the first time in his life, he wanted to be worthy of someone's caring.

A soft knock on the door jarred him out of his thoughts. "Yes, come in," he called, already standing.

Allison stepped inside, her face aglow with happiness. "Am I interrupting your writing?"

"Not at all. I was hoping you'd come up. Well? How'd your visit with Rory go?"

"Wonderful." Her smile grew brighter, but as he drew near, he saw her eyes were swollen.

"You've been crying."

"Buckets!" She gave a shaky laugh and waved a hand in front of her face. Her other hand remained behind her back, hiding something. "Hard to believe I had any tears left after blubbering all over you last night. But it felt good to finally tell her. So, I wanted to thank you."

"Thank me? For what?"

"For listening, for being here, for being you. You've helped me in so many ways since you got here, sometimes I don't even feel like the same person I was three weeks ago. So, I brought you something." She moved her hand from behind her back and held out a canvas bag.

"What's this?" He took the bag from her.

"The bookstore delivered the books you asked them to find. Plus, I added something you might like."

Reaching into the bag, he lifted out one of several leather-bound books. Opening it, he found the yellowed pages filled with handwriting.

"Marguerite's diaries," Allison said. "Or rather, the English translations my great-grandmother did. I've decided to let you read them, as long as you promise they won't leave the inn."

"Absolutely." Something warm moved through him as he looked up at Alli. "Are you sure?"

"Positive. After yesterday and this morning, I feel as if you're almost part of the family now. Adrian even asked if you might want to use the weight room downstairs."

"You're kidding." The gesture of **acceptance** startled him.

She stepped closer and laid a hand on his cheek. "You've become a very special friend to me, and it feels so good to finally trust someone again. To let myself care for someone."

He closed his eyes as dread washed through him.

"Don't worry," she said quickly. "I'm not expecting anything in return. I won't pressure you—"

"Alli, stop." Regret tightened his chest as he kissed the palm of her hand. Words backed up in his throat, and he had to swallow hard. He couldn't possibly tell her yet. She had to care for him first. Yet the longer he held his silence, the bigger the deceit. "Can we sit down?"

"Certainly."

He set the bag of books on the desk, then took a seat on the sofa. She sat beside him in the soft evening light and lengthening shadows. The innocence and trust in her eyes made his stomach churn.

"Allison, I know we said our relationship would be temporary, but what would you think about continuing to, you know . . . see each other?"

The openness vanished from her face like a wall slamming down between them. "You mean, you go back to New Orleans, and we arrange a few days together here and there? Like what you had with Kelly?"

No, he didn't want that at all. He wanted her in his life completely. But that seemed too much to ask so soon. *Take it slow,* he warned himself as he let out a breath. "Something like that."

She rose abruptly, as if ready to flee, but stopped a few steps away, her back to him. "No. I'm sorry, but . . . no."

The rejection hit him like a fist to the heart. Because she was rejecting *him.* This had nothing to do with her hatred of his family. She simply didn't want *him.* He sat back, trying to catch his breath. "I see. I just thought, we've been enjoying each other's company. At least I've been enjoying yours, so I thought—" *I thought I had a chance, for once in my life, to have something good, something golden and rare.* He stood as well, went to the desk and blindly straightened some papers. "Never mind."

"I can't keep seeing you, because . . ." Her voice broke. "I'm not sure I can keep following the rules. You'd want something friendly, convenient, but I don't think I could keep seeing you without getting . . . emotional. And that wouldn't be convenient at all. Would it?"

To his utter shock, his vision blurred. He turned carefully and found her facing him, fear and hope warring in her eyes. "Actually, it would be. Convenient. See, there's something I think I should tell you." His legs started to shake, so he leaned back against the desk to brace himself. "You see, I'm . . . I'm in love with you."

Color drained from her face and she swayed.

"Allison!" He lunged forward, pulling her against his chest, and he felt her body trembling.

"This wasn't supposed to happen." She looked up at him. "You promised we could control it. That no one would get hurt."

"I lied. I'm sorry. I didn't mean to, it just happened . . ." Smoothing her hair, he willed her to understand. "I've always been able to control my emotions, hold back. Until I met you."

She stared mutely back at him.

"I know you didn't ask for this, that it frightens you. It frightens me, too. But I want to be with you, Alli, more than I've ever wanted anything. Can't we at least give this a chance?"

Tears rose in her eyes. "What if it doesn't work?"

He cupped her face. "Surely we can find a way to make this work, and make it last, if you think you can ever love me a little in return."

Her eyes closed as a sob jerked through her body. "I'm not sure I can. I know I promised Rory I'd quit worrying about the future and live in the present, but I'm not sure I can handle something this huge."

"You don't have to be afraid. We can take it slow. You don't have to give me anything you're not ready for. Just don't push me away." He kissed her cheeks, the corner of her mouth, desperation tearing him apart. "Please don't push me away."

Her arms went around his neck, and she buried her face against his neck. "I couldn't push you away if I wanted. Oh Scott, I'm afraid to love you, but I'm more afraid to lose you. I don't know what to do."

"You do what you just said, stop thinking about the future and live in the here and now. Is that so terribly hard?"

"Yes." She lifted her head to look at him. "After all these years of holding back, it's very hard to let go. To trust fate not to kick me down again. But I'll try. I'm tired of being a coward, so I'll try."

Closing his eyes against a rush of relief and joy, he lowered his mouth to hers and felt as if he were leaping off a cliff. "No more holding back, for either of us," he said between kisses. "Whatever the future brings, we grab this now."

"Yes." She kissed him back as her tears became joyful. "No more holding back." Her heart took flight as he tightened his embrace, lifting her off her feet.

"I love you, Allison." He turned in slow circles of celebration as he kissed her neck, her cheek. They tumbled onto the bed, kissing and touching. He gazed down at her, and she could see the love in his eyes. Awed, she touched his face, let her fingertips trace the line of his nose, his beard, his lips. Had she really thought him cynical and arrogant? With his heart opened to her, he seemed so vulnerable. Love swelled within her, but the words wouldn't come, so she drew his head down to kiss his lips and show him what she felt.

No more holding back. The words made her quiver deep inside as he undressed her. When at last they lay together, skin to skin, with no barriers between them, he looked deep into her eyes. "I love you," he whispered as he moved over her.

She blinked back tears, because the words remained locked in her heart. She could feel them yearning to get out, but she couldn't say them, so she smiled at him in welcome as he settled between her thighs.

"Don't be afraid." He framed her face with his hands as he pressed inside, filling her with his body, and his love. "We'll go as slow as you want. And I'll never intentionally hurt you."

"I know." She smiled as he began to move, slowly, purposefully. Each thrust made her body and her heart ache for release. Clinging to him, she closed her eyes and lost herself to the pleasure of a joining that was somehow different from all the others. She felt connected to his soul, could feel his openness and his vulnerability. The last surprised her, because she'd never suspected he had doubts or fears. Yet it thrilled her too, that he let her see it, feel it.

He took her mouth again in a long kiss as he thrust deep, losing himself and taking her with him. When the pleasure came, she felt her heart crack open. The liberation staggered her, left her as breathless as her physical climax. She stared into space as he held her tight, and kept staring even when he shifted to lie beside her.

As passionate as he'd been in the past, he was equally gentle now. He held her in his arms, kissing her forehead and caressing her with his hands on her back and arms. Never in her life had she felt so cherished. Torn between laughter and tears, she burrowed her face against his chest and squeezed her eyes shut.

How gloriously different making love was from having sex. Now that she knew, she never wanted to go back. Sex was thrilling, but making love was . . . the moon and the stars and the brightness of the sun all rolled into one.

Whatever the future held, she had this moment. She had Scott here and now. And her heart lay open and filled with joy.

The following morning, Scott woke alone, which didn't surprise him. Allison could hardly sleep with him openly with the inn full of guests. Still, it hurt a bit that she hadn't woken him before going downstairs when they'd been so close throughout the night.

The evening had been filled with lazy touches and quiet murmurs. They'd stayed up for hours, talking and making love. She'd told him about Lauren, and he'd talked about his book. She'd asked him about his life, his childhood, his family. He'd answered evasively and encouraged her to talk about her own life instead.

If he wasn't already totally and hopelessly in love with her, last night would have done it. Her openness had fully revealed the qualities that had attracted him from the first: sweetness, honesty, intelligence, and humor. And she was a hairsbreadth away from saying the words he longed to hear.

Smiling like a loon, he rose to take a shower. There was a practical side to falling in love, he realized, humming to himself. Not the emotions, which were completely impractical, but the logistics. Since they couldn't be together at the inn, he needed to find another place to stay. He briefly considered the beach house his mother had won in the divorce settlement, but dismissed the idea just as quickly. Even though he fully intended to tell Allison who he was, he doubted she'd be comfortable there—especially since his derelict cousins liked to use the place to throw weekend parties on occasion.

Should he ask her to help him find an apartment, or

find one on his own and tell her after the fact? As for asking her outright to move in with him, he had a feeling he'd be wiser to ease her into that idea. She could move her things gradually, one overnight bag at a time.

Which brought him to the last obstacle: the tiny, little matter of telling her he'd been born Scott LeRoche.

He stood for a moment, letting the spray of the shower beat down on his back as he imagined what she'd say. In his mind, he saw her smile and call him silly for worrying as she assured him it didn't matter.

Yeah, right, buddy, in your dreams.

He'd think about it later, he decided. He had enough to deal with today already since his sister was coming to pick up Chloe. He'd deal with that first, then decide when and how to tell Allison he was the son of the man who was trying to destroy her business, a member of the family she'd hated all her life. She was jittery enough as it was without dropping that bombshell on her. Yes, waiting to tell her was definitely best.

Chapter 23

ALLISON FELT SCOTT ENTER THE room, like a shift in the air that made her skin tingle. She straightened from pouring a glass of juice for a guest and glanced over her shoulder. He stopped in the doorway, his hands in the pockets of his shorts and a contented smile on his face.

"Morning, Uncle Scott," Chloe called as she plowed through her breakfast of French toast.

"Morning," he said to his niece, but his smiling gaze remained fixed on Allison.

Heat rose in her cheeks. "Can I get you coffee?"

"Depends." He nodded to the nearly full table. "Do you need any help?"

"No. Chance has come down out of the clouds enough to be useful again."

"In that case, I'd love some coffee."

While he went to the buffet, Allison turned her attention back to the other guests, encouraging them to chat among themselves, tell where they were from and their plans for the day.

"Do you know, I think the stories about the Good Luck Ghost are true," one of the new guests, a woman from Dallas, told the others. "I had the most amazing thing happen this morning."

"Oh?" An older woman from Oklahoma City perked up. "Well, don't be stingy, honey. Tell. Tell."

"A year ago, I lost my wedding ring." The Dallas woman smiled apologetically at her husband. "I thought it had been stolen, since I'd left it in a locker while working out at my club. I've looked through everything that was in my gym bag at least a hundred times. Then, this morning, I opened my makeup case, and there it was! Sitting right there winking at me." She held up her left hand, showing off the ring. "Isn't that incredible, that it just reappeared like that?"

Her story sparked the usual debate among the guests about the existence of ghosts in general and Marguerite in particular.

Listening with half an ear, Allison poured some juice for Chloe. "So, are you ready for your mother to pick you up today?"

"Yep." The girl swirled a bite of French toast through a pool of syrup. "Especially since she agreed to take me to all the Zephyrs' home games if I don't run away again."

Scott laughed as he sliced into his pan-fried ham and pineapple. "You are such a little blackmailer."

"Please, if you don't mind, I prefer the term 'opportunist.' "

"Yeah, and the pirates of the gulf preferred the term 'privateer.' "

Chloe sighed dramatically, much to the amusement of the other guests. "The true entrepreneurs of every age are always misunderstood."

" 'Entrepreneurs'? " Scott chuckled. "What have you been doing, reading my thesaurus?"

"Well, if you were a normal guy, like Amy Sutterfield's dad, you'd keep something interesting in your nightstand, like *Playboy* magazines instead of dictionaries."

Everyone laughed as Scott shook his head. "Please, Chloe. There are some things uncles don't want to know."

"Try being a father," one of the men said.

Scott went very still, then slowly raised his gaze to Allison as if considering the idea. Her heart began to pound at the thought of having a child with him. The doctors said she could carry full term, but would she ever have the courage to try for another baby?

"Maybe someday," Scott said to the other man. "Right now, I'm content to take life a day at a time."

Allison nodded, realizing the words were a reminder of their new agreement: no holding back, but no rushing things, either.

"Hey, Chance," Chloe greeted as he came in with a fresh tray for the buffet. "Do you think I could go see the baby before I leave?"

"You bet." A smile split his face. "I'll let Aurora know to expect you."

"Cool."

"You too, Scott," Chance added. "Adrian says you were there for most of the big event, so you might as well come see the end result."

Scott looked a bit startled but pleased by the invitation. "Thanks, I appreciate that."

As the focus of the room shifted to the proud new father, Allison moved over to Scott on the pretense of refilling his coffee cup. "You don't have to go if it makes you feel awkward."

"No, I'd like to see the baby." The closeness of their bodies lent a sense of intimacy. "Can you get away later, though, after Chloe leaves? I'd like to go someplace quiet where we can talk."

A wary look in his eyes made the words sound slightly ominous, but she brushed the notion aside. "I'm sure I can manage something."

"Good." He nodded. "For now, though, I need to get my niece packed and ready to go. Chloe, you done eating?"

"All done." The girl wiped her mouth, and jumped up. He mussed her hair as they headed out of the dining room.

Allison watched them go, marveling at the kind heart that lay hidden beneath Scott's cynical facade. What a wonderful husband and father he would make . . . if she ever had the courage to take that sort of risk. If he was even thinking along those lines. Nerves fluttered in her belly, but she stilled them with a deep breath. *Think about the here and now.*

Allison stayed busy the rest of the morning with guests browsing through the shop before checking out. The steady traffic kept her from going with Scott and Chloe to see the baby, but in a way, she was glad. The last two days had held enough emotional upheaval. Seeing Scott hold baby Lauren might be more than she could handle.

So even when she found herself alone in the shop with nothing to do, she grabbed a feather duster and busied herself cleaning displays. In all, she was quite pleased with how calm she felt, and even more pleased with her family's acceptance of the man she'd decided to let into her life.

Things were going to be fine, she told herself. Just fine.

"Hello?" someone called.

Allison turned at the sound of the voice and saw a tall, elegant woman standing in the central hall wearing a bright purple pantsuit and lethal-looking high heels. The woman's stance reminded her of Chloe's pampered-rich-girl act the day she'd first arrived.

Smiling, Allison stepped into the hall and offered her hand in greeting. "Hello. You must be Chloe's mother, Diane. I'm Allison."

The woman raised a brow as she took in Allison's simple sundress, worn sandals, and scant makeup, then dismissed her with a dramatic wave of the hand. "Sorry if I'm late. You would not be-*lieve* the morning I've had. First the limo service I hired to pick me up at Houston Hobby apparently *lost* the order. If you can imagine. Lost it! I had to rent a car on the spot. Of course, they couldn't have anything sporty or even nice. I'd have settled for some boring luxury car, but no, all they had was a 'compact.' I've decided they call them compacts because they aren't any bigger than a makeup case, for heaven's sake. Uncomfortable seats, *no* acceleration, and the road noise . . . Gawd, it's so loud, you can barely hear the radio. Well, no matter, I'm here, I'm famished, and I plan to drag my reclusive brother away from the computer long enough for him to take me and Chloe out for lunch. I trust he's around."

"Mom!" Chloe gave a happy shriek from the stairs, then bounded forward to launch herself into her mother's arms.

"Ooo, baby, I missed you," Diane cooed in a childish voice against her daughter's hair. "Are you all packed and ready to go?"

"Yep. Did you meet Alli? She's really neat." Chloe turned to Allison with her head against her mother's. The nearly identical features looked completely different; Chloe with her ball cap and baggy clothes, Diane with her sleek hair and expertly applied makeup. "This is my mom."

"So I gathered." Allison marveled at the reunion. Two weeks ago, Chloe had run away from this woman, now she welcomed her with a child's unconditional love.

"Come up and see my room." Chloe tugged on her mother's hand. "I'll tell you all about the sunken ship in the cove and the ghosts and everything."

"Chloe, can't we just get your things and go? My head is splitting and I already know about the ship and the ghosts. Or have you forgotten, we used to own this place? Of course, back then, it was a dilapidated dump." She glanced around. "This is a vast improvement."

Allison went very still, certain she'd heard wrong. "What did you say?"

"A vast improvement. You've really fixed the place up."

"No," Alli whispered, "about owning the house."

Chloe's face went stiff, while Diane trailed a hand through the air. "Surely Scott told you our father, John LeRoche, owned the house until a year ago."

"Mo-*om*!" Chloe glared at her.

"But how can that be?" Ice formed in Allison's stomach. "His name is Lawrence, not LeRoche."

"Oh, that's just a name he took to piss off John. I can't believe he didn't tell you all this since he's been here, what, three weeks?"

"Mo*ther*!" Chloe grabbed Diane's arm. "We told you not to say anything."

"What?" Diane blinked, then tapped her forehead with her manicured nails. "Oh yes. I remember now. Scott didn't want anyone here to know for some reason. Sorry, I forgot." She smiled and shrugged. "Where is he, by the way?"

"I'll go get him," Allison offered in an even voice, then headed for the steps on wooden legs. Behind her, she could hear Chloe berating her mother, but the words couldn't compete with the buzzing in her head.

Anger and pain mounted with every step. She watched with detachment as her fist lifted and rapped on the door to his room. He opened it and smiled at her, that wonderful lopsided smile that she'd grown to love. Actually love! What a fool she'd been to trust fate again.

A lump rose in her throat, and she wondered frantically if it was a mistake. Maybe she'd misunderstood Diane. "May I come in?"

"Absolutely." He glanced into the hall, to be sure they were alone, then slipped a hand about her arm and started to draw her toward him.

"No!" She held up a hand. "Don't. Don't touch me." She moved all the way into the sitting area to get away from him. Her breath felt trapped in her chest, and she couldn't seem to get any air out or in.

"Allison? What is it?"

She turned to face him. "Your sister's here."

His expression turned wary as he closed the door. "And?"

"Is it true? Are you . . . are you John LeRoche's son?"

Scott closed his eyes. "I was going to tell you."

"Oh, my God." She covered her mouth.

"I swear, I was going to tell you."

"When?" she demanded. "You've been here three weeks!"

"I know, but I couldn't. Not before." He started toward her, needing to hold her and soothe her. "You've got to believe me—"

"Do not touch me!" She stepped away with her arms wrapped about her middle. "How could you do this? Was it all some kind of joke? Were you calling your father to brag and laugh behind my back?"

"Allison, how can you say that? How can you even think it! I would never use you, or any woman, that way." He moved closer, and this time when she tried to step away, he slipped a hand about her arm. "Listen to me, I'm not Peter. I don't use women, then brag about it. You can scream at me for not telling you I'm related to John LeRoche, but don't hang some other man's sins on me."

"Why didn't you tell me? Did you come here to spy on us? To help your father win the lawsuit?"

"No! It had nothing to do with him. In the beginning, I didn't tell you because I don't tell anyone. That's why I never do personal interviews. My connection to John LeRoche is nobody's business. As for my name, I didn't lie, it is Scott Lawrence. I had it changed legally years ago before I was even published."

"Changing your name doesn't change who you are. You're still his son, and you never told me. For the past three weeks, we've been—" She motioned toward the bed. "How could you do this to me?"

"Because if I'd told you in the beginning, you wouldn't have let me stay here."

She searched his eyes. "Why did you want to stay? If not to spy on us."

"For exactly the reason I said. I was in a writing slump and hoped being here would get me out of it. And it has. The book is going great. Everything's back on track for me."

"Your writing slump," she echoed numbly, as if mentally fitting the pieces together. "You thought your slump was because your family lost Pearl Island. So you came here to use Marguerite."

"You knew from the beginning I hoped her charm would help. If it didn't bother you then, why now?"

"I didn't know you were a LeRoche then."

"Does that matter? Hell, you claim to be one of Henri's direct descendants. If that's true, you're as much a LeRoche as I am."

"It matters because you lied."

He started to explain that he'd hoped she'd come to care for him enough to accept him anyway. But looking in her eyes, he realized she'd closed herself off from him completely. Nothing he said would change her mind. "Don't do this, Alli. I'm begging you—" His throat closed around the words. "We're so close to having something special, don't throw it away over things that have nothing to do with you and me personally."

"It has everything to do with us, because what we came from is part of us. Your side of the family stole our inheritance and spread so much slander about us we've lived on the fringe of acceptable society for generations while you've lived in the lap of luxury. And now, when we finally have a chance to regain what was taken from us, your own father is trying to drive us into bankruptcy so he can steal it back. You've known that for weeks, yet you said nothing." She shook her head. "If you'd lie about something as basic as who you are, how can I trust you about anything?"

"You *can* trust me." He nearly got down on his knees and begged her to listen, but he stopped himself. What good would it do but postpone the inevitable? He'd known all along it wouldn't last, but God, he'd hoped it would last longer than this.

"Fine." He turned away, unable to look at her without touching her. "If you want to play this out like some modern-day version of the Hatfields and McCoys, go ahead. Wallow in it."

He felt her standing there staring at him a long time. Finally she headed for the door, and he told himself to let her go—squeezed his eyes against the tearing pain in his chest.

"Allison." Her name slipped past his lips of its own will. He looked over his shoulder and found her standing with one hand on the doorknob, her back to him. "It doesn't have to be like this. I know you're scared, but don't use this as an excuse to run away."

She turned her head and he saw the tears streaming down her cheeks. "I trusted you, and you lied to me."

"I never meant to hurt you."

"Well, you succeeded." She opened the door. "I want you gone. I'm going to go down to the apartment for a while, and when I come back up, I want all trace of you gone."

"Allison—"

"No." She held up her hand. "Just go." The moment the door closed, he collapsed onto the settee and buried his face in his hands. What a fool he'd been. What an utter fool!

Chapter 24

SCOTT LOST HIMSELF IN HIS work. Rather than return to New Orleans, where too many people knew how to find him, he moved into the beach house on Galveston. The only person who knew he was there was his mother. He'd called her out of courtesy to ask if he could stay there, and to be sure no other family members were planning a visit in the near future.

Assured of his privacy, he set up his laptop on the student desk in his old room upstairs where he'd done some of his very first writing, and dove into the story. When he wasn't writing, he swam laps in the pool, pushing himself to the point of exhaustion, anything to block out memories of Allison.

In those moments when reality intruded into his conscious mind, he told himself he didn't care. Her rejection could only hurt if he let it. He'd never wanted to get tangled up in a relationship in the first place. Loving someone gave them carte blanche to rip your heart to shreds. He was glad he'd gotten out of it before she'd become any more a part of his life.

As for the pain that knifed through him at unexpected moments, he assured himself that it wouldn't last. It couldn't.

By the third week of his self-imposed exile, he'd reached a state of total numbness. Nothing touched him. Nothing mattered. He worked to block out reality, yet couldn't care less what happened with the book. Normally, his work and his privacy were all he cared about. Now he had them in abundance, and they meant nothing.

   Ironically, he thought *In Deep* was shaping up to be the best thing he'd ever written.

   The day he finished the rough draft, he decided it was time for a break. He opened a bottle of Chardonnay and carried it and the phone out to the back deck. The afternoon sun pierced his eyeballs, and he realized he hadn't been outside for a few days. Since he didn't want to risk running into one of the St. Claires, he'd taken to calling taxi drivers to pick up anything he needed and deliver it to the house.

   Taking a seat in a deck chair by the pool, he stared out at the gulf where sea gulls dipped and screeched at the surf. His mind drifted back to the day he and Alli had ridden horses along the beach. He could see her so clearly, laughing and happy, her lithe body atop the gray mare, the sun on her face and the wind in her hair.

   Then she'd seen the beach house, and her laughter had faded. She'd refused to even ride by for fear that someone might be out on the deck where he now sat, and she'd be forced to wave.

   Heaven forbid she should have to be nice to someone named LeRoche. He snorted and took a drink of wine. What a sap he'd been to think he could overcome generations of animosity. Closing his eyes, he leaned his head back and tried to relax as the sun warmed his bare chest and legs. Adrian had been right when he'd said Allison felt more deeply than most people. She also didn't forgive easily, and he'd bet money she never forgot.

   How sad that her very capacity to love so completely was what kept her from loving at all. Her greatest strength was also her greatest weakness. And the quality that made him fall for her in the first place was what made her unobtainable.

   The ache rose hard and fast, tightening his chest and throat, all the more painful after days of numbness. Squeezing his eyes shut, he fought the need to be with her. To see her, touch her, hear her voice. If only he could find some way to open the locks she'd put on her heart. But he couldn't. Only she could do that, and she was too angry, or too afraid, to even try.

He rubbed a hand over his face, and realized he hadn't trimmed his beard in days. No doubt his hair could use a trim as well. The last time he'd bothered to glance in the mirror, he'd looked like hell.

In need of a distraction, he picked up the phone and punched in his agent's number. When Hugh's voice came on the line, Scott lifted his glass of wine toward the gulf. "Say cheers, pal."

"Scott?" Hugh nearly shouted. "Good God! Where are you? I've been trying to reach you for weeks. Do you have any clue what this little disappearing act did to my blood pressure?"

"Aren't you going to ask what we're drinking to?"

"Only if you're calling to say you finished the book."

"How about the rough draft?"

"That depends. Is it any good?"

"It's fabulous. Or will be when I finish filling in a few holes."

"What size holes?"

"Mostly background color, polishing, that sort of thing." He decided not to mention the book had two ghosts, one of which played a much larger role than he'd ever intended. Ever since the day he'd gone down to see the ship, Captain Jack Kingsley had lived in the back of his mind. His story—or rather Scott's imaginary version of his story—had spilled out onto the pages. "It needs work, but what I have so far will knock Penny's socks off."

"It better, since she's about to have a coronary."

"She's too young to have a coronary."

"She's an editor," Hugh said. "They age quickly."

"True."

"She's also not the only woman looking for you."

"Oh?" Scott went still.

"Does the name Allison St. Claire ring any bells?"

He leaned forward, bracing himself against a wild rush of hope. "What does she want?"

"Not much. Your head on a platter. Your skin nailed to the wall. And the diaries she says you stole."

"The diaries?" His mind raced. Could he have accidentally tossed Marguerite's diaries into the car the day he left the inn? He'd unpacked his clothes and most of his books, but not all of them, so it was possible.

"You should also warn me," Hugh said, "the next time you piss someone off that badly. Here I innocently call down there looking for you, and sweet little Allison, the epitome of Texas friendly, nearly flames me to a crisp. What possessed you to steal the woman's diaries?"

"It's a long story."

"Well, I trust you'll take care of it, so she'll quit calling here leaving messages for you."

"What messages?" Hope stirred again, the sadistic beast.

"That she wants her diaries back."

"That's it? That's all she says?"

"I'm afraid it would offend my gentlemanly sensibilities to repeat the rest."

"Yeah, right." Scott snorted. Hugh had the sensibilities of a sailor and they both knew it.

When they finished their conversation, Scott went straight upstairs to the bedroom he was using. The place was a wreck with the bed unmade, clothes on the floor, books and papers stacked everywhere. He wondered why he hadn't noticed before. On a shelf over the desk, he spied the book bag Allison had given him and let out a curse. He knew what had happened. The last research books he'd ordered were ones he hadn't needed after all, so he'd forgotten about them.

Pulling the bag down, he opened it and groaned. Sure enough, there were Marguerite's diaries. He sank to the chair and debated what to do. The quickest solution would be to call the taxi company and have one of the drivers deliver the volumes safely back into Allison's hands. Yet the more he stared at them, the more the secrets within the pages whispered seductively to him.

How accurately had he portrayed Marguerite and Jack?

What had his distant uncle, Henri LeRoche, really been like?

And—far more important—if he could understand Allison's anger toward his family, could he find a way around it?

Unable to resist, he thumbed through the volumes until he had them stacked in chronological order. Then he climbed into bed with his back against the headboard, his glass of wine on the nightstand, and began to read. He skimmed through the first few volumes, since the ramblings of an adolescent girl held little interest. Although some of the historical insights about New Orleans in the early 1800s piqued his interest, especially once Marguerite took to the stage. Her wealth grew apace with her fame, and—much to her amusement—men fell at her feet in droves. With no intention of becoming a rich man's mistress, she turned them all away, until Henri came into her life.

Scott's focus instantly sharpened as he read through weeks' worth of entries, detailing Henri's relentless campaign to prove his love was real, that it had nothing to do with her stage persona or the stories of her birth. *What a total bastard*, Scott thought, long before Marguerite realized the same. He wanted to shake the woman for not seeing the truth right from the start, but reminded himself she was still quite young at that point in her life and remarkably innocent for someone who had been raised by a prostitute. Not innocent in knowledge, but in nature. She found humor and happiness in everything around her. His heart ached knowing the painful lessons she was about to learn.

By the time Jack Kingsley was first mentioned, Henri had nearly succeeded in obliterating that innocent spirit. God, the things Marguerite had endured! Scott's stomach rolled with anger. No wonder Nicole hadn't fought harder to prove her legitimacy after the man's death. She'd probably thought: "Fine, he doesn't want to claim me, I don't want to claim him, either."

Scott could certainly understand that, since he'd basically done the same thing.

The more he read about Jack, though, the more the hair on his arms stood on end. The man who unfolded to him through Marguerite's words bore more than a passing similarity to his imaginary Jack. Never in his life could he remember anyone telling him that Jack Kingsley had an illegitimate son by a barmaid. Even so, he'd put it in his book, claiming one of his characters was a descendant of Jack's. And here it was. In Marguerite's diary. Jack had had a son. By a barmaid.

Though Jack never married the mother, and clearly had little liking for the woman, his son had meant the world to him. Since Nicole was about the same age, Jack and Marguerite talked of their children often. Other things, too, jumped off the page. Like the fact that Kingsley hated talking about himself, rarely giving Marguerite any facts about his past.

His reluctance had caused Marguerite to doubt his love, but Scott could understand it all too well. Couldn't she *see* he was ashamed of his past and felt unworthy of her? The man might have been a blockade runner, willing to face Union gunboats, but he was a coward when it came to love. *How could she not see that!*

Exasperated with Marguerite's lack of perception and her inability to trust her own judgment, much less trust

Jack, Scott tossed the diaries aside, determined to get some sleep since it was the middle of the night by then. Two people that stupid deserved to die apart rather than grow old together. Idiots. Total idiots. He lay awake and fumed for nearly an hour before he turned the bedside lamp back on and continued to read.

By the time color stained the eastern horizon, he felt weighed down by sorrow. Marguerite and Jack had been so close to overcoming all the obstacles that lay between them, but had let their chance at happiness slip through their fingers.

Gazing out the window, he turned the whole story over in his mind, wondering what had happened after the diaries ended. He knew Henri had concocted a story for the authorities to explain the incident: Marguerite had tripped and fallen down the stairs while trying to run away with her lover, who happened to be a Union spy. *Lying bastard.*

Nicole had probably known the truth but either hadn't told anyone, or no one would listen. She'd gone on to achieve wealth and fame on her own, but had died a destitute divorcée in the cottage her father had built to banish her from Pearl Island.

But what had happened to Jack's son?

Acting on a hunch, Scott called Paige at the tour boat office and asked her again for the name and number of the woman in Corpus Christi, the one whose father had been so enamored of Jack Kingsley's story.

The champagne cork popped toward the ceiling amid a chorus of cheers. "Gather round, folks," Chance called.

Allison joined the others—Rory, Adrian, Bobby, and Paige—around the kitchen island in the basement apartment. She still couldn't believe the whole sordid business with John LeRoche had ended so abruptly. They'd all been braced to go to court and endure months of suits and countersuits. But that morning, Chance's attorney called to say John wanted to settle in their favor. By afternoon, they'd agreed to an amount so huge it left all of them staggered.

When the glasses were filled, Chance held his up. "To success."

"To brothers-in-law who know how to hire good lawyers," Adrian countered.

"No." Rory smiled. "To Marguerite for bringing us good luck."

"To Marguerite," Allison agreed.

Paige and Bobby, who had dropped by for an impromptu visit and been drawn into the celebration, lifted their glasses as well.

"Congratulations," Paige said. "I know how much this inn means to all of you. Although I wonder what made John LeRoche change his mind."

"I asked Malcolm that very question," Chance said, referring to their attorney. His gaze flickered toward Allison, then away. "Apparently we have Scott to thank."

Allison went still at the mention of his name. The mood in the room dimmed as everyone glanced at her. "It's okay." She forced a smile, tired of people walking on eggshells around her. "I can handle talking about him."

Although nothing could be further from the truth. Just the sound of his name tore at her heart.

"Well," Chance said cautiously, "when it was over, Malcolm chatted a bit with the opposition, hoping he could wheedle out some hint of what made John cave so unexpectedly. The other attorney, who's dropping LeRoche Enterprises from their client list, by the way, came right out and told him Scott called several times last month, carrying on a heated argument with his father through the law firm."

"He passes messages to his father through an attorney?" Rory asked, clearly stunned while Allison digested the news that Scott had been making these calls while staying at the inn. At least that explained why he frequently closed the door to the office while on the phone.

"Apparently that's the only way they've communicated for the past ten years," Chance explained. "This particular argument ended when Scott threatened to cause a public relations nightmare for LeRoche Enterprises by depicting the shipping company as environmental rapists in one of his books if John didn't settle favorably with us. John threatened to sue him if he did. So for the past month, John's lawyers have been convincing him that with the financial problems he's been having lately he was better off losing the suit to us now than risking bankruptcy down the road."

Allison stared at the counter, remembering how she'd accused Scott of spying on them to help John win the house back. But the opposite was true. He'd been fighting for them, choosing them over his own family.

Hope tried to open her heart, but past pain slammed it closed. If only he'd been honest earlier . . . She understood the initial deception, but not how long he'd let it continue.

Adrian draped his arm over her shoulder in a reassuring hug. "You okay?"

"I'm fine." She summoned a smile and lifted her glass. "I suppose we should make one more toast. To Scott Lawrence, for proving that the pen really is mightier than the sword."

"To Scott," the others echoed awkwardly and drank.

Lauren began to fuss from her carrier on the sofa and Rory went to check on her. The others followed and talk turned to the bungalows they could now build with the money from the settlement. Rory, as usual, had big plans and visions for turning the island into a full resort, not just a place to stay while visiting Galveston, but a destination in and of itself. For once, Chance didn't play devil's advocate. He just watched his wife with the bemused expression he sometimes got, as if he'd been hit by a happy truck.

Allison sat slightly apart from the others, struggling with confusion. For weeks, she'd been devastated by the pain of Scott's betrayal. Yet, beneath the shock, the longing remained, pulling her under until she feared she'd drown in sorrow. She missed him, dammit. She missed Scott Lawrence.

But she missed a man who wasn't real.

Or was he?

If only she knew what to think.

Enough, she told herself with a little shake. Nothing changed the fact that he'd continued to lie even when he learned how she felt about such things. She could never bring herself to trust him now.

But was that really why she'd sent him away? Or had she jumped on the first excuse to play the coward?

Whatever the answer, it was done and she needed to get on with her life—a life that would now be filled with the security she'd always wanted. She should be happy.

Although turning her attention back to Rory, who sat on the sofa bouncing Lauren on her shoulder with Chance at her side, she felt only the gaping hole of emptiness inside her. For one brief, shining moment, she'd thought she had the opportunity for that with Scott. She thought she'd found something worth risking her heart, risking hurt, risking everything for.

Needing a little space to herself, she headed for her bedroom on the pretext of working on her bridesmaid dress. Rory's wedding was a ways off, but working on the plans gave her something to think about other than Scott.

Rather than go for a full bridal gown confection, complete with acres of gauzy net, Rory had wanted something more personal and understated. So Alli had gone with her over to the Bouchard cottage and hauled down boxes from the attic. Together they'd picked out two of their grandmother's dresses from the 1920s. For Rory they'd selected a tea-length gown made of dusky pink silk covered in ecru lace. For Alli they'd picked a lavender dress in a similar drop-waist style, but without the lace.

Lifting the lavender gown off the end of her bed, she took a seat in the chair beneath the window with Sadie curled up at her feet. She'd barely taken a stitch on altering the hem when Paige knocked on the frame of the open door. "May I come in?"

"Of course."

Paige came forward and sat on the end of the bed, her expression earnest. "I've been needing to talk to you all evening."

"Oh?" Allison frowned.

"The whole reason Bobby and I came over is because"—she bit her lip—"Scott called me today."

Alli's stomach fell. To hear his name had been a shock, but to hear that he'd actually spoken with someone in her intimate circle had all the longing she'd tried to suppress welling up inside her. "What did he say?"

"He wanted to talk to me about Jackie Taylor, but he also asked if I'd deliver a message. He has the diaries you're looking for and claims he didn't even realize it until he talked to his agent yesterday."

"And?" she said, anger and hope playing tug-of-war.

"He said you could come pick them up anytime."

"Pick them up?" Allison gaped as anger won. "What—he thinks I'm going to drive to New Orleans to pick up property he stole from me?"

"Actually . . ." Paige's eyes held sympathy. "He's here in Galveston. At his family's beach house."

Scott was in Galveston? Her heart raced at the thought. She stared blindly into space as she realized that with a five-minute drive, she could see him, talk to him. Five minutes.

"Alli, he sounded so miserable. He asked how you were, and I could tell he's hurting as much as you are. Maybe you should go see him."

"No!" She jerked her attention back to Paige. "That would only make things worse." If she saw him, she'd start wanting him again on so many levels, physically, emotionally. She shook her head. "Definitely not. The situation is hopeless."

"Why? Because your families don't like each other? Trust me, I know all about having your family disapprove of who you love. Although I think your family is more willing to accept him than you realize."

"They were willing before—" She closed her eyes against temptation. "Paige, he lied to me. *Lied!*"

"People do that on occasion. Sometimes because they think they have to, other times because they're lying to themselves as well. Look, I don't know what all happened between you two, but I do know when I see two people who are crazy in love with each other. The two of you were good together. You made each other happy. Surely everything else is incidental."

Oh God, how she wanted that to be true. How she wanted a chance to work things out; for the Scott she'd fallen in love with to be real. She squeezed her eyes shut to hold back the tears. "I don't know."

"Go see him, Alli. Talk to him."

The thought made her ache with yearning. Did she dare risk it? Could she handle seeing him again? "I'll think about it."

Chapter 25

SCOTT HEARD THE DOORBELL AND lifted his head in surprise. The movement sent the air mattress rocking beneath him. Squinting against the sunlight, he wondered if Allison had finally built up the courage to face him. Several days had passed since he'd spoken to Paige, but the prickly feeling on his neck told him it was Allison at the door.

Great, he thought. She would pick a day when he felt like hell from too much work and not enough sleep. Of course, that described all his days lately—which was why he'd been trying to relax in the pool.

To wash off the sheen of sweat, he dove underwater and glided to the edge. Water sloshed off his body as he hoisted himself up. He gave his skin a brisk rubdown with the towel and grabbed his shirt. If only he had five minutes to make himself presentable, he thought as he padded barefoot through the air-conditioned house. In the white marble foyer, he stopped, took a breath, and rolled his head to loosen his shoulders.

It didn't help. The instant he opened the door and saw her standing there, his gut tightened with a shock of need. She wore a sleeveless sunshine-yellow dress and stood with her arms crossed as she stared at the ground. She looked up and his heart tumbled into her clear gray eyes framed in dark lashes.

"Allison," he greeted her in a remarkably calm voice.

Her eyes widened a bit as she took in his open shirt and wet swim trunks. Then she frowned when she noticed that his hair had grown longer and he'd shaved off his beard a couple days ago. Of course, he hadn't bothered shaving since, so he assumed he looked as ragged as he felt. "It's good to see you."

She looked away. "I came for the diaries." Her utterly flat voice killed any hope that she'd come to work things out.

What had he expected, though? For her to throw herself into his arms and beg him to forgive her for kicking him out of her life without letting him explain?

"Of course. Come in." He stepped back. She hesitated, and he gritted his teeth against a surge of anger. "You know, it won't kill you to breathe the same air as me for a few minutes."

Her chin went up as she stepped inside. Without a word, he led her to the great room at the back of the house with its soaring, two-story windows and all-white decor. The room reflected his mother's taste, which ran toward the expensive, sleek, and utterly cold.

"Can I get you anything to drink?"

"No." Her posture remained rigid.

He ground his teeth against the urge to curse and shake her, or beg her to talk to him. Instead, he let out a sigh. "Wait here. I'll get them."

Leaving her standing in the middle of the room, he went upstairs where he took a minute to slip on a pair of dry shorts, then grabbed the canvas bag. When he stepped back onto the open metal landing that overlooked the great room, he stopped for a moment, struck by the sight of her. She stood in her simple yellow dress with her back to him, gazing out the wall of glass at the swimming pool and beach beyond. She was the only spot of warm color in the room.

God, he missed her. And even knowing it was hopeless, he still wanted her.

She turned as he headed down the stairs, and for a fraction of a second, he thought he saw a reflection of his own longing in her eyes. He'd wondered many times what he'd say if this moment ever came. Words had always been his ally, but they abandoned him now when he needed them most.

Crossing to her, he held out the bag. "I assume Paige explained I took them by accident."

"Yes." When she opened the bag to glance inside, he saw her hands tremble. "I shouldn't have accused you the way I did. I'm sorry."

The apology renewed that spark of hope, dammit. Was there anything more painful in life than hope? "Allison, do you think we could sit down and talk for just a minute?"

"I . . . I can't." Tension radiated from her body as she clasped the bag to her chest. "I need to go."

"Do you hate me so much you can't even sit and talk this out?"

"I don't hate you." She pressed a hand over her eyes. "I wish I did. Oh God, I wish I did. If only I could hate you, I'd quit wondering if it might have worked." A ragged sob escaped her. "I have to go."

She turned to flee, but he grabbed her arm. "Allison, wait."

"No! Please . . ." She bit her lip to regain control. Seeing him again was so much harder than she'd imagined. "Please don't touch me. I can't stand it."

"Why not? If you don't hate me—"

"Because I still want you." She turned back, drinking in the sight of him standing there with his damp black hair and black beard stubble. He'd never looked more desirable. "I don't even know who you are, but I remember the illusion and I want it to be true. I want you to be Scott Lawrence and in love with me. Why can't you be who I thought you were?"

"I am Scott Lawrence," he said with quiet force. "And I never lied about loving you."

She searched his face, wanting desperately for the

words to be true. "I wish I could believe you."

"I love you, Allison." He cupped her face and stared into her eyes as if willing her to believe. "Dammit, I love you so much, it's ripping me up inside."

She shook her head as tears tumbled down her cheeks.

"Please believe me." He pressed his forehead to hers. "I am Scott Lawrence, and I love you with everything that's inside of me. *I love you.*"

A sob went through her as she circled her free arm around his neck. His lips moved over her face until his mouth covered hers. Desire rushed through her as she kissed him back, welcoming his taste. The need to touch him one last time outweighed reason. She pushed his shirt aside to run her hands over his sun-heated flesh and taut muscles.

"I want you so much," she cried against his chest. "I can't stop wanting you."

"You don't have to stop." He took the canvas bag from her, set it on the glass and chrome coffee table. His fingers fumbled as he worked the buttons down the front of her dress. "Don't ever stop."

Cool air brushed her skin as the dress fell to the floor. His hands covered her breasts, making her arch with need. Together, they stumbled toward the sofa, shedding the last remnants of clothing. He pulled her down with him, kissing her neck, her shoulder, her breasts.

She couldn't stop touching and kissing his body. Even as grief clogged her throat, she climbed on top of him, running her hands and her mouth over his torso. His body quivered as he pulled her to him for an openmouthed kiss, both of them ravenous. She reached between their bodies, took hold of him. Lifting her hips, she pressed his hardened length to her, desperate to feel him inside her again.

"Alli, no!" He jerked back. "I don't have a condom."

"I don't care," she wept and sank down hard and fast, taking all of him at once. He bucked to unseat her, but only drove himself deeper. She leaned forward to whisper in his ear. "Love me one last time. Please love me."

"I do." With a groan, he pulled her mouth to his for a soul-stirring kiss. His hands ran over her body, caressing and encouraging. As the pleasure built, she arched back, losing herself in the feel of him hard and deep inside her. He cupped her breasts, making her moan, before he trailed one hand down her stomach to where they were joined.

The moment he touched her, bright spots of pleasure danced through her. She looked down at him and saw the determination in his eyes as he focused all his attention on pleasing her, even as he gritted his teeth to hold his own climax at bay.

No, she wanted to moan. *Come with me. Be with me.* Tightening her muscles, she rode him harder, wanting the emotional connection they'd shared.

But it was gone. She'd thrown that closeness back in his face, and now even as he tried to please her body, he didn't trust her not to hurt him again. She didn't know how she knew, she just felt it, felt him holding himself back from her. The loss crashed through her. She wanted all of him. Leaning forward, she kissed the pulse point in his neck the way that made him shiver, and ran her hands over him, desperate to recapture what she'd rejected. She could feel the connection, the mutual joy, so close, *so close*.

She tightened around him, but her efforts sent her over the edge without him.

An instant after she peaked, he pushed her hips up so he could pull out, then he clasped her to him as his body bucked and he released his seed against her stomach. *No!* she wanted to scream, devastated that he gave her physical pleasure but denied her the rest. Denied her the emotional connection.

The loss broke the last of her control, and grief came gushing out of her in a torrent of tears—all the love and anger and fear. She balled a fist and hit his chest. "Why couldn't you be real?"

"God, Alli, I'm so sorry." His arms tightened around her and he rocked her back and forth. "I'm so goddamned sorry."

He held her like that as she cried, held her until her throat ached and her eyelids felt like sandpaper, until everything inside her felt hollowed out. When she finally subsided, she couldn't bring herself to look at him. She felt too exposed to face anyone, even herself.

A long moment passed in horrifying silence. Finally, he kissed her forehead and shifted out from under her. "Wait here," he whispered hoarsely.

She lay numbly, staring at the sunlight shining with blinding brightness off the white marble floor. By the time her sluggish brain thought about grabbing her clothes and running, it was too late. He came back in the room, walking toward her fully nude, carrying a white washcloth and a towel.

"Thank you," she croaked and reached for the cloth.

He pushed her hand aside and nudged her onto her back so he could wash her stomach and between her thighs. She draped an arm over her eyes for a pretense at privacy.

"Since that isn't exactly the most reliable way to prevent pregnancy, mind if I ask when you had your last period?"

"It ended two days ago."

"Well, we have that in our favor at least." When he finished, he dropped the towel to the floor, but didn't move. "You'll tell me, though, if there's a problem."

"There won't be." Although, suddenly, she almost wished she would get pregnant. She pushed the thought aside as irrational.

"Are you ever going to look at me?"

"No." Her voice sounded as raw as it felt.

"Allison . . ." He sighed. "I never lied about how I felt. If you can bring yourself to believe that, maybe we still have a chance."

She squeezed her eyes as they threatened to tear up again. "I don't think we do."

"Because I'm John LeRoche's son? If I could change that, I would go down today and have a blood transfusion. If it helps, I assure you, he's not a part of my life. He's a part of my past."

"It's not just that. It's . . . I don't know. I can't *trust* you." She covered her face with her hands. "You *lied* to me."

He rubbed his brow in frustration, searching for some way around the wall she'd put between them. His gaze landed on the canvas bag, and he narrowed his eyes as a thought struck him. "Alli, when did you first read Marguerite's diaries?"

"What?" The unexpected question made her look at him in surprise.

"How old were you?"

"What does that have to do with anything?" She sat up and scooted into the corner of the sofa, but she couldn't stand up unless he moved and he wasn't budging. She finally settled for wrapping her arms about her raised knees.

"I think it has a lot to do with the problems we're having," he said, "because you won't let go of the past. I'll admit, Henri was a total bastard. He misled Marguerite right from the beginning. But all that happened a hundred and fifty years ago so I'm having a little trouble understanding why you can't get past it."

"Because it's still affecting us," she insisted passionately. "He disowned his daughter, and people have been whispering behind our backs ever since."

"You're right. He was a bastard about that, too."

"Then you accept that Nicole was legitimate?"

"I do, which I guess makes us cousins—albeit very, very distant ones, thank God." He tried for a smile, but she didn't return it. "I still say that has nothing to do with us. I personally haven't stolen anything from you or your family. Besides, you own the house now, and from what I hear you just got a huge settlement from my side of the family, so the score has evened up a bit."

"Yes." Her voice turned subdued. "I suppose I should thank you for helping out. We heard about what you did."

"You're welcome. Although, for the record, it was an empty threat. I may not like my father, but I don't hate him enough to intentionally try to destroy him."

"Oh." Her brow dimpled in a frown, and he wondered if his statement pleased or disappointed her.

"If we can get back to my question, how old were you when you read the diaries?"

"About fourteen, I think. I don't know, I read them more than once."

He softened his voice for the next question, knowing it would upset her. "Did you read them after you lost the baby?"

Her back jerked straight. "I don't see how that has anything to do with anything." Pushing at him, she tried to swing her feet to the floor.

"Hang on." He braced his hands on the sofa arm and back, trapping her.

"You have no right to bring that up." She shoved against his chest with balled fists. "I spilled my guts to you, opened up parts of my life I've never shared with anyone, and all the while, you were lying to me."

He started to argue, but saw more than fury in her eyes. He saw vulnerability. "Would you like to get dressed before we talk about this?"

"I'd like to leave."

He stood and she scrambled off the sofa. Gathering her clothes, she struggled into them as he pulled on his shorts and shirt. While her back was to him, he picked up the canvas bag and sat back on the sofa. She grabbed her purse and fumbled for the keys, then looked about for the diaries. When she saw him holding them her back straightened.

"Give them to me." She held her hand out.

"No." He raised a brow. "Not until you sit down and answer my questions." He watched the struggle on her face as she weighed the odds of wrestling the bag from him.

Apparently deciding against it, she sat back down with her arms crossed. "Okay, yes, I reread some of them while I was recovering."

"Which ones?"

"Starting with when Henri first came to Marguerite's dressing room backstage."

"The ones where she let herself believe she was in love with a man, only to learn later that he'd seduced her into marrying him with lies. Just as Peter seduced you into sleeping with him with lies."

She kept her gaze fixed on the opposite wall but he saw her throat move as she swallowed hard.

"So now you've lumped all three of us, Henri, Peter, and me, together in your mind. We're all liars who seduce women out of selfishness or greed. And any woman fool enough to fall for us is going to suffer dire consequences."

She finally looked at him, but said nothing.

He leaned forward, bracing his forearms on his thighs. "I'm not Henri, and I'm not Peter. I kept my name and my relationship to John LeRoche hidden from you, but that wasn't to hurt you. I never meant to hurt you." He searched her face, then sat back suddenly. "Hell, what's the use? Even without all this, I never had a chance with you. You deserve better."

"Why do you do that?" She frowned, finally looking at him, looking into his eyes. "You're always cutting yourself down, saying you're selfish and cynical, but you're actually sweet and generous, hardworking and responsible."

He raised a brow. "Sweet?"

"Kind," she corrected.

His chest tightened. "You make me want to be the man you think I am, because you made me believe that, for some people, commitment can work. If I can take that leap of faith, why can't you forgive me and accept me in spite of my parentage?"

"Because I don't know if what I see is real or an illusion."

"Or are you just too afraid to believe, to take a chance?"

"I . . ." He saw the battle of emotions that waged in her eyes before she looked away. "I don't know."

"Allison, let go of the past. Have the courage to give us a chance."

She pressed her fingers to her lips when they started to tremble. An eternity passed as he waited for her verdict. "All right," she whispered at last. "I'll try." He sagged in relief as she turned and gave him a shaky smile. "I can't promise anything, but I'll try."

"You won't regret it." He gathered her against him and held her close as his heart pounded. "I swear, we can make this work."

"You have to help me, though." She pulled back enough to gaze up at him. "Because it's not just the name. I've thought about it a lot since the lawsuit ended, and I think I could get past your relation to John LeRoche. You're right, it's not something you can control and you aren't the one who tried to hurt us. Quite the opposite. I think what really scares me is feeling like I don't know you. For those three weeks we were together, you rarely talked about yourself, or let me past the surface."

He shook his head against a sense of déjà vu; she sounded just like Marguerite in the diaries. "I couldn't share very much without risking your finding out I was a LeRoche."

"I know. But now that the big secret's out, there's no reason for you to hold back." She cupped his jaw as hope kindled to life in her eyes. "If I felt like I knew you, it would be easier for me to trust you."

He leaned back. "There's not that much to tell beyond what you already know."

"I know a few sketchy facts. I have no clear picture, though, of what your life has been like, how you became the man you are."

A familiar dread crept into his stomach, the same queasiness he felt when anyone wanted to get close to him. "There's no reason for us to have long, drawn-out conversations about my childhood."

"Was it that bad? You weren't abused, were you?"

"No, I wasn't abused. It's just that that was then, this is now. I don't believe in revisiting the past."

"But"—confusion lined her face—"the past is part of who we are. If I can't get to know all of you, I can't really know any of you."

"That's not true." The last thing she needed to hear was what a rebellious teenager he'd been, or how many times his father's money and influence had kept him out of juvi-hall. Especially since that would bring up the name John LeRoche more times than he thought wise around her. "Considering the fact that you hate my family, I think talking about them would be a bad idea."

"It might be awkward at first, but what else can we do? If we're going to have any chance of working this out and making it last, I'll have to accept them as part of your life."

"That part of my life wouldn't have anything to do with us."

"Of course it would." Disbelief shone in her eyes. "Unless we're back to talking about a short-term affair."

"I want more than that, and you know it."

" 'More' as in the possibility of marriage down the road?"

His lungs locked up and he stared at her several seconds before he remembered how to breathe. "You said you didn't want marriage and kids."

"I guess I lied, too, then. To both of us." She managed a weak smile. Her gaze dropped away though when he just kept staring at her, too panicked to respond. "Since that day, when you first asked me to have the courage to risk caring, I've thought about it, and I've decided that, yes, I want what Chance and Rory have. I want commitment and a family and everything."

Marriage. Commitment. Total sharing. He blew out a breath as his mind raced. He'd been thinking in terms of reconciliation and building slowly from there, not jumping past the word "relationship" all the way to marriage. "Okay, then. I'll admit, the idea has crossed my mind a lot since meeting you." Crossed his mind along with the word "impossible." But here she was saying it was possible, even with her knowing who he was. "If you can handle the thought of marrying a LeRoche, I'd like to consider it. Although, for the record, your name would be Lawrence and I don't have a lot of contact with anyone but my sister and Chloe."

"Okay then." She nodded. "I'm willing to work on my animosity toward your family, with your help. I assume I'd at least meet your mother, and surely you have aunts, uncles, cousins."

The bands about his chest tightened even more. She wanted him to throw the doors to his life wide open and let her walk right in. The problem being, the minute she saw the mess laid bare, she'd likely turn around and walk right back out. "You don't have to meet them," he insisted. "It would be uncomfortable for you."

"I'd learn to deal with it, because they're part of your life."

"No they're not." Sweat broke out on his brow. "They're part of my past. You would be my present and my future."

"So your relationship with your family and your relationship with me would be totally separate?" She leaned back. "What about things like Thanksgiving and Christmas? Don't you even see your mother then?"

"Okay, I suppose if we got—" He waved his hand as the words stuck in his throat.

"Married," she supplied.

"Yes, if we did that, it would be inevitable you meet my mother, but she wouldn't be part of our lives. I'd still visit her on occasion, but you wouldn't have to go with me."

"That's ridiculous. Scott, you can't compartmentalize your entire life. And you're not being fair. You're asking me to work through a lot of old anger, on top of my fears about relationships in general, yet you're not willing to give anything in return."

"Wait a second. How did we skip tracks from talking about your trusting me, to where we'll be eating Thanksgiving dinner?"

"We didn't skip tracks. It's all related. You're obviously not comfortable being open, but I can't be the only one who has to face scary demons inside myself."

"Gawd! What is it with women!" He stood and began to pace. "Why do you always want men to open up and bare their souls? I think I've faced enough 'scary demons' just falling in love with the one woman in the world who is most likely to eat my heart for lunch. Isn't that enough?"

She sat there, staring at him. "No. It's not."

Silence stretched between them as the hopelessness became clear. She wanted all or nothing. Yet life had taught him all about the disillusionment that occurred when he let people too close. As much as he hated the thought of her walking out on him, he couldn't let her all the way in. He flat-out couldn't do it. "I guess we really don't have a chance, do we?"

Her face crumbled and she closed her eyes. "No, I guess we don't."

He watched as she reached for the canvas bag and her purse—and he wanted to break something. "Why can't you just accept me as I am now and forget the past?"

"Because it's clear you don't trust me." Her eyes filled with tears. "I would be willing to try, if I thought you were."

Helplessness welled inside him as he watched her head for the archway to the foyer. "Allison, wait . . ." He blew out a breath. "I just . . . I'm not good at sharing. That doesn't mean I don't love you."

"I know." Tears slipped down her cheeks. "But if you can't share your past with me, how can we survive the future?"

He had no answer for that.

"If you change your mind and decide you want to talk, I'll be at the inn." She turned and walked away.

"Allison!" he called just before he heard the front door close behind her. "Goddammit!"

He turned to the window, balled his fist, and punched the metal frame in a burst of fury. A shock of pain raced up his arm and he stared down in horror. He knew instantly he'd fractured a bone. Stumbling to the sofa, he cradled his hand to his chest, rocking back and forth to control the pain. He'd broken his goddamn hand. One of the stupidest things a writer could do!

Yet, part of him didn't even care. He was close

enough to finishing the book he could do it one-handed. It meant nothing, though. Without Allison in his life, he simply didn't care about anything.

Why couldn't she just accept him?

Chapter 26

HE DIDN'T CALL. FOR DAYS after her visit to the beach house, Allison felt a surge of hope every time the phone rang. Each time ended in crushing disappointment, followed by anger.

They'd come so close to working things out—she'd seen the look in his eyes, and believed he did love her—but then he'd pulled away. How could he expect blind faith from her yet offer so little in return? Was his love not strong enough for him to take some emotional risks? Or . . . was he as frightened of getting hurt as she was?

She thought of calling him a dozen times a day, to try again, but each time she reached for the phone, fear stopped her. He knew how to contact her if he wanted to reconcile. If he didn't, then calling him would only stir up more agony for both of them.

So, she threw herself into planning Rory's wedding and picking out the decor for the new bungalows they were building. That, at least, helped for a while. Until October arrived, with its cooler weather, and she knew the time had come to accept that it really was over. The knowledge came with a fresh wave of pain. Scott had only been part of her life for a few brief weeks, but so much inside her had changed during that time that to have him gone left her feeling empty.

Empty, but not destroyed. He'd won her heart and then he'd vanished from her life as completely as if he'd died. That should have crushed her, and it did in some ways. She physically ached every time she thought of him, but she didn't want to curl up and die herself, the way she had after losing her parents and again after Peter's betrayal and the loss of the baby.

She had her family, friends, and a thriving business. She would survive and her heart would heal. In time.

In time . . . but not today, she thought as she drove toward Houston Hobby Airport to pick up her aunt. The bright autumn day offered a relief from the scorching summer heat. As she neared Houston, the coastal plains and urban sprawl gave way to upscale shopping centers and triple-decker overpasses.

She reached the airport and pulled through the passenger pickup area. A smile broke over her when she spotted her aunt waiting by the curb. The Incomparable Vivian Young looked every inch the New York actor with her black pantsuit and regal stance. A dramatic streak of silver swirled through the flame-bright hair she wore in a neat twist up the back.

Pulling to a stop at the curb, Allison stepped out. "Aunt Viv!"

The imperial head turned and the aloof expression vanished into a bright smile. "Allison!" They came together in a tight hug. "Oh heavens, it's good to see you."

Alli stepped back, laughing. "I didn't realize how much Rory has grown up to look like you. Except she's taller. A *lot* taller."

"Like your father," Vivian said.

"And not nearly so . . . sophisticated."

"Now the artlessness is all Aurora. I'd say she was a disgrace to the family if she weren't such a delightful child."

"Not quite a child anymore." Allison grabbed the larger of the two bags and headed for the trunk of the luxury sedan. "She's married with a child of her own now."

"True. And I can't wait to see this grandniece of mine."

"Oh, Lauren's adorable. She already has all of us eating out of her hand." Allison stowed the luggage and closed the trunk. "Do you want to drive?" she asked, since the car belonged to her aunt.

"Heavens, no. I've been riding in cabs so long, I've probably forgotten how."

Allison slipped behind the wheel and headed back onto the crowded, multi-lane freeway. "Rory's so excited you were able to come down for the wedding," Alli said, moving with ease through the bumper-to-bumper traffic. "It feels like ages since we've seen you."

"It has been ages. And I would have come for the first wedding, if she'd given me more notice."

"It was rather rushed." Allison smiled. "The minute Chance found out she was pregnant, he hauled her before a judge to say 'I do.'"

"So Aurora married a Chancellor." Vivian shook her head. "Talk about a mismatched pair."

"Yes, but it works for them. They're very happy together."

"And what about you? Adrian mentioned a while back that you were seeing someone."

"That didn't work out." Alli tightened her grip on the steering wheel, determined to keep the mood light. "I can't wait for you to see the inn. We're vacant this weekend, because of the wedding, but business has been booming."

For the rest of the drive, Alli filled her aunt in on everything but her relationship with Scott. Through it all, she managed to keep her tone bright. Her life sounded so perfect, no one would ever guess how empty she felt. That would change, though. In time. She just needed time. And work. When she stayed busy, she could almost push Scott from her mind.

"Do you want to swing by the cottage and drop off your bags, or go straight to the inn?" she asked when they reached the causeway that connected Galveston to the mainland.

"The cottage first," Vivian answered. Her expression turned melancholy as they began the ascent onto the high, long arch of pavement supported by tall pillars. A variety of ships, from pleasure boats and deep-sea fishers to large ocean-going vessels skimmed the sun-speckled water. "I've missed this. There's no place on earth quite like Galveston."

The causeway brought them down onto Galveston's main thoroughfare. Traffic slowed as they reached the Historic District, where palm trees and oaks shaded stately mansions from a bygone age. "I've always thought of this town as a charming old diva," Vivian said. "Full of stories from the past."

"Yes, she is." Allison smiled at the description.

"I've been missing it a lot lately."

"Oh?"

"I'm thinking about moving back, retiring from Broadway."

"You are?" Alli nearly ran a red light in her surprise.

"Now that *Hello, Dolly!* has closed, it's become blatantly clear I've joined the ranks of 'character actors.'" The blasé tone didn't hide the twinge of hurt ego beneath. "The good starring roles are going to younger women."

"That's absurd. You're still young, and as beautiful as ever."

"Well, I don't feel young. I gave up a lot for the stage and I've had a good career, but lately I've started wondering if I'd be happier with more in my life than that. You know what they say, 'Life is that thing that happens while you're busy doing something else.' I mean, look at you, all grown up into a beautiful woman. And Aurora married and a mother. I've let too many things pass me by. I can't help but wonder how different things would have been if I'd had a little less ambition . . . and a little less pride. Mark my word, work makes a cold bedfellow when you get to be my age."

Work. The word struck home as Alli turned off the main road toward the cottage. As she grew older, work would be all she had left, since she was right back to wanting nothing to do with relationships, marriage, or falling in love. Yet here was Aunt Viv telling her not to make that mistake. Coincidence or intended lecture? "How much did Adrian tell you?"

"What?" Vivian asked.

"How much did Adrian tell you about Scott?"

Her aunt stared at her blankly. "I have not a clue what you're talking about."

"Oh." Allison felt her cheeks heat. "Never mind. It's just . . . from what you said, it sounded like you knew."

She felt her aunt studying her. "For what it's worth, I was talking about choices I made when I was your age. I chose career and pride over a man I was absolutely mad about."

Reaching the cottage, Alli pulled around back, under the covered carport, and set the brake. The tiny backyard where she'd played as a child lay before her, tangled and neglected. Tucked in the corner stood the old oak with the swing hanging from a stout branch. A grass-lined path led to the back door into the kitchen that had known generations of laughter, voices, and occasional tears. An ache rose in her heart, so sweet she wanted to cry. Even though she'd lost her parents, her life had held such joy. Scott's life—or what little she knew about it—seemed so empty in comparison. He had his writing, but nothing else. Everything in her longed to help him fill the void with happiness. If only he would let her.

Unfortunately, he'd pushed her away by closing himself off. *It's over*, she told herself for the thousandth time. *You have to move on.*

But move on to what?

"Do you regret it?" she asked her aunt. "Not having a family of your own?"

"No." Her aunt turned to her as if sensing her need to talk. "I made the right choice for me. The theater has always been my first love, and what I had with my young man was mostly lust and a whole lot of really great sex."

"Aunt Viv!" Alli blushed.

"Don't be too shocked, dear. Your generation didn't invent the concept, you know. As for your situation, whatever it is, only you know what's right. I will say this, though, if pride is the only thing standing in the way, I'd toss that out in a heartbeat."

"It's not pride." *It's fear.* "I'd do whatever it took, if I thought it would do any good."

"Have you tried?"

"Actually, I did." Her heart ached at the memory. "The ball's in his court now, and the game appears to be over."

"In other words, you tried but not hard enough." Vivian shook her head in disapproval. "Do you have any idea where I'd be today if I'd tucked my tail and run home the first time a director yelled 'next'? The things in this world that are worth having come with a price tag. Only you can decide what *you* want, and what you're willing to sacrifice to get it."

Anything, she wanted to say. "But what if I fail?"

"What if you succeed?" Her aunt raised a brow. "Life doesn't come with any guarantee but this: the surest way to fail is to stop trying."

"It's just . . ." She swallowed the knot in her throat. "It takes courage to keep on trying."

"That it does, my dear. That it does."

Scott tried to find a comfortable sitting position on the sofa. He shifted again, tugging on the collar of his shirt.

"You'll need to be careful with the wire, sir." The cameraman—or kid, rather—pointed to the tiny microphone clipped to the shirt placard.

He nodded as the kid moved behind the camera they'd set up in the den of the beach house. He hated interviews, hated them with a passion. Why had he agreed to this? Because last spring, sitting around the breakfast table at the Pearl Island Inn, October had seemed like a lifetime away. Now that it was here, he wanted to bolt right out of his skin.

"Jorge, how are your light readings?" Keshia Prescott asked the kid as she took her seat.

"They suck. I can't work with solid black clothes against all that white."

Scott watched Keshia's face as she tried to figure out a tactful way to ask him one more time if he'd consider changing into a different shirt. He looked right back and raised one brow. Sighing, Keshia gave Jorge a helpless shrug of apology.

While the kid muttered curses and adjusted the lights, Scott rolled his head in a vain attempt to relax his shoulders. Any minute, the questions would begin and he'd have to answer off the top of his head. He wouldn't be able to write his answers out, think about them, and rewrite any he didn't like. They'd just go straight into the camera to be aired the following Saturday. The queasiness in his stomach brought back everything he'd felt that day when Allison had asked him to talk about himself. He'd frozen up inside rather than having the guts to do what she asked.

Weeks had passed before he'd realized the full extent of the mistake he'd made. He'd had the gall to criticize Jack Kingsley for lacking the courage to bare his soul to Marguerite, yet he was ten times worse.

Okay, so he'd been a juvenile delinquent from a dysfunctional family. Big deal. If Allison could forgive him

for lying to her about being related to John LeRoche—
and she had seemed willing—surely she could forgive the
rest.

Couldn't she?

Gawd, the awful doubt returned full force, twisting
his insides into knots. Weakness and insecurity were so
unattractive. And embarrassing. He didn't want to be
Scott LeRoche, the screwed-up kid. He wanted to be Scott
Lawrence: the cynical but successful writer, rich, famous,
and self-assured.

Unfortunately, Allison had been right when she'd
said that if they couldn't share their pasts, they had no
future. He should have just laid everything on the table
when he'd had the chance, no edits or rewrites. Instead,
he'd blown it in a moment of sheer panic. And now it
was too late.

Or was it?

He eyed the camera. He might not have the guts to
call her on the phone, not after this much time had passed,
but there was a way he could let her know he wanted a
second chance. The idea had his stomach churning like
mad, but at least it didn't require talking directly to her.

"All right, Mr. Lawrence," Keshia said. "We're ready
to begin."

"Wait." He braced himself. "I've changed my mind."

"About doing the interview?" Her eyes widened.

"No. About what you can ask."

"We already went over that." She managed a chilly
smile, and he commended her for her patience. He knew
perfectly well he'd been a trial from the moment they'd
arrived. "I agreed not to ask any personal questions."

"I know, but I've changed my mind." He took a deep
breath. "Ask me anything you want. Anything at all."

Chapter 27

THE DAY OF RORY'S WEDDING dawned bright and clear, with a pleasant breeze off the cove. Shortly after sunrise, the small wedding party gathered in the shade of an ancient group of oaks with Ellen and Norman Chancellor to one side holding six-month-old Lauren. Paige and Bobby were also there. Allison stood with her brother and aunt determined not to cry, but her sister looked so happy, nervous, and beautiful, her eyes started to prickle the moment the minister said, "Dearly beloved . . ."

Rory and Chance stood with the minister beneath the arbor they'd erected for the occasion, flanked by pots of blooming flowers. Rory's vintage dress added a touch of romantic nostalgia. Rather than a veil, pink roses and baby's breath adorned her hair. Chance stood beside her, tall and handsome in his pearl-gray suit, with so much love shining in his eyes, Allison's heart squeezed with joy.

For this one day, she was determined to put her own sorrow aside.

When the ceremony ended, they headed inside where she and Adrian had laid out a champagne breakfast in the music room. They'd spread an antique lace tablecloth over the grand piano to create a suitable stage for one of Adrian's extravagant wedding cakes. Lauren wound up in Allison's lap during the cake-cutting, and the little bundle of energy giggled each time a camera flashed.

"You silly little goose." Allison laughed at her niece. "They aren't taking pictures of you."

Lauren bounced with excitement as her great-aunt

took a seat beside them. "I swear, they should have named that child Joy."

"She is that," Allison agreed, as Lauren reached for the flowers adorning her hair. As Rory's bridesmaid, she also wore a circlet of roses to complement her lavender gown. "No, no, sweetie, don't touch."

Lauren scowled mightily for a full second, then squealed in delight when Sadie trotted over to check on her.

When the time came for Rory and Chance to leave for their honeymoon in New Orleans, Alli passed Lauren to Ellen and went downstairs to help her sister change out of the wedding dress.

"I can't believe we're leaving Lauren behind," Rory said as Allison worked the row of tiny buttons down the back of the gown.

"It's only for two nights, and you know Ellen will be in grandmother heaven the whole time you're gone."

"True." Rory stepped out of the gown. "She's been trying to convince us that one full day and two half-days isn't a proper honeymoon and we really should take longer. Until Lauren's weaned, though, that's the most I can handle."

While Alli carefully folded their grandmother's gown, Rory slipped on the sleeveless blue dress and jazzy jacket Aunt Viv had brought from New York.

"How do I look?" She studied her reflection.

"Like a cover model." Alli smiled as their gazes met in the mirror. "I'm so happy for you." Tears sprang unexpectedly to her eyes.

Rory turned and pulled her into her arms. "Dang it, I knew today would be hard on you."

"It's not hard because of that," she assured, knowing her sister was referring to Scott. "It's just watching my baby sister get married."

"Remarried."

"It's still emotional."

Rory's arms tightened around her. "I wish things had worked out for you and Scott."

"Well, we can't all live happily ever after."

"I was so sure he was going to be 'it' for you."

"Until we found out he was John's son."

"No, even after that, I thought it would work. So did Adrian."

Allison pulled back, startled.

"Well, it's not like we can choose our parents, and he did help us win the lawsuit."

"True, but . . ." Alli shook her head. "You're the one who threatened to chop him up into little pieces if he broke my heart."

"I know, and for a while I really wanted to, believe me. Then I remembered how happy the two of you were together, and I just kept hoping things would work out." Rory took her hands. "I want you to be happy."

"I will be." *Someday.* "Last time I checked, a broken heart wasn't fatal."

"Maybe you should call him. If there's any chance—"

"There isn't." The statement was flat and final. She had to let go of the longing before it choked her. Yet her aunt's words echoed in the back of her mind: *So you tried, but not hard enough.* "The problem is, I really blew it, Rory."

"What do you mean?"

"I . . ." She struggled with how much to tell, since she hadn't confided in Rory or Adrian about that day at the LeRoche beach house. But she needed to talk about it. "I went to see him."

"When?" Rory asked.

"Right after the lawsuit was settled. He contacted Paige, told her he was staying at the family beach house and he wanted to see me." She turned away, reliving that day and all the emotions, from anger to hope to despair. "At one point, I thought we were going to work it out. I thought all I had to do was have the courage to let go of the past, trust Scott, and everything would be fine. So I tried."

"What happened?"

"*He* wasn't ready to trust *me*." A humorless laugh escaped her. "Ironic, don't you think?"

"And . . . ?"

"And, I got angry and left."

"Alli . . ." Her sister stared at her. "Trust doesn't come easily for everyone. You of all people should know that. Plus, it takes time, not a single conversation."

"I know. I know." She rubbed her head. "I realize that now. Unfortunately, then, I thought building up the courage to love was a one-time deal. Face your fears, say the words, and win the grand prize."

Rory snorted. "Don't we all wish?"

Alli nodded, realizing how foolish she'd been. "I blew it, Rory. I pushed for too much too soon and I blew it."

"Maybe you can try again," Rory offered hopefully. "I mean, at this point, what do you have to lose? You're already miserable."

"True," she admitted.

"Courage and love and trust just take practice, that's all. It'll get easier for both of you, if you'll give it a chance."

She studied her sister, envying her faith in life. "I'll think about it."

"Good." Rory nodded.

"Right now, though"—Alli picked up her sister's overnight case and held it out to her—"you have a plane to catch."

"That I do." Rory's wedding-day glow returned as

she gathered the bouquet she'd decided was too pretty to leave behind.

The others were waiting outside when they stepped onto the veranda. Rory and Chance kissed Lauren good-bye before reluctantly handing the baby over to her grand-parents. On the lawn, Paige passed out birdseed, telling everyone to form a line between the house and the limo Mr. Chancellor had hired.

"Alli!" Rory called.

She turned and saw her sister at the top of the stairs, looking at her intently, as if willing her to be happy. Then she glanced down at the bouquet and her lips curved.

"Rory, no—" Before the words were even out, the bouquet was arching through the air with a flutter of rib-bons. Alli lifted her arms on reflex, and the flowers landed in her hands. She couldn't help but shake her head at her stubbornly optimistic sister.

The couple dashed through a hail of birdseed for the waiting limo, then waved out the back window as the car drove away.

"So," Aunt Viv said, nodding toward the bouquet, "does Aurora know something the rest of us don't?"

"No. It's just her way of telling me not to give up."

"Sage advice," Vivian said as they climbed the steps to go inside. The Chancellors gathered up Lauren's things and said their goodbyes. Bobby and Paige stayed long enough to help clean up, then headed out as well.

"The house seems so empty with no guests," Allison said, staring about the music room.

"Well, we have two couples checking in tomorrow," Adrian said. "Until then, I plan to collapse on the sofa and watch football. Aunt Viv, you care to join me?"

"As long as I can put my feet up." Vivian glanced at her Louis Vuitton pumps.

The phone in the office rang as they started for the back stairs. "I'll get it," Allison said. "You two go on."

Absently twirling the bouquet, she headed for the office. "Pearl Island Inn."

"Allison?" a youthful voice asked. "Hi, it's Chloe."

"Chloe?" Her heart skipped a beat.

"You're not still mad at me, are you?"

"Of course not. I was never mad at *you*." A thousand thoughts flew through her mind: the girl had run away again, or Scott was hurt, in the hospital, dead. "What is it, though? Has something happened?"

"Nothing much. Mom let me go to soccer camp this summer, and that was really cool, but now I'm back in school, which is as boring as ever."

"I see."

"Anyway, Uncle Scott asked me to call and let you know he'll be on TV this afternoon and he wants you to watch."

"On TV?" Alli's heart started pounding. Did he also want a second chance? But why would he have his niece call for him?

"Yeah, some interview on a news station in Houston. Hang on, he made me write it down."

Allison listened numbly as the girl rattled off the time and local channel number for Galveston.

"You got it?" the girl asked.

"Yes, twelve noon on KSET." She checked her watch and saw the time was already past eleven-thirty.

"Then, after you watch it, if you want to call him, here's his phone number."

"Hang on." Allison's hand shook as she grabbed a pen and wrote the number down, surprised to see it was a Galveston exchange. Was he still at the beach house?

"I guess that's it," Chloe said. "Before I go, I just wanna say I miss spending time with all of you."

Allison's eyes stung. "We miss you too, sweetie."

"I think Uncle Scott misses you, too. He sounds really sad."

Alli pressed a hand to her lips.

"Well, I better let you go." Chloe sighed.

"Okay. Take care." She turned the phone off and sank to the chair, afraid her legs would buckle. Several minutes passed as she stared into space, dazed. Had Scott stayed in Galveston to be near her? If so, why hadn't he called? She glanced at her watch and realized how much time had passed.

Jumping up, she raced downstairs, holding the circlet of roses in place. Adrian and her aunt sat side by side on the sofa, their feet on the coffee table, eating wedding cake and drinking champagne as they watched the pregame show.

Allison snatched the controls from her brother and started switching channels.

"Alli! What are you doing?" Adrian demanded. "The Cowboys were about to kick off."

"Sorry, sorry. But I have to watch this." She took a seat in the big armchair, clutching the controls in one hand, Rory's bouquet in the other as the image of Keshia Prescott filled the screen.

"Good day, and welcome to a very special edition of *Book Talk*." The pretty news anchor smiled into the camera. "Earlier this week, I had the distinct pleasure of visiting with suspense author Scott Lawrence at his family's beach house in Galveston about his upcoming release, *In Deep*. Lawrence has a reputation for being intensely private and enigmatic, so I was surprised when the afternoon turned into one of the most candid interviews I've done." Turning in her chair, she nodded toward a screen beside her. "Watch."

The camera zoomed in on the screen as the taped interview began to play. Allison could barely breathe as she found herself back in the white den. Keshia sat in a chair before the windows with the swimming pool and beach behind her, while Scott sat on the very sofa where they'd made love. The memory of what they'd done on that sofa made her cheeks heat, but she brushed that aside as she took in Scott.

He'd trimmed his beard so it once again looked the way it had when she'd first met him, but his hair hung in loose waves nearly to his shoulders.

"Wow, talk about a stud muffin," Aunt Viv said. "Although I can't believe they let him wear solid black and sit on a white sofa. The cameraman must have had a fit with the lighting."

"Scott always wears black," Allison muttered absently.

"Scott?" Aunt Viv asked. "As in *your* Scott?"

Allison didn't answer as Keshia finished thanking Scott for agreeing to the interview and asked him to talk about the book.

"*In Deep* is set on an imaginary island off the coast of South America," Scott said, his voice the same deep rumble that had soothed and seduced her at will. "But I drew heavily on some of the history here in Galveston. Mostly the stories about the sunken ship at Pearl Island." He gave a short summary of the legend of Pearl Island and how he'd incorporated bits of it into his fictional story.

"I had a chance to read an advance copy," Keshia said, "and I really like how you wove in the ghosts. They added a touch of romance not always found in your books. Well, tragic romance, since that part doesn't end happily."

"Most ghost stories don't." A corner of his mouth lifted in a crooked smile, and Allison's heart bumped in response.

"True. The book was excellent, by the way, sure to please your many fans."

"Thank you."

"On a more personal note, I wanted to ask you about the book's dedication." Keshia opened a copy of the book she had in her lap. " 'To Allison, for teaching me the true treasures in life have nothing to do with sunken chests of pirate gold.' "

Alli covered her mouth as emotions swelled inside her: surprise, hope, fear. And longing. So much longing.

"If I'm not mistaken," Keshia continued, "isn't one of the owners of the Pearl Island Inn named Allison?"

"Yes." Scott shifted his weight, as if trying to sink back into the sofa.

"You stayed there while researching the book, correct?"

"Yes." Scott cleared his throat, and crossed an ankle over the opposite knee, creating a barrier between him and the camera.

Vivian laughed. "Talkative fellow, isn't he?"

Allison ached, watching him and feeling his discomfort.

Keshia smiled, but her eyes held impatience. "When we first set up this interview, you said no personal questions, but before we started you changed your mind and said I could ask anything. I suppose my first question would have to be why the change of heart?"

"I, um—" He burrowed down a bit more and propped an elbow on the armrest so he could press a fist to his mouth, creating another barrier to hide behind. "Allison, the woman I dedicated the book to, claims I have a problem being open. So, I thought I'd give it a shot. Sort of a practice run."

"I take it you two became involved on a personal level then."

"Oh yeah." His laugh held no humor. "Until she, um—" He cleared his throat. "She dumped me."

Keshia blinked in surprise, but recovered quickly. "For not being open?"

He gave one curt nod.

"Why is that a problem for you?"

The cameraman zoomed in tighter on Scott's face and Alli could see the lines of strain about his eyes. "A lot of reasons. Mostly because Lawrence hasn't always been my name. I was born Scott LeRoche."

"LeRoche? As in LeRoche Enterprises?"

Scott nodded. "John LeRoche is my father, which is one of the reasons I never answer personal questions. The few people who know assume my success is somehow due to family money or connections, especially since I was only twenty-four when I sold my first book. But nothing could be further from the truth. John tried to pressure me into going to work for him. I told him to stuff it and he cut me off, which was fine by me. I was still pretty hostile toward him for the way he treated my mother during the divorce. He had his own reasons for finally wanting to wash his hands of me."

"And what reasons were those?"

"Look, I . . ." He sat forward abruptly and scrubbed his face with both hands. The cameraman adjusted the angle, creating a feeling of intimacy. Alli felt as if Scott were sitting right before her, talking straight to her. "I really loved my dad when I was a kid. That might surprise most people, because he can be a dictatorial tyrant, but with me, he was different. I think he really got off on having a son. My sister's older, and he never had time for her, but with me, he always made time."

He smiled sadly. "I can remember going with him to his office, a big intimidating place that looks down on New Orleans and the Mississippi River. He'd sit behind his massive desk, giving orders to men who basically groveled before him, and I thought he was God."

"So, you and your father are close."

"Were," Scott stressed. "Past tense."

"What happened?"

Scott blew out a breath. "As I got older, I realized that while he doted on me, he treated my mother and sister with impatience and neglect. He and my mom fought constantly, and if I got upset on her behalf, he'd tell me women were just whiny and demanding by nature. I bought that at first, because the mighty John LeRoche knew everything. But it bothered me, too, because, well . . . she was my mom and I hated to see her hurting."

"What is your relationship with your mother?"

"Strained." He raised a brow, as if the word were an understatement. "When I was young, she resented me because of my closeness to my dad. Even after that closeness was severed, she still blamed me for everything that wasn't right with her world, but she started relying on me more and more to fix whatever was making her unhappy. She and my sister still do that, but I don't blame them. The older I got, the less John was around, so they didn't have anyone else they could count on."

"What severed your closeness with your father?"

"The day I realized why my mother cried so much. He'd been cheating on her. Repeatedly. For years." Scott looked at Keshia with incredulous eyes. "She wasn't being whiny. She was betrayed. Here was this man I thought was perfect, and he was a lying cheating bastard."

He rubbed his temple as if to forestall a headache. "I left the house while they were in the middle of a screaming fight, and started walking through the neighborhood, wandering down the streets until I wound up at a house that was under construction. It happened to be the home of a senator, but I didn't know or care at the time. I was in a rage. And I . . ."

He scrubbed a hand over his face. "I trashed the place. Someone called the cops, and I was arrested. I remember thinking, 'Oh man, my dad is going to be so pissed.' But he wasn't mad. He was embarrassed. He made a sizable contribution to the senator's campaign to get the whole thing swept under the rug, but never said a word to me.

"I don't know why, but his lack of reaction ticked me off." Scott frowned as if thinking it through for the first time. "I guess because I realized he didn't really give a flip about me. I worshiped him, but to him, I was just an object to show off, proof that he was man enough to produce a son. He didn't, and still doesn't, care about anyone but himself.

"When I realized that, I wanted to get back at him for . . . I don't know, everything. Neglecting my sister, cheating on my mother, but mostly for not being the man I thought he was. I had counted on him, and he let me down. So I . . . very stupidly started getting into trouble on a regular basis."

"What sort of trouble?"

"God, you name it." He laughed. "Car theft, possession of marijuana, skipping school, going to bars when I was underage. The thing is, I kept wanting him to *do* something about it. At that point, he wasn't even living with us. He and Mom were getting a divorce, and the only time I saw him was when he had to bail me out of trouble. I just wanted . . . I don't know, for him to get mad, try to stop me, something. Instead, he paid people off and pretended the problem didn't exist.

"By the time I graduated high school, I had no respect left for him. He, however, was so delusional, he actually expected me to go to college and follow in his footsteps as CEO of LeRoche Enterprises. When he came by the house for one of his rare visits, I told him I wanted to be a writer, which is the only thing I've ever wanted to be. And *that* was what finally pissed him off. We had a huge scene with Mom bawling in the background where he threatened to disown me, clearly thinking it would bring me to heel.

"Instead, it freed me in a way I can't explain." He looked amazed. "I quit living my life just to tick him off, and started living for myself. I even changed my name as a way of beating him to the punch of who was disowning who—and because I wanted to leave all that mess behind. Scott LeRoche was an angry, screwed-up kid, and I'm not proud of that. In fact, the only thing in my life I am proud of is my writing. Which is why I don't generally talk about anything else in interviews." He looked at Keshia. "Surely you can understand that."

"Actually," Keshia said out of camera range, "I think a lot of people would find it admirable that you walked away from that much wealth and became your own person."

"My own person?" He raised a brow. "Or an imaginary person. Allison fell for Scott Lawrence. Not Scott LeRoche. I'm not sure she'd care much for the person I used to be."

"If she's watching the show, is there anything you'd like to say to her?"

"No." He laughed, sitting back. "I think I've had all the sharing I can handle for one day."

Allison sat stunned as the interview turned back to writing and his books, then wrapped up and cut to commercial. When she turned to Adrian and Vivian, she found them both staring at her.

"You dumped that man?" Aunt Viv demanded. "Are you crazy!"

"It wasn't quite that cut-and-dried." Her heart pounding, she glanced down at the scrap of paper in her hand, on which she'd written his phone number. "I need to call him."

"Not so fast." Adrian stood and blocked her path when she started for the phone. "What are you going to say?"

"I don't know." Her mind whirled with too many thoughts. "That I'd like to meet with him, see if we can work things out." *Tell him that I love him, and his past doesn't matter.*

"Then you'll go running over to see him on his turf where he has all the advantages." Adrian shook his head. "No way am I going to let him off the hook that easy after what he's put you through. If he wants to work things out, he can damn well come here."

"Adrian . . ." She gaped at him, then gestured toward the TV. "You call that easy?"

"Like he said, practice run. He didn't have to face you while he said any of that, and he didn't have to face your family."

"What are you talking about?" Fear crept inside her chest.

"You two don't have a chance in hell of making things work long term until he realizes that in this family you're accountable for your actions. If you make some jackass mistake, we don't act like nothing happened. His family might not work that way, but this one does." He grabbed the piece of paper from her hand and headed for the phone.

"Adrian, no." She ran after him. "Please don't interfere. Let me handle this."

"Like I let you handle things when he first checked in? I've been kicking myself ever since for not interfering the night he took you to the Hotel Galvez."

"I'm an adult. I can make my own decisions."

"And I'm your oldest male relative. If he wants to marry you, which he damned well better, he has to go through me."

Her mouth gaped. "You can't be serious. No one does that anymore."

"Believe me, Alli. Men appreciate something more if they have to work for it. So, I'm going to make him work a bit, because you're my sister, and you deserve to be appreciated."

"Aunt Viv, help me." She turned to her aunt, who

was standing by the sofa, taking it all in with avid interest. "Talk some sense into him."

"Sorry, but I agree with Adrian. You make this too easy, and that man will spend your whole marriage holding back, while you keep waiting for him to leave you. Make him work for it, and you'll both be a lot more secure in the long run." Vivian smiled. "Besides, it's so much fun to watch men squirm."

Alli held her hands out, pleading for reason. "You've both been drinking champagne for most of the morning. I'm not going to trust you to make a decision that will affect the rest of my life. I love this man, do you hear? I *love* him."

"Then why aren't you with him?" Vivian asked.

"I don't know." Her head ached with confusion. "A lot of reasons."

"Allison," Adrian said quietly. "If you won't do this for your own peace of mind, do it for mine."

She gave him a questioning look.

"Think about it," he said. "If Peter had had to jump through a few hard hoops to get to you, he never would have gotten close enough to hurt you. Don't ask me to stand by and wonder if I'm giving another user free access to my sister."

She struggled with what to do, but realized they were right. Scott needed to know she accepted all of him, the good and bad. Just as she needed to know he honestly loved her, loved her enough to fight for her. With a silent prayer, she nodded.

Adrian picked up the phone and punched in the number. "Hello, Scott." He smiled into the phone and Alli's heart nearly stopped. "This is Adrian St. Claire. Nice interview."

Alli buried her face in the bouquet, imagining Scott's reaction. Had he been waiting by the phone, hoping she'd call?

"Yes, Allison's here. She'd like to talk to you, but I think you and I have a few things to settle first, if you'd care to come over . . . Yes, now would be fine . . . I'll be waiting." He turned off the phone and grinned. "He's on his way."

Alli lifted her head. "How did he sound? Was he angry, embarrassed, what?"

"I think . . . 'wary' would be a more accurate description."

"I've changed my mind. I can't do this to him. As soon as he gets here, I'll talk to him privately."

"You will not. I'll meet him on the veranda." Adrian pinched her chin. "But don't worry. I'll only make him suffer a little before I let him in to see you." He winked at their aunt. "Too bad we don't own a shotgun."

The blood drained from Alli's face as Adrian headed up the stairs. She turned and found her aunt smothering a laugh. "He was joking, right?"

"I don't think so. In fact, I do believe he inherited your father's flare for the dramatic. Speaking of drama, where's the best place to watch this act unfold?"

Allison's mind raced as she tried to think of a place where she could call out to Scott if things got out of hand. "Marguerite's sitting room, in the tower. It has access to the balcony over the veranda."

"A turret with a balcony?" Vivian grinned. "Oh, that's perfect."

Chapter 28

IF A MAN EVER NEEDED luck, Scott needed it now. He stopped the car and looked up at the inn. The gargoyles snarled back at him, zealously guarding their domain. This was such a mistake, he told himself. He should put the car in reverse and head back. Not just for the beach house, but all the way back to New Orleans. He needed to stop fooling himself that Allison would still want to get back together.

He hadn't even been able to watch the interview, but had sat before the blank screen of the TV watching the clock and picturing her reaction. With every minute that ticked by, nausea had grown.

He had to see her one last time, though, and Adrian did say she was willing to talk to him.

He looked at the porch and saw something move in the shadows, reminding him of six months ago when he thought he saw Marguerite's ghost. When the figure stepped forward, though, it didn't transform into the ethereal Allison. It turned into her brother. Adrian moved to the top of the stairs and took up a stance with his feet braced shoulder-width apart, arms crossed over his well-muscled chest.

Resigned, Scott got out of the car and headed for the porch. A few dozen sparrows pecked at something in the grass. As he crossed the lawn, they took flight with a noisy flutter and settled in the hanging baskets. At least no guests were around to witness whatever would happen next.

He stopped at the bottom of the stairs, looking up at Allison's brother. "So how do we do this? Do I suffer through a few insults first, or do we go right to the part where you try to break my face?"

"Nothing quite that barbaric." Adrian grinned. "I just want to know your intentions."

"My 'intentions'?" Scott stared at him, wondering if he'd stumbled onto the set of some antebellum melodrama. "Are you joking?"

"Not at all."

"All right." He took a deep breath. "I intend to ask Allison to forget common sense and marry me, but if you think I'm going to ask your permission, you're nuts. This isn't the Old South, and you're not her father, so I don't need your permission for anything."

"No, but if you marry Allison, you'll be part of this family whether you like it or not. You might have noticed we're a tad closer than your family seems to be."

"I noticed." An unexpected longing, hot and sweet, rose up inside him. To be part of what he'd seen from the outside, the open affection and unquestioning support. Would Allison's family really accept him?

"So," Adrian said, looking entirely too smug for Scott's comfort, "if you want to make Allison happy, and make a marriage between the two of you work, you do need my blessing. And that's what you're going to ask for. Right after you tell me why I should give it."

Scott blew out a breath, thinking a physical fight would be so much easier. And less painful. Summoning his courage, he met Adrian's gaze head-on. "I love her. I think I have right from the beginning. Nothing like this has ever happened to me. I thought I could control things, but when it comes to Allison, I can't control anything. Gawd." He scraped both hands through his hair. "Do you have any idea how frightening that is?"

"Not a clue." Adrian's mouth quirked with suppressed laughter. Scott's whole life hung in the balance, he felt nauseous, dizzy, and the bands of tension around his chest made it hard to breathe—and Adrian found it funny.

Scott narrowed his eyes, dearly wanting to hurt the man. Just one quick jab to the face. "I know I lied to her, and that hurt her. I never meant to, though. She said she can't trust me, but if she'll give me a chance, I'll try to be what she wants, even if it includes being more open about things." He rubbed his forehead in frustration. "Look, if you'll just let me talk to her so I can tell her all this, then she can tell me once and for all if I have any hope that someday she'll feel half of what I feel for her."

"Scott?" Allison's voice drifted down to him. He looked up and found her standing on the balcony with the turret beside her, like a vision from a fairy tale. The breeze ruffled her dark curls adorned with a circlet of flowers. "You don't have to wait for someday. Because I already love you."

"Oh, thank God." He bowed his head as relief rushed through him in one big, drowning wave. When he looked up again, she was gone. For a split second, he thought he'd imagined the whole scene, then he saw Adrian holding the front door open, like a butler welcoming him inside.

He headed up the steps, one at a time, picking up speed as he passed through the door, until he was running across the hall and up the stairs. She met him on the landing before the stained-glass window and flew into his arms. He crushed her to him, lifting her off her feet before he set her down and cupped her face. "Tell me again, so I know I heard right."

"I love you." She gazed intently into his eyes. "I'm so sorry for what both our fears have put us through. I never should have pushed you that day—"

"No, I shouldn't have been such a coward."

"You didn't have to be afraid. I don't care about any of the things you mentioned in the interview, except that your past makes you a better person in my eyes, not a lesser one. I still want to know you, though. And love you. For as long as you'll let me."

"Forever, I hope. If you can forgive me for being stupid."

"Only if you forgive me."

He kissed her hard, then pressed his forehead to hers. "I have missed you so much. Every day, I told myself it would get better, that I'd get over you. But it was a lie. I'll never get over you. Never!"

"I've been the same way. But I thought you didn't want to try."

"You have no idea . . ." He gave a shaky laugh. "I wanted to try, but I was sure you wouldn't want me once you got to know me. I'm still not sure."

"Oh, Scott." She rested her hand on the side of his face, smiling into his eyes. "You are so worth loving."

He kissed her again, softly this time. Then he raised his head and steeled himself. "Okay, here's the deal. We bungled the no-strings-attached, no-emotions-involved concept pretty badly, so I think this time, we should try the opposite. Marriage and the whole nine yards. The next time you get hurt or scared, I don't want it to be so easy for you to walk away or kick me out."

She opened her mouth, but he pressed a finger to her lips.

"Before you answer, though, I have to warn you up front, when I do something, I do it all the way or not at all. I don't believe in giving up once I set my sights on something, otherwise, I never could have gotten published. So, if we get married, there'll be no quickie divorce a year or two later. I'm not like my sister, I don't believe in changing spouses as often as I change shoes. I'm talking total commitment, or nothing." He removed his finger. "Okay. Now, you can answer."

"Yes." She laughed, then held up her hand when he started to pull her to him. "Wait! I have a warning of my own. I want what my sister has, I want you to be part of my family and I want a family of our own."

"As in a baby?" His eyes widened.

"Not right away, but yes, I want children." She saw the fear flash across his face, and smiled at him. "I've watched you with Chloe. You'll make a wonderful father."

"Okay." He nodded. "But you have to promise to help me out on the finer points of being a father."

"You'll have all of us to help you out."

He nodded, looking nearly as dazed as Chance had been when Lauren was born. "Then let's do it. Right now." He grabbed her hand and turned to go downstairs.

She dug in her heels. "What, start a family?"

"No, get married. You're even dressed already." He frowned at her dress. "Although why are you wearing that dress and carrying a bride's bouquet?"

She looked down and laughed, since she'd forgotten she was holding the bouquet. "Rory and Chance renewed their vows this morning and I was her bridesmaid."

"Oh, that explains it. I thought I was hallucinating. But as long as you're dressed and have the flowers, let's go find a judge."

"No."

"No?" He paled.

"We need a license, silly."

"Oh, license. Right. I knew that."

"And"—she cupped his face—"I want the whole family here, so we have to wait until Rory and Chance get back from their honeymoon. If I'm only going to marry once, I want to do it right."

He pressed a kiss into the palm of her hand. "Just as long as you don't change your mind."

"I won't." She smiled. "I love you."

"Thank God. And thank you, Marguerite," he called to the house. Alli frowned in confusion and he smiled. "For making me the luckiest man alive."

Epilogue

"OH MAN, I FORGOT TO tell you something!" Scott sat upright in bed.

"Hmm?" Alli murmured sleepily, her body exhausted from a day of packing boxes.

Scott turned toward her, propping his weight on one elbow. "I can't believe I didn't tell you this, but with everything that's been going on, I flat forgot."

"Well, we have been rather busy lately." She smiled as she ran a fingertip over his bare chest. They'd been together constantly for the two weeks since he'd proposed. Once he'd calmed down, Scott had decided he wanted to give her time to get to know him and be completely sure about marrying him, but not too much time, since he was more than ready to tie the knot.

She was eager as well, and her certainty grew with each passing day. The more sure he became of her love, the more he relaxed his guard, showing her how much he needed that kind of total acceptance. She'd always had that with her siblings, but watching him experience a family's love for the first time made her appreciate it even more.

So, they'd set the wedding date for New Year's Day, thinking it an appropriate time to start a new life together, and were currently in the process of moving Scott into the Bouchard Cottage—an irony since the Bouchard descendants now lived in the mansion. Aunt Viv might be thinking of retiring, but she wasn't ready to leave New York just yet. She'd offered to let them live there until more permanent plans could be made. Alli wouldn't of-

ficially move in until after the wedding, though so far they
hadn't spent a night apart.

A week after Rory and Chance returned, she and
Scott headed for New Orleans to pack up his things. He
planned to keep the townhouse, for all of them to use as
they wanted, but his official residence would be Galveston
so Allison could be with her family and continue to work
at the inn.

It was at the townhouse that Alli met his mother for
the first time. She and Chloe had been packing up Scott's
office when DeeDee LeRoche came by, full of complaints
and hurt feelings that Scott hadn't so much as called to
let her know he was back in town. He was such a horrible
son, she told Allison, he never thought of anyone but himself. And if he was moving to Galveston, what was wrong
with living at the beach house? she wanted to know.

After half an hour with the woman, Alli decided
DeeDee wasn't intentionally cruel, she was simply self-
absorbed and a bit of an airhead. A very stunning and
surgically well-preserved airhead. When Scott introduced
Allison as his fiancée, his mother didn't recognize the
name until he explained the St. Claires were the new owners of Pearl Island. Then she'd just looked horrified and
asked why in God's name anyone would want to buy that
derelict old pile of stones. When Scott finally walked her
to the door, Alli overheard the woman tell him, "Divorces
are so messy, why don't you just live together?"

Unfortunately, Alli had still been standing in the middle of the office with her mouth open when he returned.
He'd taken one look at her expression, cringed and said,
"Okay, I know you love me, I've got that part down, but
are you sure you can handle my family?"

Laughing, she'd opened her arms, hugged him close,
and assured him she wasn't going to call off the wedding
just because his mother was a rude ditz.

That had been hours ago. Now the boxes were packed

and ready for the movers. Beyond the French doors to the balcony, night had fallen. Only an occasional shout or rowdy laugh could be heard in Scott's quiet corner of the French Quarter. She snuggled closer to him in the big sleigh bed and suppressed a yawn. "What did you forget to tell me?"

"That I found Lafitte's treasure."

She pulled back, her eyes wide as sleepiness vanished. "What?"

"Well, not found it literally, but found out what it is."

Sitting up, Alli gathered the covers over her naked breasts. "Well? Tell me."

"Bobby's friend, Jackie Taylor, in Corpus Christi—"

"The one who owns the *Pirate's Pleasure*."

"Yes, her. She's a descendant of Jack Kingsley."

"You're kidding." Alli's eyes widened. "I knew she was named after him, but I didn't know she was related. I wonder why she didn't say anything when she came to Pearl Island last year."

"Because Bobby was right when he said her father's treasure hunts are a sore spot with her." Scott scooted up to lean against the headboard. "In fact, I had a hard time getting her to talk to me at all. I called her purely on a hunch after reading Marguerite's diary. At first, she denied any connection. Then she admitted to being a descendant but told me quite bluntly that there was no treasure, and even if there were, she had no clue where it might be. So I badgered her a bit more and asked why Marguerite would have mentioned Jack having it if it didn't exist. And that's when she told me."

"What? Just spit it out."

"It's a powder horn."

"A powder horn?" Alli rocked back.

"Remember when I told you that Jean Lafitte had a very flowery way of writing?"

"Yes."

"Well, he was also fond of making speeches and grand gestures. When the authorities finally ran him off Galveston Island, some of his men decided to give up piracy and stay in Texas. One of those men was Jack Kingsley's grandfather, who was apparently very close to Lafitte. Before Lafitte left Galveston, he presented his friend with a powder horn as a memento of their greatest adventure together, the Battle of New Orleans. As he handed him the gift, he referred to it as his 'dearest treasure.' "

Alli frowned. "Why a powder horn?"

"That's what I wanted to know, but Jackie claimed she had no idea. However"—he wiggled his brows—"you don't write as many books as I have without learning how to do research and track down obscure facts."

"What did you find out?" She settled in beside him, against the headboard.

"The powder horn was given to Lafitte by Andrew Jackson at a celebration ball following the battle." Scott draped an arm over his raised knee. "Jackson made a big deal about the horn having great significance because it had been given to him by George Washington during the Revolutionary War, and Washington had even carved his initials into it. Personally, I think if it really was Washington's powder horn, Jackson was issuing Lafitte a sneaky insult, because Jackson hated Washington's guts."

"Then why did Washington give Jackson the horn?"

"During the Revolution, Jackson, who was a boy, carried messages for the militia. On one occasion, Washington stuck a message inside the powder horn."

"Ah, so it was a way of hiding messages in case Jackson ran into the British."

"Exactly." He nodded. "Now, whether Lafitte knew about Jackson's animosity toward Washington is anyone's guess, but he made one of his elaborate speeches about being profoundly honored and how he'd always treasure a gift from such a mighty leader of men, blah, blah, blah. Hence it became known as"—he held out his hands—"Lafitte's Treasure."

"That is such a wild story."

"Yeah." Scott cocked his head in amusement. "To think that all this time, people have been looking for a chest of gold, but the treasure is something that has historical value rather than monetary value."

"Do you think it went down with Jack's ship?"

"I do." He smiled slowly. "And I'll bet you Marguerite's necklace is inside it."

"Oh, my goodness." Alli's heart raced at the thought. "If only we could get to it."

He played with the ends of her hair. "Have any of you thought of raising the ship?"

"That would cost a fortune."

"If we can find enough evidence that the powder horn is really down there, I bet we could get funding."

" 'We.' " She smiled as she repeated the word. "I like the sound of that. I hope you meant it to include the whole family."

Surprise lit his eyes. "I did, actually."

"See, you're learning." She leaned over to tease his lips with a kiss. "We'll make a family man out of you yet."

"I don't know." He gave a mock frown as he gathered her in his arms. "I think I need more practice. Tell me how it's done again."

"You start by saying 'I love you' several times a day."

"I love you." He kissed her as he lowered her to the mattress and settled his body over hers. "Several times a day."

"Yes, you certainly do." She laughed and wrapped her arms around him. He was so right, she thought with a sigh. The true treasures in life had nothing to do with chests of pirate gold. They had to do with family and love.

Read on for an excerpt from Julie Ortolon's next book

Don't Tempt Me

COMING SOON FROM ST. MARTIN'S PAPERBACKS

Chapter 1

JACKIE TAYLOR HAD LITTLE USE for fairy tales and even less for charming princes, which was why it really irritated her when *he* came striding back into her life. One minute she was minding her own business, straddling a work bench as she repaired a sail for her charter ship, the next she looked up to find Adrian St. Claire filling the open doorway of her dockside shed. The brilliant sun of the Texas coast silhouetted his six-foot-plus frame, broad shoulders and narrow hips as he strode toward her with cocksure grace.

"Damn," she muttered under her breath.

"What's that?" Tiberius, her first mate, glanced up from his end of the work bench and followed her gaze. A wide smile split his face, his teeth a startling white against his coffee-colored skin. "Weeell, A-drian," he said in his distinctive Caribbean accent. "What are you doing in Corpus Christi, mon?"

Jackie knew exactly why the man was in Corpus, but refrained from kicking him out . . . yet.

"It was a nice day for a motorcycle ride," Adrian said. "So I thought I'd head down the coast from Galveston and see what's shaking on your stretch of beach." As he moved out of the glare of light, she saw that the red T-shirt he wore tucked into faded blue jeans did a fine job of showing off his hard torso. He'd pulled his black hair into a ponytail, and a small gold hoop earring glinted in the shed's dim light. The two men shook hands, Ti as massive and steady as an old frigate while Adrian made her think of a clipper, sleek and beautiful and rigged for racing.

She told herself she had no use for men who collected female admirers just by walking down the street, but her body was far from immune to his appeal.

Adrian nodded toward the slice of bustling dock visible through the door. The *Pirate's Pleasure* rocked in her mooring just out of view. "From all the tourists snapping pictures and picking up pamphlets, I trust business is going well."

"It would be if the harbor didn't charge a fortune for our slip," Ti said with good humor, as if the slip rental was their only financial worry.

Adrian turned to her and his smile shifted, became sensual. "Jackie. Long time no see."

For a moment, she lost herself in clear blue eyes surrounded by long black lashes. His features were so perfect, they would be "pretty" if he didn't exude all that male sexuality. His sheer presence should have made her feel more feminine in contrast. Instead, he made her more aware of her calloused hands, too-thin build, and the fact that she'd cut her hair boyishly short since the last time she'd seen him.

She raised her chin, feeling peevish. "I gave you and your sister my answer on the phone. And the answer was no."

His brows shot up in surprise. "Well, now, that's cutting right to the chase, isn't it?"

Ti flashed her a questioning look, since she hadn't confided in him about the St. Claires' request.

"I find a direct approach saves time," she said. Securing the large needle in the sail, she thrust the canvas aside and rose. "Now, unless there's something else you want"—*besides my great-grandfather's letter*—"I'll let you be on your way."

A slow smile curved his lips, making her stomach flutter. "What if the 'something else' I wanted was to take you to dinner?"

"Right." She snorted. Conscious of her first mate hanging on every word, she crossed to a water cooler by the door. Beyond the shadows of her shed, tourists wandered the pier, buying fresh shrimp off the backs of boats or checking out the various rigs for charter. Their voices mingled with the rhythmic rush of waves underfoot and the incessant cries of seagulls. Unseasonable heat hung heavy in the air for so late in the year, and the denim shirt she'd tied at the waist over a sports bra and shorts stuck to her skin.

After filling a paper cup with chilled water, she spared a glance at Adrian as he came up behind her. "I have no desire to waste an evening listening to you try to talk me out of something I have no intention of giving you."

He said nothing at first, but she could feel his gaze on her. "I think the question here is what am I prepared to give you?"

She turned and found him leaning against a worktable, all long muscles and cat-like grace.

He wiggled his brows playfully. "I'm here to make you a proposition."

Her heart pounded even as she laughed in his face. "Don't even try to sweet-talk me, pretty boy. We both know I'm not your type."

Rather than take offense, he looked genuinely curious. "And what would 'my type' be?"

"Tall, blond beach-bunnies with Barbie-doll figures," she tossed back.

Amusement danced in those incredible blue eyes of his. "That's just packaging, sugar. But if it comes with a personality and some brains, absolutely."

The man was impossible to insult. But then she should have remembered that from their brief association a year ago. He and his two sisters had hired her ship as part of the entertainment for the annual Buccaneers' Ball.

The event had been held at the bed and breakfast they owned on Pearl Island, a small private island just off Galveston. During the few days the *Pirate's Pleasure* had been anchored in their cove, Adrian had flirted with her shamelessly. Not that she took any of it seriously. He was clearly a man who enjoyed flirting.

"Now, about dinner . . ." he said.

"In case you misunderstood, that was a no." She downed the cup of cold water and crumpled the paper cup.

"I was thinking somewhere quiet—"

"I'm not going out with you."

"—where we can discuss what my sisters and I are willing to offer in exchange for your help."

"No."

"Or . . . I can plead our case here." He leaned closer and she caught a whiff of him. Oh God, he even smelled good; like soap and wind and sunshine. His gaze dropped to her mouth, then lifted back to her eyes and held. "Although, I think we'd both be more comfortable talking over seafood and a nice bottle of wine."

She shook her head in exasperation. "Do you ever take no for an answer?"

"Honestly?" He cocked a brow. "I'm not sure. It's not a word I hear too often."

"I just bet you don't." Narrowing her eyes, she contemplated hefting him over her shoulder, walking out onto the pier, and tossing him into the Gulf. Considering his size, she didn't think she'd get too far with that plan. "Okay, what the heck. I'll have dinner with you. It's your money and your time, if you want to waste them, that's your business."

"Great." His eyes lit with pleasure. "How about The Wharf? Early enough to enjoy the sunset. Unless you'd rather go somewhere else."

"No, The Wharf is fine." Perfect in fact, since it was

right at the end of her pier. She'd be close enough to home to ditch him if he became too annoying.

"I'll pick you up around six, then," he said. "I assume you still live onboard your ship."

"I do."

"Until this evening." With a nod, he strode past her, back out into the sunshine. She watched as he wound his way past tourists and fishermen to the black Harley he'd left parked at the end of the pier. In spite of the warm fall weather, he donned a black leather jacket, but left it unzipped. Then, with a move that made her pulse hum, he swung a leg over the seat, kicked the engine to life, then had it roaring with a few twists of his wrist. After a final wave toward her, he zoomed off down the busy four-lane road that skirted the beach.

She couldn't help but shake her head in amusement. He was persistent, she'd give him that. And more gorgeous than any man had a right to be. The Gene Fairies must have been in a wicked mood the day they made Adrian St. Claire or they never would have unleashed all that sex appeal on womankind.

"Care to tell me what that was about?" Tiberius asked from behind her.

"Adrian and his sisters have been bitten by the treasure-hunting bug."

"Ah . . ." He stretched the word out. "The allure of Lafitte's missing treasure. I guess we are lucky you've not been cursed with more requests to help find it, since it supposedly went down with your great-great-grandpappy's ship."

"Well, at least this is a new spin on an old tale." She crossed back to the bench and swung a leg to straddle it. Taking up her needle, she resumed mending the sail. "The St. Claires want to go after the real 'treasure' rather than chase some fool's dream of sunken chests of gold."

"Sunken gold is hardly a fool's dream." Ti swept the

air dramatically with his big, calloused hand. "The sea floor is littered with many riches. Spanish doubloons, precious jewels, and artifacts worth a king's ransom to the right collector. Or have you forgotten the thrill of finding lost booty?"

She sent him a mutinous glare.

"Eh . . . ?" He smiled back, his eyes twinkling. "I remember a little girl who used to love diving for old coins and gold rings."

Bittersweet memories stirred at his words. How exciting the world had seemed back then, with one adventure after another. "I'm not a little girl anymore."

"No." He nodded. "But when it comes to finding lost treasure, you were better than your father—and many people thought he was the best."

"For all the good it did us since he always spent every dime we made on those dives going after bigger prizes." She stabbed the needle through the canvas. "I'm through chasing legends and dreams, Ti. Reality works just fine for me."

"If you say so." He resumed sewing, but under his breath, he started singing an old sailing ditty about the treasures of the deep blue sea.

Jackie rolled her eyes, but joined him on the chorus, the song building in volume as their needles kept time to the music.

At six that evening, Adrian rang the bell at the *Pirate's Pleasure*. And it literally was a bell, mounted on a wooden sign that had the name of the ship emblazoned in gold script and a pocket that held brochures. He assumed the bell was the appropriate way to announce his presence since a tall, chain-link gate prevented people from walking up the ramp to the main deck.

As the clanging sound faded, he searched for signs of life on board. The Baltimore schooner wasn't that large compared to other tall ships, but she was still a grand wooden-hulled vessel with three masts, a quarter deck, and forecastle. A beautifully detailed mermaid decorated the bow, just beneath the jibboom, while red and gold railing crowned her sleek black body.

Jackie appeared on deck, striding toward the ramp and stealing his breath. She might not be a classically beautiful woman, but God, she made his pulse pound. Too bad the proposal he was about to make her was strictly business. If she accepted, she'd be a venture partner and strictly off-limits for the kind of things he'd like to do.

"You're punctual," she said, glancing at her black dive watch.

"And you're ready."

"You sound surprised."

"I have two sisters. I'm astounded."

Laughing lightly, she came down the ramp wearing a yellow chambray shirt tucked into well-worn blue jeans. The soft, buttery color brought out the gold tones of her tan skin and hazel eyes. He studied her hair as she came through the gate and locked it behind her. A year and a half ago, her hair had hung in a thick, mahogany-colored braid down her back. Since then, she'd cut it short—very short—except for a few wispy fringes around the face and nape.

"Great haircut," he said.

Reaching up in a self-conscious gesture, she finger-combed the fringes by her ear. "Yeah, well, this is what you get when you tell some scissor-happy hairdresser you're sick of messing with long hair. *Whack!* All gone."

"I meant I like it." He cocked his head, surprised by her defensive tone. "It sets off your eyes." And the rest of her exotic features. There was nothing subtle about Jackie Taylor. She had thick black brows over hazel-colored cat's eyes, slender nose, high cheek bones, a

square jaw, and a lush mouth he'd fantasized about frequently. "You hungry?" he asked.

"Ravenous."

"Me, too. *Always*." He added the last in a playfully
seductive tone, hoping for one of those spunky comebacks
that always cracked him up. Most men would probably
call him nuts, but he liked the way she verbally jousted
with him rather than fall at his feet. He'd never had a
woman turn him down before. The experience was . . .
intriguing. And liberating. It gave him the freedom to flirt
as outrageously as he wanted without the fear of setting
wedding bells off in her head.

They started down the pier toward the restaurant at
the end. The docks seemed almost deserted after the bustle
of midday. Ships rocked in their berths, their rigging ping-
ing in time to the waves. A salty breeze off the gulf ruffled
their shirts while billowing clouds held the first blush of
sunset.

"So, is that why you became a cook?" Jackie said, as
if the suggestiveness of his remark had gone right over
her head. "Your appetite?"

"Chef," he corrected. "But yeah, my appetite may
have had something to do with it. The aunt who raised us
worked nights, so if we were going to eat something besides TV dinners, we had to fix it ourselves. And since
I've always enjoyed indulging my senses, I figured if I
was going to cook, I might as well go 'all the way.' " He
put enough sexual connotation in the words to be sure she
got it this time. "What about you?"

She thrust her chin out. "Indulgence is a waste of time
and money. When I'm hungry, I grab whatever's cheap
and easy."

"Cheap and easy? Mmm . . . I could be talked into
that."

She stopped and faced him, fists on hips with the surf
at her back and the wind playing in her short hair. "You

know, as much as I'm enjoying this little double entendre thing you have going here, let's get one thing straight. We are not on a date. We are going to dinner so I can get it through your head that I'm not going to help you."

"I thought we were going to dinner so I could proposition you."

She turned as if to stomp back to her ship but he slipped a hand about her elbow, stopping her.

"Sorry, you're right." He tried not to grin and failed. For all her bluster, she barely came to his shoulder. "Since this really is a business dinner, I'll try to behave myself."

She studied him a moment before nodding. "All right."

"Although, if it weren't a business dinner, I'd be compelled to ask . . . has anyone ever told you, you have a great mouth?"

Her head snapped back. "A smart mouth, you mean."

"No, I was being quite literal."

"Come off it." She laughed and blushed. Actually blushed. Imagine that. Jackie Taylor could blush. "My mouth isn't anything but big."

Adrian stepped closer, just enough to invade her space. "Your mouth is a work of art. I can't imagine any man alive who could look at your lips and not want to kiss them."

She tried to glare at him, but the color in her cheeks spoke more of pleasure than embarrassment. "You call this behaving?"

"Behaving is a new concept for me. It may take me a while to get it right." He tugged gently on her arm and smiled when she fell in step beside him. "Let's see, what were we discussing? Ah yes, I remember. Food." He glanced at her sideways. "My *second* favorite subject in life."

Jackie rolled her eyes, refusing to ask him what was

his first favorite subject. He was a man, so she knew the answer to that.

They reached the restaurant and Adrian held the door as she stepped into an atmosphere designed to please tourists; fishing nets hung from the ceiling while old-fashioned life preservers and brass portholes filled the walls between photos of proud fishermen weighing their big catch of the day.

An impossibly perky hostess glanced up from the bamboo hostess stand. "Hi," she greeted with a manufactured smile until she saw Adrian. Then her jaw actually dropped.

"Two for dinner," Adrian said, seeming unaware that the girl was about to drool on his feet. Not that Jackie blamed her. The man looked particularly drool-worthy in a pale blue shirt open at the collar, unbuttoned gray vest, and dark blue Dockers.

"Two. Yes, of course." Perky Girl grabbed two menus. "If you'll just . . . follow me."

Jackie trailed behind as the hostess led the way. Being early evening during the off season, the tables and booths were deserted. Although a few locals were gathered around the bar in the middle of the room, swapping fish stories.

"I guess you get your pick of tables." The hostess smiled up at Adrian.

"How about the one in the corner with the killer view?"

"Oh, good choice," Perky Girl sighed in admiration as if he'd just announced the cure for cancer. As they took their seats, she handed each of them a menu, never taking her eyes off Adrian. "Sandy will be your server this evening, but can I get you anything while you're waiting? Water perhaps?"

Or my body, Jackie added silently, reading the invitation in the girl's eyes.

"Water would be nice. Thank you." Adrian smiled and the girl nearly melted before hurrying off, eager to serve.

Jackie turned to Adrian. "Can I ask you a question?"

"Certainly." He casually opened his menu.

"Do you do that intentionally, or does it just come naturally? You know, like breathing?"

"Do what?" He frowned.

She resisted the temptation to whack him over the head. "Send women into a swoon."

Amusement registered, crinkling the corners of his eyes and carving long dimples to either side of his mouth. Her insides stirred in response. "Jealous?" he asked.

"In your dreams, buddy boy." She snapped open her own menu. Any woman fool enough to fall for a man like Adrian deserved to have her heart broken. Unless that woman liked to share which Jackie didn't.

Their server, Sandy, arrived—a no-nonsense woman who refrained from openly drooling—and they placed their orders.

"Okay." Jackie folded her hands on the table. "Down to business."

"Naw-ha. Our food hasn't even come. First we eat, visit, watch the sunset, then we'll talk about the offer."

"Well, if you're planning to offer me part of the salvage rights, save your breath. I'm not stupid. Texas doesn't grant salvage rights, so the minute you and your sisters brought the Texas Historical Commission into this, you lost everything that was on that ship. If you wanted to go after Lafitte's treasure, you should have just gone after it yourself."

"Are you kidding? The bulk of the shipwreck is buried under sand and silt from the nineteen hundred hurricane. Do you know how much excavating it would cost?"

"I have a pretty good idea, which is what confuses me. Why is everyone suddenly so hot to go after a worthless treasure? I explained to the writer guy—"

"Scott Lawrence." Adrian supplied the name of the famous suspense novelist who had called her a few months ago claiming to be researching a new novel. He'd started out asking if she were by any chance descended from Jack Kingsley. She'd been startled at first that he knew and tried to deny it. She knew the minute she admitted it, he'd start asking about the treasure. Sure enough, that was exactly what he did.

"I explained to Scott Lawrence that the so-called treasure is nothing but a powder horn. It's not gold. It's not some valuable jewel. It's a stupid powder horn my ancestors jokingly referred to as 'Lafitte's treasure.' So what's the big deal?"

"Ah, and here's our first course." Adrian smiled as the server brought an appetizer of shrimp cocktail and a bottle of wine. Jackie drummed her fingers as he went through the ritual of tasting the wine. When the woman was gone, he turned back to her. "So, how do you like running a charter ship?"

She narrowed her eyes, wondering when he planned to answer her question. Of course, since Lafitte's treasure was her least favorite subject, she shrugged it off. "The hours are abysmal, tourists can occasionally be a pain in the butt, and I barely make enough to cover my expenses."

"You hate it that much, eh?" He grinned knowingly, as if he could see through to the truth: That her ship meant the world to her, and she would fight to the death to keep her business going. Or until bankruptcy, whichever came first.

"How about you?" She dipped a chilled shrimp in cocktail sauce. The shrimp was fresh, but the sauce fell flat. "Do you like running a B and B?"

"Most of the time." He popped a sauce-drenched shrimp into his mouth and wrinkled his nose. "Too bland.

Mind if I doctor this up a bit?" At her nod, he rummaged through the condiments on the table, adding a little of this, a little of that, and topping it off with a squeeze of lemon. "I could do without getting up before dawn to start breakfast every day of the week, but it beats the heck out of filling orders off a menu in someone else's kitchen." He tried another shrimp. "Mmm, better. Try it now." He dredged a shrimp through the sauce and held it to her mouth.

She pulled back with a wary frown.

"Come on . . ." he coaxed.

She narrowed her eyes slightly, then opened her mouth and took the shrimp. *Oh yes, much better.* The tangy flavor lingered on her tongue as she swallowed. "So, who's cooking while you're gone?"

"My sisters, Rory and Alli. They aren't exactly slouches in the kitchen, although they're no match for me."

"You should get that ego checked." She raised a brow. "I think it might be growing."

"No, it's always been this big," he said, straight-faced.

She shook her head, thinking his charm would be so much easier to resist if it weren't so genuine. It lulled her, in fact, as effectively as the wine over the next hour. Their conversation flowed easily between bits of blackened redfish and creamy pasta. By the time they'd finished dinner, other patrons were scattered about the restaurant. Candles had been lit, lending a touch of romance to the rustic decor. Outside, the sun had already melted over the horizon so that only the white crests of the waves shone in the lights from the pier.

Jackie relaxed back in her chair as the server cleared away their plates and asked if they wanted dessert. When Jackie said no, Adrian ordered something for himself and two cappuccinos. Then, taking up his wine glass, he leaned back as well but turned slightly toward her. She had an odd sense of intimacy, as if they were lounging side by side somewhere private, rather than sitting at a table in a semi-crowded restaurant.

He studied the wine in his glass. "How much do you actually know about the powder horn?"

The question jolted her. In the past hour, she'd almost forgotten why he'd taken her to dinner.

"Now, don't get all stiff on me," he said in a lazy drawl. "I just want to know if you're aware of the whole story."

She flopped back and crossed her arms over her chest. "I know the powder horn once belonged to Jean Lafitte. He gave it to Jack Kingsley's grandfather before sailing for South America. Several of the pirates who had followed Lafitte from New Orleans to Galveston decided to stay in Texas and start a new life. Jack's grandfather was one of them. In an impromptu ceremony, Lafitte presented the powder horn to Reginald Kingsley, or Red Reg, as a memento of their adventures together. Since Lafitte liked to refer to the horn as his most 'treasured possession', my family called it Lafitte's treasure as a joke. Unfortunately, the joke has gotten out of hand over the years."

"Do you know why Lafitte called it that?"

"No. I only know that every treasure hunter out there thinks there's a chest of gold somewhere, and that—as a Kingsley descendant—I should know where it is. Only, there is no chest of gold. It doesn't exist."

"What if . . ."—Adrian swirled the wine in his glass, then looked up and caught her gaze with his—"I told you the powder horn was worth more than gold?"